MY
So-Called
SCOUNDREL

#3 Blakeley Manor Series

BY

FENNA EDGEWOOD

WOLF PUBLISHING

My So-Called Scoundrel by Fenna Edgewood

Published by WOLF Publishing UG

Copyright © 2023 Fenna Edgewood
Text by Fenna Edgewood
Edited by Chris Hall
Cover Art by Victoria Cooper
Paperback ISBN: 978-3-98536-154-0
Hard Cover ISBN: 978-3-98536-155-7
Ebook ISBN: 978-3-98536-153-3

WOLF Publishing - This is us:

Two sisters, two personalities.. But only one big love!

Diving into a world of dreams..
  ...Romance, heartfelt emotions, lovable and witty characters, some humor, and some mystery! Because we want it all! Historical Romance at its best!

Visit our website to learn all about us, our authors and books!

Sign up to our mailing list to receive first hand information on new releases, freebies and promotions as well as exclusive giveaways and sneak-peeks!

WWW.WOLF-PUBLISHING.COM

Also by Fenna Edgewood

The Blakeley Manor Series

Two families, from very different worlds, are about to converge at Blakeley Manor...

Upstairs...

The Blakeley family is famed for their infinite fortune—and their infinite eccentricities. As the Blakeley siblings reunite to host a Christmas house party, they are plunged into scandal as each one forges a passionate new alliance that crosses the boundaries of all propriety.

Downstairs...

Four very different siblings—a lady's maid, a housekeeper, a gardener, and a groom—are tied together, not only by the love and loyalty they share but by dangerous secrets that could cost them not only their employment...but also their hearts.

#1 Lady Briar Weds the Scot

#2 Kiss Me, My Duke

#3 My So-Called Scoundrel

Prequel: The Countess's Christmas Groom

MY
So-Called
SCOUNDREL

Prologue

He had no business stopping when he heard the woman cry out. He had just escaped trouble.

But she was a woman, and she had screamed—a gasping, ragged scream he was all too familiar with. A scream that signified fear.

And the street was dark, and there was no one else around.

He could continue walking. Pretend he had not heard. Perhaps that is what most gentlemen in his position would have done.

After all, he suspected the scream would not come again. He might eventually convince himself he had never heard it at all.

But then, Leigh Blakeley was not most gentlemen. He liked to believe he was hardly a gentleman at all.

So, he stopped. Turned around. Looked down into the shadowy alley and saw exactly what he expected to see.

Two men and a woman. That was ordinary enough.

But one of the men had the woman by the throat, while the other standing beside her had a hand clapped over her mouth.

Leigh spotted the two men's free hands and did not like where they were roving. He was sure the woman did not like it either.

They were young men, perhaps in their early twenties. A little younger than himself then. They were laughing, as young men often did. Clearly, they were enjoying themselves.

Even from where he stood, he knew there would be tears in the woman's eyes. She would not be laughing. But the young men did not care. She was simply sport to them.

He felt a familiar icy chill descend over him as he prepared for what he had to do.

"Let her go."

He cast his voice loud enough that it would carry to the men, but not loud enough to wake the people sleeping in nearby buildings. It was a working-class neighborhood, to put it delicately, and while many would be working at night, there were many who would be rising early.

The young men were turning to the source of the voice. They had not yet complied.

He had not expected them to.

"Let her go. Do it now, and I may let you go as well."

There, that had gotten their attention. He heard confused laughter. Saw them look at one another, obviously thinking, *Who the devil does this man think he is?*

"Bugger off!" one of them shouted. The one with his hand around the woman's throat. "Can't you see we're busy? Find your own whore."

Well, he had tried. He would not waste any more words.

They were watching him, waiting for him to walk away or, perhaps, waiting for him to make empty threats.

Instead, Leigh did neither.

There was a song in his heart as he curled his fists and charged down the alley toward the men.

Chapter One

Blakeley Manor, March 1818

Marigold Spencer lay in bed with her eyes closed, contemplating her life as a walking disaster.

She was a disaster. It bore repeating. A disaster of epic proportions.

Furthermore, this was not merely her personal opinion.

Had not Lady Fulford said only yesterday, after the incident at the modiste's, that it was a blessing in disguise they could not present Marigold at court? For she would most likely trip on her gown and fall upon the Queen's feet instead of curtsying daintily.

Of course, Lady Fulford had said it with a sigh and a quick smile to temper the blow, but Marigold had seen her elder sister, Laurel, the newly minted Duchess of Dareford, nodding her agreement before she had caught herself.

Admittedly, Marigold *had* had the bad luck to have brought down an entire wall of shelves of fabric at the modiste's shop when she had casually leaned against them. But she had fervently apologized!

Of course, after that, she had tripped on the hem of the rich lace ballgown that was being sewn for her as she attempted to step onto the dais in front of the panel of mirrors. The lace had ripped, the bottom half of the dress had dropped to the floor, and the modiste had squealed as if she felt true physical pain at seeing her creation so destroyed. And then...

Well, then Marigold had realized the rumbling in her stomach that she had believed was simply butterflies at being taken out dress shopping was something else altogether. Probably the result of the calf's head soup that Lady Fulford had insisted she enjoy a generous serving of at dinner. Lady Fulford raved that her cook was a genius in the kitchen, but there was something about the head of the calf staring up at Marigold from the serving plate, with its tongue still in place, lolling dreadfully, that had turned her stomach even at the time.

And then her stomach had turned over entirely. All over the poor little modiste's elegant shop.

Well, the less Marigold remembered about that part of things, the better. Certainly, she and her sister would not be patronizing that particular modiste ever again, though she had no doubt Laurel had left a tidy sum by way of apology for the mess.

She perked up, suddenly thinking of the unexpected good that might come of her disastrous expedition yesterday. After witnessing Marigold's mishap at the modiste's shop, surely Lady Fulford would start to have second thoughts about introducing Marigold to society. After all, think of the humiliation that might result—not only to Marigold, but to Lady Fulford herself.

When a young woman was this unlucky and awkward, how could one bring her out for a Season? Perhaps Marigold would be left alone to her own devices. Perhaps her family and Lady Fulford would even, dare she say it, believe she might be considered firmly on the shelf? Of course, Marigold was only twenty-two years old, but from what she understood, to the *ton* that was practically as ancient as Methuselah.

Well, being left to her own devices would be a very welcome turn of events, indeed. She could easily come up with her own ideas to fill her time suitably and practically. Why, she had already begun working on some very promising plans.

With a little groan of contentment, she shifted against the mattress, pulling the sheet and counterpane more snugly beneath her chin. There was something to be said for being the sister-in-law of a duke. She had never experienced the luxury of such wonderfully soft sheets pressing against her skin before. She loved to slide her bare feet across the finely weaved linen, so cool and silky and refreshing.

Of course, she had known such sheets existed. She had helped to inventory the manor's linens alongside her sister, when Laurel had been the housekeeper at Blakeley Manor. But there was quite a difference between touching a costly sheet with her fingers, recognizing its superior quality to the ones her own family used, and sliding her nearly naked body around beneath them, reveling in their softness as they covered her from head to toe, and she drifted off into blissful slumber.

She had been reluctant to accept all the privileges that had abruptly fallen to her as the sister of a duchess. But this was one she was happy to indulge in. A large four-poster bed with a huge feather mattress and these heavenly, heavenly sheets!

She opened her eyes to look appreciatively at the bed she lay in, the crackling fire burning in the hearth and illuminating her view. The dark green Harrateen hangings, the gleaming mahogany carvings... the man lying at the foot of the bed.

She bolted upright with a gasp.

There was a man in her bed.

Well, she allowed, perhaps "in" was putting it rather strongly. He was draped across the foot of the bed which, Marigold being rather petite, was fortunately quite a distance from where she lay.

His face was turned toward her. His eyes were closed. His hands clutched the counterpane, as if he had fallen asleep afraid he might slip off.

He was a young man. Her age or a few years older. His hair was dark. She might even have guessed it to be black, but where the fire-light touched it, she saw a tinge of red mixed with the dark strands. A very dark auburn then.

His cheekbones were sharp, his nose bold and angular. But his lips were soft, bow-shaped. Almost feminine. Full and slightly parted.

He was a well-formed man, too. A muscular chest and shoulders filled out his jacket. Perhaps not so tall as her lanky brother-in-law, the duke, but of an average height. It was difficult to say when the man was draped so awkwardly.

He looked so rakish and handsome, lying there in her bed, that Marigold felt her heart do a strange somersault. Not, thankfully, anything akin to the butterflies she had experienced at the modiste. No, this was something else entirely. It was not altogether an unpleasant sensation.

Then she spotted the blood.

It was pooled beneath the young man. It had soaked through the counterpane. The maids would never be able to get the stain out.

She was already sliding out of the bed, stepping toward the stranger. He did not stir at the sound of her approach.

No, he lay still and motionless, as if he were... as if he were dead.

Marigold's heart leaped. It was bad enough that there was a strange man in her bed. He most certainly could *not* be dead.

She leaned over the man, careless of waking him, hoping now that she would, and peered closely, watching for movement, for the sign of his chest rising and falling gently.

But he was ever so still.

She leaned closer, bending down toward his face, then placing a finger in front of his lips.

She breathed a sigh of relief. Yes, there was breath still there. Faint, but he was breathing, in and out. At least, for now.

She squared her jaw. She must turn him over and see how severe his injuries were.

The idea of calling for assistance came to her, and then she dismissed it quickly. Her sister was expecting her very first child. Marigold could not risk the shock. Not after what Laurel had already endured. Her brother-in-law was a solid, trustworthy sort, but he would be sleeping beside her sister. She could not trust him to leave the room without disclosing to his wife what was happening. As Lady Fulford had returned to London, that left only the staff.

She could call for one of the servants—her former friends and colleagues. They would be only too glad to help. It would be wonderfully exciting for the young footmen and maids. Though, that would also mean the entire household would soon know that Marigold had woken to find a strange man in her bed. If not the entire estate. And the nearby village. Perhaps even half of London, if the servants communicated with their counterparts at the duke's house in Town.

And then? After word that a strange, bleeding man had been found in a would-be-debutante's bed? Then Marigold would be ruined, and her Season would be at an end before it could even begin. Lady Fulford and Laurel would be devastated. Marigold would be... thrilled.

She shook her head sadly. No, not yet. She may have no other choice but to call for assistance. Even if she were ruined, she would prefer the news not circulate thanks to those below stairs, but because she broke the news gently herself to those relevant few.

The young man was lying on his stomach, his face pressed sideways against the bed.

Marigold clambered up beside him, took his left shoulder in her hands, gritted her teeth, and lifted. She lifted as gently as she could, but even so, she immediately found he was heavier than she had expected.

She let go, breathing hard, and the man's body sagged back against the bed.

She would have to be less gentle. Well, he had not woken yet, so hopefully he would not.

She tried again, this time managing to push him up onto his side. Then with a great shove, the young man fell onto his back... revealing an open jacket, beneath which were a waistcoat that had once been a dark gold, and a fine linen shirt which had once been entirely white. Both were soaked through with blood.

She steeled herself, glancing at the little table by her bedside where a stack of books lay. Had she not just been re-reading Daniel Defoe's *The Life, Adventures and Piracies of the Famous Captain Singleton*? Was it not full of wonderful tales of bloodshed, grievous wounds, and the surgeons who healed them? Had she not been contemplating her usefulness in just this sort of situation?

She slid off the bed and marched about the room, grabbing garments that looked as if they might do, a basin of clean water, and the little flask of brandy her brother-in-law had given her jokingly as a welcome present a few months back.

7

She unfastened the flask and took a hearty swig, pretending she was a fierce pirate, used to the sight of blood. She would not faint. She would not swoon. Nay, she would treat this man, and by God, he would live to be grateful to her!

She wrenched open the stranger's waistcoat, then began to pull aside the white shirt.

This, finally, was when she encountered slight resistance. The man let out a groan of pain, and she paused, realizing that after lying pressed against the bed, the shirt had become quite stuck to the poor man's injury, like whitewash to a building. Wincing in sympathy, she stayed her hand. Then, soaking a cloth in the clean cool water, she gently patted the shirt until it was quite moist and tried again.

This time, the shirt peeled back much more easily, and for the first time, Marigold could see the wound beneath.

She let out a breath she had not realized she had been holding and felt a rush of relief. It was not as bad as it might have been. In fact, for the amount of blood, she had been expecting something much worse and gorier.

Dafoe would probably have described it as only a graze. A flesh wound. Oh, she had no doubt it must sting, but whoever had injured this young man had not come close to killing him.

It was not a bullet wound as she had feared, but a long slash across the center of his chest, just below the breastbone.

She swallowed hard as her eyes trailed up the man's chest. He was a wonderfully shaped specimen. That was undeniable. He was not particularly tall for a man—she could see that now. But what there was of him was impressive. The flat plane of his stomach, the well-defined, carved chest muscles... and oh, goodness, the fine auburn hairs curling, damp and plastered against his skin.

She gave her head a well-deserved shake. If she was going to play the part of a surgeon, she must act like one and not gape at her patient.

She eyed the slash. It was still oozing blood a little but looked as if it could be bandaged. The worst of the blood loss seemed to be over.

She eyed the man's face. His eyes remained closed. If he had let out

8

a groan at the sensation of the shirt peeling away, he might wake up for this next part. But it could not be helped.

She picked up the clean petticoat beside her and began to tear it into strips.

When she had prepared what she hoped was an adequate bandage and cleaned the dried blood away from the wound as carefully as she could, she began to dress it.

It was all going well until she had to lift him to wrap the cloth around his back. She managed to get the cloth beneath him, and in her relief may have let go of his torso a little too suddenly. She winced. She would have to work on her gentleness with patients, she chided herself. As the man's body hit the bed, he let out another groan–this one so loud that Marigold's eyes darted to the door. She hoped the night footman would not happen to be passing.

She bit her lip, waited a moment, then continued binding the wound. She was determined to do a more than adequate job and so had to lift the man one more time, work the bandage under and around one more time.

Then there was the matter of fastening it tightly.

She may have been a little overzealous there. As she was tying the bandage, grinning to herself that all had gone so well, she realized the young man's eyes had opened. He was staring up at her.

"Oh, good evening."

"Who the bloody hell are you?" he wheezed, already fumbling around to try to sit up.

She put a hand on his upper chest and gently pushed him back.

"Don't even think about it," she chided. "Stay still while I finish."

"Finish what?" he demanded. "Butchering me? I feel as if I were a pig that had been slaughtered."

"You would be feeling a great deal worse if you were. I am no butcher."

She saw his eyebrows raise and enjoyed watching the fine arches curve.

"Oh, no? My latest seductress, then?" the young man drawled.

Marigold frowned. Evidently, her patient's spirits were already returning. The man eyed her up and down in a way that caused her to

9

suddenly realize she was still in her nightclothes. She was not even wearing a robe, for heaven's sake.

She felt herself blushing hot and resisted the impulse to cross her arms over her chest. Instead, she put the final flourish on her knot, yanking tightly without attempting to be gentle.

The young man let out a shocking string of curses, then lay panting hard for a moment.

"I admit," he said finally between breaths. "You aren't ordinarily my type, but I suppose you were unbearably charming, so I made an exception and things became too... vigorous between us?"

Marigold rose from the bed with a huff, taking delight in the pained expression on his face as the mattress trembled.

"Your seductress? Do you normally take women as lovers who knife you in your sleep?" she demanded. She tossed her head, her unbound hair falling over her shoulders. "Perhaps you would make an exception for me, good sir, but I would most certainly not do the same for *you*."

This was a lie, she admitted to herself. Could she imagine taking this young man as a lover to bed? It was as titillating a fantasy as any good novel and left her skin swimming in gooseflesh. But no, she would not allow herself to follow that thread. Not now. Possibly not ever. She had more important things to deal with than silly young men. Especially ones who went around getting themselves stabbed and then wandered into strange houses bleeding.

The young man smiled politely. "In that case, would you care to explain to me just what you are doing in my bedroom?"

"Your bedroom?" Marigold exclaimed. "Well now, that is rich! This is not your bedroom." She narrowed her eyes. "I believe you must have suffered a head injury. I admit, I did not think to examine that part of you."

"Oh, no?" the young man replied, all innocence. "Not when you could strip me bare to the waist. I suppose my head was uninteresting by comparison."

"All of you is uninteresting to me," Marigold snapped. "I tended you out of sheer Christian duty and good will, but now I believe I shall call for the night watchman and my brother-in-law and have you thrown out. Good luck finding your way to the village. It is a two-mile walk."

"I know precisely how far it is," the young man replied mildly. "I walked it often. To visit a paramour whose father owned the haberdashery."

Marigold rolled her eyes. "I do not need to hear more bragging about your exploits with women. I would be much more interested in hearing how you came about that wound."

"Would you?" the man mused. "Well, funnily enough, that too involves a woman..."

"In that case, never mind. My interest has evaporated." Marigold took a threatening step toward the door. "Would you care to provide me with your name before I summon the footman? I don't suppose you wish to thank me for caring for you when you were half dead and bleeding all across my bed. Oh no, wait, I am supposed to believe this is *your* bed..."

"It is Leigh Blakeley," the young man interrupted. "And it is my bed. Well, was."

Marigold gaped. "I beg your pardon?"

The man was sitting up on his elbows, inspecting the bed more closely. "Those hangings... are they blue or green? It is difficult to tell in this dim light."

"They are green," Marigold replied frostily. "Dark green."

"Not a deep royal blue?"

"Decidedly not. They are green. I look at them each night. I believe I would know."

"Ah, that's the issue then," he said, sounding satisfied. "Right house. Wrong room." He shook his head ruefully. "I've climbed through that window a hundred times or more. I must have been truly out of my head to pick the wrong window."

"Well, you were bleeding. Profusely. And apparently blind to the fact that the bed was already occupied. Though I'm sure it is not the first time that you have been so sadly deluded." Marigold inspected him closely. "You truly are Leigh Blakeley? The younger brother of the Duke of Dareford?"

"So my mother told me." The man grinned cheekily up at her.

Was it her imagination or had his eyes darted, just for a second, a little lower? This time, Marigold did cross her arms across her chest. Then she lifted her chin in the air and marched across the room to fetch her dressing robe—a sky-blue wool, which felt reassuringly warm and heavy as she pulled it on. And very concealing.

"You missed your brother's wedding. And your sister's," she snapped as she tied the belt of the robe around her waist.

"And my other sister. Though that was not quite a wedding, was it? More of a roadside stop."

Marigold narrowed her eyes. "Not entirely ignorant of your own family's affairs, after all, I see."

"There have certainly been a great deal of them. Family affairs, that is," the youngest Blakeley son drawled. For a man who had been knifed that evening, he was remarkably composed. Marigold could not help being once more impressed. He was infuriating, yes. Impressive and infuriating and altogether too certain of himself—especially when it came to women!

"You mentioned a brother-in-law, and so I surmise you are my new sister-in-law's... sister?"

"How wonderfully astute of you. And yet when you came to, your initial guess was that I was your—how did you put it? Oh, yes, your seducer. Seductress," she corrected. *Do not blush, Marigold,* she warned herself. *Do not even think of blushing as that word passes your lips, and you look down at that firm bare chest.*

"Yes, I've often been called the sharpest Blakeley. Ironic, isn't it?" He smiled wryly, glancing down at the bandage.

"Perhaps a little too sharp for your own good."

"Touché, Sister. For we are related, are we not? I was correct?"

"You were," Marigold acknowledged. "I'm the duchess's younger sister, Marigold Spencer."

The young man eyed her keenly. "You Spencers have been picking us off one by one, haven't you?"

"I could say the same about you Blakeleys," Marigold retorted, her eyes blazing. "In any case, I believe it is safe to say that it is at an end."

"Oh, certainly," he agreed. "I'm an incorrigible rogue. Lock up your daughters and all that."

Marigold sniffed. "I don't see what good that would do since you clamber through windows into women's bedchambers."

"My bedchamber... at least... well, yes, I see your point." He chuckled. A deep, low rumbling that made Marigold's goosebumps return in a flash.

"Do you think you can find it in yourself to rise? Or do you require assistance?" she asked, purposely making her voice chill. She made another gesture toward the bell by the door.

For the first time, Leigh Blakeley frowned. "Now, see here," he said slowly. "This is all deucedly awkward. Of course, I didn't mean to come crashing into your room or to bleed all over your bed."

"No, I suppose you intended to crash into your own room and bleed to death in the comfort of your own bed. Entirely alone," Marigold said blandly.

Leigh smirked. "Yes, something like that." He looked down at himself. "Honestly, I hadn't realized how bad things were. I thought it was merely a scratch. It hardly hurt at first. I rode here with scarcely any pain at all." He scratched his head. "I suppose the brandy might have masked it."

"You rode here?" Marigold exclaimed. "On a horse?"

"That is the usual way, isn't it? Or do you ordinarily mount a unicorn?"

"A centaur, in fact," Marigold retorted. "It's in the stable."

Leigh raised his eyebrows. "Fascinating. You are fierce for such a little thing, aren't you?"

"Though she be but little," Marigold muttered.

She should have known better. Leigh grinned broadly and added to the quote, "'She was a vixen when she went to school.' Are you? A vixen, I mean, Sister?"

"You know Midsummer Night's Dream by heart?" Marigold was, once again, impressed despite herself.

"Of course. I am an Englishman, am I not?" He gave her a dazzling wink, momentarily throwing her off guard. "Shall I call you Helena or Marigold?"

"Neither. Miss Spencer will do very well. Or *Sister*," she added. Though she did not feel like this man's sister. Not in the least.

She suddenly realized she was instructing a noble lord of England on how to address her—a girl who, until a few months ago, had been a housemaid—and suppressed a hysterical giggle.

She touched the bell string.

"Don't pull it," Leigh said sharply. "Wait. Please." He pushed himself up on his elbows, then gripped the foot of the bed, and slowly pulled himself to a full sitting position. He was wincing, but Marigold made no move to help. She had a feeling she knew what he was about to ask. If he could sit up by himself then...

"I'll go. By myself. I do not require assistance. Please, let me leave your bedchamber, which I so rudely invaded. My room is just next door. At least, it was the last time I checked."

Marigold frowned. "Can you even stand?"

"Of course, I can stand." She watched as he pulled hard on the closest bed poster and tried to rise. His face turned a sight paler as he slowly made his way upright. "There. You see?"

"And walk?"

"Oh, you are demanding, vixen." He groaned and let go of the bed post, taking a step in her direction. "Of course, I..." He faltered, started to fall.

Marigold darted forward, wrapping an arm around his waist before she could think twice. "You stupid man. You'll rip your bandage open!"

"No, no, it's fine," he protested. But his arm had found its way around her shoulders, and he was gripping her quite tightly, almost painfully.

"I shall escort you to your room," Marigold decided. "And then return to my own. And we shall say no more about it."

She felt him take a great shuddering breath. Then he nodded. "Very well. That might be best."

She thought again about asking him how he had become injured. Then remembered what he had said about it involving a woman. No, she'd rather not know, she decided. It was sure to be tawdry.

She steered Lord Leigh toward the door of the bedroom, then opened it, and peered out into the hall. The night lamps were lit. The corridor was blessedly empty.

"Hurry," she whispered. "Before the footman wanders by."

She heard him grunt his assent. They stepped out into the hall.

Marigold tried to ignore all the sensations that were flooding through her and focus simply on watching her patient put one foot in front of another.

But it was no use. Her hand was tingling where it touched the fabric of his shirt. Through the linen, she felt his hot skin pressing against her arm, the muscles of his back against the palm of her hand, the outline of the bandages she had wrapped around him. She had touched him—intimately. He had been in her bed.

Do not blush, Marigold, she all but screamed to herself. *Do not think such thoughts. It will all be over in an instant, and you can return to your bed.* Oh, but not to sleep. There was no chance she could sleep after all that had transpired. She would pick up *Captain Singleton* then and read, she decided. Read until morning. Read until all thoughts of Leigh Blakeley had flitted out of her head.

Flitted out until she had to see the man again at the breakfast table.

Well, at least then he would be decently clothed. And well behaved. *Better* behaved.

"Here we are." He stopped so abruptly that Marigold walked another full step, her arm pulling away, his sliding off her shoulder. For a second, she felt bereft.

Then she raised her chin. "Well, then. Good night to you, my lord."

"Good night to you, Sister," he replied solemnly. "And thank you. For your solicitous assistance."

"Think nothing of it." She turned to go.

"Perhaps," he started from behind her. "I might beseech you not to make mention of this to my brother. Or his wife. From what I understand, they are... in a delicate situation?"

"A delicate situation..." She grasped his meaning. "Oh, yes."

"I would not like to cause them any undue alarm." She heard him clear his throat. "Or my mother."

"Oh, of course not."

She turned back to face him, suddenly realizing, suddenly understanding for the first time that evening just who she was dealing with.

The black sheep of the Blakeley family had finally come home. The prodigal son had returned–fallen bleeding into her bed, to be sure— but returned.

The youngest son who could not be bothered to return for his siblings' weddings. Who had waited months to come to see his long-lost mother, even after she had been presumed dead for years.

Marigold had heard the tales. Lady Fulford had made no attempts to hide her annoyance with her youngest godchild and seemed to find relief in telling Marigold the absolute worst stories about young Lord Leigh's numerous escapades. Brothels, gaming hells, even prisons. There was no end to what he would or wouldn't do.

Leigh Blakeley was a scoundrel. A womanizing rogue. Ha! That was putting it mildly. He was, to use a stronger term, a notorious rake. A libertine. A dangerous man.

And he had nearly charmed her. More than he knew.

Yet, perhaps in the end, it would turn out that he had helped her, too.

"Welcome home, Lord Leigh," she said quietly, then pushed open the door to her own room, and closed it without another word.

Leigh stood in the hall a moment, looking at the closed door.

What a very strange girl.

He supposed he had been quite abominably rude to her at first. When he had woken up, he had to admit he had been in a fair amount of pain. To distract himself, he had made silly jests at her expense. He supposed he may even have suggested they had... He groaned. Yes, he had, hadn't he?

Well, there was nothing for that now. The girl probably under-stood. She had brothers, hadn't she? Though likely more mannerly ones than he.

She seemed quite cool and practical for such a young thing.

She was, as he had observed, quite fierce.

He stared at her door. But she was also rather pretty. Was he truly acknowledging this? She was commonly pretty. She had a sweet face, beneath all that fierceness and those blazing eyes.

But she was just another young woman. Certainly no beauty.

He wondered what his brother had planned for her.

Miss Spencer was a full-figured girl with ample curves. While she was below average in height, she made up for it somewhat with her strong presence. She also had a gorgeous mane of golden hair. It had been the first thing he had noticed about her. Well, that and the stridency of her voice and her disapproving glare. Very well, the third thing he had noticed about her. It fell around her shoulders in a wild cloud—and she had seemed not even to notice or to care.

The same could be said about those ample breasts. She had not even bothered to cover herself up, though he had been able to see her nipples puckering, ripe and taut below her nightdress. Of course, she had been rather preoccupied, tending to him and then sparring with him. She had slipped on a robe as soon as she had seemed to notice the effect she was unintentionally having.

He couldn't help it. He thought again of those heavy full breasts. The pink tips of her nipples straining against the thin white muslin nightdress she wore.

He stifled a groan. Good God. She's your sister-in-law, man, he chided himself. But it was too late. He felt himself hardening.

Cursing his debased impulses, he pushed open the door of his room and stumbled in.

Chapter Two

" I 'm delighted you've returned, of course."

Leigh watched his elder brother pace across his study. The room had once been their father's. His brother had made few changes to it. Leigh appreciated this.

"But?"

"There is no 'but.' I'm delighted. And Laurel will be, too. I cannot wait for you to meet her." The Duke of Dareford, or "Dare" as he was known to his family, grimaced. He was a tall and handsome man, just past thirty, in possession of a strong angular jaw that ladies quite admired, an elegant Roman nose he had inherited from his father, and the trademark Blakeley dark hair and eyes, which he shared with their elder sister, Katherine. "That said, I'm sure Kat and Briar would appreciate being given the opportunity to introduce you to their husbands in the near future as well."

"Yes, well, one thing at a time." Leigh waved his hand. He frowned. "Something in this room has changed." He pointed to the smaller desk in the corner. "There. The desk is bare. Where has your secretary gone? Or has he simply become monkish in his habits and cleared all traces of himself from view?"

"No, he is gone," Dare said a little sharply.

Leigh raised one brow. "Without notice?"

Dare gave a short barking laugh. "Oh, I gave him notice all right."

"Giles, was it not? I thought you were fond of the man." He had always seemed a little too greasy for a duke's secretary to Leigh, but a nice enough fellow. In need of a good wash behind the ears, perhaps.

"He was a scoundrel," Dare said coldly. "And I do not use the word in jest."

"You mean such as when you call me that?" Leigh joked. "He had a ridiculously pompous name, did he not? Belonged to an esteemed family, though. Younger son, I suppose."

"Ambrose Bartholomew Giles. Seventh son of a baron. He came highly recommended and did his duties well enough, was agreeable enough... until he was not."

Leigh began to understand. "Trouble with a serving girl, I suppose? Ungentlemanly conduct?"

Dare's mouth became a hard, flat line. "The girl is now my wife. Ungentlemanly conduct in the extreme. Utterly egregious."

"Bloody hell." Leigh was shocked despite himself. "I hope you gave him the rough send-off he deserved. Or should we track him down together? My wedding present to you."

Dare quirked his lips. "Very kind, but the matter is past. He was not pleased at how quickly he was shown the door, and I certainly did not provide him with a reference. But there was no violence involved." He paused. "Sad to say."

"Very restrained of you. Though I'm not surprised." Leigh grinned. "Big brother the peacemaker."

"Blakeley Manor is well rid of his sort. He is London's problem now. From what I have been given to understand by a friend–" Dare gestured to a letter lying on the desk behind him. "Mr. Ambrose Giles is now seeking a bride on the marriage mart. Evidently, his family has given up on his potential to foster a career and is hoping he will catch a rich wife instead. Though I sincerely pity any woman who has the misfortune to become that bastard's wife."

Leigh wrinkled his nose. "How distasteful."

Dare gave his younger sibling a knowing look. "Indeed. What precisely turned your stomach? Giles's intentions? Or more likely it was my mention of the word 'wife' or 'marriage mart.' Perhaps both?" Dare shook his head, with the hint of a smile. "Some men wish to settle down, you know, Leigh. It is not a torment for them to consider. Myself included, of course. I know you can hardly believe it, but all your siblings are very happily shackled." The duke shuffled some papers on his desk. "We got rather off course just now. Where were we? Oh, yes. Then there is the matter of Mother."

"The matter?" Leigh frowned. "You make it sound as if she were a problem to be solved."

Dare looked at him thoughtfully. "Of course, she is not. But there is a component of a puzzle to her return. Have you seen her?"

Leigh nodded. After lying in bed for hours without a wink of real sleep, he had gone to her as soon as he thought it reasonable to think she would be awake. "This morning. She was affectionate. Warm. Though frail."

She was very frail—so thin in his arms as they had embraced. But she had smiled at him in that way she had always done and gripped him tightly, as if she were afraid to ever let him go. He had nearly cried on her shoulder like a little boy, too. It had taken everything he had to hold back. She was his mother, and he had believed her to be dead. Now she was back—but she had changed so very much. Whereas once she had been a healthy, blooming woman who no one could rightfully describe as delicate or frail, now she was most certainly both those things. Her hair was still tinged with the familiar red—there was that much. But she was looking decidedly... well, old. It was damned uncomfortable, Leigh thought ironically, to have to confront one's own mortality in an aging parent.

"I still cannot believe she is really here. Alive," he said abruptly. "I cannot believe you found her." Or that it had been Dare to finally discover one of their parents' whereabouts, rather than himself. That stung a little, but only a little. After all, his siblings had no idea he had continued the fruitless search.

"Not simply a ghost that might vanish with a strong breath of air?" Dare remarked. "I felt much the same way the first few weeks. But she is back. Though we have no idea how or why she disappeared in the first place. Or what happened to Father," he added quietly.

Leigh felt his brother's eyes watching him steadily.

"Why did you not return sooner?" Dare asked, his voice even.

Leigh cocked his head. "Are you sure that is all you wish to say on the matter?"

"What do you mean?"

"I mean I missed your wedding."

"You missed Kat's wedding, too."

"I notice you do not mention our youngest sister."

Dare's mouth turned up in a rueful smirk. "A highway handfasting, or whatever the Scots call it, does not seem like much to miss." His face turned serious. "But you did miss yet another opportunity to meet your newest nephew and greet Briar's husband at Christmas. He is a fine man, all things considered."

As Dare doted on their sisters, but was particularly protective of Briar, Leigh knew this meant the laird was a deserving one. Their younger sister must be very happy indeed.

"Yes, well." Leigh decided to be honest. "I tried to be. I had hoped to be here to see you wed. Then for Christmas."

"But? You were captured by pirates and held in the brigs? They've only just released you because you managed to charm their captain by teaching his parrot Latin." Dare cocked one eyebrow. "No? Am I close? Let me try again. You lost everything you had in a casino in Venice and had to seduce the owner's daughter and beg her to help you return home, which she did by hiding you in an empty wine cask and smuggling you aboard a merchant ship bound for London?"

Leigh crossed his arms over his chest.

"Very well. Last attempt. You were caught sneaking into the tower of a lovely French maiden, and after a perilous sword fight with her furious fiancé, you were left for dead and only just managed to find your way back to England?"

This was closest to the truth. It did not escape him that all his brother's guesses were predicated on the assumption of Leigh's absolute frivolous nature.

"Your postulations are very dependent upon my skills of seduction," Leigh noted. "I suppose I should thank you for the vote of confidence. But no, sadly, there were no beautiful women responsible for my delayed homecoming."

He would not share the details on what he had been doing before returning, he decided. Let Dare think what he liked. Let him imagine his younger brother leading a rogue's existence. He would not share the truth until there was more to share.

"What's this about beautiful women?" a familiar voice crowed sharply, followed by a distinctive rapping sound Leigh could not quite pinpoint.

The two men jumped and turned toward the doorway of the library. Dare leapt to his feet as he recognized the visitor, with Leigh following suit more slowly.

"Lady Fulford! How delightful to see you."

The venerable white-haired dowager countess looked past the duke to eye Leigh shrewdly. "I see our prodigal has returned, Dareford." She lifted the object she held—a silver-headed cane—and then pounded the floor with a clatter, clearly hoping to elicit another jump, but Leigh simply smiled.

"How good to see you, Lady Fulford. It has been too long. You are looking as spry and beautiful as ever."

"Oh, ho ho! So, it was me you were both discussing just now?" Lady Fulford demanded, her gaze eagle-like. But there was a twinkle in her eyes. She gestured to Leigh. "Come and kiss my cheek, dear boy. I never could stay angry with you for long."

He obliged her, coming to kiss the soft wrinkled cheek. He felt an odd pang as he did so. Yes, he had even missed Lady Fulford. He had missed them all. Perhaps this time he would stay home for a while. At least a month.

"Even when you shattered my very best crystal vase with a cricket bat," Lady Fulford continued. "Well, what have you to say for yourself, young Blakeley? Where have you been?"

Leigh could not resist. "From going to and fro in the earth, and from walking up and down in it."

He heard his brother make a choked noise from behind him.

Lady Fulford's face was truly unreadable for an instant. Then she clucked her tongue. "Shocking. Absolutely shocking. But I would expect nothing less from you, young man."

"The devil can cite Scripture for his purpose," Dare said with false moroseness.

"Indeed, Duke. Indeed." Lady Fulford nodded, then linked her arm firmly through Leigh's. "Well, dear boy. Lead the way. I am not as young as I used to be. You may have noticed that. It is why I have this infernal cane with me now."

"Nonsense. You are as youthful and lovely as you ever were," Leigh insisted.

Lady Fulford *hmphed*. "Considering I was forty-seven if I were a day, on the very day you were born, my boy, you have never seen me as youthful and lovely as all that."

"Some women are youthful and lovely no matter how many years they put behind them, Lady Fulford," Leigh said truthfully. "You are such a rare woman."

"Aha! I am a rare woman. That we can both agree upon." Lady Fulford sighed. "I was lovely once. It is best not thought of. There are other qualities I have developed in beauty's stead."

"Far more valuable ones, I am sure," Leigh said quietly.

"Indeed." Lady Fulford looked at him shrewdly. "So, it is not simply female exteriors you value these days, Blakeley? I venture you may be growing up a little."

"Come now, Lady Fulford. This is Leigh we are talking about, is it not?" Dare jested.

Leigh tried to smile. "Dare has the right of it, I'm afraid. Incorrigible to the bones." He patted the dowager's arm. "Now tell me, please. Where am I leading you off to?"

"Why, to the family meeting, of course!" Lady Fulford narrowed her eyes. "Surely your brother told you about it."

"I did not have the chance," Dare said quickly. "I was about to when you appeared."

"Like an angel of light," Leigh quipped. "Blinding us both with your radiance."

"I shall rap your knuckles with my cane if you keep that up," Lady Fulford warned.

Leigh grinned. "What is this family meeting all about?"

"It is about your sister-in-law." Lady Fulford sighed dramatically. "The dear girl has been pushed and pulled every which way until I am sure she is close to making a run for it."

"Dare's wife's sister?" Leigh asked curiously. The girl he had met last night. He lifted a hand to his chest, then managed to resist patting the bandage she had put there. With her bare hands on his bare skin. God knew, but somehow, the act of having his wound dressed had become oddly erotic. What the devil was the matter with him? It was all because of that nightdress, he told himself. When he saw his sister-in-law today, he would be sure to put all thoughts of it far, far from his mind and behave like... well, if not the perfect gentleman, then at least... gentle. As well behaved as was possible for him, he amended. There was no point in reaching for the stars.

"That's the one. Miss Marigold Spencer. A sweet, clever but rather frumpy, plump girl. Do not get me wrong. She will have her pick of suitors once I have finished with her. Any debutante I take under my wing is a success. There are no ifs, ands, or buts about it."

"Marigold was Lady Fulford's companion for a little while," Dare explained to his brother.

"Yes, a very little while," Lady Fulford said. "And before that, she was employed as a housemaid."

"A housemaid?" Leigh quirked an eyebrow. "What an unexpected path her life has taken."

"Yes, well, her sister went from housekeeper to duchess, might I remind you," Lady Fulford replied.

"Marigold and Laurel both worked at Blakeley Manor, Leigh. As did both of their brothers," Dare remarked.

"Good Lord. You and my sisters are marrying all the help. Why, there won't be anyone left by the time you're through," Leigh teased.

"Yes, well." Leigh watched his older brother shift uncomfortably. "They are quite an unusual family."

"Their father was dear friends with your mother growing up," Lady Fulford confirmed.

"Was he really? Who was this man?" Leigh asked curiously.

"William Spencer, the vicar's son. He married a widowed Scottish noblewoman who had a young boy of her own. They had three children together–Laurel, Marigold, and Ashley."

"The young boy–this is the man Briar has married? The laird?"

Dare nodded. "Wren Spencer. The laird of the Renfrew clan, yes."

"And Kat married this Ashley Spencer?"

"He worked as our groom. They met over a Christmas house party."

Leigh was amused. "Not the man you were probably hoping our widowed sister would meet and fall in love with at the Christmas party you hosted, but I take it he is a good sort?"

"He is an honorable man of excellent birth," Lady Fulford announced. The twinkle appeared in her eye again. "Very well-formed for a man, too."

"Oh, he is, is he?" Leigh winked at her. "That's important. No less than my sister deserves. A proper, well-formed man. Well, if you say he is of excellent birth, then he must be. I have never seen you hesitate to disparage someone who is not." He grinned.

"I do not disparage those less fortunate," Lady Fulford said primly. "Though they are many."

"Yes, well," Dare said hastily. "The family meeting is to discuss Marigold's future. You may as well come along. It will be an excellent opportunity to introduce you to both girls as they weren't at breakfast this morning."

Dare's wife had broken her fast in bed with only her younger sister present. Leigh understood the new duchess was with child, but the proceedings were not going as smoothly as one might have hoped so far.

"Here we are," Lady Fulford said majestically as they reached the drawing room. The doors had already been opened, and a liveried footman stood to one side, his arms folded neatly, his chin held high. He was clearly avoiding eye contact with the formidable Lady Fulford, Leigh noticed. She probably terrified the servants. She certainly had terrified him when he was a boy. And yet, he had still brought his cricket bat into her house. Oh, the daring.

The trio entered the room which was already occupied by two

ladies sitting together on a comfortable chintz settee. A tea service had been arranged on a nearby table.

"Oh, there you are, Dare," one of the women said, rising, and smiling at them. "Lady Fulford, how lovely to see you. And you must be Leigh. I am so happy to meet you at long last, Lord Leigh. Welcome home."

Leigh looked at his new sister-in-law with appreciation. She was not what he had expected, but he could immediately see what had appealed to his brother. The new Duchess of Dareford had a calm poise and confident demeanor. She was tall and slender, gowned in a peacock-blue silk gown with few ornamentations, and her silver-blonde hair was pulled back and arranged in a simple chignon.

It was a very unusual shade, he noticed. Whereas, he thought, as he cast his gaze toward the other woman still seated on the sofa behind the duchess, her sister's tresses were a much warmer tone. A true buttercup yellow.

What was more, he observed with amusement, it was wild in a way her older sister's was not. All those curls and ringlets, twisted and pinned every which way, as if her maid had lost all patience by the end. It was fortunate that Grecian styles were in vogue. The soft mass of curls suited Miss Spencer. They framed her heart-shaped face, lending her an air of sweetness that Leigh suspected would immediately be lost the moment the lady in question opened her mouth.

Sure enough. "How good of you to make an appearance, Lord Leigh. Finally!"

There was silence for a moment.

"Marigold! Really!" The duchess hissed at her sister, blushing a little.

Miss Spencer rose from the sofa and stepped toward Leigh and Lady Fulford with a shrug. "Well really, it is not as if anyone else were chiding him for missing your wedding."

"You don't know that," Leigh said mildly. "Lady Fulford could have been chiding me all the way to the drawing room. Not to mention whacking me repeatedly with her cane."

"I have not had an opportunity to do so yet, Miss Marigold, but I certainly shall remedy that every chance I get now that you have so faithfully reminded me of my duty," Lady Fulford reassured the girl, lifting her cane and giving a light jab to Leigh's ribs.

The jab was clearly meant as a jest but, in fact, was quite painful. The carved head of the cane landed precisely where Leigh was bandaged. He choked back a cry, swallowed hard, and closed his eyes for an instant. When he opened them, he saw Miss Spencer looking back at him with what looked almost like sympathy. Of course, she was also trying unsuccessfully to hide a smirk, so it was difficult to say for certain.

"Oh, this young buck. Carrying on all across the Continent, I'm sure," Lady Fulford grumbled. "Take me to an armchair, boy. I grow weary of standing. And pass me some tea."

"Yes, Lady Fulford," Leigh said obediently as he was expected to do. In truth, he enjoyed waiting on the old lady. After all, next to his own mother, there was no woman he respected—or feared—more.

"But we are not here to discuss the incorrigible Blakeley," Lady Fulford continued. "Although I agree that his future should be next on the agenda." Leigh did not like the sound of this. "We are here today to discuss"—she paused for dramatic effect—"Marigold's Season."

"It sounds like the title of a terrible play no one would be interested in going to see," Miss Spencer muttered, sinking back down onto the sofa and rebelliously kicking the leg of the chair next to her. "Or one of the Egerton family's dreadful themed musicales."

Leigh snorted. So, Miss Spencer had already had the misfortune to be dragged to one of those. This must be the third generation of Egerton daughters. None of them could sing or play an instrument worth a damn. He could remember his mother begging him to be good during an Egerton musicale when he was no more than seventeen or eighteen. He believed he had snuck out and kissed one of the Egerton maids instead. Time much more well spent.

Lady Fulford ignored her. "Now, Duke, Duchess, you know I shall take the lead on many aspects of Miss Spencer's debut, being an old hand at all this. But of course, a duke's patronage goes much further than a worn-out dowager's ever could. And so, I believe a grand ball shall be in order to help launch—"

"Just a moment, Lady Fulford," Dare interrupted. "If you will.

There is something Laurel and I wished to mention. And I am afraid to say you will not be at all pleased."

He glanced at his wife, then stepped forward to take her hand, drew her to a settee across from where Miss Spencer sat, and pulled her down beside him.

"Lady Fulford, Laurel and I will not be able to be Marigold's patrons this Season, I'm sorry to say."

"Good Heavens! Whyever not?" Lady Fulford exclaimed, looking more scandalized by this than by Leigh's quoting of the Devil earlier. "You are Miss Spencer's brother-in-law! Her nearest family! What is the meaning of this? Surely, you must see that the girl needs a proper entrance into Society!"

"We could not agree more, and we want to support Marigold in every way we possibly can, Lady Fulford," the duchess said quickly, leaning forward. "But I'm afraid that..." She fumbled, paused.

"What Laurel is trying to say," Dare said. "Is that her physician is on the verge of recommending complete bed rest. He wishes her lying-in to begin... well, as soon as possible."

"I am not interested in lying in bed for four or five months, as you may well understand," Laurel interjected, her face set stubbornly. Then it fell. "But I have agreed to compromise. I will not be able to travel back and forth to London. I am to avoid traveling by carriage or horse at all, unless absolutely necessary."

"Goodness gracious," Lady Fulford breathed, looking decidedly alarmed. "My dear, things are truly as delicate as that?"

Leigh watched his sister-in-law bite her lip, and his brother's face turn pale.

"After the last... complication," the duchess said quietly, gripping her husband's hand tightly with her own. "After what occurred back in the autumn, I mean, well, Dr. Pearson believes we cannot be too careful this time."

"Yes, I see. Of course, of course," Lady Fulford murmured. She leaned forward unexpectedly and took the duchess's free hand in both her wrinkled ones. "I shall be praying for you, my dear one. You will get through this in good health. Both yours and the babe's, I'm sure of it."

She released the duchess's hand, looking almost surprised at herself, then shook her shoulders. "Well then, I suppose we shall have to do this ourselves. Really, it is providential that you have returned at such an auspicious time, Blakeley."

"Is it?" Leigh asked weakly. He did not like where this was going.

"Indisputably." Lady Fulford nodded vigorously. "I am determined Miss Spencer shall meet with nothing but success this Season. She shall do so with you by her side. You compared yourself to the Devil earlier, my dear boy, though only in jest, I know. But the truth is, you shall be a knight in shining armor, carrying our damsel in distress through the perils of none other than the *ton* of London itself. Of course," she added, sitting up straighter, "I shall be there as well. A helpful advisor, guiding every step."

"You wish for me to escort Miss Spencer to London? To chaperone her during her Season as a debutante?" Leigh clarified, horror growing in him with every word. "You wish for me to appear on the marriage mart? Me? The last unmarried Blakeley son?"

"Oh, pah! You make it sound as if they shall tear you to pieces," Lady Fulford scoffed. "Your brother has settled an incredibly generous dowry upon Miss Spencer."

"Much too generous. He needn't have done it at all," Miss Spencer declared loudly.

Lady Fulford ignored her and continued, "I assure you that she shall be the center of much of the attention. The mamas of the *ton* will be glad to see you make an appearance, certainly," she admitted. "But I will protect you from the worst of them." She perked up. "Unless, that is, you are ready to take up your mantle of duty and finally…"

"No, no, no," Leigh said hastily. "I am not ready to take up that mantle. Not ready at all."

"Nor am I," Miss Spencer muttered loudly. "Nor am I, Laurel. Does anyone care? No, of course not. They simply want to dump me in lace gowns and push me out to dance."

Leigh looked at her sympathetically. "Terrible thing to be a woman, isn't it?"

"What would you know of it?" Miss Spencer snapped, her eyes fiery. "You have been one yourself, have you?"

"No, but I have known a great m–" Leigh began innocently.

"All right, that's enough of that, Leigh," Dare interrupted. "Lady Fulford, Laurel and I were going to suggest that perhaps it would be best to wait until next year when we can help you with Marigold."

"Oh, yes!" Miss Spencer exclaimed excitedly. "Let's! Let's wait another year. At least one. Perhaps two. Perhaps never."

"Nonsense!" Lady Fulford rapped her cane on the floor three times in quick succession. "She is already twenty-two! Do you know how old you will be next year, Miss Spencer?"

"I believe twenty-two is usually followed by–" Miss Spencer began.

"An unspeakable age!" Lady Fulford declared. "I cannot even say the words. Why, I was married at eighteen, Miss Spencer. Eighteen! Before my very first Season was over, I was up in front of the altar."

"But were you happy?" Miss Spencer muttered.

"I was happy because I had found a good, well-to-do man to care for me and remove the burden from my mama and papa," Lady Fulford said virtuously.

"He died rather young, did he not?" Leigh inquired helpfully. "Widowhood has suited you very well."

"He died when he was meant to die and no sooner. And married or unmarried, I did my duty in all things," Lady Fulford said cryptically.

Leigh was quiet. Lady Fulford and her husband had never had children. He wondered now if they had tried. He glanced at his sister-in-law. She was looking distractedly down at the floor. Though this was her sister they were discussing, evidently there were more pressing things on her mind–which was understandable.

"What is the reason you are refusing Miss Spencer this boon, my lord?" Lady Fulford demanded loudly, drawing Leigh's attention back to her. She gazed at him hawkishly, no trace of a twinkle now. "You have finally returned to the bosom of your family. After over a year dallying God-knows-where. You have missed three weddings–"

Leigh opened his mouth to say Briar's did not really count, then thought better of it.

"And even your own dear mother's homecoming."

"Well, I'm here now, and that's what really counts, isn't it?"

"Not to mention other events," the duke said quietly, surprising Leigh completely. He realized what his brother meant and colored.

"I am truly sorry about that," he said—and he meant it. "I am here now, and I hope to be able to support you both."

"We could use your support in supporting Laurel's sister," Dare said softly, not meeting Leigh's eyes.

"You truly think I would make a suitable chaperone for a young girl?" Leigh asked in disbelief. "Despite what you all think of me?"

"Well, I don't," Miss Spencer announced loudly. "And what are you, after all, three years older than I am? Four?"

Leigh ignored her. "You have no idea how awkward it would be for me to appear within those circles again. The uncomfortable encounters. The familiar faces."

"Yes, I suppose it might be awkward to see all those women again who you dallied with," his brother said sharply. This time he did meet Leigh's eyes. His own were cold. "Of course, you are thinking only of yourself. Your own discomfort. Rather than Miss Spencer's—"

"Miss Spencer is obviously fine with not having a chaperone or a Season!"

Dare ignored her. "Or even Lady Fulford's disappointment."

Leigh was thinking quickly. He felt like an utter bastard. He had expected to be raked over the coals by his brother, of course. Even though the fact was that he had been away on family business, he could not mention any of that. He had to accept Dare's judgment, and he had planned to. But this! Being roped into escorting a naive young girl like Miss Spencer to London for months of unbearably boring social engagements. Having to converse with and drink with and dance with people he couldn't care less about.

"She is not even my own sister," he complained—and instantly wished he hadn't.

The room immediately felt frostier.

"Well, really," Lady Fulford murmured disapprovingly, shaking her head, and Leigh felt hot shame go through him. "I am glad your mother is up in her room, rather than present to hear you say that."

"You are correct, Leigh," Dare said, his voice deceptively soft. "Marigold is not your own sister. You were not there for either of ours.

Not when they needed you. I was." He rose to his feet. "Forget you were even asked. Do whatever you were planning to do with your time while you were back for this little... visit. I find I could not care less."

The duke looked over at Lady Fulford, his face stoic. "I will escort Marigold, Lady Fulford. I am her brother-in-law. It is my responsibility."

"Oh, Dare," Leigh heard the duchess murmur, her voice tinged with sadness.

Miss Spencer shot to her feet.

"This is ridiculous! All this fuss over me! Laurel cannot go with me. Lord Leigh won't. And I shall not allow Dare to go."

"We shall make do," Lady Fulford proclaimed. "We will find a way."

Miss Spencer threw up her hands. "We won't have to because... because there is no way I can have a Season now, and I will tell you all why."

Leigh felt a terrible pricking of warning in the pit of his stomach. Just below where Miss Spencer had wrapped his bandages in the dead of the night in her bed.

Miss Spencer whirled around and pointed a finger. "Because Lord Leigh Blakeley has ruined me!"

Chapter Three

Marigold watched Lord Leigh turn white as a sheet and thought she might burst with pent-up laughter.

The very idea that a man who prowled the drawing room like a dangerous jungle cat was now turning pale and wan because of something she had said was nearly enough to send her hiccupping. *Get a hold of yourself, Marigold,* she scolded. *You've never become hysterical in your life. Now is not the time to start.*

"What!" she heard Lady Fulford exclaim.

"Oh, Marigold, what are you saying?" Laurel burst out, her voice sounding pained. "How can you say such a thing?"

"Leigh, I swear to God..." Dare took a threatening step toward his younger brother. "If there is an iota of truth to this..."

"There isn't!" The dark-haired rogue exclaimed. "I mean..." Marigold watched as he tugged frantically at his cravat as if it were a noose.

"He means he was in my bed last night," she said sweetly. "All alone. Just the two of us."

She was shocked at her own nerve. She really was.

She resisted the urge to sneak another look at Lord Leigh. The heat of his gaze upon her was making her palms itch. His injury was certainly a superficial one indeed, considering how well he was holding up today. With all the blood he had spilled on her counterpane (she had been forced to make up an embarrassing lie to explain its state to her maid), by rights he should be in bed. Yet there he stood, slim and sleek as a racehorse, ridiculously well put together for a man who had clambered in a window, bleeding, mere hours ago

"Oh, good heavens," Lady Fulford said. "She is telling the truth. I can see it in her eyes. I believe I may need smelling salts."

"I believe I may need them, too," Laurel said faintly. Marigold rushed to sit in the spot beside her sister that had been vacated by the duke.

"Oh, Laurel, don't say that. It will all be all right. You know I didn't want a Season, anyway," she whispered reassuringly.

Laurel stared at her. "Yes, but this... Marigold, when it gets out... you will be utterly ruined."

"Yes, well, it can't be so bad, can it? I wasn't sure I wanted to get married."

"Ever?" Laurel was still staring. "But just think of the scandal this will bring down on us all, Marigold. If Her Grace finds out..."

Marigold had not even thought of the dowager duchess.

"You'll have to marry her. I certainly won't allow you to have ruined my sister-in-law under my own roof and get away with it, you bloody bastard," Dare was growling.

"Marry me!" Marigold heard herself squeak. "I don't want to marry him! Why must we get married?"

"Oh, for God's sake," Lord Leigh said, putting up his hands. "Dare, take a step back. I am not going to fight you." He looked at Marigold almost beseechingly. "Are you going to tell them the truth, or shall I?"

Marigold heaved a sigh. This was not going as well as she hoped.

"Oh, very well. It is true that Lord Leigh was in my bed last night," she began. Lady Fulford let out a pained moan. "But," she continued hastily, "not in the sense you are all imagining. Nothing improper occurred. That is to say, nothing improper beyond his lying bleeding at the foot of my bed."

The room burst into an uproar with everyone talking at once.

"Well, *I* didn't make him bleed if that's what you are wondering,"

Marigold said loudly. She cleared her throat for quiet. "He was already bleeding, and I tended to his wound, then helped him back to his room."

"I had climbed in the wrong window by mistake, you see," Lord Leigh added helpfully. "I was trying to surprise you all, Dare. But I cut myself, climbing in—" He looked at her quickly. "I suppose I must have fainted. It was silly, really. Never done anything so stupid in my life."

"Oh, haven't you?" The duke was still glaring.

"It's true," Marigold said quickly. She was becoming tired. Perhaps Lady Fulford would still agree to forgo the Season. After all, there had still been a man in her room, hadn't there? Wouldn't that be enough to warrant ostracizing her for most of the beau monde? "I bandaged him with one of my petticoats. He woke up while I was wrapping him up. That's all there was to it. Very silly, really." She looked meaningfully at Lord Leigh, as if to drive home that it was *he* who was very silly, not herself.

"Very silly, indeed," Laurel murmured. "Oh, Marigold. Why did you not ring the bell for a servant? Or call for Dare or I?"

"I didn't want to worry you," Marigold muttered. Which, as it turned out, she had still wound up doing. Probably in a much worse way than if she had simply roused them in the night. Then she thought of Lord Leigh's true injury. A knife wound, not a cut while climbing in the window as he had falsely claimed. It was not as if they would find broken glass if they ever thought to look.

She reconsidered. Perhaps she had spared them from some worse worry. She would have to get to the bottom of *that* matter on her own.

"I am very disappointed with both of you," Lady Fulford announced. "Very disappointed. You should have called for your sister at once, Marigold. And you, Blakeley, whatever were you thinking?"

"Well, I wasn't, you see. I was lying there, bleeding..." Leigh began.

"There is no excuse for such behavior. Regardless of how much blood you lost," Lady Fulford decreed. She struggled to her feet, cane in hand. "I do not know what to make of this. I really don't. I am exceedingly disappointed. Poor Miss Spencer. I do not know what will become of her prospects. You truly may have ruined the girl, whether you intended to or not. Even if this ridiculous situation does not become publicly known, which we must pray it does not, it demonstrates a worrying misguidedness of character on both your parts."

Marigold pursed her lips stubbornly. She was close now. She could feel it. Her Season was about to be called off. She did feel a little regretful that Lady Fulford would not get her Season after all—for it was evident she had been looking forward to it much more than Marigold. But that couldn't be helped.

Marigold was a disaster.

Hadn't last night shown that to be true even more clearly? Hadn't Lady Fulford just declared her to have a misguided character? She would have been miserable in London. What was more, she would have surely made a fool of herself—and brought shame upon Laurel and Dare and Kat and Briar and all of them, too.

And after the events of the last year, had they not already been through enough? What with their encounter with that dreadful gaming hell owner Caleb Bryce, who essentially kidnapped the dowager duchess and tried to bully Laurel into marriage, surely a little peace and quiet was in order?

She glanced over at Lord Leigh, expecting him to appear as full of relief as she was. But instead, she saw his eyes were fixed on Lady Fulford, and his expression was puzzling.

<hr />

Later, Leigh was never sure if it was the genuinely sad expression he saw cross Lady Fulford's face, the disappointment on his brother's, or the wistful one on his sister-in-law's that made him do what he did next.

"Lady Fulford," he began. "Please, sit back down. I will do it. I'll do whatever you all want me to do. I'll chaperone Miss Spencer. I'll see to it that she has the best damned Season of any debutante who ever went to Town. I swear to it. No one need ever know about my atrocious behavior last night, I assure you all. It need not impact Miss Spencer's prospects in any way."

Lady Fulford was staring at him in amazement. Dare's mouth had actually dropped open. The duchess was smiling at him, grateful and serene.

Miss Spencer was glaring and looked as if she would like nothing better than to kick him in the shins—or jab him in the ribs again with Lady Fulford's cane.

She was very pretty when she was furious, he thought reflectively, which must be a great deal of the time. Her cheeks flushed, her lips parted, a rebel curl falling over her forehead. Yes, she was small—she came to no more than chest level on him—but certainly she was fierce.

And then everyone was talking all at once, and Leigh sank onto a nearby leather armchair, his wound throbbing and his head spinning. Oh, God, what had he done?

Chapter Four

Marigold lifted a pale-pink pelisse off her bed and began to fold it glumly.

"Here now, stop that," her sister exclaimed. "Sally had already folded that neatly."

Marigold looked down at the coat. Her sister was right. She was refolding a garment that had previously been perfectly folded. She stared at it as if she had forgotten what to do with it.

"Here, give it to me." Laurel sighed, holding out her hands. "I'll do it."

Marigold passed over the pelisse silently.

Laurel eyed her as she refolded the soft wool coat. "Are you really so reluctant to return to London?"

"I don't wish to leave you," Marigold replied evasively. "Are you sure you will be all right without me? In your condition?"

Laurel smiled. "I believe it is a common one for married women. I will do very well without you, Sister. After all, I still will have my husband by my side. As well as his mother, of course."

"Yes, but..." Marigold hedged. She bit her lip. "You know what I mean."

"After the last time, you mean?" Laurel sat down on the bed with her hands in her lap. "Pray God, it was the first and last time we will have to go through that."

"Yes." Marigold could think of nothing better to say. At least her sister had lost the child early on. That was the only comfort—and it was a small one.

At least her sister was still alive and had not perished in childbirth. She might think that secretly, but she could never say it.

"Perhaps," Laurel said carefully, "going to London will be good for you, Marigold. For then, you will be thinking less about me and my well-being and more about your own." She rose from the bed and stepped over to stand beside Marigold, peering down at the open luggage that lay over the bed.

Marigold opened her mouth to protest, only to feel her sister's cool hand touch her cheek.

"Marigold," Laurel said softly. "I am scared, too. But I do not want you to carry this fear as well. I need you happy. If that means distracting yourself in London with Lady Fulford, well then…"

"Happy?" Marigold exclaimed. "Distracted, yes. Happy, no."

"Well, distracted then," Laurel said. "I will gladly settle for distracted. Go to London, Marigold. Try your best to see this through. Wear pretty gowns, attend lovely soirees, and meet the creme de la creme of England, and do not think of me… much." She smiled wryly. "We will still write to each other, of course."

"Daily," Marigold said, lifting her chin. "Perhaps twice a day."

"A trifle excessive," Laurel said, laughing. "But very well. If that will help."

"I want constant updates on your health," Marigold said warningly. "Constant. And accurate. Spare no details. I want to know everything."

Laurel's lips twitched. "Everything? Every time I use the *bourdaloue*, perhaps?"

"Very well, perhaps not everything," Marigold conceded. "But everything important. Anything of substance." She paused, biting her lip as she debated the question. "Have you felt…?"

Laurel was already shaking her head. "Not yet," she said softly. She sank back down onto a clear spot on the bed and began fiddling with the clasps of one of Marigold's jackets. "I believe it is too early. But within the next month or so..."

"And I will not be here for it," Marigold said quietly. "Are you sure...?"

Laurel turned to face her. "I am. Please. Go. I promise you that I will call you back if anything should occur. Good or bad. And when I draw closer to my confinement–"

"I will be there," Marigold promised.

"Of course," Laurel said hesitantly. "You may be unable to return, I suppose."

"Why is that?" Marigold demanded, placing her hands on her hips.

"What if you are engaged? Or married? What if your husband wishes for you to return to his country home with him forthwith?" Laurel fretted.

"Then I shan't marry him," Marigold declared, tossing her head. "Obviously, the first thing my husband must learn is that my sister comes first. Family comes first. If he cannot understand that, then my husband he shall not be."

The two sisters looked at each other for a moment, then burst out laughing.

"You shall never wed," Laurel wheezed from between bouts of laughter.

"I don't need to wed to be happy, Laurel," Marigold said, clambering up beside her sister on the bed, ignoring the mess, and squeezing Laurel's hand.

"I thought the same thing," Laurel murmured. "I was happy before I was married."

"But?"

"But I am even happier now," Laurel confessed.

"Even with...?"

"Even with that loss, yes." Laurel was quiet a moment. "I cannot regret it. Not even the pain. Yes, not even if that sort of pain should come again," she added, answering the question Marigold had been wondering about.

"But it won't," Marigold whispered. She squeezed her sister's hand tightly. "It won't."

Chapter Five

M arigold felt a cold chill come over her as she leaned against the balcony rail staring out over the ballroom.

This had been a terrible mistake.

All these men, congregating and preening, casting appraising glances at the women around them. Casting appraising glances at *her*! She could hear the whispers. She had caught bits and pieces of what was being said about her. None of it had been particularly kind–and those were only the few words she had managed to overhear.

The extremely generous dowry the duke had settled upon her had been a curse, she thought glumly. It made her a target. It made certain Marigold would not be able to get away with hiding on the edges of a room behind a fan like the shy pretty girls she had seen. No, her dance card had been filled moments after she and Lady Fulford had greeted their hosts and entered the ballroom.

Was she interested in any of the suitors so eager to lead her in a dance? She could hardly remember a single one. Yet she would spend the next three or four hours being swept around the room in their arms, each one apparently hoping to suss out whether she had what it would take to become their wife.

Marigold shuddered. She had no wish to become anyone's wife.

Certainly not a man she hardly knew. Oh, Lady Fulford had explained the courtship rituals of the *ton*. She would not be expected to marry anyone—or even become engaged—after a single waltz. No, the next step would be to have suitors come to call. Many would bring flowers or other tokens of their esteem. They would crowd Lady Fulford's drawing room, fighting like peacocks for her attention. At least, that was what Lady Fulford clearly expected to happen. Next would come carriage rides in the park—carefully chaperoned of course. Garden parties, teas, and other outings. All social occasions designed to allow Marigold to get to know her future husband. It was all very genteel, very civil.

But she wanted none of it. She had thought she might, just might, be able to go through with it for her sister's sake. After all, Laurel made marriage look so very, well, cozy. Passionate, yes, but also intimate. Her sister and the duke were very much in love, but it was clear that they were also dear friends who cherished one another's companionship.

That part of things seemed rather nice. Particularly since Marigold had to admit that she was rather lonely. First Ash had married, but that was all right as Marigold had still had Wren and Laurel. Then Wren had vanished, only to turn up married. And lastly, Laurel had been swept off.

Well, not swept off exactly. Laurel and Dare had been engaged for months. Then Laurel had swept Marigold along with her when she finally did wed, making sure her younger sister had a place at Blakeley Manor and spending as much time with her as she could.

But it was not the same. Laurel was a duchess now. She had duties and responsibilities alongside her husband. She had to split her affections and her time.

Gone were the afternoons the two sisters had spent below stairs in the workrooms chattering away together. Gone were the Sundays after church spent wandering through the village, shopping and browsing, then picnicking in the hills, or lying in the sitting room of their small cottage reading books.

Their family of four had disintegrated. Everyone had scattered; everyone had found their place.

Everyone but Marigold.

And now, here she was, being given a generous opportunity to find her own place in the world. To find a suitable husband—and one from the highest ranks of English society! She should be pleased. She should be flattered. She should be grateful.

She should not be imagining sneaking out of the ballroom and into the nearest library where she would hide in a corner, preferably behind some sort of concealing curtain or screen, and curl up and enjoy a good cry.

She straightened her back.

"Very nice," Lady Fulford said approvingly from beside her. "I was just about to suggest you do that. Your gown and your—*ahem*—decolletage are much improved by proper posture."

Marigold glanced down at herself. The gown she wore did reveal a considerable amount of decolletage. She looked like a lemon in it. A lemon covered with icing. Or perhaps two iced lemons, she amended, her heart sinking as she looked down at the expanse of cleavage greeting her. Her bust had been squeezed and squashed and now swelled up to greet her, pale mounds of flesh draped in bright yellow satin, trimmed with white bows. The skirt of the gown was little better. White satin with an overskirt of lemon-colored lace. And at the bottom were more rows of ribbons and lace.

Ribbons and lace and cleavage in your face, Marigold quipped, biting her lip to keep in the nervous laughter. That was what her would-be suitors would all be thinking.

Lady Fulford was giving her an appraising look. "Perhaps the yellow was a trifle too..."

"Yellow?" Marigold suggested. She had protested the idea of a yellow-haired girl wearing a yellow gown. It made her look sallow and washed-out, but Lady Fulford had insisted she looked simple, lovely, and virginal.

"Well, yes," Lady Fulford admitted. "Tomorrow you shall try the lavender."

"Tomorrow," Marigold agreed. Tomorrow and tomorrow and tomorrow. Ball after ball after ball. Their schedule was as full as her dance card. More so because there were also afternoons to fill, and Lady Fulford was a firm believer in not wasting opportunities.

She opened her mouth to say she thought she was coming down with a fever, but when she looked at the older lady, her annoyance fell away, and she pursed her lips together. Lady Fulford was all prickles and thorns until you got to know her. And then she was as kind and loyal a friend as anyone could wish for. More than a friend—Marigold considered her close to family. A stately godmother from a fairytale, perhaps.

Had Cinderella protested having to go to the ball? Had she wanted her life to change so drastically? Perhaps her stepsisters were not as bad as the story made out. Perhaps they were even...

"Heavens! Who is the young lady in that horrid yellow gown?"

The feminine voice carried from behind them. Marigold started to turn, but Lady Fulford's hand clamped down on her arm.

"Goodness, do you mean Miss Scullion over there? Haven't you heard? She's a proper Cinderella. Raised up from the kitchens, where I imagine she slept on the hearth covered in soot."

Peals of laughter erupted, without any attempt to stifle the sound.

Marigold counted. At least three girls stood nearby talking about her.

The same voice continued, "Why, the Duke of Dareford has settled more than fifty-thousand pounds upon the little heifer! Can you imagine?"

"I can't imagine it will be enough," the first voice spoke up again coolly. "Not if she intends to wear frocks like that. Why, she's practically popping out of it! She looks as if she just came from stuffing herself with cakes in the kitchen, not mopping it."

"Perhaps if she had done more mopping, she would fit the dress," a third voice chimed in. This girl sounded bored, but her quip elicited another round of giggles.

Marigold felt her cheeks burning. She had been teased before, of course. She was a petite girl with a curvy shape, and there would always be those who delighted in mocking her softness. Usually, she was more than capable of ignoring them. She knew she was not displeasing to look at. Her body was strong and capable of getting her where she wanted to go and doing what she needed it to. There were many who could not say the same. Usually, she simply made a witty come back and strolled calmly away from whoever was trying to goad her. Besides, such childish bullying had not happened in many years. Not since she had worked alongside a particularly nasty kitchen maid.

But the audacity of these girls! The way they continued without even trying to quiet their voices or move farther away! They wished to be heard. They wanted to be cruel. They were supposed to be the beau monde! The beautiful people, the upper crust of society. But if these girls were any indication, the *bon ton* was just as crude and foul as any other class.

Marigold felt hot tears prick her eyes.

"Do not give them the satisfaction, my dear," Lady Fulford murmured. "Don't you dare, my darling."

"Oooh!" one of the girls whispered. "Look who it is."

There were gasps, and this time an attempt was sincerely made to stifle the girls' giggles.

Marigold was dying of curiosity and longing to turn around. What could possibly be causing such a stir?

Then Marigold heard the girl with the cool voice say, "Lord Leigh, it has been too long since you graced us with your presence. Miss Cora Compton, in case you had forgotten."

Marigold felt tingles up the back of her spine. He was here? Leigh was here? Standing just behind her?

She imagined the girl curtsying elegantly. She would be beautiful, of course.

And then he spoke.

"Ah, yes, Miss Compton."

There was a tittering.

"Oh, so you do remember me," the haughty girl drawled. "I must have made quite an impression, considering how long it has been since you were in London."

The gall of this girl! How Marigold longed to turn and see her face!

How would he reply? Did he know her? Had they... perhaps been close? But no. This girl must be Marigold's age or younger. Surely, she was a debutante like herself. And Lord Leigh was at least twenty-five.

There was a pause. "I can't say I recall you, no. Your brother, on the other hand, I used to play a mean game of whist at the club with. So, this is his little sister. You say we've met?"

There was a pause.

Marigold imagined Lord Leigh looking at the girl appraisingly. Was he mesmerized by her beauty? She must be very lovely, Marigold imagined, her hands trembling where they lay on the rail, to have so easily disparaged another.

Then there came a low whistle. "Devil of a thing. I thought I'd heard it said you were pretty."

And then... he must have walked away.

There was only silence behind her.

Marigold felt her heart soar. She felt dizzy. Lightheaded. She thought she might burst into giggles herself. And then she felt a playful tap on her shoulder.

"Good evening, Miss Spencer. Is your protégée free for the next waltz, Lady Fulford?" Lord Leigh asked.

"Well, I..." Lady Fulford began.

Marigold could hear the strains of a waltz beginning to play downstairs. She tried to remember who had claimed this dance. A balding young man who had stuttered and sweat as he spoke to Lady Fulford. Not that Marigold blamed the poor fellow. But she could not see herself marrying him.

"I believe I have this dance free," she said quickly. "Don't I, Lady Fulford?"

Lady Fulford was a wonderfully good sport. She hesitated for only an instant. "Why, yes, shockingly. Though your card is otherwise full."

"Of course, it is. I am not surprised," Lord Leigh said. "Why, you look utterly ravishing in that lemon concoction, Miss Spencer. You must have all the gentlemen in this room under your thrall."

Marigold blushed. She understood what he was trying to do, and it was very kind, but she could not help but still feel humiliated by what had just occurred.

She said nothing.

"Well, shall we?" He smiled, and she felt herself go very still. She must be very careful now. *She must not be charmed.*

For the first time, she allowed herself to do what she had not done up until now. She glanced at the circle of girls standing near the wall behind them.

Her heart sank, even though she saw no more than she had expected to. They were a trio of goddesses, just as she had imagined. One was tall, dark, and slim with diamonds decorating her hair and her white satin gown. She was looking at Marigold as if she would like nothing better than to strangle her. That must be Miss Cora Compton.

The girl to Miss Compton's left was flame-haired with emerald eyes. She watched Marigold with frank curiosity and a half smile. Not necessarily as cruel as Cora then, but certainly not the sort to stop a bully.

The third girl was a brunette in midnight blue, who stared at Marigold with undisguised boredom. This must be the second girl who had spoken. She was malicious because she had nothing better to do with her time, perhaps.

Marigold averted her eyes, took a deep breath, then placed her gloved hand on Lord Leigh's arm. It was solid as a rock, while hers was still trembling. She willed it to stillness as he began to lead her toward the curved marble staircase.

"Very good of you to make an appearance, Blakeley," Lady Fulford called from behind them. "I see you take your duties as a chaperone very seriously."

"Absolutely, Lady Fulford," Lord Leigh called back over his shoulder. "This beauty is mine to safeguard, after all."

He was being ridiculous, and she ought to protest, but after what had just transpired, Marigold found herself struggling to conjure up her usual sardonic reply. Instead, she felt oddly comforted by his presence. She doubted she would see him again after tonight. Lady Fulford had already begun to lament Lord Leigh's laxness in paying his attendance. He had not come along once for a stroll in the park or even paid them a morning visit, though they knew him to be in London at the Blakeley townhouse.

But he was here. Now. Tonight.

And he looked very well indeed.

She couldn't help stealing a glance at her partner. Whereas in her room the other night, his face had been lined with dark stubble, this evening he was freshly shaved, the angles of his jaw sharp as a knife but much more beautiful. Everything about him was beautiful. And yet not in a decadent way. He was elegant, yes, like his brother the duke, but there was something about Lord Leigh that was lacking in Dare. Lord Leigh looked like he would be just as comfortable below stairs as up, as content in some dirty pub in the Seven Dials as he was here in the gleaming ballroom. Most likely more. He was playing a part, and he played it well. The fashionable young rake, the privileged son. But this was not who he was, Marigold realized with a start. Who he truly *was* had something to do with the blood on her bed.

Find the cause of that mysterious knife wound and she would have a better idea of who she was really dealing with.

Abruptly, she realized she wasn't the only one transfixed by Lord Leigh Blakeley. The room was humming, and he was the cause. All eyes seemed to be upon them as they strolled down the stairs and joined the other dancers. Eyes! *His* were a dark chestnut, she noticed. No, they were darker than chestnut. The very darkest brown there was, nearly black. Fringed by thick, long lashes. Lashes tinged slightly red, like the secret hint of auburn she had caught sight of in his hair the other night. She felt a strange thrill at the thought that she had seen his auburn hair as he lay in her bed.

Bleeding, of course. At the time, she had even thought he might be dead. But still, he had been hers in that instant.

Hers in bed.

Absolutely ridiculous, Marigold. Where do you think you are going with such stupid thoughts, she rebuked herself.

Lord Leigh had noticed her noticing him.

He waited until they had taken their place on the floor and began the movements of the dance.

"Cora Compton is a notorious..." he started. He scowled.

"A notorious?" she prompted, feeling the hint of a true smile beginning.

"A notorious shrew," Lord Leigh said firmly. "She is a nasty piece of work, and you should steer clear of her and her ilk."

"Oh, I intend to," Marigold replied. "And it shall be most easy, too, because I am certain they will already be steering clear of me. We heard all they said."

"I heard most of it, too." His mouth was grim. "A great deal of pathetic childish nonsense. They knew you were listening and so decided to have their idea of some fun."

"Or they were simply telling the truth," Marigold said quietly. "Perhaps there is nothing wrong with that." She cleared her throat. "I do understand that this shade of yellow is..." She heard her voice crack slightly and cursed herself. "Not precisely flattering." She raised her chin. "There. Now that is out of the way, and you need not lie any longer."

Lord Leigh looked, if anything, more furious. "What the devil are you talking about? I did not lie."

"Certainly, you did. To spare my feelings, to comfort me. It was very well-done, too," she assured him. "You reminded me of Wren."

She watched his face go still. "Your... elder brother?"

"Yes, the one your younger sister married. It was very kind of you. Please rest assured that I am grateful. But there is no need for those sorts of eloquent falsehoods. I know who and what I am," she said, feeling calmer. "I know yellow was the worst choice this evening, but..."

"But?"

"Lady Fulford loved the yellow, so..." She shrugged.

She saw him open his mouth, then close it again.

"She is very kind, and so I am doing my best to go along with her suggestions," Marigold continued.

"Suggestions." Lord Leigh looked wry. "That is putting it mildly. Does Lady Fulford ever make suggestions?"

"Well, perhaps 'decrees' would be more accurate. But she means well. And she truly does have much more experience than I do with–" Marigold glanced around, then wished she had not. Everyone still seemed to be looking at them, even the couples dancing nearby were openly staring. "Well, all this."

"And how are you enjoying all this, thus far?" Lord Leigh inquired. "Forgive me, but I admit I did not mark you as one of those young ladies who enjoyed extravagant social functions and all the rest."

"Well, this is only my first one," she reminded him. "Very kind of you to attend, considering."

"Ah. Yes. The first." He frowned and glanced up at the balcony. "You'll surely encounter those harridans again."

"Oh, I'm sure they have many other poor girls to pick on besides me," Marigold assured him. "I'll strive to ignore them and make the best of it."

Lord Leigh looked amused. "The best of it? Is that what husband hunting is?"

Marigold averted her eyes from his. "In truth..."

"Yes?"

"In truth, I am not sure I am husband hunting. More so making the best of what is expected of me."

As well as perhaps squeezing some plans of her own into the bargain.

"And do you always do what is expected of you, Miss Spencer?"

She met his gaze and was surprised to see his eyes were smoldering, even angry.

"I think you know the answer to that, my lord," she replied. "After all," she added, feeling decidedly naughty, "you are the one who ruined me."

He groaned, and she felt a smile finally break over her face.

"Good God, girl, don't say it too loudly. Lady Fulford will have my head."

"Do you mean because everyone is watching us—and perhaps listening, too?" she whispered.

He groaned again and half-closed his eyes. It was an ordinary gesture, but in that moment, she suddenly imagined him doing so in a different place entirely. And entirely unclothed.

She gave a little gasp and tripped on her own feet.

His eyes opened. He looked concerned. "What is it?"

"Oh, nothing," she evaded. "I was just distracted."

"By the thought of my ruining you?" he asked, grinning.

His arrow had landed entirely too close to the mark.

"I believe we should change the subject. This one is becoming rather awkward. After all, we are almost siblings. You are my patron," she said primly.

"Of course," Lord Leigh replied smoothly. "Whatever you say... Sister."

Marigold squirmed uncomfortably in his arms.

"The waltz is nearly over," he reassured her. "Only a few more moments, and you will be released from this torment."

It was by no means a torment. That was the problem.

Marigold could not help it. She looked up at him, her teeth nibbling on her lower lip. She should not have done so, for she felt certain he would see the truth in her eyes.

And then the dance ended. She watched his expression become uncertain.

"I suppose I should return you to Lady Fulford."

"There is no need. I believe my next partner is approaching," she said quickly.

And so, he was. A man of middling years, pushing his pince-nez farther up the bridge of his rather greasy nose.

He approached quickly with his eyes fixed on Marigold. Only as he reached them did he glance at her partner and seem to notice Lord Leigh. She watched the man's eyes widen.

Lord Leigh gripped her arm. "What the devil... you cannot dance with this man," he hissed.

"It is too late," Marigold hissed back. She was already resigned. It was only one dance after all. She lowered her voice and added quickly, "Of course, I know he is an unsuitable suitor, but Lady Fulford did not when she accepted on my behalf. And so please kindly release me."

She raised her voice to a normal speaking tone and tried to smile. "Mr. Giles, I believe this next dance is yours."

The dance was already beginning. It was not a waltz, thank heavens, but a quadrille. Mr. Giles was taking her hand and fairly pushing her onto the floor and away from Lord Leigh as fast as he could.

"Thank you for the waltz, my lord," she called.

Chapter Six

Gowns like Miss Spencer's ought to have been against the law, Leigh thought, as he marched back toward the marble staircase. Oh, it was not the lace and ribbons which so offended his sensibilities. No, it was the sight of Miss Spencer's breasts, lifted and positioned so optimally, like cakes on a platter. Frosted cakes, perhaps, if one took into account all the lace. The sight of those quivering orbs, pale skin soft and smooth as flower petals, had been enough to send his imagination careening to forbidden places.

Thank God, Miss Spencer had been too distracted by the cruelty of her peers to notice Leigh's initial failure to find her face with his eyes. Of course, when he finally had, what he had seen there, too, had been startlingly pretty. Miss Spencer's face was flushed from her embarrassment. She glowed like a pink rose, her lips plump and red, her eyes glistening with the hint of angry tears. Her lustrous blonde hair had been piled up in a crown of heavy waves, pinned in place with pearl clips. A few curls hung teasingly around her face, framing and softening it, making Leigh want nothing so much as to reach out a finger and push one gently back behind her ear. Right before he did the same with those threatening teardrops.

Miss Compton was a jealous idiot, and it had been a pleasure to put her in her place. Of course, if the haughtiest girls of the *ton* had noticed the surprising impression Miss Spencer made, that meant they were not the only ones. The men must be noticing, too.

Yes, and right now that knave Giles was noticing her. Probably looking right down her gown as they danced.

Leigh curled his hands into fists and strode up the stairs.

He had worked himself into quite a lather by the time he reached Lady Fulford and, to his disgust, found himself a tad short of breath. The injury he had sustained a few nights ago, which Miss Spencer had bandaged so efficiently if unconventionally, was healing nicely. However, the idea of "taking it easy" and allowing himself extra rest remained a foreign concept, stab wound or not.

"We need to discuss Miss Spencer," he said in a low voice as he reached the formidable older lady's side. "I cannot say I approve of how things are being conducted."

Lady Fulford raised delicate gray eyebrows. "Things? What things?"

"Let us begin with her dance card selections. At this very moment, she is dancing with a man who should not have been allowed within ten yards of her."

Let alone have been allowed to put his hands on Miss Spencer's own hand. Upon the soft curves of her waist. He thought of all his brother had left unsaid about his former secretary's conduct. And what had he called that secretary's behavior? He believed the word had been "egregious." That covered quite a range of horrid.

Lady Fulford peered over the rail at the couples spinning below. "Mr. Ambrose Giles? The seventh son of a baron. He was employed by your brother the duke as secretary for quite some time." She frowned. "I admit, he is not suitable husband material. His income is nil. His father is stretched thin trying to keep Mr. Giles's elder brothers' families fed and clothed as it is. I do not believe he will be receiving an inheritance, and therefore, we may discount him as a fortune hunter. Miss Spencer will not be any man's purse. We are seeking a husband, not a money-hungry grub. However, I did not see what the harm was in allowing Mr. Giles a single dance."

Leigh frowned. "The harm is that Mr. Giles was dismissed by my brother for attempting to lay hands upon the woman who is now his duchess."

Lady Fulford's eyebrows arched higher. "Good heavens."

"Indeed. He is, therefore, not the sort of man I would like laying his hands upon Miss Spencer's person. Even for a single dance."

"I quite see your point, Blakeley. Believe me, had I known, I would never have permitted it." Lady Fulford whipped out a quizzing glass that Leigh had not even known she was holding and pressed it against her eye, clearly intent upon monitoring Miss Spencer carefully for the remainder of the song.

"Why on earth did she not tell me? I suppose she did not have an opportunity," Lady Fulford continued, answering her own question. "I accepted on her behalf quite rapidly."

Leigh could easily see that. "Perhaps she feared doing so would be indelicate. Or even an issue of privacy, as her sister was the lady concerned."

"Indeed, indeed," Lady Fulford murmured. "Though I hope those girls know by now that I am a woman they may come to with any matter." She glanced at Leigh with a discerning expression. "Well, one thing has been made abundantly clear, Blakeley."

"Oh?" Leigh asked politely. "And what is that?"

"Why, the necessity of your presence, of course," Lady Fulford said with something like triumph. "If you had been at the ball from the start, none of this would have happened, for we would have benefited from your natural masculine assertiveness as well as your fore-knowledge."

"Well, perhaps..." Leigh began.

"Oh, pishposh. You don't mean to tell me you would have stood by and allowed Mr. Giles to be accepted?"

"Certainly not," Leigh said hotly.

"Well then, you must simply ensure that you are there to oversee Miss Spencer at every social occasion lest something similar occur again. What a terrible thing that would be."

As Lady Fulford still had the quizzing glass to her eye and was looking down at the couples dancing, Leigh could not tell if she was being sardonic or not. He had to assume she was utterly sincere. He sighed.

"I suppose that is a logical conclusion." He frowned. "In that case, I should also like to discuss the matter of Miss Spencer's attire."

"Her attire? Whatever is the matter with it?"

"Well," Leigh began, suddenly feeling he may be getting in over his head. "I am not sure it is altogether... suitable. For such a... young lady."

Lady Fulford lowered the quizzing glass and turned. "I beg your pardon, Blakeley, but what exactly are you saying? Are you suggesting that I have decked Miss Spencer out as some sort of... some sort of..."

Leigh felt his cheeks growing hot. He began urgently praying that the next word out of Lady Fulford's mouth would not be what he suspected.

"A... a minx?"

"A minx," Leigh said weakly. "Of course not." Though perhaps Lady Fulford had hit the nail on the head more accurately than she knew. Miss Spencer was an accidental minx. Yes, that was the perfect way of putting it. "However," he said, steeling himself to the task. "The gown Miss Spencer is wearing this evening is quite..."

"Yes?" Lady Fulford sounded downright frosty.

"Revealing?" Leigh hazarded.

Lady Fulford's eyes were hawkish for a moment, then her expression became amused. "Miss Spencer is amply endowed in the region we delicately refer to as the decolletage, is she not?"

"I suppose that she... is," Leigh hedged, feeling entrapped.

"She is a voluptuously figured young woman. I believe many refer to such a form as Rubenesque."

"I believe that is the expression. Yes," Leigh agreed.

"Therefore, no matter what she wears, especially if it is to be fashionable, she will be exposing more of her..."

"Yes, yes," Leigh said hastily. "I believe I understand."

Lady Fulford raised a brow. "Do you, Blakeley? Do you understand that there is a fine line between modesty and ensuring that one's future husband has the opportunity to get a hint of one's physical charms?"

Leigh felt himself blushing like a schoolboy.

"Hmm," Lady Fulford said, regarding him. "I believe, now and in the future, you should leave matters of dress to me."

"Yes, that is probably an excellent idea."

Lady Fulford gave him a knowing smile. "You were shocked when you first saw Miss Spencer tonight, were you not? You have never had cause to see her in evening wear before this occasion."

Leigh bit his tongue hard. He would not draw Lady Fulford's attention to the fact that he had seen Miss Spencer in the ultimate "evening wear" the first time he had encountered her while stretched bleeding across her bed. No, he would absolutely not.

"I was surprised by how different she appeared," he acknowledged.

"Of course you were." Lady Fulford reached out and patted his arm. "It is the way with all men. You believed Miss Spencer was an ordinary young woman having simply seen her about Blakeley Manor under ordinary circumstances. Tonight, you have seen how she can bloom like a hothouse flower. Yet you were not alone in this observation, Blakeley. No, by no means were you the only man in this ballroom who saw Miss Spencer's potential. And that"—she raised a finger—"that is why Miss Spencer will be sure to have a most successful Season. Oh, she may not be named a Diamond. But she shall shine like a jewel nonetheless, and she will have her pick of suitable men. I shall see to that, never fear."

She raised her quizzing glass back to her eye and made a contented sound. Evidently, Miss Spencer was still in one piece, and Mr. Giles was behaving.

Leigh stared at the elderly lady's profile. The problem was that she was not wrong.

Miss Spencer likely would have her pick of any number of men.

And suddenly, Leigh found he did not like that prospect one bit at all.

Chapter Seven

L eigh had every intention of arriving on time for the ball the next evening. Until, that is, an unexpected visitor set his schedule back by a few hours.

By the time he arrived at the Norfolk ball at a fashionable and above-average-in-size townhouse in the neighborhood of Mayfair, it was half past ten, and the event was in full swing.

He greeted his hosts, swiped a glass of champagne off a passing tray, and began to scan the room for Miss Spencer and Lady Fulford. Perhaps a real gentleman would have offered to escort them this evening. But Leigh was doing the best he could. He was not about to also make himself responsible for taking them to and fro.

In fact, he was already regretting telling Lady Fulford he would attend every event with them.

That very morning, she had sent over a footman with a bound book. The man had stood there, waiting, and at first, Leigh had not known what to make of it. Then he had picked up the book and realized this was Lady Fulford's social calendar. Evidently, she had expected him to copy it onto his own so that he might follow their every move. He had skimmed the pages, his heart sinking as he did so. Most days involved two to three different social engagements. Tea parties, garden parties, musicales, and balls seemed to be the most prominent. Though he did notice, with some relief, that a few visits to the opera had been included. Perhaps so that poor Miss Spencer did not go absolutely mad from the tedium.

Or was it possible that Miss Spencer was beginning to like her taste of the *ton*?

Impossible. Not after what he had witnessed last night.

His eye snagged upon a familiar face. Miss Spencer! She was being twirled around the floor and was beaming widely up at her dance partner.

Excellent. Leigh supposed he should be pleased to see her looking so happy, especially after the cruelty she had encountered last night.

Then he recognized the man she was dancing with.

Swearing under his breath, he downed the remains of the champagne and strode off in search of Lady Fulford.

He found her sitting at one of the tables on the far side of the room, watching the dancers while chattering contentedly to a group of elegant matrons.

She rose when she saw him, smiled, and took his arm. "Walk me about the room, Blakeley. I have been sitting long enough."

"Certainly," Leigh said stiffly.

They began their circuit. He did his best to keep his eyes fixed firmly in front of him rather than searching for Miss Spencer again. The dance was perhaps midway through.

"Lady Fulford," he said, striving to put a little coldness into his voice so that she might see how serious the matter was. "I believed you and I were on the same page after last evening. And yet now that I have arrived and seen who my..." He paused, realizing he had nearly said *ward*. "After seeing whose companionship Miss Spencer is currently enjoying, I believe our communication must have gone astray after all."

"Is the bodice of her gown cut too low for you, Blakeley?" Lady Fulford said complacently. "Or is it her dance partner you wish to complain of? Perhaps you ought to take charge of her dance card and approve each and every man before she is permitted to dance with him."

"Yes!" Leigh exclaimed, before realizing she was teasing. "I mean, no. Of course not. How ridiculous." He forced a chuckle.

"So, it is her partner and not her gown which bothers you, Blakeley?" Lady Fulford inquired.

"Her gown? Her gown is very pretty, I'm sure," Leigh said. He had hardly noticed it but reminded himself to take a closer look. Surely it would not be as provocative as the yellow concoction. "But to allow her to waltz with Hawkeye Harley. Why, his reputation is notorious!"

"The young Marquess of Harley, you mean?" Lady Fulford looked amused. "I am aware of his reputation as a rake, of course, but..."

"Well then, why would you allow him to dance with Miss Spencer?" Leigh hissed.

Lady Fulford continued to look amused. "I hardly think he is going to seduce her during the span of a single waltz, Blakeley. And need I remind you that you have a similar reputation, all your own. Far more notorious, as I am given to understand."

"I..." Leigh stopped. "Do I?"

"You need not look so chagrined," Lady Fulford said. "You may find this ironic, Blakeley, but I have received something in the nature of complaints of my own—concerning your suitability as a chaperone for a young lady."

"I beg your pardon?"

"Indeed," Lady Fulford said calmly. "The ladies I was sitting with just now were expressing their concern that you of all people had been selected as a chaperone for a debutante when, in their view, you were more likely to ruin a debutante."

"Ruin!" Leigh hissed. "I have never ruined a debutante." Widows, yes. Discontented wives, sometimes—but only in his youth, before his father had taken him aside and, in one of their last serious conversations, pressed home for Leigh the sanctity of marriage. Courtesans and other such women who Leigh thought of as "free" in the sense of being free of societal conventions, free to live their own lives without the strict control of their families—those were his preferred company. But in truth, he had not had a woman in quite some time. He had been too focused on other matters.

"I've never been what you might call a rake," he insisted.

"Oh, no? Would you prefer the term libertine? Scoundrel?"

"I should prefer not being compared to Hawkeye Harley, period. Ruining debutantes is not my idea of an entertaining pastime."

"I am pleased to hear that," Lady Fulford replied. "I believe young Lord Harley has turned over a new leaf as well. From what I understand, it is a matter of necessity. His father has given him an ultimatum to marry this Season." She looked meditatively at the couple. "He certainly is a very handsome and charming young man. Miss Spencer seemed to think so. She appears to be quite happy dancing with him."

Leigh's eyes shot over to the dancers where he saw what Lady Fulford said was true. Miss Spencer seemed happy indeed. Her head was tossed back, and she was laughing at something Harley had just said. Harley looked entertained as well—and very well pleased with his choice of dance partner.

"Do you believe in the notion of the reformed rake, Blakeley?" Lady Fulford asked blithely. "Some say they make the best husbands."

"Stuff and nonsense," Leigh muttered. "Men like that don't change. Harley would be a charming husband, yes, but a philandering one. He would run through Miss Spencer's dowry at gaming hells before you could say... well, before you could say..."

"Before you could say 'I do'?" Lady Fulford suggested, a mischievous gleam in her eye.

Leigh groaned. "Surely there are better candidates for Miss Spencer than a reformed rake."

"I suppose that is up to Miss Spencer to decide," Lady Fulford replied. "I do not believe Lord Harley is as destitute as you seem to believe or as mercenary. In any case, I make the introductions, but Miss Spencer must make the final choice. Of course, if you had accompanied us to the ball or arrived on time..."

"Yes, yes," Leigh said glumly. "I could have prevented yet another incident."

They had reached the end of the ballroom, and Leigh led the way upstairs to the mezzanine.

"I admit, Blakeley," Lady Fulford said. "It is a pleasure to have a dashing young man by my side once more, even if it is simply for a turn around the Norfolk ballroom."

Leigh was struck with guilt. "How is your dance card this evening, Lady Fulford? I should have requested your very first available waltz when I greeted you. Allow me to remedy that omission now."

"Oh, pishposh," Lady Fulford said, batting at his arm. But she looked pleased. "I no longer waltz, my dear boy. But I shall remember that you said that. Yes, I shall remember when I next revise my will." She cackled heartily and swatted his arm again.

Leigh grinned. "In any case," he said. "As long as Harley brings her back in one piece, no harm is done."

"That's the spirit," Lady Fulford said encouragingly. "What's the harm in a dance? If anything, it may make Miss Spencer look more appealing to the other young gentlemen. And if Lord Harley's interest is piqued, well, we shall see..."

She continued to chatter, but Leigh's attention had dwindled. His eyes had roamed back to the dancers below. He scanned the crowd once. Then again. Then a third time.

"She's gone," he said hoarsely. "Miss Spencer is gone."

"Nonsense," Lady Fulford said. "She must be there." She stepped over to the balcony rail and looked down for herself. "There, they are right... Oh wait, no, that is Lady Miranda Fortescue. They are of a same size and are both wearing lavender this evening."

Leigh peered all around, not just at the dancers but the occupied tables—perhaps Miss Spencer had felt weary or faint, and Harley had taken her to sit down.

But Miss Spencer was not at a table. Neither she nor Harley were anywhere to be seen.

"That bastard," Leigh swore. "The blackguard." He was already stepping away from Lady Fulford. "I'll wager I know where he's taken her."

"I sincerely doubt they will be where you think, Blakeley," Lady Fulford cautioned. "I have already warned Miss Spencer of the dangers to be found on a terrace at night."

"Even so," Leigh said grimly. From past experience, he knew being aware of the dangers seldom was enough to save anyone.

"Very well," Lady Fulford said, moving in the opposite direction.

"You go that way, and I'll go this way. I am sure we shall find them soon."

"And when I do..." Leigh said darkly.

"You'll not cause any trouble, Blakeley. For all our sakes," Lady Fulford said sharply. "Or you'll risk destroying Miss Spencer's Season when it has hardly begun."

Leigh growled low in the back of his throat, hoping she would not hear him. "I'll try to exercise restraint."

"Yes, you do that. You try very hard," Lady Fulford advised.

Leigh stalked off toward the stairs. He knew precisely where the terrace doors were. He knew the exact layout of the Norfolk garden, for that matter. He could find his way through it drunk in the dark. In fact, he had. Twice. With lovely widows at the end of his stumbles. He had stumbled straight into their arms. There had been a great deal of stumbling, then giggling, then quite enjoyable fumbling, as he recalled. That had been more than three years ago. His last time in London during the Season.

He reached the edge of the ballroom. White gauze curtains covered each of the French doors leading out to the terrace. He could not tell who stood outside–if anyone even did.

He felt odd. Both angry and nervous. Would he be interrupting a lover's tryst? Did Miss Spencer think she had found true love in Hawkeye Harley after just one dance?

Well, if so, then it was time to set her straight.

He pushed open the door and stepped out.

There was no one there.

Nothing but a damp spring night. He was glad he was wearing a coat. It was certainly not the night for a young lady in a scanty gown to spend waiting outdoors for a would-be-lover. She would catch her death if she tried.

He smiled ruefully to himself. She was not on the terrace. Perhaps he should have considered a more obvious place.

He turned to leave, just as a figure emerged through the open door and closed it quickly behind her.

"Lord Leigh, I was hoping to catch you here," Miss Compton said breathlessly. "Isn't it a lovely evening?"

"Rather damp and chill, I thought," Leigh replied, frowning. "I was about to return inside."

"Oh, I suppose you are correct. It is a little cool, now that you mention it." Miss Compton gave a delicate shiver and took a step closer toward him. She wore a gown of silver satin. The bodice was very low, with a sheer piece of muslin sewn across to make it seem more modest. Leigh could not help a peek. She was not as well-endowed as Miss Spencer. In fact, there was nothing about Miss Compton that intrigued or appealed to Leigh. She was all sharp edges and cruel corners, from her slender hips to her malicious lips. It was folly to be near a young lady such as this, a voice in his head warned him. He knew exactly what sort of ploys Miss Compton was bound to have up her sleeve.

"If you'll excuse me," he said coolly, trying to step around her.

She stumbled–an artificial misstep–and reached out a hand, pressing it against his chest.

"Goodness, I nearly fell. I must thank you for catching me," she breathed, looking up into his eyes. "Yes, it is chilly. Though I suppose if I had a warm coat like yours, it might not be so unbearable." She batted her eyes up at him like a fawn. No hint of the serpent he knew lurked within.

Was she really insinuating he should offer her his coat? Leigh thought in amusement. Was this her clumsy attempt at a seduction?

"Miss Compton, this is what? Your first Season?"

"My second," she said, continuing to flicker her dark long lashes.

"Your second Season. Well, then you should know by now that I am not the sort of man debutantes should be alone on a dark terrace with," Leigh warned. "Not that you should be alone with any man out here." He frowned. What was she doing here, really? Foolish girl.

"What sort of man is that exactly, my lord? A dangerous one?" She stepped closer. They were inches apart now. There were diamonds gleaming in her black hair. Yes, she was beautiful, he acknowledged–in the way a jeweled necklace was beautiful or a polished sword. In an off-putting, dead way. She possessed a cold stark beauty. Not a flickering flame of life–like say, Miss Spencer.

63

"I don't mind danger," Miss Compton whispered, tilting her chin up.

Yes, she was certainly fishing to be kissed. She was going to be very disappointed. And perhaps very angry.

"I'm going in now, Miss Compton," Leigh said tightly. "I suggest you wait a few minutes before you follow."

"Are you really so concerned for my reputation, my lord? How very chivalrous of you."

Then she shocked him. Miss Compton lifted her hand and, reaching out a finger, trailed it over his lips.

It was an intimate and unwelcome gesture, and it took everything Leigh had not to shudder visibly.

"But I'd rather stay here. With you," she whispered as she dropped her hand and started to reach her hands up to clasp his shoulders.

He stepped back. "Not a good idea, Miss Compton."

"What's not a good idea?"

He snapped his head about, looking toward the new voice.

"Miss Spencer!"

"Lord Leigh." Miss Spencer, unlike Miss Compton, had left the door to the terrace open a few inches. She stood near it, hesitating.

"Miss Spencer, is it?" Miss Compton snapped. "You are interrupting. Go back inside."

"Ignore her," Leigh said. "Why are you here?" He scowled. "Looking for Hawkeye, I suppose."

"Hawkeye?" Miss Spencer frowned in confusion. "Who is Hawkeye?"

"Lord Harley," Leigh clarified. "I suppose you are to meet him here?"

"What? No. Lady Fulford told me that you wished to see me and that I would find you here. I suppose she did not realize you were already occupied. My apologies," Miss Spencer said stiffly. "I shall go."

She was turning back toward the terrace door when it was pushed open, and a tall young man came through.

"Ah, Miss Spencer. Fancy running into you here of all places." The young man was grinning down at Miss Spencer in a way Leigh immediately recognized, for had he not worn the same expression many a time?

Hawkeye. Lord Jack Harley. The Marquess of Harley. Whatever the deuce one wished to call the rake. For a rake he was. Though yes, Leigh would admit the younger man did have a certain charm. He must be, what? Twenty-four, twenty-five? Leigh felt ancient at a wise, old twenty-seven.

Harley was a devilish looker, too. No wonder women fell for his lines so easily. Even Miss Spencer, apparently, for she was here, was she not? Surely this meeting had been prearranged.

Leigh glared at the handsome young man. Lord Harley was tall and broad-shouldered, with thick brown hair and a chiseled jaw. He was taller than Leigh by a few inches. But then, many men were. Harley was handsome if you liked the Adonis type, Leigh conceded. If you preferred your men to look like muscular Greek statues. A little uninteresting, if you asked Leigh. But then, what did he know about what women really wanted in a man? He had never had any trouble pleasing them, but as for what their ideal of masculinity might be, he would not hazard a guess. He supposed he fit the bill for a great many women if past experience were any indication.

"Miss Spencer, I did not take you for a hypocrite," Miss Compton sneered, coming to stand closer to Leigh.

"I beg your pardon?" Miss Spencer replied. She looked at Leigh coldly. "I do not believe Lady Fulford intended for me to be here after all. I shall see you inside, my lord."

"Oh, don't go, Miss Spencer. I should enjoy more time in your company," Lord Harley complained. "Perhaps a stroll in the garden? May I offer you my coat? It is rather chilly, is it not?"

Leigh had to admire the other man's nerve. Trying to ensnare the lamb while the shepherd stood right nearby.

But then, Harley was not used to seeing Leigh as any kind of shepherd.

Leigh watched Miss Spencer force a smile. "No, thank you, Lord Harley. Though that is very kind of you."

Naive little chit, Leigh thought, biting back the remark and trying to exercise restraint as Lady Fulford had beseeched.

"I'm coming with you. Clear the way, Harley," Leigh barked. He marched past the other man and opened the terrace door for Miss Spencer.

He realized with irony that he was leaving Miss Compton with a notorious rake. A different one.

Well if she wished to leave the terrace, she could follow he and Miss Spencer. A group of three emerging from a spell outside would cause no comment.

Otherwise, her fate was her own.

"Good evening, Miss Compton," he called over his shoulder without turning around.

"You are really just going to leave me here, Lord Leigh?" he heard her whine.

"As I did not invite you in the first place, Miss Compton, I see no reason not to. If you are really so desperate for a seduction, I'm sure Lord Harley would be only too happy to stand in." He was sinking to her level in this and making an enemy. Though God knew he had worse enemies to contend with than a nettled debutante. "Good evening to you both."

Miss Spencer walked past him without a word. He followed her back into the ballroom.

For a moment, the rush of noise and burst of warmth were overwhelming.

Determined not to lose sight of Miss Spencer again, he gripped her arm. "Wait just a moment."

"I believe 'please' is customarily used at the end of that sentence, my lord," Miss Spencer said, turning to him. "That was a very strange encounter. I am not sure why you so rudely abandoned your tryst. Though your choice of companions is unexpected to say the least."

He watched her bite her lip and realized she was offended. No, not offended. Hurt. She thought he had gone out to meet Cora Compton. The idea was ridiculous.

Leigh gave a short laugh. "Miss Compton came after me if you can believe it. No, you must believe it. Please," he added, stressing the word. "Miss Spencer, I have absolutely no interest in debutantes. Particularly not the mean little bullying sort. Miss Compton is decidedly in that category. I suppose the—" He broke off and cleared his throat. "I suppose the girl wanted a bit of fun and thought chasing me would be it."

Miss Spencer studied him in silence for a moment. "I see."

"Do you? And what of you and Hawkeye? Lord Harley, I mean. You really had no intention of meeting him out there?"

Miss Spencer raised her chin. "He had suggested something of the sort, yes. Not very subtly. I did not think he was serious. I suppose when he saw me go outside, he thought I was initiating a meeting. How very provoking."

"Where the devil were you earlier if you were not with him? Where did you disappear to after the dance?" Leigh demanded. "Lady Fulford and I were searching for you."

"Yes, and Lady Fulford found me immediately," Miss Spencer hissed, her cheeks turning pink. "In the retiring room. Is it a crime to retire, my lord?"

Leigh felt his cheeks growing hot. "Oh. Of course. So... not the terrace?"

"Not the terrace," Miss Spencer said through clenched teeth. "I should have found you both shortly. There was no need to go looking for me."

"Well... when I didn't see you or Hawkeye, I thought..." Leigh stopped lamely.

"I suppose it is rather sweet that you wished to protect me," Miss Spencer said, tilting her head consideringly. "That you believed me to be in *need* of your protection."

"Yes, well." Leigh tugged at his cravat and studied her. "I believe what I am most in need of at this moment is a stiff drink and a break from this blasted crowd."

"Good luck finding either," Miss Spencer said with a sigh.

Perhaps it was her coolness under pressure, or the fact that Harley had clearly been taken with her enough to propose a tryst after a single dance—the bloody bastard—but Leigh found himself wishing for some uninterrupted time of his own in Miss Spencer's company.

And after all, was he not her chaperone?

"Come with me," he instructed. He turned and began to walk. Would she follow?

He glanced over his shoulder to see she was trailing behind, though her expression was reluctant.

"Should we not find Lady Fulford?"

Leigh shrugged. "She will be all right for a few minutes."

"Very well." She followed him out of the ballroom and down a long corridor that led to the main foyer, then up to the second floor. "Are you sure we should be doing this? Wandering through a stranger's home?"

"The Norfolks are not strangers to me. I have known Lord and Lady Norfolk all my life. My parents were their good friends. I suppose my mother will be still," he amended. "I grew up with their children. This ball is being held in honor of their granddaughter, Victoria Peel."

"Oh, yes. I believe I recall Lady Fulford saying something about that. She was absent when we went through the receiving line, but her grandparents were very welcoming."

Leigh was amused. "Everyone is afraid of Lady Fulford, so of course they are. But you really don't recall Victoria? You've mixed up everything and everyone already, haven't you? Which ball is for which debutante and which garden party is for which social cause?"

"Perhaps," Miss Spencer admitted. "This is only my first week, but already things have begun to blend together. Countless parties, countless names. But I am doing my best. For Lady Fulford's sake."

"Yes well, perhaps it's best you did not remember Victoria," Leigh said, amused. "You've already had one run-in with her and her lot the other night."

"Have I?" Miss Spencer quirked an eyebrow. "I don't recall."

"She was one of the girls who was with Miss Compton," Leigh explained. "The brunette. Miss Victoria Peel. They are cousins. Now do you recall her?"

"Ah yes, thank you for the reminder," Miss Spencer said wryly. "I believe I recall her now. They are cousins, you say? Yes, I believe I can see the resemblance."

"I didn't think you'd forget that encounter so easily. Though none of them are worth a moment of your time or consideration," Leigh said quietly. "Ah, here we are." He lifted the latch on a door and pushed it open.

He led the way into a tastefully decorated room. The decor was masculine in tone, with dark burgundies and browns. A large leather settee lay to one side with two fawn-colored armchairs nearby. A broad mahogany desk flanked by tall bookcases dominated the other side of the room. A row of wide sash windows lined the far back wall. Rich chocolate-brown damask curtains were drawn back on either side, providing a spectacular view of the moonlit night and the terrace and gardens below.

"Lord Norfolk's study," he explained to Miss Spencer as she followed him in.

"The quiet is a relief," she murmured.

He watched her draw a deep breath, the curve of her soft breasts pressing against the confines of her gown, and said a silent curse.

He should not have brought her here. He should not have drawn her away from the safety of the crowd. Chaperone or not, their meeting here could easily be misconstrued. Furthermore, he thought ruefully, and perhaps most importantly, Lady Fulford would not like it.

Well, it was too late now. He would get what he had come for and then have her back to the ballroom before anyone had noticed they were gone.

He stepped toward where Lord Norfolk's sideboard lay and picked up a crystal decanter. Pouring a generous quantity of amber liquid into a glass, he picked up the glass and drained it quickly, feeling the heat go through him. Ah, that was better. He was not used to these trumped-up social events anymore. They were more draining than he had remembered. He must be getting old.

He began to pour a second glass. Then he recalled his companion.

"I say, would you like a drink?" he asked quickly, turning. Norfolk was a whisky man, but surely there would be a bottle of sherry or port amongst the bottles.

Miss Spencer had already crossed the room. She was standing at the windows with her back to him, surveying the view.

The room was lit only by moonlight, Leigh now noticed for the first time. The light was so bright, no other had been needed as they entered.

He stared up at the moon as Miss Spencer was doing. It was a magnificent spring night, though chilly as had already been established.

He supposed, if he had been more accommodating, he might have been down in the gardens embracing a willing, slim dark-haired female under the stars right now.

His gaze wandered back to Miss Spencer. She was the opposite of Miss Compton in every way. Petite in height, with a form some might describe as "plump" but which he would call voluptuous. A decadent goddess with a mind as sharp as knives. And that hair. So different from her sister's. A golden shade as warm as the sunshine. A few more curls had fallen out of her coiffure and now trailed down her back like a lovely waterfall. She was all sweet curves and sensual feminine soft-ness. Her brand of allure was all her own, and the more time Leigh spent in her company, the more he felt himself entranced. She was bright and clever, yet full of innocence.

Oh, she would never be lauded as a Diamond of the First Water. Because people were sheep and had no taste of their own, he thought disdainfully.

But make no mistake, Miss Spencer radiated her own perfect beauty.

He thought again of the reason why they were here this evening and felt cross. He was to help her find a husband. To protect her and guard her until she did.

Well, he could certainly do the latter. He'd happily thrash any man who stepped out of line, Harley included.

He was not sure about the former, however. He did not have the heart for it. Though he knew Lady Fulford did.

"What was that?" She turned so quickly that she caught him off guard. She was smiling as if to herself. Wide, full lips turned up so pleasantly that he caught himself smiling back.

"I asked if you would care for a drink," he said, trying to hide his disconcertment.

"Oh! That would be very nice. Anything but champagne, please."

She glanced back at the windows. "Isn't this a lovely view? The Norfolks have a very large garden for this part of London."

"Mayfair is a world to itself," Leigh reminded her as he fished through the crystal bottles. "Everything is bigger. The gardens. The houses. The *amour propre.*" Aha! A madeira. He pulled out the stopper and sniffed. A hint of citrus and the crush of spice. Yes, the warm, sweet fortified wine seemed the perfect choice for Miss Spencer.

He stepped over to her with a glass outstretched in his hand, but she did not notice him at first.

"The moon looks incredible tonight," she murmured, still gazing outside. "Shining over the tops of the townhouses. You know, Blakeley Manor is a lovely place, but there is something about being in the city that makes one feel rather..."

"Cosmopolitan?" Leigh said, grinning a little.

"Yes, something like that. As if one were part of the larger world. A sense of, well, I suppose excitement."

"Well, Blakeley is rather out of the way. My parents preferred a rustic quietude."

"Oh, my family enjoyed that as well," she assured him. "Do not mistake me. I loved our pretty, peaceful cottage. I cried when Laurel and I locked it up for the last time. Of course, a new family has settled there now. A couple with three small children. I hope they will be as happy as we all were."

Leigh stared. He had forgotten for a moment who Miss Spencer was. Who she had been before this. She was not just some privileged girl like Miss Compton who had spent her entire life leading up to this point, every step carrying her toward the moment she would become a debutante and join elite society. No, Miss Spencer had actually *worked* for a living. If he was another sort of gentleman, he supposed he might feel disgust at the very idea. Surely, it was in large part the reason those girls disdained her. She had been a housemaid, after all. And despite Lady Fulford's best efforts, everywhere she went, people knew at least something of her past and were whispering about it.

But to Leigh, this newly remembered detail was fascinating. He had never been a true believer in the superiority of nobility anyhow—especially when it was rarely accompanied by a strong sense of *noblesse oblige*. The fact that Miss Spencer had so easily been able to walk in two worlds was impressive, not distasteful to him.

Everything about Miss Spencer was different. She was a true Cinderella. And like the stepsisters in the story, the girls who had never had to strive for the privilege of attending a ball were the ones most eager to bar the door to those who had.

And yet, the slipper did not quite fit, for Miss Spencer evidently had no real longing to be here. She was participating in the marriage mart scheme out of a sense of obligation and gratitude. Or so it seemed to Leigh.

"What do you really want, Miss Spencer?" he asked curiously, unable to predict the response.

"Oh, I said anything would do," she said, turning abruptly, evidently thinking he still meant the liquor.

She turned rather too abruptly—and to be fair, he was standing a little too near.

"Oh!" Miss Spencer's arm knocked against his. The glass in his hand wobbled, steadied, wobbled again, and then sloshed heavily all over the girl.

A red stain spread over chest, her skin, the bodice of her gown. Fortunately, the majority landed on Lord Norfolk's costly rug. Damn the rug, Leigh thought.

"Oh, dear! Of course, I should be so clumsy," Miss Spencer exclaimed, looking down at herself. "Please tell me you have a handkerchief, my lord. Preferably a dozen."

Leigh set down the glass on the desk nearby, already fishing in his pockets. "I have at least one." And it was clean, too. He pulled it out and handed it to her, congratulating himself on his restraint in not trying to clean her himself, then watched fascinated as Miss Spencer began dabbing at her breasts.

"It is no use," she said after a moment. "I cannot get the gown clean. I am not sure my maid will be able to either. Such a pale lavender. What a pity, for it is such a pretty gown, too, and this was the first opportunity I have had to wear it." He watched her settle for wiping away the wine from her skin, transfixed by the sight of the red droplets being mercilessly scrubbed from the soft white expanses.

"It looks very fetching on you," he said hoarsely. "I meant to mention it earlier."

"You need not pay me compliments, my lord," she said, frowning.

At the dress or at him? He could not tell.

"I have received at least a hundred this evening already. All false, I am sure. I do not require more to feed my vanity."

"Mine are not false," he promised. "Why do you say that? I am sure the others were sincere as well."

She lifted her head, and he saw her expression was wry.

"Why do you look at me that way?" he asked, feeling awkward. "You are a very pretty girl, and I am sure I am not the only one to say so." He begged himself to shut up. To stop talking. What he said was true but there was no reason for him to confess it, and besides, she clearly thought he was simply being dissembling.

"Mmm." She seemed to be contemplating her next words. "You know, my lord, I have not had to be so obsessed with my own appearance in a very long time. Not since I attended school on the estate where some of the girls would tease me for being plump."

Leigh felt his temper rise at the very thought of this.

"When I was young, I actually allowed what they believed about me to bother me. Then I grew up a little and took some of my mother's wise advice to heart, and I realized no one's opinion of my appearance mattered much besides my own. And I like how I look. I do not believe I am unpleasant to look upon."

That was an understatement, Leigh thought.

"But more importantly, I believe that my body is strong and capable. *I* am strong and capable. I would rather be useful than pretty. I would rather be clever than beautiful. Beauty fades, but what is in my mind will be there forever. Look at Lady Fulford. She is so accomplished and so formidable. She does not need a man to tell her that she is."

Leigh opened his mouth, then closed it again. She was right, of course, and he wanted to say he agreed with her—but also to assure her that he believed she was more than pretty. But to do so would have lowered him in her eyes at that moment. So, he kept quiet.

She continued, "I suppose it was foolish of me not to realize that most of this—this Season, this spectacle—would be about, well, how women look. It is all superficiality without any substance."

"Is it?" Leigh colored. He knew she was right, of course.

She gave him a sardonic look. "They do not call it the marriage mart for nothing."

"Yes, but that goes for men as well," he countered, suddenly prepared to defend this strange time-honored tradition. "There are many young men here searching for brides, but also young women seeking them out as husbands. And there is more to it than balls, of course. The courting that takes place behind the scenes is real enough and often based on mutual amiability and respect." God, he hoped that was true.

She did not seem convinced. "I have noticed that people assume when a man pursues a woman, he is seeking pleasure. But when a woman pursues a man, she is after his money. At least, this is true in most cases. But here, amongst your *ton*, I feel as if anyone who shows interest in me is doing so because..." She stopped.

"Yes?" he encouraged.

"Well, your brother was very generous to settle such a large dowry upon me. But I rather wish it had not been so very large."

Leigh understood. "I am sure you have already encountered would-be suitors who see you for yourself and for whom your dowry would be only a small part of things."

"Really? Perhaps you are more naive than I gave you credit for, my lord." She smiled.

"What do you want?" he asked bluntly. "What do you want in a man?"

She seemed surprised by the question. "I did not think I wanted a man at all," she responded. "A husband, I suppose you mean, for women are not allowed to simply *want* men, are we?"

He did not answer. He had certainly encountered enough women who believed they were, or who did not believe in asking for permission.

"I suppose I would not mind seeking a man—a husband—for reasons of *pleasure*," she said, looking back out the window, for which Leigh was grateful as he felt as if he might choke as the word "pleasure" passed her lips. "A man who might be my equal."

He noticed she did not say, "Someone who would see me as *his* equal," and he felt a glow of pride at that. Oh, Miss Spencer had spirit all right. Was there any man worthy of this young woman? That was the question.

"Someone who is capable, who has more skills than those you would find in the ballroom. Real, practical skills. A man who believes in being useful, not simply..."

She stopped, turned her head back, and met his eyes, looking chagrined.

"Not the wastrel youngest son of a noble family who has only known a life of privilege, you mean?" he asked drily.

He was hurt in spite of knowing that was not what she had meant. She had not meant him specifically. Even so, she was pure and lovely and innocent, and he? He was drunk and bitter and renowned as a scoundrel. He shouldn't be particularly surprised if she did think of him in such a negative light.

He watched her eyes widen.

"Of course, I did not mean you," she said hurriedly. "Oh, Lord Leigh, of course I was not even *thinking* of you."

Sadly, hearing this did not soothe his ego.

He could not resist.

He waved a hand. "No matter. But you know, Miss Spencer, I may be a scoundrel and I may live a life of idleness." Though far less idle than perhaps she supposed. "But you mentioned skills and pleasure, and it is in those two areas you may be surprised to hear that I quite excel."

"Oh?" Her eyes had widened still more, he noticed. Good.

She cleared her throat. "I am not quite sure what you..."

He took a step closer toward her. "Women may want men, Miss Spencer. They may simply *want*. I have encountered enough who do."

"Have you?" she asked faintly.

He was close enough to see the stains of madeira on her lavender gown. Close enough to see the faint roses of embarrassment blooming in her cheeks.

"Yes. Women who want. Women who take what they desire. Women who rail against the idea of the marriage mart just as much as you do." He shrugged. "I have known some who have been of the *ton*. I have known some who have escaped its confines to live more freely. Some who were never a part of it in the first place. But all had one thing in common—they were women who were not ashamed to take their pleasure."

"And they wanted you, my lord, did they?" she said very quietly, her eyes steady. "All of them?"

"I possess a certain skill set," he replied, trying to be modest. "Like you, I may not be the most handsome man in the room." Was it his imagination or had her blush deepened? "But I am well-formed enough, I suppose."

"You are most handsome," she said quietly, dropping her eyes to the floor. "I do not believe you are unaware of this, my lord."

He shrugged, then realized she could not see him shrug with her head down so modestly. He reached out a hand and placed a finger under her chin, lifting her head very gently.

"Am I making you embarrassed, Miss Spencer, with all this talk of pleasure? You were the one who mentioned it in the first place, I believe. Or was this not the sort of pleasure you had in mind?"

He watched her straighten, her lips firming. "I am still not sure what sort we are even discussing, Lord Leigh. You are being rather cryptic."

He smiled. "What other kind of pleasure is there to be taken between a man and a woman?" He studied her. "Is that what you are afraid of, Miss Spencer? Of missing out on that sort? You wonder if you truly wish to marry. You see these old men clamoring around you, and it frightens you. You wonder if you will wind up with a husband who knows nothing of how to give or receive pleasure. A man who has claimed you merely for your dowry."

"I should never marry such a man," she said, raising her chin.

He was goading her now. He should not. But he could not resist. Was it the whisky or his own wicked heart?

"Ah, but what if you decide not to marry at all?" he continued. "Then what will you ever know of pleasure?"

"You have just said there are women who..."

"Ah yes, but will you be such a one? Does that ability lie within you, Miss Spencer? The ability to take what one wants and damn the cost?"

He knew it lay in him.

"You are being very silly," she whispered, meeting his eyes. "All this silly talk, my lord. Bragging of your skills in bed. Almost as if..."

Her eyes were gray, he realized with a jolt. As gray as a stormy sea—and right now, just as tempestuous.

"As if what?" he breathed, stepping another foot closer to her.

She was such a pretty little thing. A small soft woman whose head would fit perfectly beneath his chin. Her body looked so pliant and curving. All those curves that had probably never once been touched, never been appreciated.

"You did not wish for me to go out on the terrace when Lord Harley asked me tonight, my lord," she whispered. "And yet here I am with you. Why do I suddenly feel as if this room is much more dangerous than the terrace?"

He reached out a finger and touched her cheek. "No danger," he assured her. "Only pleasure. Just a little taste. No more than that. We might call it... instructional."

"Very well—" she started to say, or at least, he believed that was what she was about to say as he leaned down and kissed her.

Her lips were firm and warm and just as soft as he had known they would be. He kissed her gently, thoroughly, breathing her in. She smelled of lilac soap and green grass and warm sun.

Within an instant, he knew the kiss had been a mistake. When her arms slipped around him, trembling. When she stood on her tiptoes and circled the back of his neck with her small hand, pressing her lips more fiercely against his. When he heard a small breath escape her, like the fluttering of a little bird.

He had kissed countless women before. None had ever caused him to feel this way. None had ever tasted as sweet and as pure as summer. None had ever made him question all his choices leading up to this moment. None had ever made him feel so alone. None had ever made him wonder why he had chosen to be alone.

Hazily, he knew he should break the kiss and back away slowly.

Preferably run from the room and out of the house and back to the Continent. Or Scotland. Perhaps Scotland would be far enough away.

Instead, he brought his arms to her waist and lifted her up, ignoring her little murmurs of protest and holding her so she was raised entirely up off the ground. He watched her eyes go as wide as saucers, saw her mouth form a perfect O, and smiled down at her.

She felt exactly as he had imagined she would in his arms, her petite voluptuous body snuggled closely against him. He placed her carefully upon Norfolk's desk, ignoring the warning cries in his head, and then positioned his mouth over hers once more.

"Open your mouth," he growled playfully, brushing his lips against hers.

She did as he commanded, her lips parting as he thrust his tongue inside her. He felt himself grinning. She tasted of lemonade, not champagne.

And then he was lost in the feel of her as she clung to him, wrapping her arms around his shoulders, her fingers sliding through his hair.

He deepened the kiss, his tongue becoming bolder, stroking against hers in a shameless mimicry of the act he longed to indulge in but knew he could not. She kissed him back fervently, moving her tongue against his, following his lead, his instruction.

His cock was already hard and sore with need. He felt her writhe gently against him and came to a hasty decision. If he was already damned for kissing an innocent debutante, he may as well be a little more wicked.

He grasped her thighs and, before she could protest, raised them around his waist, pressing himself against her core, his hips wedging her legs firmly open, then kissed her more intensely, his tongue thrusting and darting against hers. She moaned. Did she feel the same burning heat that he did? Did she long for more?

He imagined raising her gown, laying her down along Lord Norfolk's desk, freeing his cock from his trousers, and entering her gently. She would be tight. Hot and tight. The sounds of pleasure she would make would be... absolutely indescribable.

God, but he wanted her. How he longed to free the tips of her breasts, straining against the damp satin of her dress. He imagined sliding the dress down on one side, just a little. Just enough for one red swollen nipple to come free, then popping it into his mouth and suckling as she gasped above him. God, it would be good. So good to taste her. She would taste so good everywhere. The dampness of the wine surely echoed by the sweet dampness that lay between her thighs.

But no. This had to stop here. Now. Already he had lost more control of himself than he had meant to.

And it would be wrong, incredibly wrong, a choice he could never come back from.

He had promised Miss Spencer a kiss. This was decidedly more than one.

Rubbing his cock against her, feeling her soft round thighs pressing around his hips as she angled herself more closely–that was not supposed to be in the equation.

He paused. Licked her lower lip once, gently, then broke the kiss.

He looked into her dove-gray eyes and saw her aching and trembling with the same want he felt.

"I believe," he said, swallowing hard. "The lesson has been learnt."

She nodded slowly, already composing herself.

"An excellent lesson, Lord Leigh," she said with surprising calm. "I thank you for allowing me to sample your... skill set."

She was patting her gown and looking across the room at the door. She longed to be free of him, perhaps. He suddenly knew with a pang that he had taken advantage of her. He had behaved as a cad. Worse than that damned Harley.

"I believe we should return to the ballroom now. If you would please..." Miss Spencer gestured with her hand, blushing, and he realized he was still standing between her legs, preventing her from slipping down off the desk.

He stepped back quickly, offered her his hand, and was relieved when she accepted it.

"May I escort you back to the ballroom, Miss Spencer?" he mumbled, feeling like a sheepish schoolboy.

"That would be very nice, thank you," she murmured.

He paused. He could not help it. "Marigold..." He stopped. "I am sorry. Miss Spencer."

She stood beside the desk, looking up at him thoughtfully. "Oh, so you do know my Christian name."

He gaped. "Of course, I do. I mean, yes."

She smiled. A sweet smile. Had he truly been permitted to kiss those lips? Had his tongue really been in that mouth? It already seemed an impossible dream, so distant had she already become. And yet her smile was kind and reassuring.

"It is all right, my lord," she said gently. "You need not say what you are about to say."

He frowned. "And what was that?"

"You were about to apologize, I suppose. For carrying our sparring too far."

"Well... yes." Is that what it had been? Sparring? He already longed to spar with her again. In word or deed.

She nodded composedly. God, he envied her composure. Ordinarily, it was he who was the calm and cool one. What the devil was happening to him?

"I thought as much. There is no need. It was... an enjoyable interlude. I believe I understand the lesson you wished to impart, and I promise I will take it under consideration." He was baffled. Then he saw her eyes widen. "There is only one thing."

"Yes?"

"The stains on my gown," she reminded him, looking down at herself. "How shall we explain them to Lady Fulford?"

"Ah." Leigh bit his lip. What an excellent question. One he should have considered before now.

He saw her brighten. "Never mind. I have an idea. Let us return."

When they stepped back into the ballroom, Miss Spencer pointed toward Lady Fulford. The older woman sat at a table talking animatedly, but when she caught sight of them, she rose and walked over quickly.

"Where have you been, Miss Spencer?" she hissed, clearly more upset than she seemed. "And you, Blakeley. You were to see to the safeguarding of our charge. Not her disappearance!"

"It is my fault, Lady Fulford," Miss Spencer said meekly. "Lord Leigh found me and brought me back."

"Brought you back? Brought you back from where?"

"I had snuck off for a moment of blessed quiet," Miss Spencer explained. "Out into the house." Leigh watched her strive to look abashed. "I was sitting in Lord Norfolk's study, sipping a glass of madeira, when Lord Leigh crashed in, all a panic. I knocked the glass and, well, you can see the results." She gestured to her gown, which Lady Fulford suddenly seemed to notice for the first time.

"Gracious," Lady Fulford gasped. "I shall fetch your shawl at once. Better yet..."

"I will fetch it," Lord Leigh promised.

He began to move away just as Miss Spencer ventured, "Perhaps we might make an early evening of it? Just this once?"

"I believe that would be very wise," he heard Lady Fulford reply.

He told himself not to look back. He would fetch the shawl, escort the ladies to their carriage, then make his own departure.

This had been... how had Miss Spencer put it? An enjoyable interlude. His lips twisted wryly. For such an innocent, she was capable of a shockingly worldly manner.

Yes, it had been enjoyable. More than enjoyable if he were being honest.

It could not happen again.

Chapter Eight

Marigold sat quietly across from Lady Fulford in the carriage and stifled a yawn. She refused to be rattled by her evening. Yes, it had gone in quite a different direction than expected.

But on the positive side, she was returning home much earlier than expected, too.

And that meant she might finally be able to put a plan into motion that she had been waiting upon ever since arriving in London. With the flurry of dressmakers' appointments and fittings and visits to the haberdasher, the milliner, and other shops, the week previous had been exceedingly full. Once properly outfitted, Marigold had been whirled into another week full of social engagements—and she knew this would not stop for the foreseeable future. Lady Fulford had literally months of events written down in that social calendar of hers. Until Marigold found a husband, of course. Then the social schedule would slow, courtship rituals would commence, and finally culminate in marriage. After which, Marigold might finally have a well-needed rest.

It was truly bizarre, but marriage was beginning to look like a more appealing prospect simply when compared to nights and nights of balls and fetes and having one's feet trod upon by strangers.

Perhaps she should settle down after all, she thought glumly. Then she perked up. First, she would see how she could manage her personal endeavor amongst Lady Fulford's packed schedule.

It was half past midnight. If she rested now, she could rise early–very early–and sneak out before Lady Fulford awoke for the day. Lady Fulford was an early riser, but Marigold had noticed after a ball that the older lady spent a few extra hours in bed each morning. Very understandable, considering the balls often lasted into the wee hours, and Lady Fulford was not exactly a debutante herself.

She would take a hack and not Lady Fulford's carriage, of course. It was a daring plan, and she was sure Lady Fulford would call it foolhardy for an unwed young lady to go anywhere alone, especially without even a maid, and at such an early hour. But then, Marigold was not a typical young lady, was she? She was hardly even a lady at all.

This was not to say she did not believe she possessed "good breeding." Her parents were fine people. Her mother had been a Scottish noblewoman. Her father had been a vicar's son. She came from a good family and had received an above-average education. Not at the estate school where she had attended for a few years until becoming bored, frustrated, and bullied mind you, but at home, from her father and mother.

Her father instructed the children in music, the arts, a little Latin, a little Greek. Her mother taught them–yes, even the boys–sewing, needlework, ancient history, modern history, as well as mathematics. Marigold loved her history lessons, and if she recalled them as well as she believed she did, they might serve her well today.

As for the history of that very evening? The history now established between herself and Lord Leigh? She would not dwell on it.

She said her goodnight to Lady Fulford and made her way to her room on the second floor where her lady's maid helped her to undress and climb into bed.

Despite thinking she would not be able to fall asleep, slumber came easily. Before she knew it, she was waking in the dark. She checked the timepiece beside her bed. It was just after four-thirty. The same time she had risen almost daily when she entered service at Blakeley Manor.

If she hurried, she could be out of the house before most of the servants were stirring for the day.

She dressed quickly in a simple lawn day dress and found a heavy wool cloak in her closet.

The streets were quiet but fortunately a few hacks were rolling to and fro. Marigold was able to flag one down without any trouble. Getting the driver to accept her destination without a fuss was another matter.

The kindly driver looked her up and down and frowned. "Not accustomed to taking ladies to that neighborhood."

"I know it is a very rough one, but my aunt lives there," Marigold explained, hoping desperately he would accept the little white lie.

The driver hesitated, then gestured for her to get in, and the hack had rolled away.

A short while later, Marigold was faithfully deposited on a street in the neighborhood of Seven Dials. She paid the driver and waited until he had driven off before looking around her. The morning was turning out to be a grim and gloomy one. In the gray light, she spotted the building she was looking for just across the street. She crossed over quickly to where a large old stone church stood. Off to one side was a moss-covered arch leading to a shadowy courtyard. Marigold marched quickly toward it.

At the back of the church, alongside a cluttered-looking graveyard, was an unsightly annex. A wooden sign hung next to the door, creaking in the wind. In the dim, Marigold could not clearly make out the words written in faded white paint, but nonetheless, she knew what they would say. The Dispensary for the Poor of St. Giles.

With a little sigh of satisfaction, she continued her march toward the door and, upon reaching it, rapped confidently.

It was pulled open almost immediately by a short figure with close-cropped brown hair streaked with gray who scowled up at her. For a moment, Marigold was taken aback. She could not tell at first if the figure was a man or a woman. The person's face was lined and weary, but all this spoke to was a middling age and a challenging life.

The figure spoke. "We have patients sleeping. Kindly cease your racket," they declared harshly.

Harsh or not, it was clearly a woman's voice. Marigold smiled. "You must be Miss Barry. Maggie."

The woman scowled even more deeply as Marigold had expected her to. She had not been counting on a warm reception. Not after hearing Miss Barry described in lavish, grisly detail by the Duke of Dareford. She had anticipated having to fight and claw her way to acceptance and was fully prepared to do so.

"Do I know you?" the woman demanded, narrowing her eyes.

"Not yet," Marigold said cheerfully. "May I come in? I have a proposal for you."

The woman was clearly unwilling. She stood in the doorway for so long that Marigold was finally forced to add, "We are not yet acquainted. My name is Miss Marigold Spencer. I believe you know my brother-in-law. The Duke of Dareford."

The woman's eyes widened slightly, and she grunted, then held the door open wide enough for Marigold to squeeze inside.

"Thank you," she said as graciously as she could manage, once she was standing inside. She peered around her curiously. Yes, it was everything she had hoped it would be. Just as gritty and gloomy and grimy as Dare had described.

The two women stood in the front room of the dispensary, which seemed to serve as a combination of a waiting room, office, and library. No one was waiting there right now, but from behind the door leading into the corridor, Marigold could hear soft murmuring. There must be patients sleeping or trying to sleep in one of the rooms toward the back. And down the corridor must also be a room for a doctor's surgery as well as a storage room for medicines and supplies.

"It is very quiet this morning," Marigold observed quietly. "I do hope I did not wake any of your patients. I admit, I expected you to be busy even this early in the day."

Miss Barry grunted again but looked surprised. "We usually are," she admitted. "It is an uncommonly quiet morning. I don't suppose you are here as a patient? The duke's sister-in-law, you say?" She peered at Marigold suspiciously. "What brings you to such a place as this so early in the day, Miss Spencer?" Then she brightened. "Perhaps you wish to make a donation to our work?"

"I do," Marigold acknowledged. "Of a sort." She bit her lip. This was the part she was most uncertain of. She had already dropped Dare's name once. Would she have to do so again in order to get what she wanted?

"I wish to work with you, Miss Barry," she announced. "Here in the dispensary."

The older woman's eyebrows shot up. "Absolutely not."

"Why not?" Marigold retorted. "You know nothing about me yet."

Miss Barry sniffed. "And I do not need to. I can tell everything I need to know by looking at you, Miss Spencer."

"And?" Marigold challenged.

Miss Barry gave a sneering smile. "You are soft and privileged. Your stomach turns at the sight of blood. One morning of someone vomiting at your feet, and you would be racing for the door. Let alone the sight of lesions or boils or even, dare I say it, *death*." She shook her head. "You belong in a ballroom, not here."

"Let me see," Marigold said, putting a fingertip to her mouth. "A soft, privileged young lady who some believed was better suited to a ballroom than to a medical establishment. Why, I do believe I sound like *you*, Miss Barry."

Miss Barry's face turned red. "What are you on about?"

"Well, you *are* Miss Margaret Barry of the Barry family of pawnbrokers, are you not? Your father grew up in the Seven Dials and became a very successful businessman. As his wealth grew, so too did his hopes for his family. He wished for his only daughter to have the very best of everything—including her pick of husbands. And so, after moving his family out of the Seven Dials and into a stately home in Grosvenor Square, he applied to the patronesses of Almack's for a voucher. Shockingly, this was granted. All seemed set for his daughter's first Season amongst the *ton*." Marigold paused. "Shall I continue?"

Miss Barry said nothing.

"But of course," Marigold said, her voice gentle, not judging. "There was to be no Season. For Miss Margaret Barry was nowhere to be found. Her father was beside himself. Had she eloped? Where could she have gone? The *ton* was all a twitter with speculation. But Miss

Barry never returned to settle any of the rumors. In fact, she never returned home at all."

Miss Barry frowned. "That's not true. I do return home from time to time."

Marigold hesitated. "I suppose your father is glad to see you," she ventured.

Miss Barry gave a short laugh. "It took five years, but yes, he was eventually *willing* to see me. His health declined. I suppose once he realized he was mortal and could no longer hold out any hope I would comply with his ridiculous scheme."

"Did you ever tell him where you had been?" Marigold asked quietly.

The other woman tilted her head. "Do *you* even know where I was?"

"It is true that there are gaps. I only know part of the story. But then, I suppose that's how you preferred it." It was Lady Fulford who had told her of the marvelous Miss Margaret Barry, quite accidentally and without realizing the impact it would have upon Marigold. They had both heard Dare's tale of tracking the clues the dowager duchess had inadvertently left all over London, from the docks to the dispensary and elsewhere. When Lady Fulford heard the duke mention a Miss Margaret Barry, she had immediately put two and two together and realized that the woman from the dispensary was the young up-and-coming girl who had fled rather than attend Almack's.

Or at least, that was how Lady Fulford had seen it. Marigold had interpreted the story quite differently. As a heroic tale of a woman leaving to seek out her own destiny.

"My own patroness recognized your name when it was mentioned by the duke," Marigold explained. "When I heard the story of how a would-be-debutante had gone from nearly having a come-out at Almack's to becoming a... well, to working to help the poor and needy at this dispensary, I was..." She paused.

"Yes? You were what?"

Marigold lifted her chin. "I was inspired. You see, I never wanted a Season either. Never in my life did I expect to get one. My circumstances are not so different from your own, Miss Barry. And I want to do what you do."

"Oh?" Miss Barry stepped forward, looking alarmingly adversarial all of a sudden. "And what is that?"

"Women are not permitted to practice medicine," Marigold said slowly. "Officially."

"Officially it is against the law, yes," Miss Barry snapped. "So, then? What am I? What can I possibly do here?"

Marigold studied her carefully. "Officially, I suppose you work at this dispensary as a nurse or a midwife. Perhaps both. Unofficially, however..."

A door leading off down the corridor suddenly slammed shut. Marigold had not even realized it had been opened.

"Unofficially, she does everything. Absolutely everything that must be done in a place such as this," a booming male voice said.

Marigold turned to see a brown-skinned beaming man with dark hair and spectacles had emerged from the back of the dispensary.

"She is indispensable to the dispensary, you see," the man said. He had a lovely deep melodic voice and spoke an accented English that Marigold had only heard a few times, most recently from foreign guests at the Norfolks' ball. The guests had been from India. She supposed this man, too, was from that faraway land.

"Dr. Arpan Bannerjee is the official resident physician at the dispensary," Miss Barry declared.

"Officially, yes," Dr. Bannerjee said, grinning and tapping the side of his nose. He winked at Marigold. "And who might this young lady be?"

"I wish to become Miss Barry's apprentice. And yours. If you'll have me," Marigold said immediately. "If you are still reluctant, my brother-in-law is the Duke of Dareford."

"In other words, if we don't do what you say, you'll make sure we don't see a farthing of his money again," Miss Barry said sourly, folding her arms over her chest.

She was so short and stout and fierce, not to mention sour that she reminded Marigold of a character from a fairy story. Rumpelstiltskin, perhaps.

"No, not at all," she vowed. "That would be cruel indeed. Not only to you and Dr. Bannerjee but to your patients. It is more than evident that the neighborhood desperately needs the dispensary."

"Oh, and you are familiar with the Seven Dials, are you, Miss Spencer?" Miss Barry said sardonically. "You grew up in these parts, perhaps?"

Marigold flushed. "Not at all. But I read the papers. Moreover, I did not grow up quite as privileged as you seem to believe. Appearances can be deceiving as I'm sure you're well aware. I am not the coddled young lady you presume me to be. Although my brother-in-law is a duke, I worked for a living as a housemaid before this. As did all the members of my family, including my sister, who was a housekeeper before she married the duke."

There was silence for a moment.

"Just like a fairy story," Dr. Bannerjee finally exclaimed, sounding delighted. "I shall have to tell my sons about the duke who married his maid."

"Oh, you have children?" Marigold inquired.

"Three children. Two boys and a girl," Dr. Bannerjee said proudly. "They remain in India with their mother for now."

"Oh!" Marigold was surprised.

"Dr. Bannerjee came to England to study medicine," Miss Barry explained. "That was how he and I met."

"Well, Miss Spencer," Dr. Bannerjee said, looking her up and down contemplatively, but not at all in the semi-lascivious, semi-appraising manner she had already grown used to enduring from would-be-suitors at balls and the like. "You seem like a capable, clever young woman."

"I am. That is precisely how I should prefer to describe myself," Marigold said, standing up straighter and squaring her shoulders. "Not to mention hardworking. And very much *not* put off at the sight of blood," she said emphatically, looking at Miss Barry.

"*Hmph*." Miss Barry looked at Dr. Bannerjee. "Do not even think of it. We take enough risks here as it is."

"What risk could there be in allowing a charitable English maiden to apprentice as a nurse or a midwife," Dr. Bannerjee asked soothingly. "It is done all the time."

"Ha!" Miss Barry looked mutinous. "We hardly know this girl."

"I suppose you receive offers of help from strange young ladies quite frequently," Marigold said with false innocence. "I suppose you already have all the help you could possibly need."

"In fact, we are understaffed and quite desperate for assistance," Dr. Bannerjee assured her in his beautifully accented English. Besides his evident accent, there was something familiar about the way he spoke. It reminded her of the duke, in fact. She suddenly wondered if they had attended the same school.

"Oh dear me, how dreadful," Marigold said sweetly. "In that case, perhaps you might take me on and try me out as it were. I promise, I am a fast learner."

Dr. Bannerjee caught her eye and winked slyly, then nodded toward Miss Barry, who was staring off toward the tall bookshelves that lay along one wall near two small desks.

"We have the funds we need to keep going but have had trouble finding competent staff, it is true," Miss Barry said slowly, frowning. She turned to Marigold. "How soon can you start?"

Marigold stared. "I... I could begin as soon as tomorrow." She would have to tell Lady Fulford the truth or else make up a very, very convincing lie. Or something in between. In any case, she would figure something out. She had to.

"Excellent." Dr. Bannerjee was beaming again, displaying bright white teeth. "Well, I must see to my patient. Maggie, my dear, perhaps you might come and help me. She is very near."

"Near?" Marigold inquired.

"Near to delivering a baby," Dr. Bannerjee explained. "And a fine healthy baby it is sure to be. The next time, you may observe. I look forward to seeing you soon, Miss Spencer."

And then he was gone as abruptly as he had arrived.

Miss Barry stood there, arms still folded, and looked at Marigold.

"You truly need not be afraid that the duke's patronage might cease whether you allow me to assist you," Marigold said falteringly. She wished to be honest about this.

Miss Barry's lips twisted. "Oh, I know. He doesn't even know you are here, does he? Your brother-in-law."

Marigold gasped. "How did you...?"

Miss Barry gave a dry chuckle. "Perhaps we are more alike than I thought, Miss Spencer. Although I doubt even *you* are daring enough to do just what I did to achieve my place here."

Marigold was exceedingly curious but knew this was not the time to ask. There would be more time to spend alongside the fascinating Miss Barry—and Dr. Bannerjee—and it could not come quickly enough.

She left the dispensary—before Miss Barry could change her mind—and walked back toward the street to hail a hack.

This was it. Marigold would have a Season, yes. But she was determined to find something all her own in London, too.

A sense of purpose. A career. Few would understand. But they did not have to. Her mind flickered briefly to Lord Leigh. What would he say if he could see her now? Would he be shocked? Disgusted?

If he was anything like his brother, he would probably put his foot down and insist Marigold leave Seven Dials at once. Men had ridiculous double standards when it came to the women in their lives. But he was not her brother. He did not have a say in her life. He was a temporary presence.

Although that was rather a pity. Because for the first time last night, Marigold had felt truly beautiful in a man's eyes. And she wondered just how much more of Lord Leigh Blakeley's skill set there was to sample.

Chapter Nine

A few hours after departing the Norfolks' ball, Lord Leigh Blakeley was at a vastly different venue. A little hole-in-the-wall pub in the worst neighborhood in London. The locals called it Seven Dials after the junction of seven roads which formed the centerpiece of the slum. In this area of Covent Garden, the Great Plague had first reared its terrifying head. William Hogarth had famously depicted the neighborhood in his none-too-elegantly titled illustration "Gin Lane," so named because it was said one in four houses in the slum functioned as a gin shop.

Lifting his smudged glass, Leigh poured a dram of whisky back, enjoying the flash of warmth as it spread from his throat to his stomach. One got what one paid for, of course. The liquor here was cheap and the taste more acrid than what Leigh was used to, but it was not completely unpalatable. No hints of charred caramel or toasted almond. But it did the trick.

Abruptly, he found himself recalling the similar blaze of heat he had felt just a few short hours before. Only that one had been caused by a woman.

Despite seeming deceptively ordinary in many ways, Miss Marigold Spencer had an unnerving effect upon him. Her kisses had sent flames of liquid fire flowing through him. And left him wanting much, much more. His skin tingled as he imagined what it would be like to let Miss Spencer lay her hands anywhere she liked on him. Would she be daring in her exploration? Would her touch be gentle, tremulous? Or bold and firm?

He shifted on the hard wooden bench. He did not need any of that sort of firmness just at the moment.

His attraction to Miss Spencer was... problematic. He had always been the sort of man who wanted what he could not have. Telling Leigh he could not have something simply served to make him want it more. So, perhaps if he broke down this attraction, he would find that was all that lay beneath it. He could not stand the prospect of another man claiming Miss Spencer. The idea of her being wed by the end of the Season had set fire to his blood somehow.

Yet, as he had no intention of wedding the girl himself, he needed to set aside this stupidity. It would serve neither of them.

Claimed she would be, he told himself. And not by him.

He jumped as a glass was dropped heavily onto the table before him.

"Drunk for a penny, dead drunk for a two-pence?"

"I generally like to keep my wits about me before I go out like a lamb to the slaughter," Leigh said genially. "But oh, what the hell." He picked up the glass of cheap gin, looked at it for a moment as he thought of the terrific hangover it was bound to bring on, then tossed it back.

Across the table, his uncle had taken a seat.

Tall and lanky, dark-haired with a salt-and-pepper beard, Lord Royal Blakeley would as soon kick someone's arse than be called a "lord." If one looked closely, they might eventually notice that his clothing was well-made and finely tailored, but certainly not the sort of thing one expected the son of a noble family to wear. He looked like a man who had known a hard day's work in his time. A man who would do difficult things without a word of complaint. Sharp and hard and not a little rough around the edges.

Royal Blakeley was the black sheep of his family. Similar to Leigh in that respect. Both nephew and uncle shared a devil-may-care attitude and healthy disregard for authority. But when Royal's elder brother and his wife—Leigh's parents—had gone missing more than six years earlier, he had shown his true colors. Not that anyone had ever truly doubted the curmudgeonly fellow held great love for his family.

"Bloody good to see you," Leigh observed. "And in one piece. At least, so far as I can tell."

Royal Blakeley smiled dryly. "Ah, as far as you can tell." He shrugged nonchalantly in a way that reminded Leigh of his older brother. His uncle and brother bore a very strong resemblance to one another and always had, though their approaches to things like duty were where they sharply diverged. Growing up, Leigh's father had marveled at the fact that his eldest son looked more like his younger brother than himself.

Leigh looked more like their father, Alistair. So his mother had always said.

"Well, you are back. So, the task must be done." He leaned back in his seat, folding his hands behind his head.

His uncle's face hardened. "It is indeed."

"So, that leaves my bit then," Leigh drawled. "I'll get straight to it."

His uncle frowned. "It need not be your task alone."

Leigh shook his head. "I knew you would say that once you'd arrived back in England. But we agreed. You've done your share. More than admirably. Now let me do this thing."

"And then it will be finished," his uncle confirmed.

"Done and done," Leigh agreed.

"And then we can tell them all?"

"And then we can tell them all, yes. At least, the parts they need to know." Leigh stood up. "I'll see you back at the house."

His uncle looked surprised. "Starting already?"

Leigh shrugged. "I already reek of cheap gin, so why not?"

"Wonderful lure, that," his uncle agreed. "Very well. Try not to get yourself killed."

Leigh grinned. "I always do."

<hr />

There was something rather invigorating about sustaining a blow from another man. When the other man was in fact three other men and all were intent upon trying to kill you, however... Well, that was another matter.

Leigh still felt invigorated. Though his body would not thank him for what he had put it through in the morning.

He had stepped out of the bustling gin shop, walked a few blocks alone in the dark, making sure to stumble every once in a while.

Just like clockwork, a gang of ruffians had come across him and set upon him.

Not just any gang of ruffians, mind you. That was key.

These were the friends of the lads Leigh had encountered a few nights back. Clearly, they wanted their revenge, and Leigh was more than happy to give it to them in this particular case—especially since it meant he would be getting something he wanted in the bargain.

So far things were playing out perfectly. Now to see if his true mark would learn of the commotion and take the bait.

"That's what you get for messing with the Kestrels," one of the men snarled just before landing a jab to Leigh's stomach.

He winced. He could feel the spot where the knife had landed already beginning to burn. With any luck, it would not tear open a second time. He did not wish to be dripping blood when he arrived at his destination. That would be heavy-handed.

He punched back, feeling his fist collide with the other fellow's jaw and hearing a satisfying grunt of pain.

"Ouch. That musta stung, Kip," another of the three louts observed. "He shoulda left well enough alone, aye, Ned?" The man who had spoken stepped to the side and tried to grab Leigh's arms from behind. Leigh dodged and whirled back around, fists raised and grinning.

"Shoulda done just that," the biggest fellow agreed, glowering at Leigh. Evidently, he did not enjoy fighting a man who took such delight in the thing. "Now he's in the sinker. Done for."

Leigh cocked his head to the side. "Taking an awfully long time about it," he couldn't help remarking. "Considering it's three to one."

The large man called Ned frowned, then shot his fist forward, surprising Leigh with his quickness. The blow landed on his jaw.

"That's more like it," he said almost happily, touching his jaw. There would be a nasty bruise there later. His valet could cover some of the worst of it up, he supposed.

The big man shook his head in perplexity. "He's mad, he is. Seems to enjoy it."

"I'll enjoy seeing you all look like fools in another moment," Leigh replied cheerfully.

"Touched in the head," the man called Kip agreed with a nod. "Thinks he'll get the best of us. Loony."

"Perhaps not I, but they might," Leigh said, nodding his chin toward the end of the alley which had suddenly grown even more shadowy.

A second group of men entered the brick arch between the buildings and now were rapidly approaching.

The three men surrounding Leigh all swore in turn.

"You've crossed a border, unless I'm much mistaken," Leigh noted. "Entered another lord's land. Not polite. Not polite at all."

"We crossed Little Earl to Great Earl when we tagged him," one of the men observed sheepishly. "I wasn't certain, so I didn't say nuffin."

"Bloody, bloody hell," Ned swore. "You stupid lout, Kip. And this bastard knew it, too."

He drove his fist into Leigh's softest parts, finally eliciting a groan.

"We're in for it. Steady now, men."

The larger group approached. There were five members in the opposition party, and Leigh decided it would be unsportsmanlike to join such a great number, so he leaned back against the alley wall with a hand to his stomach. It was bleeding a little, he noted, observing the stain on the linen shirt beneath his waistcoat, but nothing too troubling. Nothing that would entitle him to seek out Miss Spencer's ministrations a second time, sadly.

When two of the men who had initially set upon him were lying prone on the cobblestones, and the third had scampered, the group of five turned to Leigh.

One of the men from the new group stepped forward. A burly fellow with a raggedy brown cap.

"I suppose I ought to thank you," Leigh said politely.

"Only doing what the lord and master commanded," the man replied. "He wants to see you. Now."

"I'll wager he does. Well happily, I am at your service." Leigh grinned and bowed with a flourish. The five men stared. They did not appreciate a flare for the dramatic, but no matter. Leigh had enjoyed himself and, in the end, wasn't that what mattered?

And he would continue doing so. All the way down the dangerous trail he followed, right up to the day of vengeance.

He followed the men down the alley, already knowing where they led.

Chapter Ten

Marigold awoke to a sharp tapping on her bedroom door. She had fallen asleep just after recalling she still had no idea how Lord Leigh had sustained the injury she had treated. That fateful night already seemed so long ago.

Having realized the hour was still early after arriving back at Lady Fulford's from her visit to St. Giles, Marigold had decided–with only a slight pang of conscience–to take advantage of her new life of privilege and go back to bed for a few hours. Lady Fulford would assume Marigold was exhausted from the late nights they had been keeping.

She rubbed the sleep from her eyes and sat up slowly. The tapping came again.

"Miss, are you awake?"

It was her maid. She called her reply, and the door opened slowly.

"Lady Fulford would like to see you at your earliest convenience, Miss, if you please," the little brown-haired maid explained.

Marigold eyes flickered before finally landing on her timepiece laying on the bedside table. It was a little before ten o'clock.

"Surely, there are not callers already," Marigold exclaimed.

The maid shifted uncomfortably. "There is one visitor already with Lady Fulford, yes, Miss."

It was very strange, but no matter. Lady Fulford made a point of taking her breakfast no later than nine o'clock. Marigold would simply make do without.

She rose and dressed quickly with the help of her maid, then walked down to the morning room.

Lady Fulford's morning room was prettily decorated in shades of leaf-green and yellow. The room was east-facing as most were. As Marigold entered, she was met with bright sunshine spilling in through the tall windows and, for a moment, felt a burst of the happiness that comes from simply being alive to enjoy a beautiful, sunny day.

Then she saw who Lady Fulford's very early caller was and her happiness vanished instantly.

"Good morning, Miss Spencer," Miss Cora Compton twittered from where she sat on a settee across from Lady Fulford.

Lady Fulford turned. "Good morning, my dear."

Marigold forced a smile. She came slowly into the room and took a seat at the other end of the settee near Lady Fulford.

"Miss Compton, you appear to be acquainted with Miss Spencer, though I do not believe you have formally met," Lady Fulford observed. "I am pleased to introduce you now. Miss Marigold Spencer is my special protégée this Season. As I am sure you are aware, her sister has married the son of a dear family friend, the Duke of Dareford. Therefore, Miss Spencer is like family to me."

There was no mistaking the warning.

Marigold watched Miss Compton, but the information did not seem to surprise or unsettle her.

Lady Fulford turned to Marigold. "Miss Spencer, may I introduce to you Miss Cora Compton. I believe she caught your eye the other night." *That was one way of putting it*, Marigold thought.

"Well, now that introductions are out of the way," Lady Fulford continued. "Miss Compton has something that is apparently quite urgent she wished to discuss with us."

"I wished to discuss it with *you*, Lady Fulford," Miss Compton stressed, leaning forward a little. "There was no need for you to summon *her*."

"Yes, but as you mentioned it pertained to Miss Spencer, I decided we should include her in the conversation, Miss Compton."

Marigold did not like the sound of this. She swallowed and, though she knew it was a nervous fidget, began to smooth out the wrinkles in the skirt of her dress.

"As you wish." Miss Compton's eyes may have narrowed a little, but she continued to smile complacently. Like a prim pussycat that had swallowed a canary whole, Marigold thought desolately.

Whereas Marigold felt like nothing so much as a schoolgirl about to receive a scolding from her teacher.

It was an unpleasant sensation. Miss Compton seemed to be the constant creator of those. Marigold thought of the terrace and how Miss Compton had all but thrown herself at Lord Leigh. She sat up a little straighter, remembering how that had played out. And what had next transpired. Lord Leigh did not want Miss Compton. He had kissed her, Marigold. Odd how that thought gave her something like courage.

At least for a moment.

"I am very sorry to inform you of this, Lady Fulford," Miss Compton said, not looking sorry at all. "But your protégée was observed by a reliable witness walking in the neighborhood of Seven Dials." She paused. "Alone. At night."

She met Marigold's eyes, her expression already triumphant.

"It was not night," Marigold protested, feeling anger rise up in her. Just how did Miss Compton know any such thing? Was she following Marigold? Spying on her? Who was this "reliable witness"? For surely that was simply a cover for Miss Compton herself, was it not?

"Aha!" Miss Compton crowed. "So, you do not deny it?"

"I would never lie to Lady Fulford," Marigold said, straightening her back and meeting the older woman's gaze. Nevertheless, she felt herself flushing guiltily.

"Ah, then I am sure you asked for permission before you snuck out in the dead of night to visit the most loathsome part of London," Miss Compton sneered.

"Thank you, Miss Compton," Lady Fulford said mildly. "Is that all?"

"All?" Miss Compton seemed shocked. "Your ward—or protégée as you call her—was sneaking about alone at night in..."

"Yes, I believe we both heard you the first time," Lady Fulford interrupted. "And who did you say it was that observed Miss Spencer again? A reliable witness, was it? They must have been very zealous indeed to run straight to you."

Miss Compton raised her chin and looked self-righteous. "I cannot disclose who brought the information to me. With Miss Spencer's very best interests at heart, of course. However, I can assure you they are a very trustworthy sort of individual and would never tell an untruth about such a serious matter."

"What serious matter? I did nothing wrong," Marigold interrupted hotly. "It is not as if it were against the law to visit undesirable neighborhoods."

Lady Fulford put a steadying hand on her arm and squeezed very gently. "I see, Miss Compton. Well, no one is accusing anyone of telling untruths. As you have just heard, Miss Spencer has made no attempt to deny her journey." She paused for a long moment, and Marigold watched her look at Miss Compton much like a hawk must look at a mouse just before it eats it. "What I should like to know most, Miss Compton, is why you immediately assumed that Miss Spencer had traveled to Seven Dials without my consent."

Miss Compton gawked.

"You seem to be insinuating, not very subtly I might add, that I am an inadequate guardian. That I have failed to supervise the young lady in my care properly. That I am incompetent, perhaps." Lady Fulford's tone had turned decidedly frosty.

Miss Compton paled slightly. "Not at all," she stammered. "But Miss Spencer's reputation..."

"A young lady's reputation must be safeguarded above all," Lady Fulford agreed. "Like your own, Miss Compton. And yet I understand, from speaking with Lord and Lady Norfolk, that you nearly catapulted your way into scandal yourself when you were found alone with a young man on their terrace, during the ball they recently held for their granddaughter and your cousin, Miss Victoria Peel."

Marigold watched in fascination as Miss Compton's face changed rapidly from white to red.

For a split second, she felt a prick of conscience. After all, had she not also been alone with a young man at the Norfolks' ball? And had she not done something so scandalous with Lord Leigh that, if the fact ever emerged, it would be very damaging to her own reputation? She thought of how loyally and ruthlessly Lady Fulford was coming to her defense and was ashamed at her own lack of judgment.

However, it was simple to remedy the matter. She would never allow herself to be with Lord Leigh alone again. Nor would she ever, ever accept another of his outrageous offers to teach her anything about the ways of the world!

"You seem to be intent on turning this around, Lady Fulford," Miss Compton said angrily. "Rather than accepting my gesture of good will toward you both. However, if you truly knew where Miss Spencer was going when she made her ill-advised trip to such a calumnious place, perhaps you would satisfy my curiosity and tell me what on earth in Seven Dials was worth risking a young lady's life and reputation."

Marigold felt a moment of panic.

"Miss Spencer was conducting her visit to the neighborhood in order to perform charitable works, of course," Lady Fulford said calmly.

"That is true," Marigold burst out. She looked at Lady Fulford, her eyes wide with relief. "I was visiting the Dispensary for the Poor of St. Giles. They do wonderful work there, and I wished to help. They have agreed to take me on as a volunteer."

"A dispensary?" Miss Compton appeared disgusted. "One of those places for the destitute, you mean? Full of ill and dying people? *That* is where you were sneaking off to?"

Marigold opened her mouth to protest Miss Compton's use of the word "sneaking" before remembering she had indeed been doing so. Though if she had known this would be Lady Fulford's reaction to the truth, she would not have bothered.

"I think it is very noble that Miss Spencer wishes to aid the poor," Lady Fulford said. "We participate in a great many charity bazaars and dinner parties to raise money for good works, without ever performing such works ourselves. Have you not noticed, Miss Compton?"

Miss Compton glared.

"However, I believe you were unduly hasty in your enthusiasm to begin, Miss Spencer." Lady Fulford patted Marigold's arm gently. "You may recall that I asked to accompany you to the dispensary, at least the first time. I suppose you simply could not wait for me to rise this morning. But that is of no consequence, for this morning you were in fact watched over without knowing it. One of my footmen noticed your departure and made sure to follow you." Lady Fulford shot Marigold a very keen look before turning serenely back to Miss Compton. "So you see, Miss Compton, she was in no danger whatsoever. A foolish mistake for a country girl to make, but not one which is likely to damage her reputation. Certainly not when the *ton* learns Miss Spencer's true motivations were simply Christian charity. And I am sure you can be counted upon to put that about."

Marigold was doing her best to control her facial expressions. Had Lady Fulford truly just told multiple lies for her? "I should indeed have waited for you to rise, dear Lady Fulford. My enthusiasm got the better of me, but that is no excuse for my folly. It will not happen again, I assure you. I am sincerely sorry for causing either you or Miss Compton any concern."

"It is of no consequence, my dear girl," Lady Fulford said briskly. "Well, Miss Compton, if that is all? Or did you have more to tell us? Perhaps your little spy witnessed other events of note that you would like to share?"

Miss Compton rose quickly to her feet, scarcely hiding the fury on her face. "Indeed not. I believe I will say good day now, Lady Fulford. Miss Spencer."

Once she had gone, Marigold was surprised to hear Lady Fulford let out a heavy sigh. "Oh, that girl," the elderly lady exclaimed. "What a little weasel she has grown up to be. Had your best interests at heart, did she? I'll eat my hat if she did."

Marigold giggled, then put a hand to her mouth. "I really am very sorry to have caused you distress and embarrassment, Lady Fulford.

After all you have done for me, too. I am not deserving of such kindness or loyalty." She shifted on the settee. "How did you know?"

"How did I know you had gone off to do something relating to good works, you mean?" Lady Fulford replied, her gaze once more becoming hawkish.

Marigold nodded nervously.

"Well, because I know *you*, my child." Lady Fulford smiled. "Where else would you possibly have been going? On some assignation? To meet a lover perhaps?" The white-haired dowager snorted. "*That* is what the likes of Miss Compton or Miss Peel would have been doing, not you." Her lined face turned somber. "However, Miss Compton is not incorrect about one thing. Seven Dials is a terribly dangerous place for a young woman to visit, let alone to walk alone in the dark—whether it was the dark of night or the dark of morning."

"It was the dark of morning, I assure you. But I am certain you are right," Marigold replied meekly. "I was simply so eager after the ball..."

"Ah, so you had been plotting this for some time. Yes, I see." Lady Fulford gave a sigh of resignation. "The social outings bore you, I know. You need something else. Something more stimulating. Once you find a husband, he will be the center of your life. And then you will have children to occupy your attention. But in the meantime, I know the Season can be a bit tedious for a clever, bright young woman such as yourself."

"That is it exactly," Marigold said in relief. She would not argue about the husband and children part of things. "I need a purpose. I need to feel useful." She debated saying she also longed to *learn* something. But how would Lady Fulford react if she knew Marigold was actually hoping to be trained as a nurse? That she hoped to not only assist with caring for the sick but, one day, to perform medical tasks herself?

And that she had absolutely no plans to cease any of her "charitable work" even if she did, by some miracle, manage to attract an acceptable husband?

"*Hmph.* Well, you are not afraid of hard work. After your time as a housemaid, I suppose you are quite used to it. I cannot say I see anything terrible about that, though I am sure many would." Lady

Fulford tilted her head and looked at Marigold keenly. "Precisely how frequently were you hoping to serve such a higher purpose, Miss Spencer?"

"Three times a week?" Marigold said hopefully. "Perhaps four?"

"Three will be more than sufficient," Lady Fulford decreed. "You are volunteering a modest portion of your time, not offering to run the place single-handedly. You will travel by carriage from now on, with no exceptions. A reliable footman will accompany you. He and the driver will await you outside for the entirety of every visit. They will be only a short distance away should you ever require assistance. You will visit the dispensary only during daylight hours. These are the conditions I demand."

"That seems very reasonable," Marigold said carefully. "Are you sure you will not require the carriage?"

Lady Fulford shrugged. "There is still the town coach, the chaise, the landau." Her eyes twinkled suddenly. "And if I am feeling particularly bold, the barouche."

Marigold, who had been used to walking most everywhere before her sister's momentous marriage, was a trifle overwhelmed by this list of conveyances.

"You will not allow the likes of Miss Compton to depress your spirits in any way, my dear," Lady Fulford declared abruptly, evidently misinterpreting Marigold's silence for unease. "Your reputation remains intact. Miss Compton's own is precarious, and she must be aware of that, which is why she is jabbing out, hoping to hit another young lady who she perceives as vulnerable." Lady Fulford sat up proudly. "Well, you are *not* vulnerable. You are exceedingly well protected, having both myself and Blakeley by your side. A rather daunting pairing if I may say so myself."

"Incredibly daunting," Marigold agreed, smiling at her patroness. "I am very grateful to have you both." Well, that was true. If only Lord Leigh would kindly stick to doing his duty and nothing more.

"You know, my dear," Lady Fulford said, looking contemplative, "as a girl, I was always fascinated by the story of Agnodice. She was a woman who lived in ancient Athens and wished to practice medicine. Have you heard the tale? An outstandingly brave woman. She disguised herself as a man so that she might work as a physician. However, as you might imagine…"

Annoyance crossed Lady Fulford's face as a knock at the door interrupted the tale. A timid-looking footman announced another guest had arrived.

"The Marquess of Harley, Your Ladyship," the footman stuttered.

Lady Fulford's white eyebrows shot up. "Goodness!" She looked at Marigold. "My, my. I must say, I was not expecting him to be your first caller this morning. Kindly show Lord Harley to the drawing room."

Clearly Miss Compton did not count as their first caller.

Marigold looked back at the dowager with wide eyes. What could Lord Harley possibly want with her?

Chapter Eleven

he Viper's Den, London
    "Ah, the overlord at last! Shall I kneel and kiss the ring?
Swear fealty?" Leigh jested as he was shoved, none too gently,
into the third-floor office where a large man sat smoking behind an oak
desk.

"I save the ring-kissing for my mistresses," the man behind the
desk said. "Fealty. Well, that is another matter."

He rose to his feet and approached Leigh, inspecting him with idle
curiosity. "Who are you that I should accept your fealty in the first
place?"

Leigh had heard Caleb Bryce described as an intimidating man.
Even fear-inspiring. Bryce was the owner of the Viper's Den, a notorious gaming hell and select club which catered to various tastes. But
he was much more than that. Over the last two decades, the older man
had become something of a king of the London underworld. Perhaps
not the only 'royalty' that those nefarious nether regions had to offer,
but certainly one of the people at the very top of the dais.

Bryce was fifty or a few years past that, with unusually dark-red hair
now seasoned liberally with gray. He had a barrel-like, muscular

physique that reminded Leigh of a prize fighter. He dressed well. Even a little on the ostentatious side, with a bright-green silk waistcoat that reminded Leigh of a dandy. But there was nothing else of the dandy about Bryce. He was a stone-cold prince of power who could crush a man just as easily as welcome him through the doors for a night of drink.

Perhaps Leigh should have been frightened. Even intimidated.

But fear was not in his nature.

Caleb Bryce had crossed the Blakeley family, and Leigh was here to remind him that they had not forgotten.

"On second thought, it seems a tad early in the day to be swearing anything," Leigh commented. He glanced at the clock on the mantel. Half past three. Most were still abed. Yet for him, the day had now well and truly begun.

Bryce raised his eyebrows but said nothing. He strolled back to his desk, snubbed out his cheroot, then turned back to Leigh.

"My men picked you up because I owed you a boon," he said conversationally. "Do you know why that is?"

"There was a girl," Leigh began. He grinned. "There always is. Isn't there?"

Bryce did not reply.

"The girl was in an alley. There, that's not how the story usually goes, is it? Two men were being... let us simply say 'ungentlemanly' toward her." Leigh shrugged modestly. "I was happening past. I saw her. I decided to do something about it."

"Most men would not have bothered," Bryce observed.

Leigh nodded. "I'm not most men."

He saw a flicker of a smile cross Bryce's face. "The girl was one of mine. I do not hold with the mistreatment of women. Even whores. Do you know who the men were, treating her so... ungentlemanly... as you put it?"

"Not yours," Leigh replied. "Some other chief's, I take it?"

Bryce smiled slightly. At this point, Leigh thought, he clearly believed Leigh was a cocky fool. A young gentleman out for a lark, thinking himself a hero of the night.

"You might say that, yes," Bryce replied coolly. "And then you went and got yourself into trouble with them again tonight. Because you had helped the lady, my men knew I would prefer it if they helped you—and then brought you here."

"Walking where angels fear to tread," Leigh said sadly. "Deep in my cups, I'm afraid. It's a shameful habit."

"Indeed," Bryce replied. "Well, see that it doesn't happen again." He began to walk back around his desk.

"Is that all? Is the session with the lord concluded?" Leigh asked. "Back to business, is it? Burning the midnight oil and all that?"

"I had to satisfy my own curiosity, you see," Bryce said. "It seemed rather odd that my people should encounter you twice in such quick succession. But now I've laid eyes upon you."

"Harmless, am I not?"

"A silly drunk young lord," Bryce said dismissively. "So, yes, now it's back to real work."

"Ah, yes. Then you have confirmed I'm just an everyday fool and not a threat to your... empire?" Leigh asked casually. He approached the desk and watched Bryce frown slightly. "I take it, then, that you have no idea who I truly am." He chuckled. "Funny, here I thought you were the one man who was supposed to know who *everyone* was."

Bryce scowled. "I make it my business to know everyone of consequence. Especially if they enter my domain."

"My face isn't familiar? I do favor my pater rather than my frater, it's true. Alistair Blakeley. That was my father's name."

Leigh watched the larger man's face lose color.

"Blakeley, you say?" Bryce managed. He pulled back his chair and sat down heavily.

"That's right," Leigh said cheerily. "And from what I understand, it's a fortunate thing for you that we Blakeleys are such sympathetic, charitable people. Or else you'd already be in Newgate. Or somewhere even lower down."

"Is that why you're here? Belatedly seeking revenge?" Bryce said coldly. "Here I thought your brother had demonstrated a certain grace in pardoning my blunder."

"Oh, he's full of grace," Leigh assured him. "Though blunder seems rather an understatement. But no, no. Rest easy, Mr. Bryce. I'm not here for vengeance. At least, not upon you. The way I see it is you did a damned cowardly thing, but in the end, we got my mother back. True, you preyed upon a vulnerable gentlewoman when her family believed her to be dead. Her life and freedom evidently meant little to you. You claim you never mistreat a woman. Well, I'd say what you did to my mother came bloody well close to it."

Leigh realized he was becoming more heated than he had intended. He cleared his throat. "But Dare informed me of the whole story. You believed you were getting some sort of revenge of your own by doing what you did. You had lost your sister and believed Dare to be responsible. You pinned the blame on the wrong man, but in the end... well, all's well that ends well."

Bryce nodded slowly. "And yet here you are."

"How astute of you. Yes, here I am. In your delightful establishment. And you must be asking yourself why. Why is Lord Leigh Blakeley here, speaking with me, when I would rather he be anywhere else?"

"The question did come to mind," Bryce replied, narrowing his eyes.

"Well, Mr. Bryce, the way I see it is—you owe *me* a boon. Not the other way around."

"Ah."

"'Ah' indeed."

"You meant to be set upon by those men tonight," Bryce concluded. "You wanted me to find you."

"I was not sure you would allow me entrance to this magnificent venue if I simply appeared at the door and demanded an audience," Leigh replied. "Of course, I might have found other means."

"But none so entertaining," Bryce countered, a glimmer of something like amusement in his eye.

"Precisely." Leigh grinned. "I'm glad we're singing from the same song sheet."

"What exactly is it that you want, Blakeley? I do not have your father held hostage. I can assure you. You are welcome to search the premises if you wish."

Leigh was very certain he was the opposite of welcome, but that was all right. He did not need to accept that kind offer.

"As my father is dead, I feel quite certain you are correct."

He watched Bryce's eyes enlarge. "Your father is dead? You seem quite sure of that."

"I am," Leigh said.

"And the person or persons responsible?"

"Two dead. One soon to be," Leigh said cheerfully.

"I presume that is where I come in?"

"You presume correctly."

Leigh glanced around the room and found what he was looking for. A second chair. He grabbed the wooden seat and pulled it up near the opposite side of Bryce's desk, then sat down, leaning back with a sigh of relief. There was some pain now, he admitted to himself, where his earlier injury had been reopened. Well, his valet would just have to bandage it for him when he finally made his way home.

Bryce leaned over his desk. "Who, may I ask, is the odious villain you are endeavoring to locate?"

Leigh spoke a name.

Bryce whistled and leaned back in his chair. "That's a large ask, my lord. Even for you. I must..."

There was a banging noise, and the door flew open.

A woman ran into the room, quickly followed by a large manservant who looked out of breath and annoyed.

"I must speak with you, Bryce," the woman said, her face flushed. "You must not keep putting me off so cruelly. I swear to you that it is urgent that we speak." She was a striking, dark-haired woman who clearly did not believe in sparing the rouge or the kohl. Dressed to catch the eye in a brightly colored silk gown with an ermine pelerine draped overtop.

Leigh sat back in his chair. Clearly this was a family matter.

"Damn you, Carlotta," Bryce swore, rising from his chair so swiftly it fell over behind him. He pointed at the woman. "Get her out of here. I told you never to let her in here again, Hector."

The tall manservant looked pained. "Indeed you did, Mr. Bryce. I'm sorry to say that she slipped past us. Won't trouble you again."

"She'd better not," Bryce snarled. He glared at Carlotta. "How many times must a man tell you he is done with you for you to accept it, woman?"

Leigh watched the blood drain from Carlotta's face.

"It is only that..." she whispered.

"I don't give a damn what you have to say that is so urgent," Bryce snapped cruelly. He snapped his fingers. "Hector, take her. Gently mind you, so she doesn't call the night watchman down on us like that other time. Oh, you'd like nothing better than to see me in chains, wouldn't you, you foul-hearted wench?"

But the spirit seemed to have gone out of the woman. She dropped her eyes to the floor, and when Hector took her arm, she allowed him to lead her out.

Bryce picked up his chair and sat back down.

"Where were we?" he said shortly.

"I was just thinking of how you never mistreat a woman," Leigh said slowly.

Bryce scowled. "She can go to the devil."

"She hurt you. Badly," Leigh guessed. "Another man?"

Bryce grunted. "I'll never know for certain. She enjoyed toying with me."

"You could not forgive, for love's sake?" Leigh asked, thinking of how the woman's face had fallen.

Bryce gave a derisive snort. "Love? Gluttony for power more like. She wanted to 'rule' with me. To have a hand in everything I did."

"Is it so very wrong for a woman to want that? To wish to be your partner?" Leigh asked cautiously.

"She was a weakness I had indulged far too long. She is gone now," Bryce replied brusquely. "Now. We return to you, my lord. You wish for my help in killing one of the most powerful men in London."

"Such a nasty word. I said nothing about you doing any killing," Leigh said. "I simply need a location. Then, I'll pay a visit. We'll... chat." And so they would. For the first minute or two.

Bryce studied him for a moment. "It could be dangerous for me to even find out that much."

"This is not some rival lord of another gang we're talking about, Bryce. I believe it should not be too difficult for someone like you to manage."

"No, but they have powerful connections," Bryce countered. He looked as if he were about to say more, then shook his head. "Very well. I'll see what I can do."

Leigh rose from his chair. "I know what you're thinking, Bryce. And you had best not repeat the performance. You strung my brother along, and in the end, it was a child who led him to the truth faster than you did. So, I'll say this once. Sooner would be better. For both of our sakes."

"A threat, Blakeley? I thought Newgate was off the table."

"It is. There are always other options," Leigh said.

"Perhaps you'll find him yourself before I can," Bryce said. "You never know. Goodnight, Lord Leigh Blakeley. You may leave the way you came in."

Leigh nodded his understanding. Not through the center of the building, where all Bryce's guests were currently still in the thick of a night of hedonistic pleasures, but down a staircase, through a servants' corridor, and out through the back in other words. In fact, that suited Leigh. He had no wish to be seen here. Or worse, to have to make conversation with anyone who thought they knew him.

He made his way back down through the building, thinking carefully. Bryce was fearful, but not fearful enough. If he did not have what Leigh needed in a few days' time, a boot to his throat would put him in the right state of mind.

He pushed open the door to the alley. A woman was there, leaning against the dirty brick wall, apparently unconcerned for her white ermine cape. No wonder, Leigh thought. She was crying.

Upstairs, Leigh might have guessed Carlotta to be thirty or thirty-five years old. Now, with her make-up running down her cheeks alongside the tears, she looked much younger.

He fished out a handkerchief and passed it to her without a word.

She stared at it a moment, then looked up at him, as if realizing for the first time she was no longer alone.

"That beastly man," she said as she snatched it and began wiping at her face. "That utter bastard."

Leigh leaned back against the brick wall next to her. "In a spot of trouble?"

She stared back at him. A gleam appeared in her eye.

"I heard the name you said," she declared. "The one you wish to find."

Leigh frowned. She must have been standing outside in the hall, listening for a moment before she barged in.

"Shameless little eavesdropper, aren't you?"

Carlotta tossed her head, black curls gleaming in the starlight. She had a certain flair, Leigh thought admiringly. He had to give her that. Already she was rallying from her earlier humiliation.

"I've been called worse," she said. "So?"

Leigh raised his eyebrows. "So?"

"I can find what you need faster than he can. If I do, I will want to be paid. Properly paid."

"Subtlety is not your strong suit, is it?" Leigh asked. "How do you think you can help me exactly, Miss... Carlotta?"

"That's as good a name as any," she answered, dark eyelashes fluttering. "Just Carlotta will do."

"Very well, 'Just Carlotta.' Answer the question."

"By telling you where this man is," she said. "I don't care what you do with him. That's none of my concern."

Leigh smiled. "Of course it isn't. So, you believe you can discover where to find a man that even Bryce claimed he may not be able to locate?"

Carlotta snorted. "Oh, Bryce can find anyone if he wishes to. But he dislikes you. So, he'll move slowly. Drag his heels."

Leigh thought quickly. What she said rang true. Why not let her try?

But... "I don't wish for you to put yourself in harm's way simply to glean information on my behalf, Carlotta. Do you understand what I am saying?"

Carlotta seemed confused for a moment, then she nodded. "I appreciate the concern. It is more than I have received from Bryce." She lifted her chin stubbornly. "But I shall be fine. I'll contact you when I have what you need. I'll list the sum I expect you to bring."

"Very well," Leigh agreed. "A race to the finish, then. May the best man or woman win."

Carlotta gave a half smile. Then she walked away, taking his handkerchief with her.

A few hours rest would do him good, Leigh decided as he fell back on his bed, clean and bandaged and full of hot tea. His head ached from the mix of cheap whisky and gin, as he had known it would. He wasn't as young as he once was. Who would have thought twenty-seven would be the start of ripe old age.

He closed his eyes.

Unbidden, a memory came to him.

It was winter and Christmastide. The entire family was traveling by coach to visit friends who lived two days' journey away.

With four children and two adults, as well as all the things small children require on such a long journey, the coach was full to the brim. Another family might have put the children in a second coach with a nursemaid. But not the Blakeleys. Everyone had piled in. Sitting close together was comfortable. They were a family that enjoyed one another's companionship. The journey was no chore, but rather, an adventure to be savored.

Leigh could remember leaning back against his mother's shoulder, breathing in her familiar scent as she ran her fingers gently through his hair.

He had fallen asleep as the coach rocked gently back and forth and the snow fell outside, listening to the soothing chatter of his brother and sisters as they played cards with their father. Eventually, he had woken up, his head resting on his mother's lap, her hands sweet and soft as they brushed his hair.

He had felt completely happy that day. And completely safe.

It was not a rare memory. There were many similar ones. His parents had seen to that.

He felt a lump in his throat. A second memory came.

A snowball fight with his father and brother when he was perhaps seven or eight years old.

Dare had not always played fair back then. He had landed a large ball of snow right in Leigh's face.

Leigh was not proud. The snow had caked his eyes and stung like hell. He had cried, frantically trying to wipe the burning snow from his eyes.

His father had approached, gently pushed Leigh's hands down, and then brushed the snow from his son's face very carefully, saying nothing of his tears.

Then Dare had come up, teasing and laughing, calling Leigh a "namby-pamby."

His father had sharply told Dare to go back to the house. Then he had spoken very tenderly to Leigh and told him there was nothing wrong with his tears. It was natural for boys and girls to cry, he said. Then he kissed Leigh on the forehead and picked him up and put him on his shoulders—as if he were a much smaller boy—and carried him back to the house.

There were dozens of similar memories. His father had been not only a playful parent who enjoyed his children's company, but also a loving, tender-hearted man.

What would he say if he could see his son today? If he could know what Leigh and Royal had done and would do to avenge him?

The lump in Leigh's throat had grown into a heavy stone. He felt as if it might choke him. He lay on the bed with his eyes closed, breathing hard, his hands curled into fists.

His father was dead. Alistair Blakeley had been dead at least three years.

When he and his Uncle Royal had learned the truth a few months back, Leigh had been shaken. Not merely because his father was confirmed dead, and all hope of ever seeing him alive again was finally, irrevocably gone. But because Alistair Blakeley had died in a terrible way, for a terrible reason. His death had been a spectacular waste. A great man and a great father had been lost, simply because of another family's despicable envy and greed.

But at least his father had not been alone when he died. He had been with their mother, even if she did not recall that now. This was one small comfort to Leigh.

He willed his breathing to slow, for his body to relax. Everything was coming together. He and his uncle would see this thing finished, for his family's sake.

And then... then surely Leigh would feel some measure of peace. As would his family.

He would go back to his mother, and he would tell her the truth. That the men who had killed his father were gone once and for all.

And then?

For six years, he had covertly searched for his parents' where-abouts, without ever truly allowing his brother or sisters to know just how deep his obsession lay. Better they think he was merely a wandering rogue. A womanizing scoundrel who squandered family money all over the Continent on gambling and drink. Had they known the truth—that their uncle had taken Leigh under his wing, taught him and trained him until he was a deadly and formidable force to be reck-oned with, and then hunted alongside him—well, perhaps they would have been repulsed, or worse, afraid.

Leigh had always been a restless spirit with nowhere to call home, nowhere to truly lay his head. This was who he was, he told himself. This was who he would always be. It had nothing to do with his parents' disappearance anymore.

Leigh was never going to be the perfect son, diligently marrying a proper young lady and siring a family of Blakeley children.

But... always was an awfully long time. The truth was more compli-cated. Perhaps Leigh would have been closer to an ideal son before his parents' disappearance. Perhaps he would have led a more settled life.

Now that his mother was back, safe in the bosom of her family, what reason did he really have to leave again? Should he not at least try to stay for her sake?

The truth was, there was a part of him that longed to rejoin his family. To remain at Blakeley Manor. To see Dare and his wife's child born. To be an uncle, a son. To take up his place in his family, to feel truly part of it again.

But another part of him felt only pain at the prospect.

With his father gone forever, it could never be the same.

The childhood memories were sweet, yes, but bitter, too. He would never feel so safe, so happy again. Those days were gone for good.

Chapter Twelve

"You wish for me to marry you? I'm afraid... I don't quite understand." Marigold stared stupidly at Lord Harley's handsome face.

Her palms were sweating. She did not think it was merely because Lord Harley looked uncannily like a chestnut-haired version of a Greek statue. Adonis perhaps. Or a young Alexander the Great.

The young man they called "Hawkeye" Harley smiled patiently.

"Which part of my proposal do you not understand? Tell me, and I would be more than happy to explain it again," he said, as if he were a tutor and she a dull student.

She stared, suddenly glad that Lady Fulford had agreed to step just out of earshot into the adjoining room when Lord Harley had politely requested a meeting alone with Miss Spencer.

"This is madness," she hissed. "You cannot truly wish for me to marry you."

Lord Harley shifted uncomfortably, drawing Marigold's attention to the way his long muscular legs filled out his buckskin trousers. Lord Leigh's were shapelier, she decided loyally. At the thought of Lord Leigh's legs, she felt herself blushing. Now was not the time. She was being proposed to, for heaven's sake!

"I am given to understand you have made a reputation for yourself as rather a... well, a rake, Lord Harley," Marigold said carefully. "And yet you wish to settle down?"

Lord Harley ran his fingers through his hair and sighed. "I must settle down, Miss Spencer. It is not that I necessarily wish to. I must."

"Or else?" Marigold inquired. "It is to be death, then? The guillotine perhaps?"

Lord Harley gave her a wry smile. "Aha, I see you have a sense of humor. Not a necessity in a wife, but I assure you that I would value it dearly." He leaned back on the settee and stretched out his arms. "No, not the guillotine. Only the blade of my father's displeasure severing my allowance at the neck, if you will."

"Ah, a rake requires funds?"

"A rake does," Lord Harley admitted. He leaned forward and lowered his voice. "I have no wish to offend your delicate sensibilities as a woman, Miss Spencer..." He paused.

"But?" Marigold prompted. "Come now, it cannot be so very terrible."

"I do not think it very terrible at all, though certainly it cannot be the marriage proposal all maidens wish for," Lord Harley said. His face was so good-natured and honest that Marigold smiled. "Will you allow me to be completely forthright with you about what I am seeking, Miss Spencer?"

"I encourage you to do so," Marigold said. "I should hope for nothing less from a man claiming he wishes to be my future husband."

"I need a wife, but I do not want a wife, Miss Spencer," Lord Harley said bluntly. "My father has demanded I wed before the Season is finished. He will provide for me and for my wife if I do so. The amount he has promised to settle on me is generous. And of course, once I inherit..."

"Yes, I believe I understand that you are exceedingly wealthy and will be even more so once your father is someday deceased. Go on. What is the scandalous part that you are avoiding telling me?"

Lord Harley folded his hands. "Very well. I wish for an open arrangement in my marriage. I enjoy my life as it is now, very much so.

I do not wish for any of that to change." He met Marigold's eyes steadily.

"You wish to be a philandering husband, and you wish for a wife who will not make a fuss," Marigold translated. "I see nothing so revolutionary about this. Only about your honesty beforehand."

"Thank you," Lord Harley said gravely. "I had hoped a woman might appreciate that part of things."

"I am not your average debutante, Lord Harley," Marigold reminded him. "Perhaps most young ladies would not respond well to such bluntness. I only say this as a caution. In case you must make this proposal again to another. Go slowly."

Lord Harley's eyes widened. "Does that mean you are refusing already? Please, I beg you, hear me out..."

"No, I am not refusing," Marigold said, holding up a hand. She felt a little like a queen. Lord Harley did not want her—she had been correct about that. Nevertheless, she clearly held his future in the palm of her hand, and there was something rather fascinating about that. She would allow herself to enjoy it just for a moment and then move on. Obviously, she would not accept his proposal. She had no wish for a husband—but even more so, she had no desire for an openly fornicating one. What possible benefit would she get out of being cuckolded?

"Of course, I realize there is little benefit to my wife in what I have just proposed," Lord Harley said as if reading her thoughts. "And while I know my reputation, Miss Spencer, I would have you know that I would treat my wife with every kindness—in other respects, I mean."

"Oh, you would, would you?" Marigold was amused. "She would not have your loyalty, but she would have your kindness."

Lord Harley licked his beautiful lips. "She would. Of course, we would need to be compatible in some respects. My father demands heirs."

"Obviously. Heirs." Marigold could not help it. She imagined being bedded by Lord Harley. It would not be... completely unpleasant. And he had said he would treat his wife with kindness. Lord Leigh had spoken of the pleasures that men could bring women. Well, this would be one way to find out in detail.

"Obviously," Lord Harley said quickly, "I could not promise my loyalty, in all honesty, no. But besides treating my wife with kindness and respect, I would also make provisions for her own freedom."

"Her own freedom?" Now Marigold's curiosity was piqued. "How do you mean?"

"Well," Lord Harley said cautiously. "Not only would my wife remain in full control of any dowry she brought to our marriage—" Already a very generous offer, Marigold knew. "But I am aware there are some women who are not simply interested in being wives and mothers."

Marigold managed not to snicker. She supposed she should be impressed by Lord Harley's attempt at liberality. "Yes, I, too, have heard this is so."

"Yes," Lord Harley said seriously. "And when we danced the other night, I could not help but wonder if you were perhaps a young woman such as this. What they call..." He lowered his voice even more. "A *bluestocking*."

Marigold cocked her head. "I suppose I am rather a bluestocking, now that I think about it." It was a rather aristocratic term for a clever, studious woman, but she supposed it now applied. "I am certainly interested in learning more about the world, how it works, and pursuing endeavors outside of the domestic sphere."

"Aha!" Lord Harley was beaming. "And I would not be averse to this as your husband, Miss Spencer. Nay, I would encourage it. I would be proud to have a clever wife. After all, if I were to be free to pursue my own interests—" Much less academic ones, Marigold thought wryly. "Then my wife would be, too. There would be no stipulations. Fair is fair." He coughed discreetly. "Furthermore, after we had produced an heir, if my wife chanced to find another man that she, well, favored, then..."

"Yes, yes, I believe I see," Marigold said hastily. "Lovers are allowed for both parties, then? Yes, I understand."

Lord Harley looked relieved. "You do not seem repulsed by my proposal."

"No, it is rather refreshing," Marigold reflected.

It could also save her a great deal of trouble. If she accepted Lord Harley's offer, her Season would effectively be over. No more balls, no more garden parties, no more dancing with inane and sweaty men.

She looked Lord Harley over carefully. He was handsome and stylish. He was not lacking in wit or intelligence from what she could perceive. He did seem kind. She hoped that was not a facade. But then, that was what a courtship period was for, was it not? She could inspect his character then, with Lady Fulford's assistance. After all, he would need to at least put on a pretense of wooing her. There would be walks in the park, dinners, nights at the opera, and all sorts of little outings.

"What you are proposing is, in effect, a sham engagement," she said, meeting his eyes. "I would not be able to be completely honest with Lady Fulford. I am not sure she would understand. Nor would your father, I take it?"

"He would understand parts of it," Lord Harley said ruefully. "Some parts all too well. But you are correct. He would not appreciate my offering my wife such great freedom. He believes a woman should remain at home. Preferably at our country estate. That is where he kept my mother."

"Kept her?" Marigold's eyes widened.

"She was not a prisoner," Lord Harley said quickly. "But he preferred that she remain there rather than joining him in Town. She obliged, but when he was gone for months on end, she was very unhappy. Even as a small boy, I recognized that much. She loved my father, and well, he hurt her. Not with his hands!" Lord Harley's eyes widened. "Please make no mistake. He is not that kind of man. Nor am I."

"No, no, I understand. He was simply, well, something like you, I take it?" Marigold assured him.

Lord Harley seemed relieved. "Yes. He is not a faithful man. My mother was heartbroken at first. Eventually resigned."

"It could not have made for an entirely happy childhood," Marigold said with sympathy.

"No, it did not." Lord Harley studied his hands in silence for a moment, then looked up at her. "That is why I am trying to do this properly, Miss Spencer. And why I have selected you. I loved my mother. I wished for her to be happy. As a boy, I did everything I could to try to make her so. I have no wish for my own children to go through something similar. Though our time together has been limited, I have seen something of your character. You seem warm-hearted and open. I believe you would be a good mother."

"Well," Marigold said slowly. "Thank you. I suppose." It was true that she would do her best to be a good mother, if she married and if children eventually came along.

If she accepted Lord Harley, she supposed he would wish for an heir right away. That might put rather a damper on things at the dispensary. But later, she would have more freedom than many women if all Lord Harley promised was true.

"I know I am doing this all wrong," Lord Harley said, twisting his fine, strong hands together. "But dash it all, I cannot simply lie to a lady and lead her on. It would be cruel."

"Yes, I appreciate that. I truly do, Lord Harley." Marigold chewed her lip. "I respect your honesty. I will consider your proposal."

Lord Harley's eyes lit up. "Truly? You respect it? You will consider it? Really?"

He leaped up from the settee. "Well, I say, Miss Spencer, that is rather bang-up of you. I knew you were a clever girl when I danced with you."

Clever. Not pretty. Not beautiful. Warmhearted. And clever.

But there were worse things to be.

Marigold smiled. He was very charming in his way. She could see why he had no trouble finding paramours.

She rose, noting how Lord Harley towered over her even more than Lord Leigh did. She could not imagine kissing Lord Harley now that she considered it. He was simply too tall.

She sighed. But she was sure they could manage if it came to that.

"Thank you for your offer, Lord Harley," she said as graciously as she could. "I believe that is what it is customary to say..."

"Yes, you are welcome, of course, Miss Spencer." Lord Harley was still beaming. "Well, this has taken a weight off my mind. I was afraid I'd make an awful cake of myself. May I call on you again soon? For your answer?"

Marigold thought for a moment. "Please permit me at least a few days to reflect on your proposal."

"Very good." Lord Harley hesitated. "I know I have already imposed on your sensibilities a great deal for one day, Miss Spencer, but if I may be so bold as to ask... Please do not speak of this to anyone?" He colored. "I mean, I understand you must discuss it with Lady Fulford but..."

"The terms of your proposal shall remain in the utmost confidence, Lord Harley. I will not spread this about as gossip. I promise you that. Whether I accept your offer or not, that will not change." She smiled up at him reassuringly.

He smiled back in relief. "I knew you could be counted on, Miss Spencer."

His smile changed to a broad boyish grin, and Marigold felt her heart nearly flip over. Nearly. She recalled Lord Leigh's, and then it truly did flip. Lord Harley may be a charming rake, but Lord Blakely was a perfect rogue with the perfect grin to match.

"And may I say, Miss Spencer," Lord Harley went on. "That I truly hope you do say yes."

He bowed and left the room, presumably to say his goodbyes to Lady Fulford.

Marigold sank down on the sofa, her mind reeling.

Was she truly considering accepting?

This was her first proposal. It was not what she had expected.

If she were to be completely honest, she had anticipated her first serious suitor being a middle-aged man. Perhaps a balding widower. With rheumatism. Who walked with a cane. And had five children.

She had also anticipated *refusing* her first proposal.

And that was the most surprising thing about Lord Harley's proposal. Not simply that he was young and handsome. But that she had been rendered so indecisive.

Perhaps this was why, when a familiar voice spoke to her from out of nowhere, she reacted without any forethought.

"Miss Spencer, you look white as a sheet. What the devil has happened? I saw Lord Harley leaving just now."

"Yes," Marigold said in a daze. "He has just proposed."

Chapter Thirteen

"I beg your pardon," Leigh said coldly. "He did what?"

"He... proposed. Oh dear, I should not have said that."

Leigh stared. For once in his life, he was almost speechless. Almost.

Miss Spencer had lifted her face appealingly. A little color had returned to her cheeks.

"But you said 'no,' of course." He gave a short laugh. "Good Lord, the nerve of that young blade."

He walked to the sideboard and began to pour himself a drink. Admittedly, it was early in the day, he had hardly slept, and furthermore, Lady Fulford did not hold with strong liquor before evening. Well, she would have to indulge Leigh just this once. After all, he had just suffered a shock.

He took a sip from his filled glass and winced. Perhaps he should not have leapt straight to whisky this time. His head still ached from the combination of cheap liquor the night before. Or was it still that same night turned day?

He realized the room remained silent.

"Miss Spencer," he said sharply, turning back to face her. "You *did* refuse Hawkeye Harley's proposal?"

"Why do they call him that?" Miss Spencer asked quickly. If Leigh didn't know any better, he might think she was stalling. "It seems a strange name for a... what is it he is again? Oh, yes, a marquess."

Leigh wrinkled his nose. "Many young gentlemen have ludicrous nicknames. Given to them at Eton or at a fencing club or while out drinking themselves into stupors." He took another sip from his glass. A little better. "They believe it makes them sound fashionable, danger-ous, or daring, I suppose. Take your pick."

"Do you?" Miss Spencer asked, looking curious.

"Do I what?"

"Have a nickname? Were you ever given one?"

Leigh took another sip. "A few," he admitted with reluctance.

"Goodness! More than one. What are they? Will you tell me?"

"Gaisgeach was one."

"Gaies-what?"

"Gaisgeach," he repeated. "It's Gaelic. It means–" He coughed. "Hero or warrior. Something along those lines." He looked down at his glass. "They meant it more ironically than anything else. I was green as grass when they called me that."

"Who did?" Miss Spencer asked curiously. "Who called you that?"

He swirled the remaining amber liquid. "Oh, the fighting men, you know." He looked up at her. "Men in Scotland," he explained. "My uncle took me there to, well, hone my skills."

"Hone your battle skills?" Miss Spencer exclaimed. "He thought you would have need of such things, did he? Here in London?"

"Well, I haven't spent all that much time in London. Not since my parents..." They were getting a little too close to home here. Leigh wondered if he should change the subject.

"Ah, yes. You preferred to travel." Miss Spencer's face took on a knowing look.

Leigh could imagine what she had heard. He frowned. "I've seen a little of the world, it's true."

"And you must have met so many interesting people, too," Miss Spencer said sweetly.

Leigh knew she must be thinking of women.

"All sorts of people," he agreed, thinking of the blood he and his uncle had spilled along the way to reach this final destination. None undeserving. None he would ever need regret. They were careful of that, he and Royal. No women, no children. No innocents.

"And the others?" Miss Spencer prompted. "Your other nicknames?"

Leigh's lips twitched upwards. "Too many to name. Not all of them nice, either." He had been called Night Wind in Constantinople. The Shadow in Venice. He was rather fond of those two, though he did not relish describing to Miss Spencer precisely how he had acquired them.

He looked up from his glass abruptly, his eyes narrowing. "You didn't answer my question."

"Oh, I must have forgotten it," Miss Spencer said. She rose from her seat quickly. "You know, I believe I will go and see what is keeping Lady Fulford. I am sure she would like to greet you."

She began to walk by him.

"Miss Spencer," Leigh said a little more sharply. "You did refuse Harley, did you not?"

She paused. She was very close now. He could smell the fragrance of her breath. Sweet, like she had been eating a ripe and juicy apple. He could see the perfect fan of her light-brown eyelashes as she lowered her eyes to avoid his.

He watched her bite her lower lip. A clear sign of indecisiveness. And possibly deception. Would she lie to him?

With a start, he realized he was truly worried she might have accepted that blasted rake Harley.

"Good God, woman! Do you not realize what sort of husband Harley would make? He is the worst sort of rake!"

"I did not say I had accepted him," Miss Spencer retorted. "And is that not rather like the living in a glass house and throwing stones?" She frowned. "I suggest a trade."

"A trade?" Leigh scowled. "What sort of trade?"

"I will tell you how I answered Lord Harley when you tell me how you acquired the knife wound on your..." She blushed. "The knife wound," she finished firmly.

Leigh smirked. "The one on my chest, you mean?" He watched her flinch ever so slightly, then nod. Was she remembering that night? Was the memory of him lying there, nearly naked in her bed, really so disconcerting to her?

He took a little step toward her, enjoying her unease. "You mean the injury I sustained before climbing through your window and falling into your bed, Miss Spencer?"

Oh, to say the word "bed" around Miss Spencer. It was an exquisite delight to see her face transform, her cheeks pinken, her lips tremble. Should he repeat the wicked word just once more and see what happened?

She lifted her chin. There was a very small dimple in its center, he noticed. "The very one."

Leigh thought again of Harley. He looked to the dimple. He thought of Harley's lips caressing Miss Spencer. Her lips. Her chin. That adorable dimple.

"Bloody hell," he swore. "It is not a fair trade."

"What do you mean?"

"I mean there is no question that you must have refused Harley. To do anything else would be... Well, it would be..." He hesitated. He had intended to finish with "madness," but clearly, that would not go over well.

"Yes?" Miss Spencer's tone was rather chill.

"Tell me you did not accept him." Good God, Leigh felt as if he were near to begging. "Simply confirm your own good sense, Miss Spencer. The good sense I know you possess in abundance." There. Much better. Appeal to her vanity.

Miss Spencer smiled. "I think not, my lord. You, my dear lord, are cheating." The smile fell away. "You do not wish to tell me where you received the injury. Very well. I shall be left to devise my own suppositions."

"And those are?"

"Oh, ever so many. Most involving you running from a jealous husband," Miss Spencer said sweetly.

Leigh's eyes narrowed. "I have never run from a man in my life. Certainly not anyone's husband."

He heard footsteps in the hall. "Really, Miss Spencer, the matter is a delicate one. I would tell you if I could but..."

"Well, then that is your answer," she interrupted, looking smug. "Perhaps in time you shall learn what transpired between myself and Lord Harley. But then, it is also a *delicate* matter..."

"What is a delicate matter?" Lady Fulford inquired, her cane rapping on the floor as she entered the room. "Blakeley, how good to see you. Miss Spencer has just had a rather remarkable visitor."

"If you are speaking of Harley, I saw him leaving as I came in, and I see nothing remarkable about the man," Leigh said frostily.

"Besides his penchant for debauchery, don't you mean, my lord?" Miss Spencer chirped.

Leigh glared.

"Balderdash," said Lady Fulford, waving her hand. "I believe those rumors are greatly exaggerated."

"They are not, I assure you. I am surprised you allowed him to be in the room with Miss Spencer alone at all, even for a moment," Leigh declared with a scowl.

"I was just around the corner, hardly out of earshot," Lady Fulford said soothingly.

Leigh longed to ask if she had overheard anything, but this would have been ungentlemanly. Not to mention desperate.

"Well, my dear, I can hardly wait to discuss the morning with you," Lady Fulford said, eyeing Miss Spencer approvingly.

Evidently, this meant without Leigh's presence. He thought quickly.

"I came to pay my compliments to you ladies, but also to ask whether your very busy schedule might allow you to attend the theater this evening with me."

Lady Fulford looked surprised. "The theater! We were supposed to attend a dinner party at..."

"Oh, I should love to attend the theater," Miss Spencer exclaimed at the same time. "What is playing?"

"I keep a box at the Theatre Royal. I believe Mrs. Mountain"–he spoke of Rosemond Mountain, the actress–"is performing as Polly Peachum."

"The Beggar's Opera!" Miss Spencer's eyes lit up. "Laurel would sing us songs from it, but I have never seen it performed."

"I suppose we may miss one dinner party," Lady Fulford said, looking at Miss Spencer with the indulgence of a fond grandmother. "I did not realize you enjoyed the theater, my dear."

"I must admit, I have not had many opportunities to do so, but I should love to attend. It is very kind of you, my lord..." Miss Spencer trailed off, her eyes narrowing a little, as if she had just recalled their earlier dispute. "Very kind indeed."

"I am nothing if not kind," Leigh said, bowing and smiling faintly. "Shall I pick you up in my carriage? Shall we say seven-thirty?"

He left Lady Fulford's feeling pleased as punch... until he remembered he was supposed to be chaperoning Miss Spencer. Not entertaining her or touring her around London. Certainly not courting her himself.

No, that was what Lord Harley was intending to do, apparently.

He swore as he stepped into his curricle and took the reins. What the devil was he thinking? He had other matters to deal with. Pressing ones. Yet, here he was preparing to take a debutante and a dowager to the theater that same evening.

And yet... as Miss Spencer's chaperone, did he not have a duty to ensure that if she chose to wed, she at least made a suitable choice? His brother and sister-in-law would expect no less of him. If they learned she was engaged to a notorious young rake, would they not blame him, at least in part?

To think nothing of Miss Spencer's own unhappiness if she should make such a fatal matrimonial decision.

It was sheer brotherly duty and human empathy which were leading him to the theater that evening.

It had absolutely nothing to do with Miss Marigold Spencer's dancing gray eyes, golden tresses, or stubborn dimpled chin.

Chapter Fourteen

Having removed her pelisse and passed it to the maid accompanying them, Marigold looked down at her gown and bit her lip nervously. It was a rather flaming scarlet. Velvet this evening, rather than silk. The sleeves of the dress were long and full at least, though of sheer gauze. They contrasted nicely with the bodice... which was all but nonexistent.

Tiny bodices with very high waistlines and long, full skirts were currently the height of evening fashion. But on a curvaceous, full-figured young woman like Marigold, the effect was perhaps unintentionally... well, Junoesque. Indeed, Marigold felt certain that the ancient Greeks would approve of her gown. But then, they also approved of sculpting ladies entirely bare breasted.

"Head in the clouds, Miss Spencer?" a familiar voice drawled near her ear. "I say..."

There was a pause.

She turned to look at Lord Leigh and had to repress the urge to swallow. Hard. He was dressed all in black, right down to his silk cravat. The dark shade suited him. He looked every bit the elegant scoundrel. And there was something of the street ruffian about him. Was it the flinty cut of his cheekbones or the slant of his jaw? *Or perhaps it was the memory of his fine naked chest, Marigold,* she chided herself. A knife-wound certainly was the ultimate dashing rogue accessory.

She had promised herself she would not think of the kiss they had shared that night at the Norfolks' ball, but now she found herself unable to keep that promise.

Everything about Lord Leigh Blakeley spoke of wicked kisses and more. The very air around him hummed with sensuality. It was certainly not her doing, she thought with a pang. No, it was Lord Leigh's devil-may-care demeanor and his easy elegance. All the women nearby must feel it, for most of them were looking in their direction.

The most scandalous urge came over her. To step close to Lord Leigh, lift her lips to his, and press his body closely against her own. She had felt that once. The press of this man's desire. She had moved it discreetly from her memory, but now it flooded back. The press of his hardness against her most intimate place. The haze of pleasure that moment had evoked.

"I say, Miss Spencer, what on earth are you thinking of? I did not really mean in the clouds literally, and yet you look positively celestial at the moment," Lord Leigh observed wryly.

"I was thinking about Lord Harley," Marigold snapped back before she could stop herself. "I mean, I see he has just come in. Across the room."

She watched Lord Leigh immediately stiffen. That had been ungracious of her, she admitted. Especially as he was their host. What had she been thinking?

She had been thinking that she would like to see Lord Leigh discomfited.

By Lord Harley? By the idea of her and Lord Harley, yes. She had to admit it. She had a very wicked urge to see if she could make Lord Leigh jealous.

She saw with delight that he was frowning now. Frowning? No, that was decidedly a scowl.

"So he has," Lord Leigh said, glaring in Harley's general direction. "But may I remind you that I am your host and companion this evening, Miss Spencer? No matter how much you may wish it other-wise. Me, not Harley. Now, may I show you to our box?"

"I thought we were waiting for Lady Fulford," Marigold began. The older lady had joined a group of chattering older ladies and gentlemen in one corner of the foyer and looked in no hurry to abandon them anytime soon.

"She knows where the Blakeley box is. She will join us soon," Lord Leigh said.

He led the way through the vestibule and up the grand staircase to the landing. Marigold had marveled at the Covent Garden Theatre's exterior. Modeled on the Temple of Minerva of ancient Athens, it was a majestic facade with its Doric portico, fluted columns, and carved reliefs of famous dramatic scenes, both ancient and modern. Now, inside the theater proper, it was even more imposing with gorgeously dressed people milling about the luxurious setting.

Lord Leigh led her through a row of beautiful porphyry stone pilasters, past a statue of the Bard himself, and through a door leading into one of the private theater boxes.

Marigold stared wide-eyed. The stage-box was ornately decorated with hangings of crimson moreen, rich silk cushions on each of the chairs, and projecting ornaments of gilt–historical figures, crowns, lyres, and so on.

With time, she had grown used to the luxuriousness of her new milieu. First Lady Fulford's London home, then Blakeley Manor, and now the new settings she found herself in, such as the grand ballrooms of *ton* families. But this was something new. She understood that it was not simply the wealthy who attended the theater. A separate entrance led onto the main floor and the galleries, where for a shilling or two, one could see the same play as the Prince Regent himself. But the Prince Regent watched from the King's own box. He entered through a private entrance, reserved exclusively for the royal family on Hart Street.

The Blakeley box was nearly as exclusive. High above the shilling galleries and the main floor.

There was a buzz of excitement in the air as Marigold obediently took the seat Lord Leigh offered. The feeling that she was used to none of this—not even the shilling galleries—and did not belong suddenly threatened to overwhelm her.

She thought of the old dispensary with its crumbling walls and general shabbiness and felt a pang of longing. That was where she belonged. Not simply an ornament on display, but a useful, productive member of a group of people trying to help their fellow man.

"You still look very far away, Miss Spencer." Lord Leigh's voice filtered in. His tone seemed gentler now. "Tell me, what are you thinking of?" There was a very slight hesitation. "Is it Harley? I swear, you may mention the man if he means so very much to you. I will... try my best not to disparage him."

"That is very restrained of you, my lord, but I was not thinking of Lord Harley," Marigold replied honestly.

"Oh, no?" Was it her imagination, or was there relief in his voice?

"No. I was thinking of something else, something you might be just as disapproving of."

"As disapproving of as Lord Harley?" He snorted. "I think not."

"Very well, then I shall tell you." She took a breath. "I was thinking of the Dispensary for the Poor of St. Giles. Have you heard of the place?"

She turned to look at him. His handsome face had shifted from the faint annoyance it had borne downstairs to genuine curiosity.

"I believe Dare mentioned it once or twice. Wasn't my mother taken there at one point?"

"Yes, they cared for her. Or tried to, before she was spirited away in the night by Mr. Bryce's men," Marigold said. "Your brother met with a woman at the dispensary, who works there as a, well, a sort of healer."

"How interesting," Lord Leigh said. "Well, I suppose there are many women healers, are there not?"

"The idea does not bother you? A woman treating the sick?"

Lord Leigh stared. "Is it not the most natural thing? Many women have the inclination, do they not?"

"But have you ever received treatment from a woman yourself?"

He wrinkled his angular nose. "All the Blakeley physicians have been men."

"Women are not permitted to become physicians," Marigold said quietly.

His eyes studied her keenly. "And yet you have that inclination?"

She was surprised at his astuteness. "I have the inclination to... to be useful. To help."

"To help at this dispensary? Just what sort of place is it?" He paused. "Well, it is in St. Giles. I suppose that tells me all I need to know." He eyed her skeptically. "Not generally the sort of place one finds a refined young lady."

"But I am not a refined young lady, my lord," Marigold replied, smiling a little. "I am a young upstart of a lady."

He chuckled, the sound deep and rich in the back of his throat, and she shivered.

"You are a fine young lady. Is that what this is all about? You feel you do not fit in amongst the *bon ton?*" He sat up suddenly. "You deserve to be here, just as much as the next girl, Miss Spencer. Don't allow Miss Compton or any others of her type to dissuade you of that fact."

"Because I have a large dowry or because my sister married a duke? I certainly did not have a place here before any of that," Marigold replied tartly.

"Well, now..." he began.

"It does not matter," she continued. "I do not care. About any of this. I have been given an opportunity to help at the dispensary, and with Lady Fulford's permission, I shall do so. But even without her permission, I... Well, I..."

"Oh, do go on," Lord Leigh encouraged. "You would defy her, would you?"

"She is not my mother, but she has been very kind to me and my sister," Marigold admitted. "I should not wish to defy her. But I feel this is... my path. So yes, I will follow where it leads, even if that requires a little audacity."

"Healing the sick and helping the poor is your path?"

"Yes, but also learning, above all else, my lord. Learning! Learning new things. How to treat the sick. How to mend the body. Does it not all fascinate you? I will admit, when I found you in my bed that night, I..." She paused.

"Go on," he urged, his face mischievous.

"Well, my reaction was perhaps not quite what you might expect of a young woman. I was excited."

"Excited? Yes, I could see that." His gaze was decidedly mischievous.

Her face flared with annoyance. "Not in that way. Well," she conceded, "not merely in that way. No, I saw the blood on you, and I wished to help. And I did help. I did not swoon or become sick at the sight of your wound, though it was fairly grievous. No, I helped. I bandaged you."

"That you did," he acknowledged, his expression begrudgingly respectful. "You did a damned fine job of it, too. My valet was a medic in the wars, and he approved. A nicely tied bandage was what I believe he said."

Marigold felt a rush of pride. "You must thank him for me."

Lord Leigh was looking at her thoughtfully. "So, you are interested in becoming a healer. Not in marrying Lord Harley."

They were back to that again.

"There is no reason I might not do both," Marigold countered.

Lord Leigh scowled darkly. "What the devil does that mean? If you are saying you have accepted the man..." He shook his head.

"Would you think less of me if I did?" she demanded, truly curious. "You hate him so very much?"

Lord Leigh sighed. "I do not hate him at all. But I have known many men like him. Some have been decent enough fellows—in their treatment of other men, at least. Hell, I may be one of them. No," he said, shaking his head quickly. "That is not true. Perhaps I was something like Harley once. Years ago. I'll admit, my reputation as a rake certainly has lingered. But truth be told, it is not wine and women and song that interests me these days." He met her eyes, his gaze steady and intense. "Like you, I have moved on to other more serious pursuits."

"I should very much like to know—" Marigold began, but at that moment, Lady Fulford swept in.

Their conversation was cut short, and the play began.

As the first strains of music rose from the pit, the theater became, if not absolutely still, then at least quieter. Marigold leaned forward in her chair eagerly as the curtain lifted and the lights on the stage flared, all thoughts of the dispensary temporarily put aside. She was here now. Perhaps she did not belong but–she snuck a glance at Lord Leigh seated beside her. Well, regardless, it was still very fine to be in such a lovely place with such handsome company about to be entertained in such a stimulating way.

If only, she thought with a pang, it was real. If only the man beside her was the one who had proposed marriage. He certainly seemed to be, if not enthusiastic, then not disapproving of the idea of Marigold volunteering her time at the dispensary.

What if this could be her future? Evenings spent by his side at the theater or the opera or quietly reading at home. Days spent engaged in truly useful work at the dispensary or another medical charity. Of course, not every evening had to be spent quietly reading... With Lord Leigh Blakeley for a husband, Marigold could easily imagine the production of heirs not as a coldhearted task simply to be completed, but a joyous, erotic foray.

She imagined undoing Lord Leigh's black silk cravat, moving her mouth against the plane of skin beneath, and then removing the rest of his clothes–all in the privacy and comfort of their bedchamber.

Oh, but it was a wonderful fantasy.

And one which would never, ever come to fruition. No matter what he may claim, everyone who knew him said the same thing. Lord Leigh was a rake who spent his time pursuing pleasurable pursuits all over the globe. He was not made to be a husband. Certainly not an attentive or faithful one.

She must think only of the opportunities she did have–like Lord Harley and his generous offer.

She turned her eyes resolutely to the stage.

At the intermission, Harley made his way over to their box.

"Good evening, Hawkeye," Leigh said coolly. "Looking for someone?"

"Oh, don't be a bore, Blakeley," Lady Fulford said, pushing him aside. "Good evening, dear Lord Harley."

Since when had Harley become a "dear" to Lady Fulford, Leigh wondered with annoyance? She had never called him a "dear." At least, not recently.

"You must be looking for Miss Spencer," Lady Fulford crooned, pushing Leigh still farther aside to make way for the young woman as she stepped shyly forward.

"I was indeed hoping to catch a glimpse of the lovely Miss Spencer," Harley admitted, smiling broadly. "May I say you are looking ravishing in that gown this evening, Miss Spencer?"

Leigh watched Miss Spencer blush prettily and felt a surge of murderous rage flow through him. If he pushed Harley over the side of the stage box, could he claim it was an accident? Oh, bother, who cared? It would be worth it, he decided. Simply not to have to see that preening male face staring so gleefully at Miss Spencer's bodice another instant.

"Would you like to walk Miss Spencer about the theater, Harley? This is her first time here, you know," Lady Fulford offered. "Just around the vestibule mind you."

"That would be wonderful," Harley said, beaming still wider.

On second thought, Leigh decided, he would wait for Harley to sweep Miss Spencer away and then push Lady Fulford out of the box. How dare she simply offer Miss Spencer up like fruit on a platter! Did she not understand the dangers here?

Leigh waited until Harley had led Miss Spencer away, then turned to Lady Fulford.

She was already looking at him. "Have you quite finished shooting daggers into Lord Harley's back, Blakeley? I suppose you would like to shoot a few into me next."

"I..." Leigh stared open-mouthed for a moment, then remembered who really had Miss Spencer's best interests at heart. "I simply fear you are not thinking ahead, Lady Fulford. Yes, Harley would be a fine catch–at least, superficially. But you and I both know that he would make Miss Spencer an appalling husband."

"Do we know that, Blakeley?" Lady Fulford inquired, not looking particularly perturbed at the prospect of Miss Spencer's eternal marital unhappiness. "They say reformed rakes..."

"Yes, yes, you have mentioned that dreadful idiom before, and it simply does not ring true."

Lady Fulford sniffed as if he had offended her. "Perhaps not in your case. But I wonder if Harley is about to turn over a new leaf. He certainly does seem taken with her. Arrived before anyone else this morning. Well, almost anyone else."

"There was a man who arrived earlier than Harley? Who was it?" Leigh demanded. Good Lord, Miss Spencer would be the death of him. Fending off these rabid suitors. Trying to protect her future. It was turning out to be a full-time occupation.

"Not a man. Simply Miss Compton, pushing her nose in where it did not belong," Lady Fulford explained.

"Ah, I see." Leigh was relieved.

"I believe he proposed to her," Lady Fulford said, leaning in and lowering her voice. "Lord Harley, I mean. Marriage, Blakeley. Now, I ask you, would a rake propose marriage to a girl so very quickly if there was not love in his heart?"

"Love!" Leigh snorted. "Lust perhaps."

"You are a cynic, Blakeley," Lady Fulford said disapprovingly.

"Until recently, I thought you were one as well," Leigh countered.

Lady Fulford looked contemplative. "Perhaps I, too, am turning over a new leaf. With your dear brother's marriage to the elder Miss Spencer and now this unexpected turn of events. Well, it's enough to make even the most pessimistic of your elders stop and wonder. Perhaps it *is* possible."

"Perhaps what is possible?" Leigh asked crossly.

There was an uncanny gleam in Lady Fulford's eyes. "True love, of course. True love which can transform even the most hardened young rake and turn him into a doting husband and father." She shook her head. "You know, Blakeley, if the prospect of Miss Spencer marrying Lord Harley is so very off-putting to you, and you are so terribly concerned for her future happiness, there is one simple solution."

"There is?" Leigh asked eagerly. "What is it?"

"Why, simply marry the girl yourself."

Lady Fulford swept out of the box, waving her fan and cackling.

The old crone, Leigh thought dejectedly. And they said wisdom came with age.

Chapter Fifteen

Lady Fulford did not return from intermission.

Instead, the lights dimmed, the play resumed, and Leigh was left staring at Miss Spencer's profile, thinking about the last thing Lady Fulford had said to him before she walked out.

It was a ridiculous suggestion. And yet... he could do it. Make Miss Spencer his. He could be the one to claim her. Harley need not ever have her.

She could be his. *His* in his home. *His* in his bed. And he would make good use of her there, too. She would know every pleasure a man could bring. He would take her in every way there was. She would be a delight in his arms, and he... Well, there was no longer any doubt that he wanted her. Badly.

But for herself, not simply so that no other man would have her.

If she were another woman, he might simply give in. Seduce the girl and be done with it, satisfy his craving. But he was not that man. And she was not that sort of girl. She was a Vestal Virgin. Sanctified. Under his protection. And Lady Fulford's, he reminded himself.

And he was no longer the rake he once was. Nor had he ever been the sort to seduce innocent virgins.

But in this case? He would make an exception for Miss Spencer if she were his bride.

What would he do with a wife? He had no intention of staying in London. At Blakeley Manor? Perhaps a lengthier visit than usual. But to settle down? Stay put? Be a husband?

He had been trained to hunt, trained to kill. The hunt was nearly over, and after that? He could not see himself simply becoming a domestic creature. That was a happiness he did not deserve, nor one he could bring to another.

And yet... And yet he could not bear the thought of what Harley would do to a woman like Miss Spencer. Break her trust. Break her spirits.

Break her heart.

For surely, her heart would become involved. If it was not already.

He snuck another glance at her curving cheek in profile. Those full rosy lips. The golden ringlets.

"Kindly stop staring at me, my lord." She turned ever so slightly toward him. "You are supposed to be watching the play."

"I've seen it a hundred times," he replied. "Dull as ditchwater."

"Well, it is not to me," she said crossly. "You are distracting me."

"Am I?" he said, his voice low and husky. "I can't say I'm sorry for that."

She met his gaze, her own uncertain. She flicked her tongue over her lips, then quickly glanced away.

Leigh smiled to himself. Good. He had unsettled her.

"Do you love him?" he whispered, leaning toward her ear.

She jumped.

"Love who?"

"Harley, that dolt. Who else?"

"My lord, I believe silence is required at the theater," she began.

He was ready for this. "Look about," he said, waving a hand. "No one else is being quiet. Why should we?"

It was true. Most theatergoers, especially those in the private boxes, had watched the play many times already. They attended not simply to see the entertainment but to be seen. Chatting quietly throughout the performances was not such a faux pas as Miss Spencer seemed to think.

"Well, Miss Spencer? Shall I get a straight answer from you this evening on anything to do with your paramour?"

"He is not my paramour," she hissed. "At least. Not yet."

Leigh frowned. "Not yet? But you are inclined to accept his proposal? Tell me this. Tell me why. Why a faithless rake, Miss Spencer? Is your heart so very smitten? Is he so irresistible to you? I admit, I had not taken you for the sort to fall in love simply because a man possesses a pretty face, and so hastily, too..."

He had gotten to her. She turned to him, her face angry. "I am not in love. He has offered me freedom. Freedom! Is that not a good enough reason for a woman to consider chaining herself for life to a man? I am expected to marry. Why should I not choose a man who will consider my wants?"

"There is no reason you should not do so," Leigh said soothingly. He furrowed his brow. "But how on earth has Harley offered you freedom? I should think it would be anything but freeing to be the wife of a reckless debaucher."

"I should not have said anything," she muttered, beginning to toy with the strand of pearls around her neck. Leigh's eye was drawn to the soft white skin of her hands, her arms, the curve of her breasts below the pearls. They were very large breasts indeed. How incredible they would feel cupped in his hands, spilling over with their bounty. Heavy and ripe.

"Why not? Why should you not discuss what is perhaps the most momentous and long-lasting decision you will ever make?" Leigh demanded, trying to clear his head. "Did Harley tell you not to speak of it?"

She flushed. "It is none of your business, my lord."

"Need I remind you that I am here to protect you and your best interests, Miss Spencer."

He watched her take a deep breath. "Very well. In that case, I must ask you to simply trust that Lord Harley is not entirely the man you believe him to be."

"Not entirely?"

"No. He has my interests at heart more than you may think. And at this stage in the proceedings–" She drew another quick breath. "I am inclined to accept his offer."

Leigh could hardly believe his ears. "The Season has only begun. You will receive other offers."

"Not like this one," she said, shaking her head. "It is... well, it is unique."

"Because Harley is handsome and dashing, I suppose," Leigh said darkly.

"Not at all," she exclaimed, then covered her mouth with her hand. "My lord, this is neither the time nor the place."

But Leigh had lost all patience. He drew her to her feet and to the last row of chairs at the back of the box, where the crimson curtains partly veiled one of the chairs.

"Here. Sit. It is more private. Lady Fulford has not yet returned, so there is nothing to fear. No one shall overhear you."

It was more shadowy here at the back of the stage box. Leigh loosened the curtain and let it fall against his chair.

"Now tell me," he said. "What has he offered?" When she opened her mouth to protest, he raised his hand. "I swear to you, I shall not breathe a word."

"I am the one who was not to breathe a word," she said miserably. "Believe me, my lord, it is very tempting to discuss the matter. But I promised I would not."

Leigh was quiet a moment. "You may trust me, you know. I will not..." Now it was his turn for a deep breath. "I will not approach Harley. I will say nothing to the man. I truly am simply... concerned for you."

There was a stabbing sensation in his chest. It was true. He cared for the girl. Not simply as a woman to lust over. He did not wish to see her hurt. Not by Harley, not by anyone. She was his. His to protect.

At least, for now.

"I will tell you only to show you that you cannot sway me," Miss Spencer said abruptly. "Lord Harley suggests an unconventional partnership. One based on our individual interests. We shall each be free to explore these however we please."

"He will be free to explore other women, in other words," Leigh surmised.

"I do not care what he does with other women as I do not give a fig about Lord Harley at all."

"Yet you will. When he becomes your husband, you are sure to care. Eventually."

"Perhaps," she admitted, looking uncomfortable. "I may begin to appreciate his friendship. His companionship."

Leigh could imagine what else she might begin to appreciate. And as a young lady who had never experienced lovemaking with another man, when Harley took her, she was sure to feel a bond begin that she had not anticipated. With a man who did not deserve her. Who would not care for her. A man who would not remain faithful to her, no matter how she clung or cried or pleaded.

"And you will receive what in return for this devil's bargain?" he demanded.

"I will retain control of whatever fortune I bring to the marriage—not that I need it," she added quickly. "But it would bring a greater measure of freedom, I must admit. And Lord Harley promises not to interfere in anything I choose to pursue, including a profession."

Leigh had to admit he was a little impressed. "Harley knew just what to say to tempt you."

"He did," Miss Spencer acknowledged. "And after only one waltz, too." She raised an eyebrow. "Am I to take it you think I should accept him, then? That it is indeed a generous offer?"

"Not in the slightest," Leigh said coolly. "I think it is a damnable thing to suggest to a woman, no matter how bold and unconventional it may be. You deserve more than what Harley is offering. Much more."

Miss Spencer shook her head. "You do understand the sort of proposals I will likely receive if I continue with the Season, my lord? They will be from men perhaps even less desirable than Lord Harley. And who is to say, even if I find a man who seems kind and decent, that he will in fact remain faithful to me? Perhaps this way is better. At least with Lord Harley, I shall know my heart is not on the line."

"There is no guarantee it will not be later," Leigh said brutally. Dammit, could she really be so blind to the dangers?

She looked at him steadily. He could not quite gauge her expression. "I believe I can say it never will be."

Leigh's mouth moved faster than his brain. "If you are not seeking a love match, Miss Spencer, and if Lord Harley's offer is truly so very tempting, then I have a second proposal for you. Here and now."

Miss Spencer looked puzzled. "I am not sure what you mean."

"I mean, me," Leigh said, racing ahead, his heart pounding. "Here is what I propose. Marry me instead, Miss Spencer. I offer you the same terms Harley has given with one caveat. I shall remain faithful. I swear it as part of the terms of our agreement. You deserve no less."

Miss Spencer's jaw dropped. "You cannot be serious, my lord," she said slowly. "Have you had too much to drink?"

He felt impatient. "I am as serious as death. My proposal is genuine. When can I expect my answer? Here? Tonight? Quickly, Miss Spencer. Surely it is not hard to see that my offer is substantially more favorable."

"I cannot believe you are serious," she said, shaking her head. "You cannot be."

Leigh's impatience was changing rapidly to annoyance. "Why can I not be?"

"What would Lady Fulford say?" she murmured. More loudly, "Are you not but another rake, my lord? I hardly know you, yet you promise me faithfulness."

Leigh felt himself losing his temper. "I do not make promises I cannot keep, Miss Spencer. Do you? Believe me when I tell you, I would remain steadfast. You may speak with any member of my family, and they will tell you, scoundrel or not, rake or not, Leigh Blakeley always keeps his word."

"Very well," she said slowly. "I believe you. My apologies, my lord."

"If I am proposing marriage, surely we can use Christian names," he snapped. "Call me Leigh. God knows I hardly hear myself spoken of anymore these days without a goddamned 'lord' in front." He met her eyes and saw them wide as saucers. "Will you permit that... Marigold?"

The name slid over his lips like liquid gold. Pure as honey and just as sweet.

It felt right. Warm and natural on his tongue. The name he had been hoping to say all his life.

He looked at her, luscious and ripe in the shadows, and felt himself stirring. God, but he wanted her. Would a taste really be so bad?

He lifted his hand and trailed a finger lightly over her bare neck. She shivered.

"Very well... Leigh," she whispered. "But as for your offer, I must give it more consideration."

He had known she would say that.

"Fine." He leaned toward her, his lips against her ear. "But do not think too long. I am not a patient man, Marigold."

He brushed his lips lower, against the tender skin beneath her ear. "You are so lovely. You look ravishing in that scarlet concoction."

"The bodice is too small," she complained. She raised her hands to the fabric, tugging at the top with unbearable modesty. "It shows too much."

"It does precisely what it is meant to. Draws the eye to your ample endowments." Leigh slid a finger down to the tops of her breast and lazily traced a circle. "It makes a man think of how to free these beauties from their bondage."

"Are you that man, Leigh?" Her voice was soft, her eyes wide.

Leigh felt as if he might go mad if he did not touch her.

He lowered his head to her breasts and licked the top of one breast delicately. "I very well may be."

He heard her gasp. "What are you..."

"Shhhh." He put a finger to his lips. "It is all right. No one will see. We are in the shadows. The curtain is blocking you."

It was probably true. He could hardly see the audience, so it was unlikely they could see him.

"I'll be... discreet. But I must touch you. If I cannot have you, naked and bare beneath me, let me at least touch you. Let me show you, Marigold, how it might be. With me in your bed," he said seductively. He could feel her shivering. "Would you not like a taste of that, too?"

"I have already had a taste," she murmured nervously. "It seemed... very dangerous." She turned to meet his eyes.

This was her mistake. He took advantage of his opportunity and pressed his mouth to hers roughly, his tongue parting her lips and diving inside with a desperate insistence.

"You are mine," he murmured. "Mine. Not Harley's. Let me show you how good it could be."

He moved his hand down, sliding over her gown, gently caressing the curve of her velvet-sheathed hips, feeling their abundance, imagining the softness she would display if he could pull the gown completely from her body and see her lavish form revealed in all its glory.

His fingers moved to her skirt, lifting the velvet slowly, exposing her calf, then her knee, then sliding up along her thigh and in between.

She met his gaze with something like panic in her eyes.

"What are you doing? We can't..." And then her eyes widened as his fingers touched her core. She was as hot and as slick as he had hoped she would be.

"You're so wet for me, Marigold. God, you drive me wild. Tell me you want this," he whispered. "Or tell me to stop, and I swear I shall obey your command instantly."

She moaned, her eyelashes fluttering as she closed her eyes, opened them. His fingers brushed ever so delicately, like the wings of a butterfly, once, twice, then stilled.

"Oh, I want..." she whispered, her hand reaching out to grip his arm. "I don't want... I don't want you to stop. Don't stop, Leigh. Oh, God, what are you doing to me?"

She felt more than half mad when he spoke of how much he wanted her. Her body was hot and flushed with heat all over.

She wondered if he felt the same. This frantic desperation. This sensual haze that made her feel drugged and dizzy.

She glanced over at him, at the front of his trousers.

"Let me touch you in turn," she whispered, hardly able to believe it when the words slipped from her lips. She felt wicked and daring, here in the shadows of the secluded stage box. Lost in lust. Lost in whatever this feeling was for Leigh Blakeley.

His hand slid more firmly between her legs, his fingers parted her, opened her, and she closed her eyes and moaned.

"Very well," she heard him say. "As you wish."

Her hand was tentative as she reached over and felt the front of his trousers. Though she had anticipated his arousal, a jolt still went through her as she felt him, hard and throbbing, his member erect against her fingers. He felt large against her small hand.

She had no idea what to do.

"I don't know..." she whispered. "I've never..."

In the shadows, she saw him shake his head. "Just touch me. You need not do anything. Touch me if you wish. But most of all, let me touch you. Let me give you this pleasure."

As she was already sopping wet and aching between her legs, there was no chance of this stopping now. She burned for him. She needed him. She needed whatever this was.

Oh, she had touched herself before, of course. She was not ignorant of what her body could do. In the night, her fingers finding the bud of her sex and bringing herself pleasure. All girls did. And boys, too. There was no harm to it.

But this... oh, this was so much more. The foreignness of his bare skin pressing against her most intimate place. His fingers, rough against the mound of her sex, sliding wetly against her sensitive flesh.

She nodded, aroused beyond all ability to reason. Her nipples were hard and peaked against the tight velvet fabric of her gown. If he tried to slide her bodice down, God knew she would not stop him, she realized. God, surely he would not. But also, oh, how she longed for him, too. She imagined the feel of his lips against her breasts as his fingers moved insistently against her and then...

He slid one inside.

She gasped, arched, and he slid in a second, spreading her, then thrusting, deeper and deeper. His strokes were steady and sure, a confident rhythm. He knew what he was about, she thought hazily. Good

Lord, perhaps rakes really did make the best husbands. Was she about to find out?

And then his wonderfully dexterous hand moved. His thumb found her clit, while he worked and stroked, sliding in and out, making small circles against her bud. She was close, so close. She needed this. She needed to come.

She clenched one hand over the arm of the chair. The other was rubbing, stroking, circling Leigh's cock through his trousers. All inhibitions were gone. There was only this, their shared bodies. Her hand pressed against him, and she heard him groan. She knew the pleasure she was giving him was not as satisfying. Oh, how would it be with him inside her? Naked and bare and hard as he slipped his length between her thighs?

And with that thought, she came. She came hard, with a sob, as he drove his fingers into her, shattering her into a million pieces, a burst of unfathomable rapture. She felt herself clenching around his hand, unwilling to let him go. And then she relaxed. It was over.

She was shaking, trembling. And her hand was still covering his cock, as hard as ever.

"Oh God," she murmured. "Oh, Leigh. That was..."

His lips found hers, silencing her words. Oblivious of who might glimpse the kiss from across the gallery. Oblivious of anything but her. She felt his fingers move away from her sex, pull her skirt back down over her legs, and felt lost for a moment. She saw him discreetly pull out a handkerchief, wipe her wetness from his fingers. She could smell herself on him. The sea-salt scent of her pleasure. Good God, let Lady Fulford not come back now, she thought desperately, while returning the kiss, elation flowing through her at the pure wonder of the moment.

And then Leigh's mouth was moving away from hers, down her neck, planting soft kisses, murmuring her name as he reached the tops of her breasts and kissed them reverently, then cupped them with his hands.

"I long to pay them the homage they deserve. They have been most terribly neglected this evening," he said, licking just above the edge of her bodice. She could feel her nipples puckering, fighting against their constraints, and gasped. "It's torture. Pure torture."

He lifted his head and sat back, looking at her.

"Is that what it is?" she asked faintly.

"Oh, indeed," he said, nodding seriously. "Would you not agree?"

"I am not sure what this has been." Yet another dangerous mistake, she feared.

"Call it a gift. A hint of what may be. On the eve of our betrothal."

"I have not said I will accept," she whispered, pushing a strand of damp hair behind one ear. In truth, she felt more confused than ever.

He nodded. "I understand. But..."

The curtain behind them pushed open and Lady Fulford's maid stood there, gasping with excitement.

"Pardon me, my lord, Miss," she said, bobbing her head quickly. "But Lady Fulford has twisted her ankle. Lord and Lady Norfolk have helped her to their carriage and are taking her home. I'm to ride along and prepare the staff. She asks if you–" The maid blushed and curtsied. "If you, my lord, would be so good as to escort Miss Spencer home in your carriage after the performance."

Marigold watched Leigh's face become smooth and expressionless. "Of course. Tell Lady Fulford that Miss Spencer is safe in my hands."

She felt a choking sound coming from her throat and clamped a hand to her mouth, then pretended to cough.

"Thank you, my lord. I shall." And then the maid was gone.

"Leigh," Marigold hissed. "How could you?"

He sat there, grinning in the shadows like the devilish rogue he was, and she swatted his arm. Then it somehow... stayed there. Her hand resting on his arm. Quite comfortably.

She left it there until the end of the performance.

Later as they drove home in the carriage, she realized she could not have said what the rest of the play had even been about.

Chapter Sixteen

"Are you sure I should not remain with you?" Marigold stood hesitantly in the doorway, holding her reticule and gloves. "I could read to you..."

"Nonsense! I can read to myself very well. No, I have everything I need, my dear. I have my maid. I have the footmen. I have my cane." Lady Fulford patted it appreciatively. "I shall be fine. Now, go. The carriage is waiting."

Lady Fulford sat on an overstuffed settee with her foot elevated on a small round stool. Her ankle was sprained but not broken, and her physician had told her she should be on her feet again within a week or two if she stayed off it and used cold compresses for the swelling.

She lifted a hand to shoo Marigold off dismissively, then paused. "Or have you simply changed your mind?"

"No," Marigold said quickly. "Not at all."

There was simply so very much *on* her mind was all. Suddenly her work at the dispensary seemed very distant. But of course, she still wished to go. She must put all thoughts of husbands and marriage and ridiculous proposals from her mind, she decided resolutely, and think of more important things.

But as she sat in Lady Fulford's grand black carriage and rolled through the streets of London, she found that easier said than done.

Last night with Lord Leigh had been... strange in the extreme. And also wonderful in the extreme, too. She felt a sharp sense of guilt for having allowed things to have progressed as far as they had. After all, what if she should accept Lord Harley?

But then, Lord Harley would feel no similar pang of guilt. Nor would he ever in the future.

Even so, Marigold thought stoutly, sitting up straighter in the carriage, she intended to be faithful to her husband whether he was to her or not.

And if that husband were to be Lord Leigh Blakeley?

Well, faithfulness would come all too easily.

But perhaps that was the rub.

With Leigh, she might lose her heart. With Lord Harley, her soul.

Either way, it felt as if she were playing with fire. And in imminent danger of getting burned.

The carriage came to a halt outside the churchyard, and Marigold stepped out.

She paused. Another carriage was stopped just across the street. How strange, for it was quite an elegant one. Similar to Lady Fulford's. Black and sleek. Clearly someone wealthy owned it.

She looked on curiously as the carriage door opened, and a girl peeked her head out. She wore a dark bonnet and a veil over her dark hair, but there was something rather familiar about her.

The girl was just beginning to step out when a hand reached out and clasped her waist. Marigold watched the girl gasp, then turn her face to the carriage door. There was obviously someone there. Even from this distance, it was plainly a man's hand.

The girl's face disappeared into the carriage. Marigold found she could all too easily imagine what the girl was occupied with doing. Something involving the lips. Decidedly.

The girl's head emerged again, followed by her whole body, and this time she made it all the way down to the cobblestones where she paused to look around.

Aha! Another carriage was rolling up. Another elegant conveyance. This one must be to pick up the girl as she was dropped off.

Marigold was smiling to herself at the romance of it when the girl finally noticed her.

Two pairs of eyes widened in unison. Even through the veil, Marigold could now make out the girl's face. Victoria Peel! The dark-haired girl had paled beneath her bonnet. Marigold opened her mouth, thinking to greet her—though surely it would have been a very awkward greeting—when the girl dashed forward, stepped into the waiting second carriage and, without any further ado, was away.

Marigold felt relieved. What on earth would she have said, in any case?

She began to walk behind the church to the dispensary entrance. It was probably all very innocent, she told herself. Evidently, Miss Peel was secretly engaged. Or perhaps not secretly and Marigold had simply not kept track. Surely there must be many betrothed couples who wished to see more of each other in private before they wed and so snuck off in carriages to meet alone. It was hardly revolutionary.

In any case, it did not concern her. After last night, she certainly had no business judging anyone else for improper conduct.

So, she put the matter from her head and marched into the dispensary.

In contrast to her last visit, this morning the clinic was bustling. The chairs in the entrance room were full of people—many of them women holding babies or with small children on their laps. The place was full of noise, and for a moment, Marigold stood still, quite overwhelmed.

"Oh, so you have come back, have you?" Miss Barry was leaning over her desk, evidently preparing to go outside to smoke the pipe she held in her hand. Marigold looked at it with interest. Dare had described Miss Barry's shocking smoking habit, and she found herself quite curious. She had half a mind to ask to try it. But perhaps not this morning.

"Of course," Marigold said cheerfully. "Here and ready to get straight to work. I may even stay the entire day if you have need of me."

"Oh, you may, may you?" Miss Barry said with a sniff. "Your governess has allowed you that great privilege?"

Marigold flushed and glanced at the waiting patients, hoping they would not notice Miss Barry's teasing.

"My..." She had best keep things simple. "My chaperone, not governess. Lady Susan Fulford," she added a bit more boldly. "Perhaps you recall her. From your... earlier days."

"Ha! Nearly said 'younger,' didn't you?" Miss Barry looked entertained. "Dash it all, I believe I do recall a Lady Fulford. Hawk-eyed woman? Looks as if she could see right into your soul or wants you to think she can?"

"That's the very one," Marigold said, smiling. "She has been very kind to me."

"*Hmph*. Well, I admit I'm surprised you've returned. Arpan won't be, though. He has a terrible habit of always thinking the best of people. I have tried to break him of it, but every six months or so, he returns to India to visit his family, and when he comes back to England, he is worse than ever," Miss Barry complained.

"I suppose that means he truly loves them and they him," Marigold commented with amusement.

"*Hmph*," Miss Barry grunted. "Well, I suppose I should get you acquainted with the place. Follow me. And you may call me 'Maggie' from here out. No more of this 'missing.'"

"Very well, Maggie," Marigold said obediently. She was nearly trembling with eagerness to begin.

Within a few hours, her mind was brimming with new information. She had been shown the dispensary's filing system. Desk drawers filled with notes and records for each patient. Beautifully handwritten in Dr. Bannerjee's case and nearly incomprehensible scribbles in Maggie's. Oh well, she was sure she could decipher them if required.

Maggie had taken her through the storage rooms, showing her where all the instruments for Dr. Bannerjee's surgeries were kept as well as clean linens, bandages, and medicines.

She had been introduced to three of the other staff. Mrs. Sharp and Mrs. Tuck, who worked as nurses—both spry women in their sixties, and a younger man in his late twenties named Nick, who seemed a jack-of-all-trades. Maggie called him an "orderly."

While they had gone about their tour, the nurses had been busily escorting patients in and out, and the orderly had brought people into Dr. Bannerjee's office, which was in the back of the dispensary.

"We shan't interrupt him while he's in the thick of things, but do please keep in mind that when you begin to assist us, Dr. Bannerjee believes in clean water and clean hands," Maggie informed her. "Where he is from, cleanliness is a virtue. It is a sacred tenet of his religion, which he holds very dear. Which reminds me, be very respectful of his religion, no matter how odd it may seem to you. He is a patient man when it comes to most things, but–" Maggie cleared her throat, and Marigold received the distinct impression she was speaking from personal experience. "He won't brook any teasing about this."

"Of course," Marigold assured her. "I shouldn't dream of it. Which religion is it, so that I may try to learn more about it?"

"He is a Hindu," Maggie said. "They worship many gods. And goddesses, too."

"How fascinating!"

"Yes, well, I think one is quite enough," Maggie said sniffing. "More than enough if you ask me. But to each their own."

"I look forward to learning a great deal from you and Dr. Bannerjee. Has he always worked with you at the dispensary?"

"He is a founding member," Maggie said with pride. "He and I met at... Well, we have been friends for some years. He saw the need in this area, and he loves England. He believes in hard work and an honorable occupation. Not that he has any need of the money. Which is fortunate, for there isn't any." Maggie snorted.

"What do you mean?"

"Oh, Arpan is the only son of a mining magnate of some kind. Gold or silver, I believe. Father is an Englishman. But Arpan's mother was Indian. They met in India. His parents, I mean. Arpan came to England when he was about ten, I believe, for his schooling. His father insisted he have the very best education, though he didn't give Arpan his name, you'll have noticed. But at least he left him wealthy and free to do whatever he liked, so I suppose that's something."

"That is certainly something to be grateful for," Marigold agreed, thinking of her proposal.

Their conversation was abruptly cut short by a woman going into labor in the waiting area.

"Happens all the time," Maggie advised as one of the nurses and Dr. Bannerjee came running as the woman cried out shrilly. "Most common thing we deal with. Sometimes they don't even know they're with child."

"Don't even know," Marigold gasped. "How is such a thing possible?"

Maggie sniffed and lowered her voice. "You'd be surprised how little most women know about the workings of their own bodies. It isn't as rare as you may think."

The poor laboring woman was being half-walked, half-carried by a composed-looking Mrs. Tuck and Dr. Bannerjee down the hall. Marigold quickly stepped out of the way.

"Perhaps you'd like to observe?" Maggie suggested, her face wry. "After all, you may benefit from the instruction, too. Sooner than you think."

"I believe I know... more than average," Marigold said, a little defensively. "My parents believed in instructing us, and we had a book of anatomy that we were permitted to look at even as children. Though I am sure I have much to learn." Then she realized exactly what Maggie had suggested. "Oh yes, of course, I should like nothing better! Really? May I? The poor woman won't mind?"

"Poor woman she most certainly is," Maggie said with a sigh. "But as she is highly distracted, I very much doubt she will mind another person in the room. Be very quiet and stay out of the way, mind you. I'll go back to see to some of the others who are waiting."

A few hours later, Marigold had witnessed her first patient brought to bed. Though she had done nothing more than fetch clean water and linens for Dr. Bannerjee and Mrs. Tuck, she was flush, fatigued, and perspiring by the end of it. The birth of a child was a marvelous thing— but nerve-racking, too! There had been some points where the babe had gotten rather stuck, and Marigold had seen Mrs. Tuck's worried face. But Dr. Bannerjee had remained calm and confident. He had spoken gently to the mother, and then he and Mrs. Tuck had worked together to actually turn the child from the inside so that it might be freed from its unwieldy position. After that, things progressed very quickly.

As Marigold slipped out of the room to carry a pile of dirty linens to the laundry, the mother was resting behind her, holding a lovely newborn little boy.

"And that's all the rest she'll get," Mrs. Sharp whispered, coming up to Marigold and peeking into the room behind. "For she has six bairns at home already, you know. Won't get much rest there, poor thing."

"Oh dear," Marigold said, alarmed. "Do the women never stay overnight? To recover and replenish their spirits?"

"Not in most cases, no," Mrs. Sharp replied, shaking her head. "There's not enough room for that, dearie. We keep only those who can't be moved. Otherwise, it's up and on your feet and out the door as soon as you can manage."

"And that woman will be up and on her feet? Today?" Despite her best efforts, Marigold could not help but be shocked.

Mrs. Sharp looked at her with a half smile. "It's the rare woman who can afford to lie abed." She patted Marigold's arm. "She's used to it, mind you. She'll be all right."

Marigold made a mental note to find the name of the mother and ask Lady Fulford to send a package to her home. If the poor lady could not have a night of uninterrupted rest with her new baby, perhaps they could help in another small way.

"Excuse me, Dr. Bannerjee," Mrs. Sharp said as the doctor came out of the room, pulling the door shut behind him. "There is another woman. Asking for..." Mrs. Sharp squirmed uncomfortably. "Well, you'd best see her yourself."

"Is she hurt? Ill? I shall come at once." The kindly doctor looked exhausted, Marigold noticed, but he said nothing about going home or taking a break.

"No, no, nothing like that," Mrs. Sharp said hastily. "She is with child." She coughed discreetly. "But plainly does not wish to be."

"Ah, I see," Dr. Bannerjee replied. "Well, show her in there, if you please, Mrs. Sharp." He gestured to a small room across the hall that had a small table and desk alongside cupboards full of supplies.

"Very well, but then I must return to Maggie," Mrs. Sharp said, shuffling her feet a little.

"I understand." He turned to Marigold, his eyes inquiring. "Perhaps Miss Marigold may accompany me to speak to this patient?" As soon as Dr. Bannerjee had learned her Christian name, he had declared it much more lovely than her surname and asked permission to use it instead. Marigold had gladly assented.

Marigold nodded. "Of course."

"Stay silent, if you please, Miss Marigold," the doctor said quietly. "So as to let the patient feel at ease to speak her mind."

Within a moment, a dark-haired lady, much more richly dressed than any of the other patients Marigold had seen, was shown into the little room.

"How may I assist you, ah, Mrs...?" Dr. Bannerjee asked with courtesy. "Or perhaps Miss?"

"Miss. And I'd prefer not to give a name," the lady said shortly.

She was younger than Marigold had realized at first. Her face was very pretty. Marigold was surprised to see she wore rouge on her lips. The only women she had seen made-up in the Seven Dials so far were... Well, this woman was clearly not one of those. Or if she was, she was of a different sort.

"Very well. How may I help you, ma'am? Mrs. Sharp informed me you believe you are with child?"

"Yes, bloody unfortunately, too," the woman burst out. She bit her lip.

Dr. Bannerjee's eyebrows went up, but he said nothing of the outburst. Of course, Marigold thought, he must be used to many sorts of scenarios. Not all women would be pleased to learn they were carrying.

"If I may," he said softly. "I should like to confirm you are correct. Perhaps that will also help you, as well."

"If you like," the dark-haired woman replied. "Though it would be a miracle if I was not. I believe I can tell."

"This is not your first time, then?" Dr. Bannerjee asked as he helped the woman to the table and began his examination.

"My first time, yes," the woman said in a low voice. "Not the first time I've seen a woman with child. Or a baby born."

"Ah, I see." Dr. Bannerjee was quick and thorough. "Well, you are correct. I believe you are in the early stages yet. A few months along."

"That's what I told you," the woman said, sitting up and looking almost angry. "Now can you help me?"

"What do you wish help with precisely?"

"Well, I don't want the bloody thing. I don't want any of this. I want to get rid of it. I've heard you can do it. Will you? I can pay. I can pay handsomely."

Dr. Bannerjee shook his head, but his expression remained neutral. "You've heard incorrectly then, I'm afraid." As the woman looked likely to burst out angrily again, he held up his hand. "Do not mistake me. It is not that I do not wish to help you, but my skills do not lie in this area. It is a... delicate procedure, what you are asking for. Those who perform it have had training from others more knowledgeable. I confess, I have not."

"You have not," the woman repeated hollowly. Marigold saw the hopelessness on her face.

"Though I understand you may feel desperate, I wonder if you understand the risks involved in the procedure," Dr. Bannerjee said. "I would not wish to dissuade you but..."

"You shall not dissuade me," the woman insisted, her face flushing. "And I don't need your judgment either. There is no other choice for me. Do you see? Do you understand?" She shook her head, looking him up and down. "No, you couldn't possibly."

Dr. Bannerjee tilted his head thoughtfully. "I would ordinarily be able to recommend a practitioner to you. But the woman I know is older, and she has recently retired, given up her trade. She was a very reliable woman. I should not like to recommend anyone to you who was not, for as you know the outcomes..."

"Yes, yes, damn the outcomes," the woman said angrily. "I'm damned if I do, damned if I don't." She began to rise from the table.

"Fine. If you can't help me, I'll go elsewhere. I've heard of another. I'd prefer a woman, but if a man it has to be, so be it..."

Dr. Bannerjee looked concerned. "Are you perhaps thinking–" He named a name, and the woman nodded. "Oh, no, my dear. Please, not that fellow. You are more likely to... Well, it is not safe. Not with him. Look, if you would return in a few days, I will see what I can do..."

"You will perform the procedure yourself?" the woman demanded eagerly.

Dr. Bannerjee shook his head. "No, not that. As I have told you, it would not be safe for me to do so."

"Not safe with you, not safe with him. Either way, it does not seem as if *safe* is an option," the woman complained. She shook her head and, to Marigold, seemed even more miserable. "I don't have time. I need to leave London. And before I do, I wish this to be... taken care of."

"I understand," Dr. Bannerjee said softly. "Well if you change your mind, return in a few days, and perhaps I will have a referral for you."

Marigold had been very quiet for all this. When the woman left, wrapping her fur-trimmed cape around her and pulling the hood up over her face, Marigold did not even think she had noticed that another woman had been in the room.

"I truly would have helped if I could," Dr. Bannerjee said, meeting Marigold's eyes.

Marigold nodded. Although she had no experience with them herself, she knew such things occurred. Even at Blakeley Manor, she had heard the women below stairs talk in hushed voices of so-and-so who had died trying to bring on her monthly courses when she was with child. She could not recall many happy stories.

"It is truly a shame," Dr. Bannerjee mused.

"That she does not wish to be a mother?" Marigold asked.

The physician shook his head. "Not at all. Many women do not wish to be mothers. They are simply left with no other choice. When it is a matter of life or death, well..." He shrugged his shoulders.

"Would you wish to learn this procedure you spoke of?" Marigold asked curiously. "So that you could perform it safely for the women here?"

Dr. Bannerjee shook his head. "It is against my beliefs to conduct such a procedure or even to prescribe the herbs which might induce a woman to be brought to bed early. But if I could have referred her to a safe practitioner, I truly would have..." He shook his head sadly. "Let us hope she does not do anything rash."

"Yes," Marigold agreed.

Dr. Bannerjee studied her in silence for a moment, then seemed to cheer up. "Well, Miss Marigold, you have had an interesting first day."

He led her out and back to the entrance area. To Marigold's surprise, it was nearly dark outside. Evening had fallen without her even noticing. She had been much longer than she had planned.

"Goodness, my poor driver," she exclaimed. She hoped the footman and driver had gotten something to eat while they waited. Perhaps next time, she should suggest they bring a picnic. And a deck of cards.

She felt her own stomach grumble loudly.

"Aha, you have not had a break all day, have you?" Dr. Bannerjee asked, hearing the rumble.

Marigold blushed. "Neither have you," she reminded him.

"No, no, I do not stop. And I see you are like Maggie and I. We do not stop the work until there are no more to be helped. And even then..." He began to yawn and covered his mouth tiredly.

"There are still a few patients waiting," Marigold said tentatively. "Would you like me to stay?"

"You go home, Miss Marigold," Dr. Bannerjee instructed. "Nick and Maggie are still here. We will see to the last sufferers and then take our turns at rest."

Did he and Maggie ever leave the dispensary, Marigold wondered? Such a question would be very indelicate–after all, Dr. Bannerjee was married–so she refrained from asking. But certainly, they seemed so dedicated that it was a distinct possibility they slept there most nights. Not that she supposed there to be anything resembling romance between Maggie and the good doctor. No, Maggie's heart lay entirely with the practice of medicine. That was abundantly clear. For all her gruff bluster, Marigold could not imagine Maggie Barry ever turning away a person in need–or stopping to rest until she had cared for every last one waiting.

"I will be back soon," Marigold promised. Indeed, she was already more than eager to return, despite her weariness. She snatched up the stack of reading materials that Maggie had left her, noting a copy of William Buchan's *Domestic Medicine* in the pile. She smiled to herself. She had read *Domestic Medicine* a handful of times since locating it in the Blakeley family library a few months ago. But it was a lengthy and dense work, and so it would be good to go back to it.

She walked slowly back to her carriage, her arms full of books, thinking of the dark-haired woman. It had been a brave thing the woman had done—to come and ask Dr. Bannerjee if he could help her. Clearly, she had no other place to turn.

And if the woman was unable to find a solution to her desperate problem? Well, there was the Foundling Hospital. But the hospital was frequently overwhelmed with admissions. And Marigold had heard terrible stories about the outcomes for the infants left in the hospital's care. Most were never reclaimed, and those who remained frequently did not endure through childhood.

And the alternative? It was too awful to consider, but Marigold had read the newspapers. Some women took a step even more terrible and desperate.

Surely what the dark-haired woman had asked for was better than these options.

Marigold thought of Laurel and her happy state. How grateful she was that her sister was settled and taken care of no matter what may come. The Spencers were very privileged indeed, Marigold thought guiltily, in comparison to so many she had seen today.

And what of Lord Leigh? What would he think of what she had seen today? Would he judge the dark-haired woman harshly? Or would he look on her with sympathy and human kindness? She was inclined to think the latter, but perhaps she should ask. It would be an interesting conversation. Those seemed limitless with Leigh.

She tried to imagine having a similar conversation with Lord Harley... but could not.

Chapter Seventeen

L eigh Blakeley was supposed to be playing whist. But his mind
was anywhere but on the cards he held in his hand.

Over and over again, he replayed in his mind the moment
of Miss Spencer's climax in the theater box. The sweet sounds she had
made, the touch of her hand on his cock, the dew-petal softness of her
skin as he had stroked her.

And her breasts. Oh, Christ. The scarlet dress she had worn had
left nothing to the imagination, and as he had parted her, fingers
stroking deeper and deeper, her breasts had jiggled enticingly, full and
plump.

God, he could think of nothing else but her. What her breasts
would look like, soft and full, as he peeled the crimson silk off her.
What her nipples would look like, a ripe dusky rose or perhaps a
purplish amber.

Would they be small little buds or round berries? He rather
thought the latter. He would take one in his mouth while he fingered
the other, and then he would part her thighs and place himself
between them. All the while she begged and chanted his name...

He let out a groan, and his partner quirked an eyebrow, then
smirked. The bastard believed Leigh had a bad hand.

It was worse than that. Leigh was simply bad to the core.

He was a cad. A rotter. A bounder. The worst sort of scoundrel.

And even worse—yes, much, much worse—for the first time in his life, Leigh Blakeley was *scared*.

It was shameful to admit. This feeling of actual fear.

He was afraid she would reject his proposal.

He was afraid she would *accept* his proposal.

In short, he was an idiot who had no business having proposed at all.

This was all Lady Fulford's doing. He had half a mind to go and tell her so.

Except that would mean risking being seen by Miss Spencer.

Who he both longed to see and had been hiding from now for... well, only three days. But it felt like an eternity. Was that because he missed her? Or because not knowing was simply driving him mad?

It was all very confusing. And Leigh was not used to being confused. He was not an indecisive man ordinarily. Quite the opposite. His uncle had trained the last bits of indecision out of him. He acted firmly, with foresight and determination. Ruthlessly even, when required.

But with Miss Marigold Spencer... well, he had been ruthless, in a way. He had ruthlessly undercut Lord Harley, that was for certain. That part of things was at least rather satisfying. Though of course, Harley did not yet realize he had a challenger to contend with. Leigh frowned at this realization. Someone ought to tell Harley. Hopefully, Miss Spencer.

But then that would mean she had accepted Leigh.

And that Leigh was to become... a husband.

A married man.

Leg-shackled.

Noozed.

Caught in the parson's mouse-trap.

Tied a knot with his tongue that he could not untie with his teeth.

Leigh had once seen a courtesan in Italy tie a cherry stem into a knot with only her tongue and her teeth. Now that was a knot he wouldn't mind tying. Or trying to untie.

He imagined Marigold's red lips parting as she slipped a cherry stem between them, her white teeth flashing, glimpses of her pink tongue as she deftly slid the stem to and fro.

Leigh shivered. That was quite enough of that.

"You're not paying attention," his partner at the gaming table at White's complained. "What's gotten into you, Blakeley?"

Leigh threw down his cards. "Heart's not in it, I'm afraid. Sorry, Smithfield. Shall we continue another day?"

"Bah!" The other man looked annoyed, then studied Leigh's face for a moment. "I've seen that expression before. You need something." He snapped his fingers. "A woman. That's what you need. There's a new opera dancer at the…"

"But I don't want a woman, Smithfield," Leigh interrupted. He scratched his jaw thoughtfully. "Though it has been… some time," he admitted.

"Don't want a woman? Not even a lovely opera dancer?" Smithfield looked aghast, then his jaw dropped. "Perhaps that's the problem, then."

"What?"

"No," Smithfield declared, his eyes narrowing. "You're only just back in England. There hasn't been time."

"Time for what?" Leigh demanded. "What is it?"

"Can it be you're… in love?" Smithfield ventured, his smirk returning. "You have been attending a dreadful number of balls and things with that Lady Fulford of yours."

"Ha!" Leigh exclaimed. "In love." The idea was ridiculous. In lust, yes. He was even close to admitting this, but to do so would be to risk disclosing the object of his lust to Smithfield, and he would not dishonor Miss Spencer in such a way.

Harley would dishonor her in all ways, a nasty voice in his head said.

Shove it, he snarled internally.

"What the devil are you thinking now?" Smithfield asked.

Leigh realized he had been staring out the window. "Nothing." He stood abruptly. "Well, I'm out. Good day, Smithfield."

He strolled the street, contemplating how to spend the rest of his afternoon.

When he had been abroad with his uncle, time had been easy to fill, he thought with a pang. In some ways, he missed that. It had been... a distraction. A welcome, constant one. The hunt.

Now that his mother was back, and he knew his father was gone, well, he was simply waiting for the last step to be over and done with.

Oh, he was looking forward to satisfying his final bloodlust, sating the need for vengeance that he and his uncle had both carried for so long.

But then? He had no idea.

He could return to how he had been before his parents' disappearance. Spend his days much like he had spent his morning—gambling and bored. Or dallying with opera dancers eager for a rich and handsome patron.

He thought of Miss Spencer. Even now, she might be spending her morning with Harley. Perhaps he sent her fresh flowers every day. And trinkets and chocolates, too. Just how dutiful a suitor was he trying to be? Did he take her riding in Hyde Park? For strolls on Bond Street? Surely, he didn't take her to Gunter's for ices?

Dare had said that the way to his bride's heart had been through a chocolate ice. But Leigh had assumed he was joking.

Leigh scowled as he hailed a hackney.

<hr />

"You have a guest," Lady Fulford announced as Marigold entered the room. "And more flowers have arrived from Lord Harley."

Marigold was aghast. "More! We have hardly any space in which to put them."

"He is a very generous suitor. But perhaps a tad overzealous with his gift-giving," Lady Fulford admitted, glancing around the drawing room which had taken on the appearance of a hot house. "Though the chocolates and sweets have been rather nice."

"Please continue to enjoy them," Marigold said, a glint of amusement in her eye. "You are the injured one. Heaven knows you deserve them more than I." Especially after what she had been up to with Lord Leigh.

"If I enjoy them much more, I shall not fit into any of my ballgowns," Lady Fulford complained.

"Who is the guest?"

"Oh, yes, the guest! It seems Miss Victoria Peel wishes for a private tête-à-tête with you. I have had Matthews show her into the morning room." Lady Fulford gave Marigold a quizzical look. "First Miss Compton, now her cousin. You have certainly made an impression on those girls."

"Yes," Marigold replied uncomfortably, thinking of the carriage. "I am not at all sure why they have singled me out."

Well, at least she could deduce who Miss Compton's "reliable" witness was now. Evidently that had not been Miss Peel's first time in Seven Dials.

She stepped into the morning room, not at all looking forward to her audience with Miss Peel. Especially as this time, Lady Fulford had seen no harm in allowing the conversation to take place without her.

"Miss Spencer. You have finally arrived. Good. I wished to speak with you. Though I did not expect to have to wait so long."

Miss Peel rose from her seat with the importance of a young queen who had kept waiting for her subject.

Do not apologize, Marigold told herself firmly. *Do not say it is lovely to see her. No polite lies.*

"What did you wish to speak with me about, Miss Peel?" Marigold asked directly.

Miss Peel was even prettier face-to-face than Marigold had remembered. She had a perfectly formed oval face, eyes so bright and blue that they reminded Marigold of her sister's, and dark silky hair which cascaded around her shoulders in carefully styled curls. Her figure was... well, everything Marigold's was not. Like her cousin Miss Cora Compton, Victoria was above average in height with a slim, demure form. The sky-blue muslin morning dress she wore seemed to flow around her like a butterfly's gossamer wings, delicate and feminine.

"Let us not play coy, Miss Spencer," Miss Peel said, not returning the smile. "I know what you saw. Why beat around the bush? I suppose you want something."

"W-want something?" Marigold stuttered.

"Of course." Miss Peel crossed her arms and sneered a little. "Someone like you must want something."

Marigold raised an eyebrow coolly. "I beg your pardon?"

"Oh, please, Miss Spencer. I'll admit, you have a rather influential patroness. Who would have expected Lady Fulford to show such a soft-side for a peasant? But she is your only ally. Without her, you are alone. An interloper amongst us. Nearly too old to be a debutante in the first place, and certainly desperate to find a suitable husband who will overlook your low-born blood."

"As far as allies, you seem to be forgetting my chaperone and brother-in-law, Lord Leigh," Marigold reminded Victoria as her temper flickered to life.

Miss Peel waved a hand dismissively. "I don't think anyone is anticipating that he will remain a constant presence by your side. A man like Lord Leigh? No, now that he is in London... well, I am sure there is a great deal to distract him. Certainly, things more interesting than attending debutante balls with an unsophisticated ragamuffin of a girl."

Marigold narrowed her eyes. "You insult my birth, my education, and my appearance, Miss Peel, and yet you somehow imagine I want something from you. I'll admit, it does not seem likely from my point of view. You and your cousin are remarkably similar in character. That is *not* intended as a compliment."

Miss Peel looked at her in silence for a moment. "Very well. Perhaps I was too blunt with my words." She bit her lip, and Marigold saw a flash of panic beneath the regal exterior. "I'll admit, Miss Spencer, you have me in a very disagreeable predicament. I suppose you think I am completely under your power. But I would have you understand here and now that I am not used to being under anyone's thumb, especially not a..." She seemed to bite her tongue just in time. "I am not used to it," she finished.

"I am not sure what you are talking about," Marigold said with bewilderment. "I have done nothing to you, Miss Peel. Nor do I wish to hold power over you. The less we have to do with one another the better, as far as I am concerned."

Miss Peel pushed back a strand of dark hair irritably. "Not yet, Miss

Spencer. But you cannot mean to tell me that you saw what you saw and do not plan to use it for your own advantage."

"My own advantage..." Marigold began. Then she stopped. "Oh, for goodness' sake," she said with exasperation. "You think I mean to *blackmail* you?" She laughed. Miss Peel frowned. "I have no interest in blackmailing you. I have neither the time nor the inclination. Add that to the list of things you and your cousin have gotten very, very wrong about me and then cross it off. Now, if that is all—"

"You are lying," Miss Peel interrupted, her face twisted with confusion. "Surely you are lying. You saw me in... well, in the most compromising of circumstances..."

"Much like you saw me and did not hesitate to inform your cousin?" Marigold interjected coolly. "I am not you, Miss Peel. Thank heaven for that."

"Even so," Miss Peel went on, her face desperate. "A word in the right ear, and I would be ruined, Miss Spencer. If my father knew..."

"He will not find out from me," Marigold interjected. "Nor will anyone else."

Miss Peel stared. "And for your graciousness, you expect nothing? No assistance as you navigate the superior social milieu in which you find yourself? No demands of friendship?"

"Friendship!" Marigold laughed. "Can one demand friendship?" She shook her head. "I suppose you mean a false sort of friendship."

"If that is what you wish to call it. I could stand beside you at social functions, Miss Spencer. Speak highly of you to others. Praise your gowns, your... appearance."

Marigold could not help it. She let out a hoot of laughter. "You would be altogether believable, I am sure."

"Well, I would do my best," Miss Peel said warily.

"No, thank you, Miss Peel." Marigold shook her head. "That shall not be necessary. You need not buy my silence. You may simply have it. This may come as a shock to you, but I have no wish to ruin your life—nor that of your cousin. In fact, I have no wish to have anything to do with either of you at all. I am not sure what it was that brought me to your attention in the first place. I suppose you simply have a habit of attacking anyone who is new or different."

"You are quite different, you must admit," Miss Peel insisted.

"I know you believe I don't belong," Marigold said softly. "That my family is not good enough. But my sister is married to a duke. She wished for me to have a Season. It is thanks to her and her husband's kindness that I am here. And now that I am, I certainly will not let any spoiled young ladies like you and your cousin or any of your friends frighten me away or cause me to doubt my own worth."

Miss Peel still seemed skeptical. She was studying Marigold as intently as a still-life painter might inspect a vase. "That is all very well and good, but perhaps there is more than simple altruism at work here, Miss Spencer."

"I do not know what you mean," Marigold said a little wearily. She had hoped their audience was nearly concluded.

"I mean that you were at the same location I was," Miss Peel said slowly. "And despite what you claimed to my cousin about being involved in selfless charity work, perhaps you, too, have something you wish to hide. Perhaps you and I have more in common than I thought when I first arrived here today. The playing field is level, for you, too, have compromised your reputation. Your honor. Well, what little you had in the first place."

"Oh, what rubbish is this now," Marigold exclaimed. "I have been more than patient with you, Miss Peel, but now I should like you to leave. You would try the patience of a saint, and I am certainly not one of those."

"I am not such a naive young chit, Miss Spencer..." Miss Peel began.

"Oh ho! I think you have established that quite well," Marigold snapped.

Miss Peel flushed but took a step closer. "I can see when a girl has had a lover. And I can see it plainly all over your face. If you have something to hold over my head, Miss Spencer, well, then I swear, I will hold this over yours. I will *not* be ruined. Do you hear me? I know you have taken a lover. You were meeting him in Seven Dials, even though Lady Fulford is stupid enough to believe your ridiculous lies. You are compromised, and should you dare to spread what you saw, then I shall shout what I know from every bell tower in London."

It was clear she believed what she said. There was a look of ferocity mixed with terrified panic on Miss Peel's pretty face. She must be desperate indeed.

With a pang, Marigold realized there was some measure of truth to what the other girl had said.

"Compromised? What's this about being compromised? I say, good day, Miss Peel. I did not expect to see you here." Lord Leigh stood in the doorway, a hint of a smile on his handsome face. But his eyes were cold. "Rather a heavy topic of conversation for afternoon tea, is it not? And here I thought you young ladies were supposed to set the standards for good behavior. Conform to the height of propriety and all that."

"Miss Peel is just leaving. She has been spouting some very spurious beliefs, none of which have any relation to reality," Marigold said firmly. "When did you get here, my lord?"

"Oh, I've been lurking about for a little while. Admiring all these fine flowers," Lord Leigh said, putting a hand out to tug a petal from a rose in a nearby vase. "Rather excessive, aren't they?"

He dropped the petal onto the floor and met Marigold's eyes. She saw a strange heat there. Was he... angry? With her? But why?

Miss Peel pushed past her. "I am not sure what you have just overheard, Lord Leigh," she said in a honey-sweet tone. "But I believe your ward–your charge–whatever Miss Spencer is to you–has been engaging in improper conduct. And I mean to make this public. If I have to." She stood up straighter, squaring her shoulders.

"Oh, for goodness' sake." Marigold put a hand to her temple. "There is nothing to make public. Miss Peel, kindly recall what I said earlier and believe me when I say, I mean you no harm. There is really no need for any of these threats..."

"You are accusing Miss Spencer of impropriety of some sort? Of what precisely?" Lord Leigh interrupted, frowning.

"Of... of compromising herself. Her virtue," Miss Peel stammered, her face flushing.

"With whom?" Lord Leigh asked coolly.

"With whom?" Miss Peel's eyes darted back and forth.

"Yes, who is he that has so compromised Miss Spencer? I should very much like to know..." Lord Leigh paused.

Marigold drew her breath in sharply. She did not like this pause. She did not like it at all. What was Leigh doing?

"Considering she is my fiancée, after all."

"Your fiancée? You must be joking, my lord." Miss Peel was staring at him with undisguised horror. She glanced at Marigold.

"Yes, it is true. If Miss Spencer is compromised, there is only one man who could possibly be to blame. And I–" Lord Leigh paused for dramatic effect a second time, and Marigold felt a sharp urge to slap the smirk off his face. "I am that man."

"His Lordship is a scoundrel and a liar who is playing a cruel trick on you, Miss Peel. We are not engaged," Marigold declared. "Now, please may I see you out?"

"What do you mean, my sweeting, my pet? Of course we are." Lord Leigh stepped up to her so quickly she was startled. He lifted one of her hands to his mouth and kissed her palm tenderly. "You need not hide our betrothal any longer."

"Oh, you idiot," she said, real anger in her voice. "We are not betrothed. I will not and cannot marry you, especially now that..."

"I do not understand..." Miss Peel began.

"I suppose you have gone and accepted that fool Harley? Is that what you are saying?" Lord Leigh demanded hotly.

"You should not have spoken that name," Marigold hissed, glancing at Miss Peel who had gone from haughty to confused and now was looking rather peaked and dazed. The dark-haired girl's face had gone from flushed to pale.

"I believe I shall go, after all," Miss Peel murmured, sidling toward the door. "Perhaps a private conversation..."

They watched her leave. As soon as she had stepped into the hallway, Marigold whirled to face Lord Leigh.

━━━◦◦◦━━━

Leigh took a step back. Miss Spencer had turned on him like a wrathful Fury.

"What on earth are you doing? Announcing our engagement to the most loathsome girl in London?"

"Second most loathsome, I thought."

"It does not matter. What matters is that I have not accepted you. Unless—" An expression of horror came over her face. "Unless you believe that what I allowed to take place at the theater was an indication of my..."

"No, no, of course not," Leigh protested. "What do you take me for?"

Miss Spencer was shaking her head. "I do not know what to take you for. I have not seen you since that night, three days ago. The night you also proposed marriage. Now here you are, showing up with a sense of entitlement so large I am surprised you fit through the door."

"Well, it is a double set."

Miss Spencer emitted a sound of exasperation.

"Does this mean you have accepted Harley?"

"You should not have mentioned his name. Especially before Miss Peel. It is none of your business, my lord."

"If this is about my absence this week, I apologize. I admit, I was caught up in some business of my own..."

"I could not care less if I saw you or not, my lord. It may shock you, but I have been quite busy myself."

"Ah, yes, with your work at the dispensary."

"Yes, at the dispensary. And with helping Lady Fulford. She has injured her ankle, you know, and you did not even think to pay her a visit. Meanwhile, Lord Harley has sent us flowers, sweets, and..."

"Sweets and chocolates!" Leigh burst out. "Is that what you are after? What of more important things?"

"Things more important than showing care and consideration to one of your parents' oldest friends? Or things more important than showing due regard to your supposed future fiancée by respecting her privacy when she confides in you?" Miss Spencer demanded, her eyes flashing.

"Yes! Bloody yes! Things like this."

And then he gripped her by the shoulders and kissed her, right there in Lady Fulford's morning room.

He didn't give a damn who saw. At this point, it would work in his favor if someone else were to walk in. Let them. Let them all come.

His lips were hard and demanding. He did not coax, he took, holding Miss Spencer's body against his with a deliberate possessiveness. She resisted at first, her hands coming up to his chest and beginning to push him away. Then her lips parted, her fingers fastened around the lapels of his tailcoat, pulling him more tightly against her. Leigh resisted the urge to grin. Instead, he kissed as if his life depended upon it. If kisses could be duels, then in a strange sense, Leigh was dueling, fighting Miss Spencer for the right to possess her. He thrust his tongue between her lips, tilting her head back with the force, then snaked one arm around her waist, holding her firm, while her other hand crept to her breast, cupping and squeezing.

That was a step too far.

Miss Spencer let out an outraged gasp and struggled against him. Immediately, Leigh let her go.

"You feel so good in my arms," he panted, looking down at her. "I'm sorry. But I had to show you, dammit. How it could be. Between us. Always."

"Always?" She shook her head. "I will admit you are an excellent kisser, my lord. And yes, I enjoy your company. Most of the time. But I hardly know you. No, worse, I hardly trust you."

"Yet you trust Harley?" Leigh asked in disbelief.

She bit her lip. "At least Lord Harley has been honest with me. About what he wants, what he expects."

"So have I," Leigh said hotly. "Do you think I go about offering marriage as a hobby, Miss Spencer? I have only posed the question once."

"I am honored indeed then, Lord Leigh," she said tightly. "But that does not change the fact that the very first night we met—if it can even be called that—you had come from a fight or a duel of some kind. And you have still not had the faith in me to share just what transpired that night. I have safeguarded your secret," she pointed out. "I have not breathed a word. But it took only a moment in Miss Peel's company for you to drop Lord Harley's name, embarrassing me in the process, not to mention making a fool out of me when the news that we are not in fact engaged emerges."

"It need not emerge," Leigh said slowly. "As for that night, I should like nothing more than to tell you everything. It is not as you think. It had nothing to do with another woman. Well, not in the way you think..."

Her eyes flashed. "I see."

"There is a great deal going on in my life that you could not possibly understand," Leigh said desperately. Then immediately wished he had not.

"I see," she said again, very softly. "In that case, perhaps it is not the time to do anything so permanent as take a wife, my lord."

Leigh felt his blood flare. "Oh, you think Harley will be more forthright with you, do you? That he will make a better husband? That you will never disagree?" He gestured with his hand to the space between them. Even now he could still feel the sparks in the air. "This? What we have. What we feel. It is a rare thing, Miss Spencer. I will tell you now, frankly, that in all my time as a..." He saw her lift her chin. "Yes, as a rake if you like. I have never felt it. It is more than lust. More than desire. Though it encompasses those things, too. It is—"

"Please do not say spiritual, my lord," Miss Spencer interjected. "I think I should cast up my accounts." She shook her head slowly. "No, I believe what you said just now. About there being a great deal happening in your life besides this. You are distracted and confused, my lord. You wish to best Lord Harley by thwarting his proposal out of some misguided belief that you are jealous of him, I suppose." She gave a little laugh, and Leigh heard the sadness in her voice. "Goodness knows why, for it is my only one. But offering marriage to me? That was a mistake. Surely you must see that. Men like you... well, they do not marry. Or if they do, they certainly do not remain faithful. Not to bluestocking girls like me."

Leigh lost his temper a second time. "You are right about one thing, Miss Spencer. I do wish to best Harley—and I shall do so. Perhaps when he is out of the picture, things will become much clearer for you."

He began to stride toward the door, then paused.

"But you are wrong, you know. I was not about to say 'spiritual' just now. Though the word I was about to use is one you might call sacred. Perhaps you might even allow me the opportunity to say it to you another time."

Then he stepped through the doorway and was gone.

Chapter Eighteen

What was the word? What was the blasted word he had been about to say?

Affection not love. Desire and passion, too, yes. But not love. Surely not love.

Leigh made his way to the location where he knew he would find Harley. His mind was in turmoil. He felt pulled in two directions. Pulled between life and death themselves.

Soon, he would be embarking on the most important task of his, albeit, rather short life. He could not complete it successfully when his mind was so transfixed by Miss Spencer. This was an obsession, yes. He had felt it before and could recognize it again. A pain gnawing at him from within. Consuming him.

He and his uncle had fed such an obsession. Kindled it, nurtured it, allowed it to grow. In the end, it had led them to a kind of justice.

He had hoped it would lead him to his parents.

But no, it had been Dare who had blindly followed the breadcrumbs and become the hero—restoring their mother to her family, bringing her safely home from her long nightmarish journey.

It seemed Leigh's place was not to recover or restore, but to vanquish and destroy. He and his uncle had hunted down the perpetrators of the crimes against his parents, and soon they would no longer pose a threat to any other living soul.

But instead of this long-awaited revenge, his mind was filled with her. Thoughts of a future where she lay in his arms by night and filled his days with her sweet voice and laughter.

He had reached his destination.

He pushed open the doors of the Bond Street saloon and stepped inside.

A cacophony of strident male voices, the smell of masculine sweat, leather, and other odors filled his ears and his nostrils.

Gentleman Jack's boxing saloon was a favorite locale with young bloods like Harley. Leigh knew the marquess was a regular attender at the boxing academy and boasted of near-daily dedication to the sport.

Sure enough, Leigh caught sight of him easily. Sparring with another young man in a boxing ring across the room.

He stepped over and waited until Harley noticed him there.

Within a few moments, the match ended, and Harley jumped down. The bloody bastard had won, of course.

"Blakeley! I didn't know this was your sport," Harley said, grinning and coming over, a white towel slung around his neck. The young man was bare-chested and gleaming with sweat. He was well muscled, too. A fine specimen. But not the right specimen for Miss Spencer.

"I wish to speak to you about Miss Spencer," Leigh said bluntly.

Harley arched his brows. "Perhaps a private room?"

Leigh followed him to a small back room where Harley gestured to a wooden bench and then closed the door.

"Not a boxer, eh, Blakeley?" he said again good-naturedly. "Pistols more your style?"

"Oh, I can use my fists," Leigh said steadily, meeting Harley's gaze. "Or put a broadsword, a rapier, or yes, even a pistol in my hand, and I'll make short work of... well." He shrugged modestly.

"I like a man of confidence. I hope you aren't here to suggest pistols at dawn, however."

"The thought did occur to me," Leigh said.

Harley nodded. "I see. Miss Spencer has told you of my proposal.

I'll admit, I suspected it would be difficult to keep such an unconventional offer a secret."

"To be fair, she did try. I rather tormented her until she told me," Leigh said dryly.

"I see. Not very gentlemanly to harass a lady, but then, you are her chaperone, aren't you?" Harley said, levelling his gaze.

Leigh met it head-on. "Not a very good one, I'm afraid. But yes."

"And my proposal to Miss Spencer worried you, did it? Is that because she's on the verge of accepting?" Harley smiled.

"You would be damned lucky if she did." Leigh glowered. "She deserves a sight better than you."

"I'm a marquess, Blakeley," Harley reminded him. But his voice was mild. "You think she could do better than that?"

"I think she deserves a faithful husband who does not need to bargain her into marriage," Leigh replied.

"Ah! You wish for her to marry a man who will swear to be steadfast." Harley shook his head with a grimace. "And what makes you think she will be?"

"I beg your pardon," Leigh said hotly. "What the devil do you mean by that?"

Harley put up his hands. "I say nothing against Miss Spencer's honor in particular. I only meant to point out that it is not only men who struggle to remain constant."

Leigh was amused. "You're what? Twenty-two? Twenty-three? A year or two older than Miss Spencer, if that. And yet you have known many inconstant women in your time, have you?"

Harley was quiet for a moment. "I'm young, yes. And I know my own reputation. I am not naive, Blakeley. But yes, I have known love, fleeting though it turned out to be."

He met Leigh's eyes steadily.

Leigh was shocked at what he saw. "Whoever she was, she hurt you badly, didn't she? I am sorry."

Harley shrugged. "I savor the sweetness life still has to give."

"You spend your father's money, and you whore around London, you mean," Leigh interpreted. "Well, whatever suits you. But it won't suit Miss Spencer. Even if she has convinced herself it might."

Harley whistled. "I'm close then, am I?"

Leigh was nettled. "Not in the slightest. She'll refuse you."

"And yet, here you are," Harley pointed out. His eyes suddenly widened. "I see how it is. 'O beware, my lord, of jealousy; It is the green-eyed monster which doth mock the meat it feeds on.'"

"Shakespeare? Really, Harley?" Leigh narrowed his eyes.

"I believe Iago is a highly underrated villain," Harley said thoughtfully. "And believe me, I should know. I've learned a little something about the fruitlessness of jealousy."

"I am not jealous. Least of all, of you, Harley," Leigh insisted.

Harley grinned. "Ah, but there is something worth being jealous of, is there not? Miss Spencer's true and tender heart."

Leigh was tempted to punch the younger man, simply to shut his cocky mouth, but suspected it would not help.

"I've asked her to marry me as well," he admitted begrudgingly.

Harley's jaw dropped. "You? The infamous Lord Leigh Blakeley? You have proposed?"

"Good God, man, you started it all," Leigh exclaimed.

"Does that mean you hope she refuses you?"

"Not at all. I'm here to ask you to withdraw your offer. It has... confused the girl. Needlessly."

Harley eyed him. "I believe it has confused you more, Blakeley. You're a bit of a mess at the moment, are you not? Is that her doing?"

Leigh sank down onto the bench with a groan. "I really don't know anymore."

Harley watched him a moment, then took a seat a few feet down the bench.

"Very well. I shall withdraw my offer. If you really think it will help your cause."

Leigh put his head in his hands and groaned again. "It won't. I've been a damned fool."

Harley's hand clapped down on his shoulder. The gesture was oddly comforting. "You have it bad, old man, don't you?"

"Have what?" Leigh asked despondently.

"The disease called love," Harley said cheerily.

Leigh stared, then swallowed hard. His throat felt parched. Too dry to speak. He tried to formulate a sentence. His mouth even opened. But all that emerged was a croaking sound. Like a woodland frog.

Harley chuckled and slapped his knee. "Hit the nail on the head, did I? Well, I hope it turns out better for you than it did for me. Have you wooed the girl? Sent gifts? Flowers? That sort of thing?"

"You've rather beaten me to the punch there."

"Suppose I have. Sorry, old chap," Harley replied, not sounding sorry at all. "Well, I did have high hopes, you know. She's a clever girl. Not the usual style, but pleasant to look at. Dashed nuisance, I shall have to go looking again."

"She's a damned sight more than pleasant to look at," Leigh growled.

Harley put up his hands. "There, there. Wasn't trying to disparage the lady. Now, am I to assume by your long countenance that you are out of her favor?"

"Decidedly out."

"Does she enjoy the gifts I've sent round? Flowers, bonbons, that sort of thing? You might do something in the same vein."

Leigh thought. "No, I don't think she did, really." The thought was somewhat cheering.

Harley scratched his chin. "Doesn't care for flowers or chocolates. What of words? Have you tried to woo her? Written letters? Sonnets, poems, that sort of thing?"

Leigh narrowed his eyes. "Don't tell me you've written her sonnets, Harley."

"No, no. Not yet." Harley smirked. "Well, think, man! You have a reputation as a savvy fellow. You have been by her side more than I have. Surely you know the girl better than I do."

Leigh considered what Harley had just said. "I do know her better, don't I?"

And just what did he know? Miss Marigold Spencer *was* clever. Practical, too. And unlike every young lady of the *ton* that Leigh had ever met, Miss Spencer did not view hard work as beneath her. What had she called herself today? A bluestocking.

He straightened up on the bench. "I know where I must go."

"Excellent." Harley beamed.

Perhaps he was not such a bad chap after all.

Leigh shifted awkwardly on the bench. "Uh, as for all the effort you have expended..."

"Think nothing of it," Harley said. He sighed, and for the first time, his face fell a little. "Though I must marry this Season, you know. The pater demands it."

"Cut off without a penny else?"

"Right on the mark," Harley said woefully.

"And what of the girl you loved? Is she really so inconstant? So out of reach?" Leigh asked carefully. "Otherwise, why not pursue her instead? Make a go of it?" He had a thought. "Or is she an opera dancer or something of the sort? I suppose your father would not be keen on that."

"No, no, nothing like that. She's a proper young lady. At least, she would fool anyone." Harley looked down at his hands. "But I'm afraid that ship has sailed. Might have been a misunderstanding at first, but now I've heard she's gone off with the very worst of fellows. She'll be in a heap of trouble soon. And there's nothing I can do, even if I wished to, for she won't speak to me."

"I'm sorry," Leigh said. He thought of losing Marigold to another man—an unworthy one. Well, Harley was not as unworthy as he had thought. But she would not be marrying Harley. Miss Spencer was *his*. He would make sure of that.

"Never fear. Plenty of fish in the sea and all that," Harley said, trying to smile. "I'm sure I can find a reasonably intelligent young woman who will be pleased to become a marchioness."

"I have no doubt," Leigh said, rising to his feet. "Well, thank you, Harley. Damned gracious of you."

"Good luck," Harley said solemnly. He grinned. "With Miss Spencer, I suspect you'll need it."

Chapter Nineteen

M arigold Spencer had never looked forward to a change of
scene more than she did that day.

She took John the footman's proffered hand and
stepped out of Lady Fulford's carriage. Lately, John had been insisting
upon walking her round to the back of the church. Apparently, he and
the carriage driver had witnessed a few muggings and knifings and
decided it was not even safe for Marigold to walk that far alone. She
had not bothered to protest.

"Here we are. I shall be about four or five hours today," Marigold
said, trying for her usual cheerful tone as she stepped up to the door of
the dispensary.

As she walked inside, the familiar smell of ointments and tinctures
filled her nostrils, and she was hit with a roar of noise. Another busy
day. Good. She needed something to take her mind off things. The
prospect of a frenzied day of work without any breaks was welcome.

She stepped farther into the waiting room and froze.

"What the bloody hell are you doing here?"

Lord Leigh looked up from the desk which he had been using as a
surface upon which to fold freshly laundered linens.

"I should think that was obvious," he said, raising his eyebrows.

"I'm folding. And goodness me, do young ladies of your acquaintance generally use such strong language?"

"No," Marigold admitted. Though she had certainly used more of it when she worked below stairs. She glanced at the little old lady sitting behind her who was looking up at her with a disapproving expression. "I beg your pardon, Mrs. Brown. I don't know what came over me."

The elderly woman nodded and returned her gaze to the newspaper she was holding. Mrs. Brown's son must be in for another consultation about his rheumatism. He was a regular patient of Dr. Bannerjee's.

She walked up to the desk, noting the imprecision with which the linens were being folded. "You are doing a terrible job."

"Thank you, that is most encouraging," Lord Leigh said mildly. "Do you always speak to the new orderlies in such an encouraging way?"

"We already have an orderly," Marigold said, beginning to lose her temper. "A very competent one."

"I am sure he is a genius with laundry, too," Lord Leigh said cheerily. "Perhaps he can give me a few pointers."

"We cannot afford another orderly," Marigold hissed. She had overheard Maggie and Dr. Bannerjee discussing the need for more help just the other day.

"Oh, I'm an excellent bargain."

Marigold narrowed her eyes. "How excellent?"

Leigh glanced behind her. "Oh, there you are, Miss Barry. I was just introducing myself to Miss Spencer. Apparently, she does not believe you required an additional orderly."

Maggie looked up from the file she had been reading as she walked. "Not need another orderly? What's that, Miss Spencer? Surely you could see we were desperate for more help."

"Yes, of course, Maggie. That's not what I meant." She glared at Lord Leigh and lowered her voice. "You did not tell her we were already acquainted?"

"When I took the job? No, I saw no reason to mention that," Lord Leigh said innocently.

"Besides," Maggie said, walking over to the second desk and

putting down the file. "Mr. Blakeley was so keen to be of assistance that he offered us his services for free."

Marigold clenched her jaw as Lord Leigh smirked. "An excellent bargain indeed."

"Dr. Bannerjee certainly thought so," Maggie agreed. She looked at Leigh appraisingly, then down at the linens. "I suppose we shall see if he is competent in other areas. Laundry folding is clearly not his forte."

It was Marigold's turn to smirk. "It certainly is not."

"Now that you have arrived, perhaps you might help me," Maggie said, opening a drawer of her desk and beginning to fish around for another file.

"Of course! Anything," Marigold said, smiling with false sweetness at Lord Leigh.

"Wonderful. Please show Mr. Blakeley around. Mrs. Sharp started to give him the grand tour but was called away to see to some sutures. Mrs. Larson's little boy fell off the roof of their necessary and split his leg open."

"Tommy? Oh dear. I do hope he will be all right," Marigold exclaimed. Mrs. Larson had at least a dozen children. Marigold had not managed to learn all their names, but Tommy had impressed her with his chubby cheeks and shy manners.

"I'm sure he will be just fine. He should learn not to climb so high," Maggie replied tartly.

"I have finished up the laundry and am ready to begin when you are, Miss Spencer," Lord Leigh chirped. "Ready and eager." He bounced up and down on the heels of his feet with an earnestness Marigold found simultaneously aggravating and amusing. Perhaps because it reminded her a little of herself. Was this how she had appeared to Maggie?

"Delightful," Marigold muttered, glaring at him. "Very well, please follow me."

"Anything you say, my dear Miss Spencer. You have only to command, and I shall obey."

Marigold rolled her eyes, but she found herself sneaking another glance at Lord Leigh as they stepped into the hallway. He had dressed down for his visit, showing an impressive measure of common sense. In this respect, he looked very ordinary, wearing plain brown trousers, a white shirt which looked deceptively homespun, and a simple charcoal-colored wool coat. Even his necktie was a plain piece of linen, not silk, and was simply tied.

His trousers were well fitted. As was his thin white shirt. They did not leave much to the imagination. Marigold swallowed as she recalled the feel of that hard, muscled chest pressed up against her hand.

She felt strangely disarmed by Lord Leigh's change of clothing. He looked even more the street-urchin scoundrel, as if he had stepped right from conducting shady deals and doing dark deeds in the streets of Seven Dials. There was nothing of the aristocratic gentleman left of him. Even his jaw was faintly stubbled with dark hairs, as if he had purposely left it unshaven. He smoldered with danger, those high cheekbones sharp as daggers, the hint of a grin on his roguish mouth.

Looking at him made Marigold hungry in a gnawing, aching way that she now knew was pure desire. Every nerve in her body was tingling from his nearness.

"Would you like me to offer your compliments to my valet?" Lord Leigh inquired, cocking his head.

"What?"

"I noticed you inspecting my cravat. Clearly you appreciate this simpler style."

"Nonsense, I was simply... surprised. I thought you enjoyed dressing like a peacock." That was unfair. Lord Leigh did not play the dandy. "I suppose you simply had these clothes lying about, waiting for an opportunity like this," Marigold snapped.

He was silent for a while. "I keep a wide variety of clothing on hand. You never know when they will be useful," he said finally. "You may recall that I do not generally mingle amongst the *ton*. It may also surprise you that, in fact, this is a more natural setting for me than a ballroom."

Marigold stared. Could he be telling the truth? Was Lord Leigh more at home here than she was?

"I have attended such events only for your sake," he reminded her.

She frowned. "In that case, why are you here?"

"That, too, is for your sake," he replied, his voice gentle. His gaze was steady. Marigold found herself looking away first.

"This is the room where patients may convalesce," she said, returning to her task. She gestured to a closed door. "We will not disturb them now. Most will be resting. But Mrs. Sharp or Mrs. Tuck checks on them hourly, and Maggie and Dr. Bannerjee make their rounds every hour or two."

"Is Miss Barry also a physician then? I was not sure I should ask."

"She is not, but she performs a great number of medical duties here at the dispensary," Marigold said primly. The question irked her. She had still not pinpointed the precise source of all Maggie's infinite knowledge. Surely it could not all have come from books. "She is more akin to a surgeon."

"I see," Lord Leigh said. "Well, she seems like a very capable woman."

"She most certainly is." They moved farther down the hall. She paused outside the large storage room and frowned. "I suppose I should show you where to find everything. Or did Mrs. Sharp already take you through the organization of our supplies?"

From the corner of her eye, she saw him shake his head. "She did not. I believe she was about to when she was called away."

"Very well." Marigold sighed. She pushed the door open. "Come inside. Close the door behind you. Patients are never permitted in the storage room. If you find one in here, ask them to leave and..."

"Count the supplies?" Lord Leigh quipped.

"That would probably be wise," Marigold admitted. "Though I think theft is a rare occurrence. Most of the neighborhood values the work we do here, and you'll find patients generally very respectful."

"Still, it's easy to forget to be respectful when one has an empty belly," he said quietly from behind her as she walked in.

"Yes, that's very true," Marigold said, surprised at his astuteness. "But Maggie is incredible at sensing who is in need of a meal. We have spare food in the back that she offers, or if nothing is available, there is a charity kitchen around the corner that she will often walk them over to."

She glanced about the little room, preparing to point out the necessities, then narrowed her eyes.

"Oh, drat," she exclaimed in annoyance. Someone had left a mess. A liniment bottle had been left too close to the edge of its shelf. Someone must have bumped it without noticing, and the bottle had tipped, leaking its contents down the rack and onto the floor. "I shall have to clean this up."

She reached for a towel from the pile on one of the shelves.

"Here, let me," Lord Leigh said.

"No, it is all right," she said crossly. She was being cold to him, she knew. But she could not help still feeling angry from their last encounter. He had lied so boldly to Miss Peel. As if she was his, by right, to claim.

Not that the thought of Lord Leigh claiming her was entirely repulsive...

She began to crouch down to mop up the spill but stepped a little too closely to where the liniment coated the floor. Her foot slipped, and she let out a little squeak, her arms beginning to flail.

Arms shot out from behind her, strong hands grasped her firmly by the waist, keeping her from tumbling forward onto the floor. The momentum pulled her backwards, her body lining up flush against Lord Leigh's torso. Marigold felt a burst of hot awareness as she pressed against him, the places where his hands touched her waist igniting with sensation, as if there was no fabric separating skin from skin at all.

She took a small step back from the puddle of ointment on the floor, but that was a mistake. Her bottom pressed up firmly against the front of his trousers, and she felt the unmistakable sign of his arousal, that hard rod lining up between her buttocks like an arrow trying to find its way home on an archery target. She heard his sharp intake of breath, then felt its warmth against the sensitive skin of her neck.

His hands were still on her waist, nestling over the swelling curves of her hips.

A more modest young woman would surely have stepped away immediately, overcome with embarrassment. Instead, Marigold found herself rolling her hips against him, ever so slightly.

He let out a pained groan, and then before she could do more than gasp, he moved his hands and was whirling her around to face him.

"What are you doing?" he asked, his voice low and rough.

"I... don't know," she gasped.

He looked at her hard. "Perhaps you don't. But you are driving me wild, so I ask you to stop. Please."

She gazed back, knowing she should do as he asked.

But she did not want to.

"I thought this was what you wanted," she whispered, raising her hand to his neck and trailing her fingers over the sensitive flesh of his nape.

He let out a guttural sound, almost like a growl, and she lifted her chin, lips already parting. Later, she could not say whose lips found whose first, though she had intended to initiate the kiss.

His hands were still on her waist. Now they began to push her across the room, his lips never once breaking from hers as he moved her until she felt her back hit the storage room wall.

She opened her mouth to ask what he was doing and abruptly found his hands clasping hers, lifting her arms, pinning them over her head as he splayed her against the wall and pressed his body against hers, letting her feel his desire. A jolt like lightning went through her as they connected, and she felt her legs spreading for him. Even through the dress, the trousers, their bodies knew what they wanted and were desperate for it.

They fit together so well, she thought dimly. Like interlocking puzzle pieces. If it was like this standing up fully clothed, how much better would it be lying down in a bed, naked bodies intertwined?

His mouth was urgent, parting her lips and filling her with his tongue. She let out a little moan, and he must have worried he was hurting her, for he lowered her hands, letting them fall onto his shoulders.

And then his own moved down her body, strong hands caressing her hips through her dress before moving up to cup her breasts, squeezing gently. Marigold felt herself becoming a blaze of liquid fire. Her nipples hardened under his hands, straining against his palms.

This was torture for them both, and now was not the time or place. She had to stop it. Now.

"Leigh," she said breathlessly, breaking her lips away from his. "We must stop this."

At once, his hands fell away, and he took a step backwards. She felt a sense of loss as his body left hers but straightened up, smoothing down her dress.

"Very well," he said. "As you wish."

She studied him, trying to regain her composure from earlier. "Why are you here? Really?"

"I wanted to be where you were," he said simply.

It sounded remarkably like the truth.

She bit her lip. "You cannot waste Maggie's time, waste Dr. Bannerjee's time, simply because you wished to see me."

"I am not," he said, setting his jaw stubbornly. "I also wish to help. Can I not be useful as you are?"

"I..." she opened her mouth. The door burst open.

"Ah, there you are, Miss Spencer, Mr. Blakeley." Mrs. Sharp stood in the door frame.

"Yes, I was just cleaning up a spill," Marigold said, hurrying forward and picking up the towel again.

"We need you, Mr. Blakeley," Mrs. Sharp said briskly, ignoring Marigold. "We need strong arms. A man has just been brought in. Stab wound from the look of it. While out at the pub, of course. His wife and son managed to get him here, but he collapsed in the waiting room. Can you help?"

"Certainly," Lord Leigh said, moving quickly toward her. He was already starting to shuck off his jacket as he left the room. Marigold watched them go, then turned back to the puddle.

He had wanted to see her. He wanted to help. The warm glow she had felt at the touch of his hands had not dissipated. No, if anything, it had grown.

Well, let us see how the afternoon goes, she told herself. But she could not stop smiling as she wiped up the liniment.

A few hours later, Leigh felt things were going very well. He was down to his shirtsleeves, had been splattered with a few unmentionable liquids, and was sweaty and probably smelled quite unappealing. He took a subtle sniff near the region of his armpit and got a whiff of strong ointment up his nose for the trouble.

He glanced across the room at where Miss Spencer was standing with a look of determination, holding a patient's leg in place while Dr. Bannerjee dabbed on an herbal tincture of his own creation. Damp strands of curly hair fell over her face, she was flushed and perspiring, and her dress had clearly seen better times.

Leigh grinned. Even so, she was perfect. He was glad he had come.

"Thank you, Miss Marigold. I think that will do," Dr. Bannerjee announced. He looked down at his patient. "Now you will lie here a little while, allow the tincture to permeate the wound, and then we will bandage you up."

Miss Spencer had released the patient's leg and was coming around the table.

"You look very weary, Miss Marigold," Dr. Bannerjee noted. "Go and have a little rest. Please do not forget to wash your hands."

Leigh watched her smile. "Of course. I believe I will do that. Just a very quick one. I'll be back in a few minutes."

She noticed him standing in the doorway. "How did it go with the man who collapsed in the waiting room?"

"Maggie made quick work of him," Leigh replied. "I was quite impressed. He was no match for her."

Miss Spencer looked amused. "You make it sound like a battle."

"Considering how foxed he was and how hard I had to work to hold him down, it was surprisingly similar, but he didn't touch Maggie. I saw to that all right." He grinned down at her. He was tired. Part of him wanted to go home, have a hot meal, a hot bath, and sleep. And the other part wanted to stay right here, near her, until she finally relented and went home for the night as well.

"You look happy," she observed. "The work seems to suit you."

"As it does you," he replied. "And as do you."

"You really came here just for me?"

"Would you have preferred more flowers?"

"Heavens, no!" She wrinkled her nose. "Poor Lady Fulford's drawing room is already full enough."

Leigh grinned more broadly. "Good. I didn't think that would be the way."

"The way to what?" she said sharply.

"The way to... well, to woo you, Miss Spencer."

Her eyes widened. "Is that what you are trying to do?"

He nodded, his expression becoming solemn. "I should begin properly with the apology I know I owe you. I ought not to have said what I did in front of Miss Peel, nor drop Harley's name, either. I was brash and rude. I am sorry."

He saw her eyes flicker, then she said, "I see. Well, thank you."

"I'd like to come back here, you know," he said, lowering his voice as they walked down the hall, passing Mrs. Tuck. "Like I've promised."

"Surely you must keep your promise."

"Yes, but is that all right with you?" he asked a little hesitantly.

She paused. "You did not think to ask beforehand."

"That is true," he admitted. "I should have done so. I suppose I was afraid you would say no."

"You truly like the work? You wish to return?"

"I like both," he said honestly. "I like the work, and I like working with you."

She studied him before resuming her pace. "Yes, it has been rather pleasant, hasn't it?"

"Will you be here tomorrow?" Leigh asked, already impatient to see her again and not simply in the tedious setting of a drawing room.

She shook her head. "I promised Lady Fulford only three times a week." She smiled up at him, her face suddenly impish. "But I am planning to push that to four."

"If you married me," he said quietly, meeting her gaze, "you could come as often as you liked. Your life would be your own. It would be your decision to make. You would not have to bargain with a guardian or chaperone."

"That would be... nice," she said carefully.

"I suppose Harley offered the same."

They were interrupted by Maggie approaching. She did not look well pleased.

"Mr. Blakeley, there is a man here who says he is your valet."

"My valet?"

"Yes, he says he has an urgent message for you. Kindly refrain from having your servants, no matter how many they may be, from visiting you when you are volunteering your time, if you please."

"Of course," Leigh said quickly. "It won't happen again. It must be very urgent indeed for him to have come here." He frowned, wondering if the message was about what he had been waiting for.

He turned to Miss Spencer as Maggie walked away huffily. "It seems I must go. But I want to see you again. Soon." He grabbed her hand, raised it to his lips. "You have no idea how much."

He took pleasure in watching her color and bite her lip. "That would not be... unobjectionable," she agreed.

"Good. Keep an eye out." And then he winked and strode away.

An idea had struck him. The perfect idea. No flowers, no chocolates. No, he would make a grand gesture. One which would be sure to win Miss Spencer's affections once and for all.

Chapter Twenty

"Miss Marigold?" Dr. Bannerjee popped his head into the storage room where Marigold was putting away the last of some bottles. "I know you were about to leave," he began, sounding apologetic. "But I wonder if you might assist me with something before you go?"

"Of course. Anything. What is it that you require?"

Marigold had rarely seen the physician look hesitant, but now he did. "There is a patient in one of the rooms in the back. Her spirits are very low. I wonder if you might go and speak with her before you leave?"

"Certainly. I will go straightaway." Marigold tucked the last bottle onto the shelf and brushed out her skirt.

"She is an... unusual patient," Dr. Bannerjee said. "Maggie thought perhaps you would be the right person to speak with her."

Marigold's eyebrows went up. "I see. Well, I can certainly try."

Dr. Bannerjee led the way down the hallway. "She is a very young woman," he said in a low voice, over his shoulder. "And she is in a bad situation. Yes, very bad."

"Oh dear. I am sorry to hear that. I will certainly try to encourage her if I can."

"Yes." Dr. Bannerjee seemed about to say more but stopped himself. "She would not tell us everything, but hopefully, you will get her to share more freely."

"I hope so." Marigold pushed open the door to the last little room at the end of the hall. There was a pallet in the room and a small cupboard. Maggie and Dr. Bannerjee sometimes took turns resting in the room when they stayed overnight.

There was a girl lying on the pallet as she entered. The girl's face was turned to the wall.

Her hair was long, dark, and disheveled. She wore a very pretty dress of a fine, rich muslin material, gray with embroidered pink flowers. It was not the sort of thing one usually saw among the inhabitants of Seven Dials. Marigold was reminded of the finely dressed, dark-haired woman who had come in a few days before. This girl was younger, however. She was more on the slender side, too.

Marigold crouched down next to the little bed. "Miss? Dr. Bannerjee asked me to come and speak with you."

"Go away." The girl's voice was muffled against the wall, but even so, there was something familiar about it.

Marigold stared at the girl's prone form. She had not even thought to ask Dr. Bannerjee if the young woman was injured in some way.

"My name is Marigold," she began. "Marigold Spencer. If you are in some kind of trouble, you have come to the right place..."

The girl shifted on the bed. "Miss Spencer?"

"Yes, that is right," Marigold replied. "Perhaps Dr. Bannerjee mentioned me..."

"Miss Spencer!" The girl began to roll over, then let out a sharp yelp of pain.

As Marigold took her in, she could see why she had done so. The girl's right arm was clearly broken. Dr. Bannerjee must have seen to it beforehand, for it was wrapped tightly and in a sling.

This was not the extent of the girl's injuries. The young woman's face was bruised and puffy. Her lower lip was cut, and Marigold could see dried blood.

But that was not the most shocking thing of all.

"Miss Peel!"

Miss Victoria Peel gazed up at her with a dull expression. "Have you come to laugh at me, Miss Spencer? I suppose you never expected to find me here."

"Of course not," Marigold said. "And no, I did not expect it. But that does not mean you should not stay. What on earth has happened to you, Miss Peel?"

The girl stared back at her with hollow wide eyes. "I missed my courses," she said slowly. "My mother found out and told my father."

Marigold felt a sick feeling growing in the pit of her stomach. "And they... did this to you?"

She had seen abused women and children before, even in her short time working at the dispensary. It was a horror all its own. But she had never seen the effects on someone she actually knew.

Miss Peel turned her head so that she might look at the wall. "My father."

"Oh, Miss Peel, I am so very sorry," Marigold said softly. She reached out a hand, then remembered Miss Peel's broken arm. "You did not deserve this. Any of it."

Miss Peel turned her head back. "Don't I?" She gave a bitter laugh. "I am quite sure I do."

"Nonsense," Marigold whispered. "You made a mistake, that is all."

The girl laughed again, her voice shrill. "The worst mistake of my life, yes."

"Still, no matter how bad the mistake, they are your parents. They should not have treated you so," Marigold said stubbornly. She hesitated a moment. "Shall we contact someone for you? The... father perhaps?"

"The man who got me into this mess, you mean? I shouldn't call him the father," Miss Peel said. She shook her head slowly. "No. He won't help. He can't."

"Surely he would if he knew the trouble you were in," Marigold insisted. "If he could see you now..."

"No," Miss Peel interrupted. "You see, he is already a father. He is married." She turned her head away again. "And besides, I have no wish to be seen. By anyone."

"Oh, Miss Peel," Marigold murmured. "What will you do now?"

"I cannot go home. They've cast me out. I suppose I will walk the streets," Miss Peel said, her voice brittle and wry.

"You cannot be serious," Marigold said in horror. "There must be some safe place you can go. Your cousin, Miss Compton—could you not go to her home? Tell her what has occurred? You seem very close."

Miss Peel turned her head, and Marigold saw she was smiling faintly. "My cousin? You think she would help me?"

"Wouldn't she?"

"Her father is my father's brother. Where do you think she learned her cruel little tricks from in the first place?" Miss Peel asked, her voice dry.

"Oh." Marigold was still. "Well, then..."

"No, there is nowhere. I have no other friends. None who would take me in. Not like this. With child, bruised, battered? I think not. They would be too embarrassed. Afraid my shame would become their shame."

Marigold was thinking quickly. "Then you must come home with me. To Lady Fulford's."

Miss Peel seemed intrigued. At least, she did not protest immediately. "Do you offer that option to all your patients?"

"This is different," Marigold said. "I know you."

"Do you? I was perfectly horrid to you, and yet you would do this for me?" Miss Peel studied her closely.

"You were horrid," Marigold said frankly. "But I would not wish this on my worst enemy. Please, let me help you."

Miss Peel stared up at the ceiling. "Everything hurts. Perhaps I might just lie here. For a few days. Or weeks."

"The pain must be very bad. But your arm will heal quickly. The pain will not be so terrible in a few days, I promise." She wondered if Maggie and Dr. Bannerjee intended to let Miss Peel remain in the convalescent room. "I can certainly ask if you may stay here, if that is truly what you wish." She hesitated. "Usually only the very ill are allowed to stay. Because they cannot be moved."

"There is no room for me at the inn, is what you mean to say?" Miss Peel smiled darkly. "I understand."

"Miss Peel, you simply must let me take you home," Marigold

insisted. She could not leave the girl. The threat Miss Peel had made of turning to the streets in her desperation seemed all too real.

"What makes you think Lady Fulford would even allow me into her home? Do you know what they say about girls like me, Miss Spencer? You have only been amongst the *ton* a very short time. Have you seen many unwed young ladies with child at the functions you have attended? Have you?"

"I have not," Marigold admitted.

"No, because should anything so dire as this befall a blue-blooded young lady, she would be whisked off to the country to convalesce in secrecy. Then the child would be taken away, of course. But my parents have not even done me that courtesy."

"Would that be your preference? To go somewhere far away? To have the child given to another family?" Marigold asked quietly.

"It does sound remarkably appealing at the moment. To be somewhere far away from London where no one knows my name. Where I am not in disgrace. But it is not an option. I cannot go home. I have told you. My father would kill me if I appeared on his doorstep again." She gave a short, choked laugh. "And no. It may surprise you, Miss Spencer, but I will not give away my child. Though I am quite sure I shall make an absolutely wretched mother, I want this baby. It is all I have left."

Marigold felt a stir of rage against Miss Peel's father. No matter how angry he must have been, how concerned for his own reputation, it did not excuse the cowardice the man had shown in beating a frail young woman—in hurting his own daughter like this.

"You are better off without them if that is how they truly feel," Marigold said quietly. "Excuse me a moment. I must consult with Dr. Bannerjee."

She went quickly to the door, thinking hard.

When she stepped into the hall, she found Maggie was already there waiting. Rarely did Maggie allow herself the indulgence of smoking her pipe inside. It was asking for a fire, and if the patients saw her doing it, they would think they were free to do so as well. But most of the patients had gone home. The dispensary was much quieter now.

Maggie lifted the pipe from her mouth. "She's a little rich girl, isn't she? Do you know her?"

"I do," Marigold said. "We are not friends, but we have met once or twice."

Maggie gave her a sardonic look. "Not friends, eh? Why am I not surprised?" She took a puff from the pipe. "Well, she's in a rotten situation. Don't suppose the father can help?"

"The baby's father?" Marigold shook her head. "It does not sound like it. Is she very far along? I could not even tell..."

"It's still early. I suppose her parents found out?" When Marigold nodded, Maggie let out a low whistle. "Splendid people, they must be. They did that to her?"

"Yes. And now she has nowhere else to go," Marigold said, her voice low. "She asked if she could stay here."

She saw sympathy in Maggie's eyes, but the short, gray-haired woman shook her head. "Ordinarily, yes, but not tonight. We are full up. And Arpan needs a room in which to rest. He plans to stay all night." She nodded toward the little room. "She must have someone. Surely in her privileged circle there is someone who can take her in..."

"She says there is no one," Marigold said miserably. "How can this be, Maggie? There are so many girls in similar states. And nowhere for them to go but to kind friends or family. There must be infinitely more turned out, who we never see at all."

"Infinitely," Maggie agreed, taking another puff. "I've lost track of how many women and girls I've seen in desperate straits."

"How is it that there is no place for them?" Marigold asked desperately. "There are so many charities, some purport to help women..."

Maggie's lips twisted. "Oh, yes, if you're a pure woman, that is. Or a repentant prostitute. A young unwed girl? One from a good home? They would simply send her back."

"Have you seen the state of her?" Marigold exclaimed. "No one could call her home 'good.'" She came to a decision. "Very well. I will take her home with me. Whether she likes it or not."

Maggie eyed her appraisingly. "Good for you. And you think your patroness will let her stay?"

"She'll have to," said Marigold resolutely. "She's a kindhearted woman. She'll simply have to."

Another thought was beginning to form in her mind. The seed of an idea. But it was so preposterous, so far-fetched. She would have to consider it further when there was more time.

Running footsteps filled the hall.

It was the other orderly, Nick. Marigold had not realized he was still here.

"A messenger for you, Miss Spencer," he said, panting a little. "From your Lady Fulford."

Maggie rolled her eyes. "Not you, too, Miss Spencer."

"It won't become a habit, I assure you. How very odd. She must know I will be returning home soon."

She followed Nick back to the waiting room where she saw one of Lady Fulford's other footmen standing.

"Miss Spencer," he said, smiling. "I have some very good news."

The carriage jostled and lurched as it rolled over a bump in the road, and Miss Peel let out a little cry of pain. Marigold glanced at her sympathetically. The girl had finally been persuaded to come home with Marigold. She had been told there was no other option. Marigold was not about to let Miss Peel go out into the street, no matter how much she protested.

Though Marigold was not expecting a precisely warm reception, she did not believe Lady Fulford would turn Miss Peel away. Not when she saw her arm—and the rest of her.

As for the messenger, it seemed one could never have enough babies in a single day. For Laurel had given birth to a little son!

Marigold could still hardly believe it. As she had hoped to be present for the birth, her initial reaction had been deep disappointment.

Laurel had been brought to bed, and Marigold had not been there to help. She had been miles away in London, assisting strangers instead of her own sister and attending balls and the theater. Part of her felt furious and frustrated at herself for not insisting she remain at Blakeley Manor.

But the important thing was that mother and child were healthy. Though Laurel had been brought to bed much earlier than anticipated, by at least two months by Marigold's calculations, the delivery had gone smoothly.

The messenger Lady Fulford had sent did not have a great deal of information, but Marigold had been given to understand that the baby was very small but thriving.

She glanced across the darkened carriage where Miss Peel slouched in the corner. The dark-haired girl's eyes were closed. She had fallen asleep. Poor Miss Peel. Marigold had not yet told her about Laurel and Dare's new addition. She would find out soon enough when they arrived at Lady Fulford's, for Marigold knew Lady Fulford would not be able to keep such good news to herself.

She bit her lip, thinking of how hearing the news would make Miss Peel feel. Perhaps for tonight, she might leave out part of Miss Peel's situation and share it with Lady Fulford the next day. Surely seeing Miss Peel's injuries would suffice, and Lady Fulford would wish nothing more than to sweep the young woman off to a hot bath and a clean bed. Then Marigold could speak to Lady Fulford privately. Yes, that would be more discreet and, hopefully, more comfortable for Miss Peel as well.

With a weary sigh, she leaned her head against the cool window. A baby boy. Oh, she could hardly believe it. She felt a smile crossing her face despite her fatigue. What a wonderful thing for Dare and Laurel. And what a relief after the pain they had already been through from their loss last autumn.

Marigold said a silent fervent prayer for the new baby's health.

Wren and Briar had little Percy. What would Laurel and Dare name this new little fellow, she wondered?

The warm glow she had felt, triggered by Lord Leigh's touch, had intensified somehow. She thought of Laurel's baby, then she thought of Leigh, and she knew both were matters which deeply involved her heart.

Now this was dangerous territory indeed. Lord Leigh had

encroached upon Marigold's very heart. He had charmed, he had seduced, and he had nearly succeeded. She had been seduced by a scoundrel and was very much afraid of what that meant.

Lord Leigh truly seemed to want this marriage. To want her to accept him.

And Marigold was incredibly tempted to do just that.

But there was one very large, rather looming problem.

To marry Leigh would mean risking all. It would not be like with Lord Harley, where her heart could remain safely locked away, and where she could continue in many ways as things were now, her life remaining relatively unchanged.

With Leigh, everything would change. She could not see marrying him without opening her heart to him. And once she had done that, well, she would be vulnerable. Exposed. What pain he could potentially cause her should he decide he had made a terrible mistake.

She glanced across at the sleeping Miss Peel. The girl was just one example of what happened when a woman put her heart on the line for a man.

Oh, Leigh was nothing like the man Miss Peel had trusted, clearly. He was offering Marigold honorable marriage. The protection of his name. His intentions were good.

But even the best intentions could go terribly astray. If he cared for her but did not love her... If he promised to be faithful but could not keep that promise... If he should regret the marriage in the end, Marigold knew she would be devastated.

Lord Harley promised nothing. Offered nothing but his hand.

But in her heart, Marigold knew she could not accept Lord Harley, even though part of her wished she could.

The carriage rolled up before Lady Fulford's stately Mayfair townhouse, and Marigold slowly stepped out.

She caught the footman by the arm before he could step in to rouse Miss Peel. "Let her sleep a little while longer, please, John. Goodness knows, she needs it."

She left the footman standing guard over Miss Peel and slipped into the house to speak to Lady Fulford.

As Lady Fulford's butler swept off to inform his mistress of

Marigold's return, she stood by the table in the foyer, pulling off her gloves. Looking down at the table, she saw a note with her name on it and, picking it up, tore open the paper.

It was written in a masculine hand. "My dear Miss Spencer..." She scanned the contents quickly.

Lord Harley was withdrawing his offer of marriage. He was very eloquent and careful to give no offense—but also provided no real reason why. Still, Marigold believed she could hazard a guess.

Tucking the missive into her reticule, she turned to tell Lady Fulford of their new houseguest as that illustrious lady came down the stairs.

Chapter Twenty-One

S tanding in the shadows of a narrow alley, Leigh opened up the folded slip of paper Carlotta had passed him to see an address. The street was familiar though not the building.

"Have you met with Bryce?" she demanded, watching his face.

"No, not yet," he admitted.

"So, I am the first." When she had approached him earlier at the meeting place, Leigh had thought she looked dejected. Now triumph shone on her face. "I told you," she gloated. "I have brought you what you needed as promised."

"You have," Leigh agreed. "And for that, I am grateful."

"How grateful?" She smiled coyly, and he found himself smiling back. She was not his type of woman, and he was fairly certain that he was not her type of man. But she was charming in her way. Furthermore, she was brave and bold. Two qualities Leigh always appreciated in women.

"Very," he said, grinning. He fished in his pocket. "This is part of what you requested. I did not think you would wish to carry the entire amount on your person. If you go to my man of business tomorrow, he can see that you are provided with the rest." He glanced about. "Do you have anyone accompanying you? For protection, I mean."

The street was dark. And while she was dressed more discreetly tonight in a black silk cape with the hood pulled up over her ebony hair, Leigh felt apprehensive for her sake. She may have left the fine white ermine at home, but she was still a striking woman. It was easy to tell, if one looked closely, that her clothing was well-made and expensive. And now she would be carrying hundreds of pounds on her as well. She was too easy a target.

When she shook her head, Leigh frowned.

"Perhaps I might accompany you home," he suggested. He put up his hands quickly before she could get the wrong idea. "Merely as a bodyguard, nothing more."

She shook her head. "That is very kind. Truly. I thank you. But I have another... appointment. One in which discretion is valued."

"I see," Leigh replied. "Well, if you are certain..." He was still not comfortable with her going off alone. He considered following her at a distance. He wondered if she would notice.

She smiled slightly. "I will be all right on my own. I am more familiar with this neighborhood than you may realize, my lord." She gestured behind her at the street lined with gin shops and slum tenements. "I grew up on a street much like this one."

Leigh was not entirely surprised by the news but raised his eyebrows. "I see. You have come a long way, it seems."

"I used to think so." The dark-haired woman stared at the street behind her. "Now I am not so sure. I used everything I had to help a man rise. And when I had done so, what did I have left? Nothing."

"You mean Bryce?" Leigh said softly.

She nodded. "Oh, I was not his first woman, of course. Nor did I expect to be his last. But I—" She paused, and her voice choked. "I helped him. I gave him all my aid, all my knowledge. I watched his so-called empire grow. And then, he became tired of me. Where once he had called me clever, now I was tiresome, irritating, clingy." She smiled bitterly. "I would not have cared if he had taken other women. If only he had shared some of what was, by rights, partly mine. Instead, I was left with nothing. No, *less* than nothing. In some ways, I am worse off than I was before." She bit her lip hard, and Leigh saw her face was white.

"It does seem... unfair," Leigh said carefully. "Carlotta, are you well? You seem..."

She looked at him, hard. "Oh, so you have noticed. What one man fails to observe, another man is not so blind to." She shrugged. "There is nothing wrong with me that may not be mended. Your money will help with that."

Leigh was confused. "I hope it buys you the life you want. The life you deserve," he said, and he meant it.

"It will help. It is a good start." She tried to smile. Her kohl-lined eyes were smudged, he saw. "What of you? You mean to pursue this man? It will not be easy."

"It will be much easier than you think," he said quietly. He held up the slip of paper. "This? This was the easy part. We—I—have spent years to get here."

Carlotta hesitated. "This man... he hurt your parents?"

Leigh nodded.

She dropped her voice to a whisper though no one was nearby. "He has not been in England long, but already it is known that he is a very bad man. You must know this. He will not be alone. He will be guarded. You will not go by yourself?"

Leigh smiled thinly. "I am not a particularly good man either, Carlotta."

"You are good," she said, tossing her head. "You are better than him. Believe me, I have spent enough time around worthless men to know."

"Maybe," Leigh replied. "But I think he will find he has met his match. Do not worry about me." He did not wish to boast, and he knew she would not understand his confidence. But he was not afraid of what he would find when he arrived at the address she had provided him. "I have been well trained, let us say," he finished.

She looked at him carefully. "Very well. I wish you the best. Will you go to this address soon?"

He nodded. "Very soon."

"Then I will listen to the streets. I hope to hear it said that he is dead, and you still live."

Leigh smiled a little. "I hope so, too."

208

Carlotta pulled out a small gold filigree timepiece and let out a gasp. "I must go. I shall be late."

"You are sure I cannot—" Leigh began.

"No, no. Goodnight, my lord. And good luck."

"To you as well," he murmured as she swept away, her slippers moving silently over the cobblestones. As he watched the slim, dark figure disappear into the night, he suddenly felt Carlotta must have quite the story to tell. He wondered if she had ever told it to anyone before.

For a few moments, he stood in the alley staring at the slip of paper in his hand. Then he crossed the street to where a group of beggars stood huddled around a fire in a grate and tossed the slip in.

As he watched the paper go up in flames, he knew he was nearing the end of the road.

It was tempting to go straight to the address. But he had promised Royal he would let him know before he did.

So in the end, he turned and walked up the street in the direction of home.

⸺ ⸺

When Leigh arrived back at the Blakeley townhouse, it was past his uncle's usual hour for suppertime. He prowled about until he located Royal in the library, his head buried in a book about ancient Italian villas, a cheroot dangling from one hand, a glass of whisky on the table beside him.

"Well?" his uncle asked, raising the cheroot to his lips with one hand and closing his book with the other. "I suppose you have heard the news?"

Leigh frowned. "I believe so..."

"About the child?"

"Child?"

Royal gestured to the table, on which lay an open letter. Leigh picked it up and read.

"Dare is a father," he exclaimed in wonder. "Is it possible?"

209

"I believe it is a daily occurrence around the world," Royal replied, evidently unimpressed by the miracle of birth.

"You are a great-uncle, twice over now," Leigh pointed out with a grin.

His uncle grimaced. "You need not rub it in."

"A second grandchild. A little boy. My mother must be over the moon," Leigh mused.

"A second grandchild your father will never have the opportunity to meet," Royal said quietly.

"True." Leigh folded the letter back up. "Still, it is a new life. A new Blakeley." The news had buoyed him in a way he could not describe. He felt oddly uplifted, as if he had drunk a glass of champagne very quickly.

"We have certainly had enough deaths in this family to last us a long time." Royal placed his book on the table.

"Perhaps this signals a new beginning." Leigh shoved his hands in his pockets, frowning. "Life and death. They balance one another, don't they? You can't have one without the other."

His uncle smiled slightly. "Thinking of Maat tonight, are we? Feeling tragically melancholic? Domesticity tends to bring that on for me, too."

"Perhaps a little, yes," Leigh admitted. When he was a child, his history-obsessed parents had told him of the Egyptian goddess, Maat, who weighed the hearts of the dead in the underworld. If a heart was heavier than the goddess's special feather of truth, it was decreed unworthy and given to the goddess Ammit to be devoured. If it was found to be equal in weight or lighter than Maat's feather, the deceased was believed to have led a virtuous life.

It was all bunk, of course. Leigh's heart was a great deal heavier than a feather. But tonight, he found himself thinking of the scales in terms of life and death. He had had so much to do with death for so very long.

"I believe I may wed soon," he announced.

There was silence in the room. Then, "And who is the happy bride-to-be?"

"You'll meet her soon if all goes well," Leigh said shortly. "Look, I've learned the address. I'll go tonight."

He felt his uncle's eyes. "So, thus the sudden interest in the balance of the scales."

"Yes." Leigh ran a hand over his face. "I want it over with. Done. Do you feel the same way?" He snuck a peek at the older man's face. Royal Blakeley looked contemplative.

"Babies and weddings instead of good old-fashioned vengeance, you mean? No, I don't believe I'm quite ready to hang up the saber yet," Royal answered.

"But our task is nearly complete," Leigh reminded him.

Royal nodded. "This one, yes. I'll find another. There will always be evil men who need killing." He smiled obliquely. "But you, my lad, you need not. No, I can see it in your eyes. When one is moved by the news of a newborn babe... Well, you're a lucky man, Leigh."

"Lucky? How?" If anything, he had expected his uncle to say he'd gone soft.

"You can change," his uncle said simply. "You *are* changing. You are ready for the next part of life. I am no longer capable–no, nor interested–in changing. Death has become a part of me."

He meant killing, but Leigh would not point this out.

He felt a strange thrill at his uncle's pronouncement. Was he changing? Could he change?

"I helped to save a man's life today," he said suddenly. "The woman I hope to make my wife–she was there."

"Was she now?" His uncle eyed him keenly. "She sounds like a capable lady. Helping you balance those scales already."

"She is. She cares about other people. She sees the world as a place to learn from, not simply stagnate in, like so many people we know."

"The world has taught you many lessons as well," his uncle said in a low voice.

"Of course," Leigh said hurriedly. "You have taught me well. I've traveled by your side, done more, seen more than most men do in a lifetime. I hope you do not think that..."

"No." His uncle lifted a hand. "Leigh, it is all right to go. To travel a new path. We have done what we set out to do."

"Nearly so." Leigh took a deep breath. "I'll go alone tonight, as I've said." But not before he paid a visit first.

"Yes. You've said." His uncle's face seemed troubled, then he sighed. "I trust you to complete the task but give me the address. In case."

"Very well." He told him. "There is somewhere I must go first. Something I must do. But by dawn, it will all be over."

"When we visit Blakeley Manor, we will have a gift for them they are not expecting," his uncle said, grinning like a tiger.

"Yes." Leigh felt a pang of discomfort. But was it a gift they would want?

"There was a second letter," his uncle declared abruptly. "I had your valet put it on your desk. I did not open it, but I believe it is from that man Bryce."

"He is a little too late," Leigh said, frowning. "I had the information from another source." He did not wish to think of Bryce. To do so was to think of how poorly the man had treated Carlotta. He was glad he had paid the woman handsomely for the information. She deserved her new beginning.

His uncle shrugged. "Ignore it then."

Leigh nodded. "I'll gather what I need, then be on my way. I'll see you in the morning."

"Happy hunting," his uncle said and raised his glass.

Chapter Twenty-Two

Marigold was having a perfectly wonderful dream.

She was back at Blakeley Manor and wandering the gardens at night with Leigh by her side. He was holding her hand and tugging her rather insistently. Then it began to rain—huge, heavy droplets soaking through the thin white summer dress she wore. She shrieked, and Leigh pulled off his coat and wrapped it around her shoulders, then kissed her on each eyelid. She tipped her face up to the rain and beamed. She felt happy and satisfied, as if she had eaten the most delicious meal in the world.

They ran, laughing like children, into the orangery. She turned to Leigh just as a flash of lightning lit up the glass building, and then his mouth was on hers, kissing her as if his life depended on it. She closed her eyes as he pulled her down onto the floor of the orangery, his hands caressing her everywhere. She had no spirit to resist...

Then there came a tapping on the glass of the orangery.

Marigold frowned in her sleep. A tapping?

The tapping continued. It was most insistent.

She opened her eyes. It was dark. She was in her room at Lady Fulford's house.

The tapping came again. She looked about, then stifled a scream.

There was a man at the window, silhouetted in the dark.

For a moment, she was certain she was about to be murdered in her bed. She began to think of ways to fight off the intruder. Most involved her hitting him with William Buchan's *Domestic Medicine*. It was lying on her bedside table and quite heavy.

Then she squinted in the dark. The man had pressed his face closer to the glass and raised a hand to his eyes. He was peeping! A brazen Peeping Tom.

The face came into focus.

"You cannot be serious," she muttered, flinging back the coverlet and sliding out of the bed. "Not a bloody second time."

She paused. This time she would be better prepared, she told herself, picking up a high-necked wrapper and tugging it on before continuing on her way to the window.

"You retire rather early, don't you?" Leigh asked, climbing into the room without even a greeting. "Hardly past supper."

"We supped hours ago," Marigold told him haughtily. In truth, she had been so tired after her long day at the dispensary that she had gone to bed even before Lady Fulford. Not that she was about to admit this.

Leigh was eyeing her wrapper with interest. "I say, what is that? I've never seen a woman wearing one before."

It took all Marigold had not to blush. Perhaps in her efforts at modesty she had overdone things a bit.

"As you have two sisters, I believe that is highly unlikely," she said, lifting her chin and pulling the wrapper tighter around her neck. "It is a dressing robe."

"A dressing robe? I do have two sisters, yes, but I have never seen something quite so..." Leigh's mouth snapped shut, apparently having noticed her facial expression. "Well, no matter." He grinned slyly. "I suppose Lady Fulford is rubbing off on you."

"Are you implying I have the habits of an old woman?" She caught Leigh looking down at the thick socks and warm woolen slippers she wore and felt a warm flush creeping up her neck.

"I suppose you didn't know I was coming," Leigh observed soothingly.

Marigold had just about had enough. "No, I most certainly did not."

Leigh had the grace to look sheepish. "I thought it would be a grand gesture."

"To sneak into my room in the dead of night and nearly cause me to have an apoplexy?" Marigold asked coldly. She frowned. "And what are you wearing? Are you about to attend a masquerade?"

In truth, he looked extremely dashing. He was clad all in black again. His trousers were even more well fitted than ordinary and made of black leather. His boots were a matte black leather as well, while his shirt and coat were similarly dark as midnight. The materials were plainer than the ones he had worn to the theater but more closely tailored. He looked dangerous, like a pirate about to partake in a duel.

"Oh, just the usual," Leigh said, glancing down at himself quickly. "Not a masquerade, no." He coughed. "I... I wanted to see you."

His mouth softened. Marigold found herself gazing at his lips, so lovely and full, so tempting. Despite herself, she found herself longing to touch him.

"I've missed you desperately," he confessed, and she felt her heart give a violent lurch.

"It has only been a few hours," she reminded him.

"Still. I missed you."

What was she doing? Were these not the words she longed to hear? Had she not just dreamed of this very thing? Of being alone in the dark with this man?

Yes, but the Leigh of her dreams was perfect in all ways. He loved her completely. She had given that dream man her heart, knowing he would never hurt or betray her.

The man in front of her? This daredevil rogue who had the audacity to steal into her room? Well, that was another matter.

Nevertheless...

"I missed you, too," she admitted.

"Did you now?" he marveled, still grinning. "It feels good, doesn't it?" He looked her up and down, then shook his head.

"What is it?" She felt panicked. For heaven's sake, why was she dressed like an old woman the night Leigh Blakeley had climbed through her bedroom window? And this time, not bleeding.

"I was simply thinking that even dressed like a miniature Lady Fulford, you still look dashedly sweet," he said, shocking her to the core.

"Sweet? I am not sweet!"

"No?" He scratched his chin. He had still not shaved. He ought to find a new valet, she thought crossly. Instead of making him look unkempt, however, the dark bristles simply made him more unbearably handsome. It was completely unfair, she thought, looking down miserably at her fuzzy slippers.

"No, I suppose you aren't sweet," Leigh was saying.

For some reason, it stung to hear him acknowledge it.

She was a little bit sweet, wasn't she? Even her siblings agreed on that.

He was looking at her. The daredevil rogue was looking at her, his eyes steady and intense. She shifted nervously in her slippers, her hands clasping the front of the robe.

"You're perfectly spiced," he said then, his voice low and husky. "Sweet, yes, a little. But well salted, too." He grinned that irresistible grin, and she shivered in spite of her warm clothes. "With a little ginger thrown in, for good measure."

He took a step closer toward her. Marigold took one step back. Her ankles hit the trunk at the foot of her bed.

"Ouch!" She refused to meet his gaze any longer. To do so was to court disaster. Or worse, seduction. Could one be seduced while dressed as a younger version of Lady Fulford?

"You make me sound like a piece of gingerbread," she said crossly.

Leigh ignored her. He was very close indeed now. She could see the rise and fall of his firm chest. She took a deep breath, trying to calm herself, and as she did so, his hand slipped around the back of her neck, clasping her gently.

"What are you doing?" she asked, tilting her head up. His dark eyes immediately homed in on her. He was standing so near that she was tempted to reach out a finger and graze it along his jaw, to feel the coarseness of that dark stubble.

"I'm trying to do things properly," he said, his lips twisting in a sardonic smile. "Can't you tell?"

"What do you mean?" she whispered.

"I mean, Miss Marigold Spencer, that I believe I have been in love with you since that very first moment I woke up bleeding in your bed."

"Don't be ridiculous. You were in no state to be aware of anything. You were injured."

"I was, that is true. And tonight, I'll finally try to tell you why. But before I do..." He looked down at her, then shook his head, and before she could stop him, lowered his lips to hers.

The kiss was sweet and brief, a quick brush of his lips on hers. Still, Marigold found herself gasping. She put a finger to her lips. Her hand was trembling.

Something was happening. Here. Tonight. Something told her nothing would ever be the same.

He was still gazing down at her.

"That was for luck," he said, grinning a little. "But it's God's honest truth. I love you. I have loved you since that night." He shook his head as if in wonder. "I have little recollection of climbing into your room. I remember opening the window and then, somehow, I got to your bed."

"You certainly did," she said, some of her ordinary spirit returning.

He grinned fully this time. "And then I woke up. In love."

"You don't know what you're saying," she whispered. Yet her heart was beating furiously. She thought it might beat right out of her chest. And she felt happy. So happy. Happier than she had in the glorious dream she had just been having.

He touched her cheek. "You saved my life, Marigold. That night, yes, but every day since. You have no idea..." He paused. "I haven't lived an entirely virtuous life before this."

"I am shocked to hear it," Marigold said drily.

He shook his head again, and his smile was almost sad. "No, I don't mean simply a debauched youth, Marigold." He hesitated.

She could not help it. She let go of her robe and placed her hand flat against his chest.

"Tell me," she whispered. "I will not judge you for it."

He lay his free hand flat over hers. It was warm and strong. She could not remember a simple touch of hands ever being so comforting.

This *was* love, she thought, and for all her bluster, the truth was she was terrified of admitting it.

"I feel as if I've spent years traveling in the darkness," Leigh was murmuring. "Chasing after something I thought would make things right. Redemption. Revenge. I don't know. I've chased evil, Marigold. I've chased evil to its very hiding place, and I've looked it in the face. And then..."

"Yes?"

"I've struck true," he said, his voice low. "I've killed evil men where I've found them, Marigold. Can you still look me in the eye, knowing that?"

She lifted her head steadily. "I know what I see. You would never have killed an innocent."

"No," he agreed. "Never. But even when trying to destroy evil... well, one can come too close."

She put a hand against his cheek. "What do you mean?" she whispered.

"I mean there was a reason I stayed away for so long. Away from my family. Not even returning immediately when I learned my mother was alive. I... I've been in quite a bad place without even realizing it. Not until I met you."

"I've done nothing, Leigh. Only..."

"You have no idea what you've done," he interrupted, his voice rough. "But believe me, you have done something. I have been obsessed. Chasing revenge. For years. Can you imagine that sort of life?"

Marigold stared. "You found the people who hurt your parents."

"Yes." His gaze shifted. Suddenly, his face was cold and hard. "My uncle and I, we found them. After more than five years. And the things we had to do to get there..." He shook his head.

"And that is why you were bleeding? That night?" Marigold thought she was beginning to understand. "You had gone after them?"

"Well, no. Not that particular night, no. That did have to do with a woman as I told you."

She felt her throat constrict. Something must have shown on her face, for Leigh added swiftly, "Not in that way, Marigold. She was in trouble. A girl in a dark alley with two men closing in on her. Up to no good, as I am sure you can imagine. I did not have to stop. I could have simply passed her by."

He was watching her carefully. "Was that what you would have wished me to do? Is that what you would have done?"

Marigold's eyes widened. "No, of course not. I would have tried to help."

He kissed her again. Soft and gentle, but with the hint of something else. They were both yearning, both holding back. Waiting for the conversation that would surely change their life tonight to end, so that something else could begin. Marigold was not sure she could wait much longer.

"That's what I knew you'd say. I suppose I was cocky. I'd hardly set foot on English soil before I hurled myself into more trouble. But I couldn't help it. There were only two of them..."

"*Only* two?" Marigold interjected.

He quirked his lip. "Yes, only two. Young fellows. But one got lucky there at the end. Had a blade I didn't see." He shook his head. "It wasn't a bad wound. I thought it would mend quickly."

"So, you left it completely untreated and thought you'd simply go to bed, did you?" Marigold demanded, suddenly thinking of how he might have climbed into the correct room, fallen into his own bed instead of hers and then... Would he have ever woken up? Or would he have lost too much blood from leaving the wound unbandaged?

She could not think of it now. The idea of this man being lost to her was unbearable.

"You see? I was reckless," Leigh said, his voice low. "I've been reckless. I sought trouble out even when I might have avoided it. Oh, I don't mean that I shouldn't have helped the girl. But I've walked a dangerous line, stepping too close to the edge on purpose."

"You didn't care if you lived or died," Marigold said softly, understanding.

"I don't suppose I really did," he admitted.

"But your mother is safe, Leigh. Surely when you found out..."

"That's the queerest part of all," he interrupted. "I thought if that ever happened, then yes, it would change things. Then, beyond all hope, it did. But nothing changed. At least, not for me."

He looked at her, and she glimpsed the sad little boy lurking behind the man's face. "Perhaps I am simply too far gone."

"Nonsense. You're right here, with me," she whispered and kissed his lips tenderly.

This time, the kiss was not as brief. He needed her. She could feel his hunger as their lips pressed together. A warm pleasurable sensation was flooding through her from head to toe.

His hands slipped to the front of her robe and began tugging it gently open. She did not try to stop him.

Then abruptly, his fingers stilled. "Wait. I must tell you..."

"What must you tell me?" she asked. Her lips still felt hot and full. She knew they should stop, that he was right, but she was loath to do so. "What is it? Why are you looking at me like that?"

His gaze was as hungry as his lips had been. "I need to know that you'll have me, Marigold. That is what I have been trying to tell you. You're the light in the darkness. I've found you, and now I'm damned if I'll let you go again."

"Marry you?" she whispered. "But are you..."

"Don't ask if I'm certain," he said harshly. "Don't ask that ever again, Marigold Spencer. I'm as certain as any man has ever been about a woman. I love you. I want you. More, do you know what I see when I look at you?"

Marigold felt her cheeks redden. The critical part of her mind flared to life, and suddenly, she could think of any number of things, none of them good. *Short and dumpy, plain and dull,* a cruel voice that sounded remarkably like Miss Compton murmured in her head before she could stop it.

Leigh's hands slipped around her waist, holding her firmly, possessively, pulling her close. His chest was a solid wall against her softness, her breasts molding against his firm body. He was strong as steel, and she? Try as she might to be practical, rational, yes, even *good,* she was helpless. Transfixed. Mesmerized by this man.

"I see my future in your eyes. *Our* future," he said, his voice husky.

"I see you. I see a home. Anywhere you are, that is where I want to be. You have dreams, Marigold. Beautiful dreams. Your work at the dispensary. The way you wish to help people, to learn how to help. Let me be a part of them. For I now know I want that future, too. A future where we work alongside one another. Help people instead of hurt them." She watched him swallow hard. "Do you... Could you see yourself wanting that, too? With me?"

She was so unused to seeing him uncertain. He was always so cocky and careless, so confident. In a way, it was unnerving. In another, it filled her with a pure certainty of her own.

This was her man. Her Leigh.

"Yes," she said, without bothering to add more. And then she stood up on her tiptoes, put her hands on his shoulders, and kissed him with everything she had.

First his lips, kissing deep and true. Then his cheeks. She pressed a soft kiss to one cheek, then the other. She moved to his jaw, licking lightly along the sharp angles of it. His stubble was coarse but soft, too. She ran her tongue along the hairs, feeling him shudder. She felt a heady rush and moved her mouth down to the little hollow at the base of his throat where she licked and sucked a moment.

Then back to his lips again. His kiss was savage, desperate as she returned her mouth to his. He pulled her to him so tightly she could scarcely breathe. But suddenly, breathing seemed hardly important. The kiss overwhelmed her. Suffusing her with pleasure. She could think of nothing but Leigh. Leigh's lips on hers. His warmth, his firmness, his scent.

She wanted him, all of him. Here. Now. She cared nothing for striving to resist any longer.

She tugged her own robe off.

The night dress beneath was nothing scandalous, but still, she saw him draw in a ragged breath as the robe fell away.

"That was what you were hiding?" His voice was hoarse.

She looked down at herself, suddenly self-conscious again. The nightgown was similar to the ones she had owned before coming to London. But Lady Fulford had insisted upon fitting her properly for her chemises and had demanded the modiste add some pretty, feminine touches to even the simplest items. And thus, even Marigold's undergarments had lace edges and scalloped borders and pretty, frilly ribbons. At the time, she had protested the details as unnecessary. Now she was grateful to be wearing something so pretty. This particular chemise had been cut quite low, the scalloped trim drawing attention to her large, full breasts.

"God, I can see all of you through it." The words were a throaty growl. "Do you know how you look?" Leigh demanded.

Marigold shook her head slowly.

"Like you've come straight from bed. Tousled. Rumpled. Like a scantily clad angel. Absolutely fucking perfect."

And then his hands were on her breasts, cupping their softness in his palms. They filled up his hands as she had known they would. She moaned as his palms raked over her nipples, unable to stand the anticipation of his touch. He caught each nipple between his thumbs and forefingers and gently pinched and squeezed, then rubbed his thumbs over the tips of her nipples until she thought she would scream.

She gripped his arms, her fingers smoothing over the fabric of his coat, enjoying the feel of the muscles beneath as he toyed with her nipples, kneading her breasts.

When he lowered his head to suck, she began to tear at his coat.

His mouth was hot and wet, saturating the thin fabric of her night dress. It felt exquisite, his lips curling around the hard, puckered nipple. He bit down gently, and Marigold gasped, her hands sliding the coat down off his shoulders, then onto the floor. She moved her hands over the front of his shirt, feeling his beautifully sculpted chest, his shoulders, his arms. The power and warmth of his body, the heat of his mouth on her breasts... She felt dizzy, intoxicated, as if she had drunk too much champagne. But this? This was far better than any champagne.

She tugged his cravat free and dropped it on the floor while his arms snaked around her waist, hardly leaving her room to maneuver as his mouth strayed pleasantly between her nipples, first one, then the other.

He was steering her, she realized as she worked. Steering her around the trunk that had nipped her ankles, steering her around the post of the large bed, and over to its side.

They were coming precariously close to falling into the bed together, she thought, her heart hammering. And she could not seem to care. No, she could hardly wait.

She pushed the fabric of his shirt up and over his chest, fingers grazing against his skin, gliding over the dark hairs of his stomach, his ribs, before forcing his head up and away from her breasts.

She had never seen a man shuck off a shirt so quickly as Leigh did, ripping the shirt over his head with undisguised frustration.

Then he stood there, bare-chested, panting, and heart-wrenchingly beautiful. And hers. He was offering to be hers. For always.

"Christ, you're beautiful, Marigold," he said, looking back at her just as admiringly.

She crossed her arms over her chest, covering the wet spots where he had sucked before she could help herself.

"Don't do that," he said roughly, putting his hands on hers. "Don't cover yourself. And Good Lord, swear to me you won't try to put that ghastly robe back on."

Marigold laughed shakily. "Very well. I won't."

She lifted her chin, then placed her hands on the shoulders of her nightdress. "I suppose fair is fair."

She slid the fabric over her shoulders, watching his face, mesmerized by what she saw. His lips had parted slightly, now he licked them, watching her hands as if they were the most fascinating things on earth.

The fabric slid down her shoulders. She lowered her arms and let it slide still farther down. Until the gown had fallen past her breasts, leaving them bare and exposed and puckering in the chill air, past the swelling curves of her stomach, and stopped on the roundness of her hips.

She left the gown there, not ready to be completely exposed before him yet. She was bare to the waist, her head held high and proud.

"I am not perfect," she said. She cleared her throat. "As you can see."

"And you think I'm perfect, do you? You're perfect to me," he said gruffly, and the look of longing on his face was all she needed to see.

She could not stand it any longer. They had talked enough. She had not realized until now how badly she wanted this. How badly she wanted him. It had been a long time coming. Perhaps, as he had said, even since that very first night.

"Take me then, Leigh. For God knows I want all of you."

He growled, a sound low and deep in his throat. Intimidating, but playful, too.

If one enjoyed playing with wolves.

Leigh did not believe there was any man alive who would not find Marigold Spencer irresistible at that moment.

She was a petite little thing, yet here she stood, bare-breasted and glorious, radiating beauty like an ancient goddess.

He drank in the sight of her curves like a thirsty man in a desert. Her breasts were as perfectly formed as he'd imagined. The nipples large and rosy-tipped. Her skin was pale but not too pale—there was a warmth there, a beautiful flush. Her hips were wide, too. Her figure full of curves, like the lines of an hourglass. Everything about her made him long to touch her, stroke her. Her hips called to him. They would be the perfect place to rest his hands from behind her as he sank into her sweet softness.

The thought of looking down on her naked form from behind was all too compelling. But he was not choosy. He would take her any way she allowed. He would sweep her up against him, push the gown from her hips, lay her on the bed, spread her legs, and then fill her. He would fuck her gently at first, then harder, then ceaselessly, until they were both exhausted and unable to do anything but sleep in each other's arms.

But... he wanted this to be good for her. As far as he was concerned, this was their true wedding night.

He had to move slowly.

Slow was not something Leigh had ever been good at.

He thought of where he must go after this and brushed it aside. He had a few hours. He would make sure they both enjoyed them. He would spend them bringing his love pleasure and delight. Then he would leave her to slumber and find her again in the morning.

He stepped toward her, pulling her against him, relishing the feel of her naked breasts against his chest. Her heart was thumping hard.

"Marigold..." He took a deep breath. "You need not fear me. Ever. I want... All I want is to take care of you. To make you happy. Do you understand?"

He felt her nodding against him. God, she was soft and sweet. Her curves fit along him perfectly.

He ran his hands lightly over her bare back. "I want to make this good for you," he murmured, placing his lips against her neck and nuzzling. "Tell me what you want."

Was this cheating? He knew what he hoped she would say.

She pushed back slightly and looked up at him, her lovely lips parted, her cheeks flushed with desire. "I want you," she breathed. "Inside me. All of you. Together as one." She hesitated, and he saw her cheeks bloom with a deeper shade of pink. "The sooner the better if you please."

He swallowed hard. "I'd be a cad to refuse a lady," he said hoarsely and, placing his hands on her hips, pushed the gown to the ground.

His fingers found her wetness nearly instantly, brushing against the soft swirls of blonde hairs between her legs, parting them, and slipping between.

"Oh, God, Leigh," she moaned, holding his shoulders.

He moved his fingers through her dampness, then slipped one inside. She was slick and hot.

Leigh did not have to look down to know he was more than ready to take her. His shaft pressed against his trousers, throbbing and hard.

But he would make this easier on her first. Besides, had he not been longing to taste her since the Norfolks' ball?

He reluctantly moved his hand away from her wetness, hearing her displeased moan as he did so, then scooped her up before she could protest and lay her on the bed.

Working quickly, he undid his trousers, pushing them down over the long shaft of his cock, feeling it bob pleasantly free.

When he looked up, she was staring at him, propped on her elbows, looking languid and lovely—a golden princess on a pearly white bed. Her long curling blonde hair fell over her shoulders, a few strands tumbling tantalizingly over her breasts. He swallowed and circled his shaft with his fist, stroking himself. It would take everything he had to resist laying himself over her right then.

He cleared his throat, straining for composure. "Are you all right?"

She nodded shyly. Her eyes hadn't left his cock.

"See something you like?" he teased.

Her pretty face was rosy with embarrassment, but her smile was coy and certain.

He climbed onto the bed, stretching out next to her, and kissed her lightly as he slid a hand back between her legs. The sound she made was heavenly music to his ears.

"You'll have to wait, my darling," he whispered, finding her ear with his teeth and nipping gently. "For there's something I wish to give you first. And something I wish to take."

"What is it?" she whispered, straining against his hand, pressing her soaked slit more firmly against him. "I can't wait. Please, Leigh."

He trailed his hand up her stomach and back to her breast, where he lightly stroked one peaked nipple, then moved his hands to her hips, gently holding her in place as he lowered his mouth.

He kissed the tops of her thighs first, feeling the silkiness of her skin. He was close now. He felt her hitch of breath as he moved his mouth, hot breath blowing gently over her woman's mound. He flicked his tongue against one damp curling hair, tasting the hint of salty brine.

Then he dove his tongue between the curls, finding the sweet wetness between and licked, long and slow. Her sensitive flesh opened traitorously for his roving mouth. God, she was soaking wet for him. He fastened on to her, licking and sucking, cupping the swells of her bottom with his hands to hold her against his mouth as he worked his tongue. Her bud was swollen and hard against his lips. He kissed it gently, flicking his tongue against it carefully, knowing the fine line between pleasure and pain.

He touched her lightly, then stroked harder. Teasing her toward her climax, not wanting her to come too soon, relishing her taste, savoring the intimacy, the power over her.

"Do you like this, Marigold? Do you like my mouth on you? Tell me, darling. Say the words."

Marigold was arching, her hips pushing off the bed, trembling with her need.

"Yes, Leigh."

"Just a yes?" he teased. He licked her bud, nipped it gently.

"More than like, Leigh," she gasped.

"Ah, that's better. For I certainly more than like this. The taste of you. The feel of you. Your cunny wet against my mouth. I love it." He lapped his mouth against her, working her clit.

She groaned, squirming against the bed–overcome with her desire.

He could push his cock inside her now, satisfy them both.

Or he could be the grown man he was and wait. Bring her to her climax, then bring her again. And again.

He had always believed himself to be a generous lover, but for once, it was more difficult than it had ever been.

He flicked a practiced tongue against her salty cleft, then slid a finger inside her. God, she was tight. He felt her body momentarily freeze, then quiver. Ever so gently, he added a second and thrust, his rhythm insistent as he licked her bud.

She thought he was filling her now. Wait until he took her completely, he thought, with satisfaction.

She was close. Her head flung back, her lips parted. He thrust into her core, delving deep inside her.

Her body jerked. She cried his name so loudly he suddenly feared Lady Fulford might burst through the door, waving her infernal cane.

Then her body heaved, trembled, and a wetness poured forth over his hand.

He looked at the puddle on the bed in fascination. He had seen the phenomenon a few times with other women but had not expected to see it tonight, with a maiden no less. And from his mouth, not his cock. Let that be a lesson to his masculine pride, he thought ruefully.

He could feel her trembling. Quickly, he moved up beside her, enfolding her in his arms.

She pressed her head against him, trembling like a leaf in a storm.

"Shhh, Marigold, love. Shhhh."

"That was..." He felt her draw a deep breath. "I can't... Is it always like that?"

She felt so good, her warm body nestled against him. He pressed his lips to her cheek.

"Not quite," he said carefully. "I think... I think it depends on who it is with."

She was quiet a moment, then her small hand stole into one of his. "And I will always be with you."

Leigh was speechless. She was right. It was what he wanted, was it not? Yet hearing her say the words... It moved him more than he could have anticipated.

"You're mine," he whispered against her hair. "Mine."

"Make me yours in every way, Leigh," she whispered back. Then she arched her body against him. Letting him feel every exquisite curve as she molded to him. His cock throbbed with need, pressing against her thigh, hot and hard.

God knew he couldn't resist that request. He moved overtop of her.

Leigh looked down at her bosom and Marigold shivered. She had always thought her breasts were far too large. They were awkward at best, too eye-catching at worst.

But now Leigh was gazing at them as if they were a feast and he a starving man.

Slowly he reached out his hands, stroking the sides of them before taking the round globes in his hands, lifting and shaping, then dropping his mouth to suck gently on one straining nipple.

He was beautiful, this man, hovering over her. His body hard and chiseled, his chest covered with a dusting of curling dark hairs.

And farther down, below his waist, that most intriguing part of him of all, brushed against her thigh, so firm and hot. A seed of wetness emerged from it as he suckled her breast, and she gasped.

"God, Marigold," he said, lifting his head and looking down at her. "This will be so good. A little pain but only a little."

He kissed her lips tenderly as his hand stroked her bare thigh, then slipped between her legs in a practiced way, as if her body had already become, in some way, a part of him.

She knew what he would find. She was still wet. Very wet. And ready. Oh, so ready for him.

Was this wantonness? Was it brazen, wrong? If so, she could not bring herself to care. It felt like sheer bliss.

Leigh groaned as his fingers stroked her cleft.

Then she saw him raise his hand to his cock, encircling it, stroking it. There was something incredibly arousing about the sight of him touching himself. She swallowed hard, watching as he guided himself to her entrance.

The feel of his cock, there, at her core, was indescribable. She wanted him inside her, filling her. The pain would be nothing. She could bear the pain. She wanted Leigh. She wanted him *now*.

He seemed to know her mind. His expression was grim, as if he could hardly contain himself.

She felt the head of his cock pushing inside her and gasped, arching her back.

"I can't hold back if you do that, Marigold, love," he said, his face straining with effort.

"Then don't," she replied and lifted her hips to meet him, forcing him farther inside her.

And then he was in, sheathing himself in a thrust that seemed to never end, his cock stretching her, filling her. He drew out, and there was pain then, yes, and an unexpected feeling of loss. But then he thrust into her again, a hard stroke that sent her trembling and quivering.

She spread her legs wide, cradling his hips, forcing him farther inside her, lifting herself to meet him. Her hands were on the back of his neck, twisting his hair, clawing at his back. She was desperate, wanting more and more.

Her breasts pressed up against his chest, bobbing and thrusting against his body as he drove into her, harder and faster, again and again.

He felt so good. His lips found her mouth, his tongue thrusting into her as hard and hungry as his cock. Marigold opened herself to him, parting her mouth and her legs ever wider, wrapping herself around him.

Leigh froze as her legs tangled around his hips. For an unbearable moment, he stopped.

Then his mouth pulled away, his arms found her waist, and he was tugging her up off the bed, flush against his chest. He was sitting up, she realized, and pulling her atop him.

He wished her to ride astride. She had heard the term. One heard a great many things about sex when one worked below stairs, and this was one she had always been curious about.

His hand was between her legs, finding the crest of her bud with his fingers and languidly teasing it. With his other hand, he pushed his cock back inside her. She moaned, biting her lip, welcoming his hardness as it filled her once more.

Then she put her hands on his shoulders, knowing without being told just what to do.

His thumb circled her most sensitive part as she began to ride him, her body moving up and down, pulling him deeper into her.

She changed her rhythm, making it faster, harder. His hands gripped her waist, almost painfully, and she knew he was close then. She clung to him tightly, rubbing herself against him, hearing him groan in pleasure as she brushed the tips of her breasts against his chest.

And then he was crying out, calling her name just as she had called his, his body warm against her as he held her tight.

As his seed spilled into her, she felt her own release find her, the bud of her sex rubbing up against him as pleasure flowed through her, rolled over her in a blissful wave.

"Oh, we must do that again," he murmured, kissing the tip of each breast, as he held her on his lap. He looked up at her and grinned, and she felt herself grinning back.

Then he pushed her off, pulled her back onto the bed beside him. There was wetness spilling down her thighs, onto the bed.

Leigh kissed her, then leaped out of the bed, going over to the basin and washstand in the corner and returning with a cloth. Tenderly, he raised the damp cloth to her thighs. She looked down as he worked, seeing the blood and what must have been his seed, mixed together.

"It did not hurt," she offered, still full of wonder at what she had felt. "Well, only a little."

He smiled at her. "I'm glad." He threw the cloth back into the basin and climbed up next to her, pulling her against him.

She closed her eyes. This. This she could easily get used to.

And she would. This was how it could be. Them, in bed together. All their days. All their nights.

He stroked her hair, and she felt as if she might purr like a cat.

"Dare and Laurel are parents," he said, and she woke from her daze, suddenly remembering.

"Yes. A baby boy. I am so glad. How I wish I had been there."

He kissed her hair. "Next time." She felt him breathe deeply. "What a marvel a baby is. You know, I felt nearly moved to tears when I found out."

She raised herself up to look at him. "You did?"

He nodded. "Strange, is it not? For a baby I have not even seen."

She touched his cheek. "Not so strange. A baby of your blood. Your family."

"Yes." He was quiet for a moment. "It was another thing that convinced me that I was changing. And that I must see you tonight."

"See me?" Marigold was confused.

"I needed to know," he said. "That I had a future, too. With you."

"Oh, Leigh." She was moved, her throat constricted. She traced his cheek with her fingers. "And what of you? Do you want children?"

He looked thoughtful. "We generally do not have much choice in the matter, do we? At least, not if we continue to do… this."

She tilted her head. "Well, a little. There are things women can do as you probably know."

"But they don't always work, do they?" he countered. He shook his head. "Whether children come or not, I will be content." He lifted one of her hands and kissed her fingertips. "As long as I have you, Marigold, I'll be happy. I won't hazard my happiness on children. If they come, they will be welcome. If *you* wish for them, then I hope we will have many."

"I should..." She cleared her throat. "I should like to continue to work first, I believe. But even if children do come, I plan to continue to explore my interests." She glanced at him. He did not appear put off by this.

"Of course, you shall," he agreed. "Whatever you like. Perhaps the children can even join you when they are older." He grinned. "Look at me, speaking of imaginary children."

"Of our family," Marigold whispered. Her heart felt very full. She kissed him, then straightened up. "Now tell me of your parents, Leigh."

There was silence in the room.

She watched him frown.

"If you do not wish to tell me tonight," she began carefully. "I will understand."

He lifted a hand. "No, it is all right. I must tell someone. Royal and I, we planned to tell the others. We shall, very soon. I may as well begin with you."

Chapter Twenty-Three

L eigh studied her face. "You know what there is to know already, I suppose?"

"I know all that Laurel and Dare have told me, and all that your mother has told them," she replied.

Leigh grimaced. "Which is not much. She seems to only recollect what occurred from the ship to the point she reached England, and then beyond. But she has been very ill. It is not surprising."

He thought of how to begin. "My parents, as you know, were lovers of antiquities. They were collectors, but acquiring artifacts was not their primary passion. They wished to see the original objects in their natural surroundings, and so they did a great deal of traveling. When they traveled, they would learn and study, speaking with locals and sketching the things they found. At times, they would make acquisitions, yes. But they did not raid and pillage like some so-called lovers of history and antiquarians do. For my parents, the context of a piece was more important than the piece itself." He glanced at her. "Does that make sense so far?"

She nodded. "Yes, but I do not see how…"

"You will." He sat up in the bed, wrapping his arms around his knees. He had never told the story. It was not something he had looked forward to doing. But she deserved to know where he had been... even if he could not tell her where he was going. Soon she would know even that. But not tonight.

"Not all were as cautious or respectful as my parents were when it came to collecting. Some would use any means at their disposal to take what they believed should be theirs by right. When it came to Egyptian artifacts in particular, the collectors' mania was even stronger. We can thank Napoleon for that, I suppose. Well, my parents made many trips to Egypt and, along the way, made friends with powerful, local people who did not believe in having their homeland simply surrender its treasures to foreigners. My parents agreed and became outspoken in their criticism of others—mostly English and Europeans—who took ruthlessly, without thought for future generations. In this way, they developed enemies."

He rubbed his hand over his face. "There was one man in particular. An Italian from a noble family. But not simply noble, he was powerful. And not simply powerful, but actually criminal. Though I do not believe my parents realized the danger he represented at the time." He shrugged. "Not that it would necessarily have stopped them."

Marigold was listening quietly.

"Well, it seems this man began to feel my parents were too much of a thorn in his side. At times, they would persuade local authorities to thwart him from making a purchase he had counted upon. At others, they would provide funds to one of the local families so that they might covertly purchase an artifact before it could be bought and removed from the country."

He looked at Marigold. "You must understand—to my parents, this was their passion. Next to us children, it was their life. But to this man and to his family, it was a business. A very profitable one. He and his men would purchase artifacts and resell them back in Italy and elsewhere on the Continent. They had quite a fine operation, supplemented by less... acceptable endeavors. I'm sure you can imagine what those might entail. They were not used to being thwarted in any way. Certainly not by an English couple who they saw as mere interference to a lucrative side business."

"And so, they kidnapped them?"

Leigh nodded. It seemed so obvious now, but the abduction had been conducted carefully and well concealed. "Under the auspices of a sea voyage. The man had his people follow my parents toward their next destination—India—which they never reached. Along the way, they vanished, seemingly without a trace. Well, my uncle and I eventually found traces."

He would not tell her how. Nor the bloodshed in the process.

The man who had orchestrated his parents' abduction, Francesco Adragna, was a ruthless oligarch. Even in Egypt, he could extend a powerful fist despite the center of his power lying in Italy. Those who had seen something had been paid well to say they had not. It had taken something other than money to get them to finally speak the truth.

"The long and short of it is that we were finally able to trace them to a villa on the Amalfi coast, owned by this family. The building was an ancient one. Picture one of our medieval castles, and you will have an inkling of where they were. Now picture the dungeon of one of those castles. Dark, mildewed, cold stone. That is where they spent five long years."

"Five?" Marigold began. "But I thought..."

"Five years together," Leigh said, his voice low. "My mother spent her sixth year alone."

He watched Marigold's eyes widen, her mouth fall open.

"They kept them as prisoners, not caring if they lived or died?" she whispered. "They were mistreated?"

"I believe they were mistreated at first. At least, my father was," Leigh answered. He did not wish to go into the specifics. "But later, they were mostly left to themselves. Abandoned. I am not sure which would be worse. To feel so forgotten. I cannot imagine the horror. The frustration." He swallowed. "They had jailers, of a sort. Their first seems to have been a somewhat kindly man. After the first few months, it seems he managed to even give them books. He saw they received adequate food. But when he was replaced, about four years into their confinement, their conditions declined again. So too did my father's health." Leigh paused. "My father died in their fifth year in that place. My mother was left alone."

Leigh suspected that his father's health had waned because he had been giving his wife much of his own food. From what he and Royal had been told, the conditions had been very poor, and the Blakeleys all but forgotten. Perhaps the Adragnas had hoped they really would starve to death. If so, they had half-succeeded.

"Oh, Leigh." Marigold had a hand to her mouth. "I cannot even imagine."

"I still do not know what this family believed they were doing. Why go to this bother? Surely, they would have killed them eventually." He shook his head. "Or perhaps this sort of torment was nothing to them."

From what he and Royal had heard, the Adragnas had done far worse to other enemies.

"How did your mother get free?" Marigold murmured. "Did you learn that?"

Leigh nodded. "It seems there was a granddaughter who would visit my mother. She would bring her sweets and books and speak with her at length. My mother was teaching her English." He had no idea if his mother would ever recall this, but so he and Royal had been told. "Well, when my father died, she began to visit more frequently. She must have come to care for my mother, and she had power in her own way. She was something of a royal princess in that place, far away in the hills where this family holds so much sway. She must have decided enough was enough, and so she helped my mother to escape."

"Oh, how bold," Marigold whispered, her eyes alight.

"Yes, it was," Leigh agreed. "And dangerous, too. I call her a girl, but she was closer to a woman. Perhaps seventeen or eighteen. She must have thought her grandfather would not care if my mother escaped—or that he would not know. The whole thing was arranged to look accidental. She had taken my mother out for a walk—a very rare thing—and then claimed she ran away."

He hesitated. "Well, my mother did escape. The girl had arranged her passage on a ship bound for France and, from there, to England. Shockingly, she made that perilous journey successfully, though over-come with exhaustion and suffering from the spells of illness you know she gets."

Marigold nodded.

"But the girl..." Leigh wished to spare her, but he could not leave this out. It would be crucial, later, when she finally learned what he had done. "The girl did not survive."

Marigold stared. "What do you mean? Surely, his own grand-daughter..."

"They were—are—ruthless people, Marigold," Leigh said. "Keeping my parents caged up like animals was only a very small part of this family's cruelty. And perhaps nothing exceeded the cruelty which they showed to one another. The granddaughter had defied her grandfather, the leader of their house. And so, she had to be dealt with."

"What did they do?"

Leigh hesitated. "I believe... I believe they threw her off a cliff."

He and Royal had discovered all this far too late to intervene. It would always be one of his greatest regrets. They had been too late for his father. And too late for the Adragna girl.

"No." Marigold's face was pale. "How could they?"

"Her own father and brother did this thing," Leigh continued, barreling on, ignoring the look of horror on her sensitive face. He was running out of time. He had to finish the story. And then he had to go and finish it once and for all.

There were tears in her eyes. "Their own daughter. Sister."

Leigh nodded. "It is the way of the men in this family. They obey, absolutely. Without question."

"But you and your uncle... have dealt with them?"

Leigh hesitated. They had dealt with all but one. The Adragna cub—the brother—had escaped. He had come to England, searching for Leigh's mother no doubt, at the instructions of his father and grandfather.

He had not located her, of course. Leigh and Royal had all but erased her trail, and Blakeley Manor was under constant surveillance, thanks to a word in Dare's ear.

Now no further instructions would ever be received. The young Adragna had begun to develop his own operations in London. He was moving fast, making powerful connections. Perhaps he hoped he would be permitted to remain and forge his own path, away from his domineering grandfather.

But if so, that hope would end tonight. Ascanio Adragna had helped to confine Leigh's parents. And then he had helped to kill his own sister, the girl who had set Leigh's mother free.

And so, Leigh and his uncle had decided. Regardless of his relative youth, he would not be permitted to live.

"Yes," Leigh replied finally. He raised a hand to touch her hair, smoothing it back behind one ear and enjoying the way she smiled sweetly at his touch. "We have dealt with them."

"And soon you will tell Dare and your sisters this?"

"Yes. Very soon. My uncle and I will return to Blakeley Manor. To see the baby, but also to share this news." He hoped she would be right there by his side when he did so. Then a new chapter would begin. One that was not spotted with blood.

"So, it is finally over," she marveled. "What a nightmare for your mother." She hesitated, biting her lip. "Do you think she will be pleased with what you have done? Do you think she will remember?"

"I honestly do not know," Leigh replied. "And whether we tell her will be left to Dare to decide. He has spent the most time with my mother now. Perhaps he will think it is best left alone. After all, she is home, and she is safe. If she cannot remember this girl... this girl who helped her. Well, perhaps that is for the best. Perhaps it will be less painful this way."

"Yes," Marigold agreed. "But oh, that poor girl. Not knowing she would be losing her own life when she helped..."

"It is tragic." Just one tragedy of many perpetuated by this merciless family. "But her family has paid the price for their cruelty." He studied her face carefully. "Now that I have told you all this... well..."

"Yes?" She looked at him curiously. "What is it?"

"Well, I know I must have shocked you. If you feel I am not the man..."

"Oh, for heaven's sake, Leigh." She leaned forward, cupped his face with both hands, and kissed him on the lips. "I know what you are about to say, and there is no need for it."

He watched her settle back in the bed, the sheets tangled around her waist, bare from the hips up, and already completely comfortable that way around him. He grinned. She was his. His wife to be. And God, what an incredible woman she was.

"No, you avenged not only your parents but the girl as well," she went on. "How could I fault you for that?" She pursed her lips together. "I suppose," she said carefully, "there is also something not altogether unappealing... about a man who would fight so very fiercely as you have done, to protect his family."

"And yet I did not protect them," Leigh said bitterly. "We did not even locate them in time to do that. This innocent, this girl, she took all the risk—and it cost her everything."

"Yes, but she died knowing she had done the right thing. And if she had not, you would have."

She shivered suddenly, and he watched her pull the blanket up over her chest, her face suddenly downcast. "It is a horrible story though, Leigh," she said quietly. "I do not think I shall wish for you to share it with me again. At least, not for a while."

"I do not enjoy speaking of it," Leigh admitted. He moved over to her and pulled her into his arms.

They were quiet for a moment.

"Stay with me all night, Leigh," she said, nuzzling her face against his neck. "Stay with me and then shock my maid in the morning." She sighed. "Oh, I am only jesting, of course. But I do wish you could stay all night."

"Soon," he promised, kissing her on the tip of her nose. "Soon we will be together like this every night. But tonight, I must leave."

"Now?" Her face was crestfallen.

"Now," he admitted. "I am sorry." His arms tightened around her. "But I must see you again soon. Tomorrow?"

"Tomorrow," she agreed. He felt her hesitance and knew where it stemmed from.

"Perhaps it would be best," he began, "if I came here in the morning and made my intentions known to Lady Fulford? And after that, we could send letters to your sister and brothers."

"*Our* intentions," she corrected. "And yes, that would be best." He felt her settle back against him, her body more relaxed. "We are to be married. I still can hardly believe it. Oh, the look on Lady Fulford's face when you tell her..."

Then she jabbed him in the stomach.

"Ouch! What was that for?"

"That was for ruining my other marriage offer," she said, tossing her curls in his face. "A very good one, too. I might have been a marchioness."

"Damned Harley," Leigh groaned, feigning hurt. "As if you care about such things as titles. Besides, you wouldn't have suited."

"No, I don't believe we would have," she said playfully and then lifted her face to be kissed.

Chapter Twenty-Four

T he night was still young as Leigh prowled the street toward the opulent, rented townhouse not too far away from Lady Fulford's own.

He felt more awake and alive than he had earlier in the evening. Above all, he was eager to see this task complete.

Ascanio Adragna was the only grandson of the Adragna dynasty. His grandfather and father had trained him well. Ascanio had a reputation as a sadist who enjoyed disturbing games of chance—not the sort one could find in a gaming hell. No, Ascanio's tastes ran to more macabre pleasures. He pursued women. Quite literally. In Italy, he had kept a luxurious estate solely for the purpose of hunting unsuspecting courtesans. When friends would come to stay, a courtesan would be set loose on the grounds. Then she would be hunted by Ascanio and his disturbed friends and used by them however they wished.

Leigh did not know if the courtesans ever saw freedom again. He certainly hoped so.

After tonight, it would not matter, for Ascanio and his evil family would be at an end. The last branch of the tree would be cut.

The young man likely believed missives from his father and grandfather had simply been going astray these past few months. Tonight, he would realize he was alone in the world. At least, for a few brief minutes.

A man stepped forward out of the shadow, and Leigh froze.

"Royal. What the hell are you doing here?" He scowled. "Is it the address? Did she give us the wrong place?"

His uncle shook his silvered head. "No, the address is good. But you're too late. He's left for the night."

Leigh cursed. "Where? Did you follow him?"

Royal smiled grimly. "Of course I followed him. Thanks to a tip from one of the servants in this house." So, Carlotta's information had been useful. It had been a start.

Royal's teeth gleamed in the moonlight, sharp and deadly like a wolf's. "You may thank me later. Now go. End this." His uncle named a location in the neighborhood of Seven Dials. A rundown house owned by the Adragna family. The address had been known to them for some time, but Ascanio had never been spotted there, and so they had written it off as a dead end. Leigh and Royal believed it was used for smuggling, but really, anything could be in the building.

"Are you hesitating?" Royal demanded. "Why not let me come along?"

"No. I'll do this by myself as we agreed." Leigh frowned. They had settled the score with Ascanio's father together. The man had been an excellent warrior, surrounded by many men. He had fought fiercely and well. That had been a satisfying fight and worth having his uncle by his side.

The grandfather had been removed by Royal's hand alone. Royal had requested this. Leigh had granted the request. He did not think the Adragna patriarch's death had been particularly quick. But then, he really did not care.

Now it was Leigh's wish to settle the last score on his own terms. He had no fear of Ascanio. The young man had a reputation of being something of a coward. Even with his men about him, Leigh had no doubt he could see the thing done.

"I'll go now," he declared. "I'll see you at home in a few hours."

His uncle nodded slowly. "Very well."

Leigh made his way to the address Royal had given him. The

building was dark. But on the second floor, Leigh could see a glimmer of light shining from behind a heavy curtain.

There was only one entrance. The front of the house was boarded up, likely to make passersby think it was simply another abandoned building. Leigh made his way to the door at the back.

Kicking it open quickly, he whirled about, evading the grasping hands of the startled bodyguard who had been standing there, likely hoping for a quiet night.

A quick blow to the top of the man's stomach just below his breast-bone effectively knocked the wind from him. As the man stood gasping, Leigh took him by the neck in a move he had learned from an old Scottish warrior. When the man was unconscious, he lowered him carefully to the floor. Chances were good the man would awaken and be none the worse for wear the next day. And if not... well, the man had chosen to work for Ascanio Adragna.

The entire thing had taken no more than a few minutes. No others had come running.

Perhaps this man was the only one Ascanio had brought along with him.

Leigh made his way through the dark building to the base of the stairs. A light came from the landing above. He could hear voices. A man's—Ascanio? Then he heard a woman's voice.

He cursed softly. He had no wish to harm a woman.

Nor had he any wish to be seen by a woman. He fished about in his pocket, then donned the black silk mask he had brought along for this eventuality. His vision was not as good with it on, but he had fought in it before. He would make do.

He began to make his way slowly up the stairs, then froze. There was a second bodyguard stationed at the top of the landing.

Luck was on Leigh's side, for the man's back was to him.

It was not very sporting, but he decided it was more humane. He crept up the stairs, and when he reached the second step below the man, raised his fist and delivered a blow to the jaw as hard as he could. The man collapsed with a low groan. Leigh caught him and dragged him quietly to the floor below.

He could simply kill both the bodyguards, but that was not his way, though his uncle might say he was being foolhardy.

He moved back up the stairs, pausing on the landing. A closed door lay before him. From behind it, the woman's voice had become louder. Leigh could not make out what she was saying. She was not speaking English. She must be Italian. But it was clear from the tone that she was beseeching someone.

Dammit, she sounded hardly more than a girl.

There was a crashing sound, as if furniture was being knocked over. Then a wailing broke out, followed by a sharp slapping sound. After that came a muffled sob.

Leigh gnashed his teeth. He could easily imagine what must be going on in the room beyond.

He had no doubt Ascanio was alone.

He stepped forward and kicked the door open. It fell in easily. The advantages of a derelict building.

Sure enough, a young woman crouched in a corner, sobbing. Blood spilled from a cut on her lip.

Ascanio Adragna stood above her. He was shirtless and licking blood from his knuckles. He wore a pleased smile as he looked down at the helpless girl that turned Leigh's blood to fire.

"I said I was not to be interrupted." He spoke with a heavy Italian accent.

"My mistake," Leigh said coldly. He waited for the young man to turn, see his mask, and recognize that Leigh was not one of his bodyguards.

Slowly, the young man faced him. Understanding seemed to dawn.

"Who are you?" Ascanio demanded.

Leigh ignored him. He looked down at the girl. "Go. Get out of here," he instructed her.

The young man's face changed from amusement to rage. "What are you doing..."

Leigh gave him a shove, propelling him into a boarded-up window. The young Adragna hit it with a smack, then stood upright, his face furious. "What do you mean by..."

"Shut up," Leigh commanded. He waited for the girl to rise, then took her gently by the arm, and led her to the door. "The other men will not bother you. Are you all right from here? Do you have a place to go?"

The girl looked at his masked face, pressed her bleeding lips together, then nodded.

"Very good," Leigh said, relieved. He had no wish to extend his rescue. But if she was lying? She was Italian after all. Had Ascanio brought her to England with him? Without the Adragna son, would she be alone in the Seven Dials?

He leaned down and spoke into her ear so Ascanio would not overhear. "If you are lying, if you cannot find a safe place, come to this address and find me. I will help you." He named the place.

She said nothing, simply moved toward the stairs and began walking down carefully.

Leigh waited until he heard the broken downstairs door open and close with a bang, then turned back to Ascanio.

The young man was a fool. He simply stood in the center of the room with his arms folded across his chest. He had not even tried to arm himself.

"Do you know who I am?" the young man demanded with the hint of a smile. "My men will see you sent to the bottom of your River Thames."

"Your men are dead," Leigh said, deciding to lie. "They'll be of no use to you."

He watched Ascanio pale.

"I hope you had an enjoyable night," Leigh said. "For it was your last. Considering how you were treating that girl, I can't say you'll be missed." He took a step forward. "Do you know who I am?"

The young man finally had the intelligence to look afraid. He shook his head.

There were so many things Leigh might have said. In his mind, he had rehearsed many speeches. Would speaking of his father, his mother, or Ascanio's own murdered sister have helped to prick the young man's conscience? Did he even have one? Leigh rather thought not.

In the end, Leigh simply slid his hand into his pocket and found what he needed.

"Good," he said. "Perhaps that's for the best."

When he was through, he cleaned the knife and pocketed it. Later, he and his uncle would return and dispose of the body. The night watchmen would be no hindrance. There was a system for these things. It helped if one was affluent and privileged, of course. Generous payments being the first step.

He felt weariness descending on him. He had done what he had come to do, and it was over. He had known there would be no real sense of satisfaction. He had learned that with Ascanio's father. And then, when his uncle had confirmed the grandfather's death.

Vengeance was not a beginning. Simply a tired old end.

Marigold was Leigh's beginning. His newfound joy.

He walked slowly down the stairs, thinking of what he would say to her when he saw her tomorrow. Had he complimented her beauty enough tonight? Had he really told her what she meant to him? Expressed it as eloquently as he had wished?

Well, tomorrow he would make her feel like the most beautiful woman in the world. And every day thereafter.

When the knife came out of the dark, he was caught off guard. Then he laughed, looking down at his black shirt. At least the blood would not show, he thought dimly, as he fell.

Leigh woke to great pain and the sensation of being pulled.

He *was* being pulled. Pulled along a darkened alley by someone with a great deal of strength. Enough to partly pull, mostly carry a muscular man in his twenties.

He caught a glimmer of sunlight. The night was gone. He had lived to see another morning.

"You bloody idiot. I tried to warn you," the man holding him muttered.

Leigh could not make out his face. The mask had fallen over his eyes. He could not seem to find the strength to push it up again.

"There were only two," Leigh mumbled. "Only two." Or were there three? He would not count Ascanio.

The other man snorted. "This is what comes from showing mercy to an enemy. Believe me, I learned the lesson long ago."

Leigh tried to open his mouth to ask if the man was not also being merciful.

But then he realized he had no idea where he was being dragged off to. Perhaps it was toward the Thames. Perhaps this man was his enemy. How did he know this was not one of Ascanio's own men?

He looked down at the street and saw his blood dripping dark onto the pavement.

Blackness washed over him again.

Chapter Twenty-Five

Leigh had not come.

Half the morning was already gone, and still he had not come.

Perhaps he had slept late. Or had been detained somewhere. Or perhaps he did not plan to come. Perhaps everything had been a lie.

Stop that, Marigold scolded herself. Stop it at once. He will come. It was not all lies.

He had obviously been detained, but whatever the reason, she need not simply sit about all day and wait.

"You certainly do have an odd way of making friends, my dear," Lady Fulford said. Her voice sounded very distant. "Marigold, my dear? Do you hear me?"

Marigold shook herself, trying to clear her head. "Yes, Lady Fulford."

"I was just saying to Miss Peel here that you certainly have an odd way of making friends," Lady Fulford said.

Marigold looked up. "Well, we are not friends. Are we, Miss Peel? Not yet."

Miss Peel sat in an armchair nearby, holding a cup of tea in her uninjured hand. Her bruised face had changed color overnight. Today it was all purples and greens. Her white sling blended well with her ivory gown. It was almost unnoticeable. As Miss Peel had not brought anything with her, she must be wearing something borrowed from Lady Fulford. The ivory suited the dark coloring of her hair. She looked very pretty. One would not be able to tell from looking at her that she was with child. Not yet.

"But she needed help, you see," Marigold said, turning to look at Lady Fulford. "And I knew you would not refuse that."

Lady Fulford looked rattled for a moment. "Did you now, my dear?" She gave a resigned sigh. "Well, you were correct. But I'm afraid it will be a dreadful mess. What Lord and Lady Norfolk will say, I cannot even imagine. Harboring their granddaughter. Such long-time friends, too. Could they have possibly known?"

Miss Peel appeared miserable. But at least she was safe, Marigold told herself. She found herself unable to think clearly about anything but Leigh. She needed some sort of distraction. Anything to get herself away from this obsessive train of thought. The chanting in her head that would not stop repeating, *When will he come? When will he come?* Worse still was the frightened voice that insisted, *He isn't coming. He will never come. What have you done? What will you do?*

Marigold stood abruptly. "I'm ever so sorry, Lady Fulford. But I forgot I promised I would help at the dispensary this morning. They are shorthanded, you see," she added lamely. "I would not have agreed otherwise, but they were so kind to Miss Peel yesterday and..."

Lady Fulford looked surprised. Then she waved a hand. "Yes, yes, my dear. Very well, run along. I shall stay and continue my conversation with Miss Peel."

Marigold nodded and began to move toward the door. Then she paused and turned back. "Miss Peel may really stay here? You will not return her to her parents? No matter what?"

Lady Fulford frowned. "Considering the state she is in, I think not. She is of age. They cannot simply claim her. No, she will remain here." She turned toward Miss Peel and raised her wrinkled head imperiously with the grandeur of an empress. "You may consider yourself under the protection of the Countess of Fulford, Miss Peel. No one shall harm you. If your family somehow learns you are at my residence and attempts to contact you here, I assure you that they shall be turned away. Unless you wish to speak with them, that is."

"Thank you, Lady Fulford," Miss Peel murmured, her eyes downcast. "I very much doubt they wish for my return."

But Lady Fulford's eyes were already flickering back and forth between Marigold and Miss Peel. "Still," she said, "I believe there is something you girls are not telling me."

Marigold repressed the urge to swallow guiltily. When informing Lady Fulford of Miss Peel's arrival and the circumstances in which she had left her parents' house, Marigold had decided that one thing was better left to Miss Peel herself to share.

"Yes, well, I believe Miss Peel will discuss the rest of that with you now," Marigold said hurriedly. "I know she may count on your kindness and discretion."

She certainly hoped so. The scandal was about to become much larger than Lady Fulford realized.

Was there a penalty for aiding and abetting the abused and pregnant daughter of a noble family? Marigold certainly hoped not. If anyone would know, it would be Lady Fulford.

She slipped quickly from the room.

The dispensary was in chaos when Marigold arrived.

There was no one attending to the patients in the waiting room. Fortunately, the two women waiting seemed to be in no distress and were chatting quietly.

Marigold nodded to them, then walked quickly down the hallway.

She could hear a woman groaning and hastened her pace. A woman brought to bed? A complicated delivery perhaps?

The door at the end of the hall burst open.

"Oh, Miss Spencer! You have come just in the nick of time," Mrs. Sharp babbled. "Not one but two emergencies! And just after Dr. Bannerjee was called away, too."

"Tell me where you need me. What is happening?"

"If you could fetch clean linens and a bottle of powder of

ipecacuanha and bring them there to Maggie." Mrs. Sharp gestured to the room she had just emerged from. "I'll go and check on Mrs. Tuck. She is with our other patient, you see. Quite alone, I'm afraid."

"Very well." Marigold gathered the items and returned to the room.

Inside, Maggie stood over a woman lying upon the table. A pile of blood-soaked clothes lay on the floor beside her.

"Goodness," Marigold exclaimed, coming over. "What has happened? I have brought what you asked for."

Maggie looked up tiredly and glanced at the items. "I told Mrs. Sharp not to bother with an emetic," she said crossly, spotting the ipecacuanha. "It will not do any good."

"What has happened?" Marigold asked again cautiously.

"Poisoning." Maggie looked down at the woman in the bed. "She's already cast up her accounts enough times. There is no point causing her to do so again."

"And the blood..."

"She was with child," Maggie said shortly.

"Accidental poisoning then," Marigold guessed.

She looked down at the woman, curious despite herself, then gasped and covered her mouth. "I have seen her before. She was here the other day."

"Was she?" Maggie sounded almost disinterested. "She is not the first and will not be the last. Dr. Bannerjee told her we could not help her, I suppose. And so, she went somewhere more dangerous and took this stupid risk."

"Yes." Marigold stared down at the dark-haired beauty. The woman's face was haggard and pale. Her eyes were closed. "Is she...?"

"She's not dead yet," Maggie replied. She touched a hand to the woman's forehead with surprising gentleness. "And where is the bastard who did this to you, my sweet lady? That's what I'd like to know," she murmured. "Always the women who pay the price for what two do. She must have been desperate indeed to try anything. Well, at least she was not further along. That is when things become dreadful indeed. Oh, the things I have seen."

"What did she take?" Marigold inquired.

"Pennyroyal tea. A great deal too much of it." Maggie rubbed her nose with the back of her hand. "Perhaps she thought she would overdo it to make sure it worked. Or perhaps the apothecary she found was a fool who gave her too much. We may never know." She peered down. "I believe she has fallen asleep. She has had a terrible time of it, but the worst may be over. She has lost a great deal of blood. She is weak, but who knows, she may come through." She clapped her hands together. "Right. Well, come along. Let us check on Mrs. Tuck."

"Mrs. Sharp went to her," Marigold said, hurrying along and following the older woman out into the hall.

"Yes, Mrs. Sharp has been here all night. She must be dead on her feet. I must send her home. Then we shall see to this other man, after which I will send you back to sit with the woman. There is not much you can do for her, but at least you can see to it that she does not fall out of bed. And if the bleeding begins again—"

"I shall fetch you at once," Marigold said quickly. "Should I go there now?"

"No, come with me first. We may need your help. Nick went home a few hours ago, and Dr. Bannerjee left to call on a woman nearing her time, drat the man's kindheartedness. I believe this one was wounded in a fight of some sort. Mrs. Sharp said sutures would be needed. If she and Mrs. Tuck have not managed it together, I may need you to help hold him down. Are you ready?" Maggie pushed the door open.

"Oh, there you are, Maggie," Mrs. Sharp said, scurrying to the door. "Mrs. Tuck has just finished cleaning the poor man off." She looked back over her shoulder. "Well, part of him off," she amended.

The man on the table had been stripped to the waist. There was a nasty gash on his stomach that Mrs. Tuck was still dabbing at, but Marigold could see that most of the blood had been wiped away.

The man's head was turned toward the wall. There was a dark cloth covering the top part of his face. A mask of some kind?

He did not seem to be awake. There was blood across his shoulders and on his cheek. Mrs. Tuck had not gotten to those parts of him, Marigold supposed.

"I was just about to begin the sutures, Maggie," Mrs. Tuck said, looking up. "But you know he is sure to wake for that part."

"They always do," Maggie agreed. "Well, come in Miss Spencer and take hold of his shoulders. Mrs. Sharp, no need for you to be here for any of this. We can manage. It is high time you went home."

Mrs. Sharp's face crumpled with relief. "Oh, do you really think so? I am rather done in."

"Yes, dear, be on your way," Mrs. Tuck urged. "Miss Spencer can help us. We'll get on very well."

Mrs. Sharp nodded and hurried out as Marigold moved to stand near the man's head.

"What happened to him? Do we know?" Maggie asked, coming to inspect the gash. "Looks like a blade."

"Yes, in and out. Clean at least," Mrs. Tuck agreed. "The wound is still bleeding, as you can see, but not as badly as it was when his friend brought him in."

"Well, let's stitch him up. No time to waste," Maggie said stoutly, never one for hesitation or abundant sympathy.

Marigold looked down at the man on the table. She had done this before. He would wake soon and likely start to scream. Marigold would have to hold him fast. She hoped she had the strength. He was a young, fit man.

She slowly pulled the black cloth from his head. The young man's hair was dark and tangled. It was caked with something, too. Probably blood or dried mud. He was none too clean. There was so much blood on his face.

She reached for the damp cloth that Mrs. Tuck had been using and began to wipe at the man's face just as Maggie turned around and let out a sound of exasperation.

"These damned windowless rooms! It's like working in a cellar!"

"Well, we were trying to save on expenses," Mrs. Tuck said meekly. "Mrs. Sharp only lit one lamp."

Maggie huffed. "Ridiculous. Let us light the other. Your sutures are much neater than mine. I will stand by you and hold him down."

"Very well." Mrs. Tuck ran to light the second lamp in the sconce on the wall as Maggie inspected the tray of materials.

The blood on the man's face was dried and held fast, but gradually it was coming away. Marigold worked as gently as she could.

"Oh, don't bother with that. His face is hardly the important part at the moment," Maggie complained as she noticed what Marigold was doing. "Now, ready to hold fast when Mrs. Tuck begins?"

Marigold nodded.

The light bloomed along the wall just as she lifted the cloth away from the man's face.

She gasped.

"What is it?" Maggie demanded. She peered at the man closely as Marigold stood gaping down in disbelief. "Rather odd clothes for a man from these parts."

"Y-yes," Marigold stuttered. She stood frozen, the cloth still poised in her hand. Her fingers felt as if they had turned to ice. She could hardly breathe.

She forced herself to take a deep, slow breath. "Maggie, I know him."

"Do you now? A toff, is he?" Maggie asked offhandedly. "Saw him at a ball, did you? What'd he do to get in this state, I wonder?"

Marigold choked back a sob. "A toff, yes. Maggie, I don't know if I can do this."

"No casting up your accounts," Maggie warned, wagging a strong finger. "You've a hearty stomach. I've seen it. You can do this. You don't wish for the poor man to die on us now, do you?"

Marigold shook her head fervently.

"Well, there's no one else. Here's Mrs. Tuck. Let us begin."

Marigold lowered her hands to the man's shoulders. She saw they were shaking. She prayed Maggie would not notice.

"Firmer," Maggie commanded. "Hold him fast."

Mrs. Tuck lifted the needle and thread. "Poor man," she *tsked*. "This won't be pleasant for him."

"Very unpleasant. Very necessary," Maggie grunted. She held the man's arms tightly. "Begin, if you please."

The sight of the needle piercing through Leigh's flesh was almost more than Marigold could bear. She choked back a sob, willing herself to hold tight.

Then she felt him stir.

"He's coming to," Maggie warned. "Careful now, he looks like a strong lad."

Sure enough, Leigh began to thrash with each pull of the needle.

At first, Maggie and Marigold did well enough, but it seemed his strength was returning to him.

"This won't do," Maggie grunted. "We shall have to stop. Look, he's bleeding again."

"Very slippery, but I can... manage," Mrs. Tuck said, her teeth gritted with determination. Marigold watched her feel about on the tray beside her for a cloth, then dab at the blood.

Maggie was whipping her head about, looking around the room for something else to use to hold Leigh down. "Bloody hell! What became of the straps we used to have?" She stopped, and for a moment, Marigold thought she looked almost frightened. "What the devil! Who's the great lump standing in the corner?"

"Oh," Mrs. Tuck said, not looking up. "That man over there? I thought you saw him when you came in. He brought in this one."

"Well, hell and damnation, if he didn't just give me the fright of my life," Maggie exclaimed angrily. "What are you doing lurking about there, my fine fellow?"

Marigold turned to see where Maggie was glaring. Near the door, in the corner where they had come in, a large man leaned. Now that the room had more light, it was easy to spot him, but earlier, he must have been in the shadows. Clearly, he had no wish to be seen.

He was scowling at them as he followed Maggie's instructions and stepped into the pool of light.

"Why, I know you," Marigold exclaimed. "Bryce! Caleb Bryce."

The man scowled, clearly displeased at being recognized. "I was about to leave when you both came in. Miss Spencer, good day. I shan't say it is good to see you again."

"Oh, so you do remember me! I certainly remember you," Marigold said hotly. "What have you done to Leigh?"

"I did nothing," Bryce said coolly. "I found him in this state and brought him here. I paid him a kindness."

"You felt guilty for what you had done to his family already, you mean, so you decided not to leave him for dead," Marigold guessed, her face flushing.

"Well, now you can help him a little longer," Maggie declared. "Get over here and stand where the girl is. She says she knows him. Perhaps that is why she is doing such a terrible job of it today. Hold his shoulders down as Mrs. Tuck works. Marigold, step back."

Leigh was groaning and twisting on the table. His eyes had still not opened. Was he feverish? Was the wound already infected? Marigold prayed not.

She stepped away as Bryce walked up to the table. He easily pinned the thrashing Leigh down.

Marigold backed up to the wall, suddenly aware of how fast her heart was beating.

"He will be all right, though, won't he, Maggie?" she asked the other woman in a low voice as Mrs. Tuck put down the cloth and picked up her needle, resuming her delicate task.

"How the hell should I..." She stopped, spotting the look on Marigold's face. "Oh, for heaven's sake. You know him well then, do you?"

The other women clearly did not recognize the new orderly who had been in the dispensary only the day before. Little wonder when he was still covered in blood and dressed so differently.

"You might say that," Marigold replied. She looked down at Leigh's bloody face and gave a little hiccup. "He is my fiancée, you see."

Mrs. Tuck gave a start. "Dear me! Maggie, did she say..."

"Yes, she did," Maggie said grimly. "You might have waited until Mrs. Tuck was finished to jolt her like that, Miss Spencer."

"Oh dear me, dear me," Mrs. Tuck was mumbling.

"Just keep doing your fine work, Mrs. Tuck. Pay no attention to Miss Spencer," Maggie instructed. "Miss Spencer, out! Now. Go and check on the woman in the other room. Sit by her and hold her hand if you like. You can at least do that much, can you not?"

Marigold nodded numbly. She knew she should not be in the room. Not while Mrs. Tuck was working. She should not have said what she had said. If Mrs. Tuck fumbled, made some mistake. Well, she would never forgive herself.

"We'll patch him up, and then you can come back," Maggie said in a low voice, trying to show some mercy. She cleared her throat. "He'll be just fine."

Marigold nodded again. She knew that tone. It meant Maggie was not certain about a patient's outcome. She very rarely lied. She almost never provided false assurances. She must have become quite attached to Marigold if she were willing to make this small effort to do so.

It was almost flattering.

But Marigold would rather have had false hope. It would have been more bearable.

She stumbled down the hall and opened the door to where the woman lay.

Chapter Twenty-Six

The dark-haired lady was still asleep when Marigold came in.

She stepped up to the bed softly, then sat down in the chair, putting her face in her hands.

The scuffing sound of footsteps roused her a few minutes later. She lifted her head to see Caleb Bryce entering the room.

"That woman asked me to tell you..." he began. He stopped. Marigold saw he was staring at the woman in the bed.

"What is it? Do you know her?"

She watched as he stepped closer to the bed.

He was a hard man with a stern face. Even before when he had been kind to Laurel, Marigold had never found him particularly likable, though there was something which made him unforgettable. Right now, he seemed larger than ever as he stood over the woman in the bed.

"What has happened to her?" he demanded.

Marigold hesitated. "She ingested poison."

Bryce's head whipped about to look at her. "On purpose? She meant to do away with herself?"

"No," Marigold said slowly. "It is... complicated."

Bryce's eyes were roaming the room. She watched as they landed on the bloody clothes on the floor near the bed. There had been no opportunity to clean the room.

"Are those from her?" he asked, his voice harsh. "She was bleeding?" His eyes flickered to Marigold. He was silent a moment, then he nodded slowly. "I see."

"Do you?"

And then he did something which shocked her.

Caleb Bryce knelt down on the other side of the bed and lifted the woman's small hand into his much larger one.

"She was with child," he said in a low voice. He closed his eyes as if it hurt him to look at the woman. "My child."

"Yours!"

"She tried to tell me." His voice sounded strangled. "I... I threw her out."

Marigold said nothing.

He looked at her almost pleadingly. "I had no patience for her. She had been... in the way."

"You thought she was coming between you and Laurel, you mean," Marigold said cruelly. "You cast her over, thinking you would pursue my sister."

Bryce did not argue. "I was a brute."

She watched him run a hand over his face. It was more lined than she remembered. Still, there was a rugged handsomeness to him. She supposed it drew women like Carlotta.

"She was carrying my child," he whispered. "She came to tell me, and I would not listen. I was a bastard. You see, she had done much for me. I... well, I did not give her the credit she had earned."

Marigold found this hardly surprising. She held her tongue.

"Will she live?" he demanded, looking up at her.

"That remains to be seen," Marigold said evenly. She suddenly remembered. "What did Maggie send you to tell me?"

"Oh, yes. That. They are finished. He is awake—or something close to it. You may go to him if you like."

Marigold was already moving toward the door. "You will stay with her?"

"Yes," Bryce said gruffly. She saw him look down at the woman's hand in his. "I will stay."

———

"Well, I suppose it is technically still morning, but this is not Lady Fulford's."

Leigh lifted his head, already grinning as he recognized the familiar voice.

"Half marks then," he begged. "After all, it is still morning you say."

"I believe I shall take marks off for arriving half dead," his beloved complained.

He looked at her, his heart already racing happily. She was dressed simply for her work in a simple flower-printed gown of pale green. Her long, curly blonde hair was braided and pulled back. A simple, practical style. It drew his attention to her high cheekbones and ripe cheeks. Like pretty red apples. Her lovely full lips were parted a little, and he realized belatedly that they were wobbling.

She came closer, and he saw her hands were curled into little fists. "You bastard," she said, her voice shaking. "You left and said nothing about where you were going or what you were doing. It was not dealt with. They were not dealt with. Were they?"

"No," Leigh admitted. He cleared his throat. "But they are now. All of them. I swear it."

He lifted his arm and winced. He raised it anyhow, reaching out for her hand. She hesitated, then put it in his.

"I am so sorry, Marigold," he said forthrightly. "I am a bastard. I deserve whatever names you wish to throw at me."

She took a step closer, her small hand squeezing around his, and he saw there were tears in her eyes.

"Bastard. Scoundrel." She gave a small hiccup. "Fiancé."

"I like the sound of that last one," Leigh said, smiling.

"You might have died," she whispered.

"But I didn't." He tried to grin cheekily, to force a smile from her. But her face was sad. "Marigold, it is over. I should have told you where I was going. Or better yet, I should not have come to you until it was over, and I was safe..."

"Not come to me?" Her face was horrified. "That would have been worse."

He squeezed her hand gently. "Very well. Then I am glad I did." *So very glad*, he thought. "But I should have told you where I was going. I am... not used to taking anyone into my confidence. That will have to change. I promise you that it will. I trust you with my life, Marigold. Please believe that."

She came closer, raising her other hand to press against his arm, and nodded slowly. "I want to." She lifted her hand to touch his cheek, and Leigh turned his head to kiss it. "Oh, Leigh..."

"Well, then, Mr. Blakeley." Maggie's voice boomed out from behind them as she swept into the room. "Or should I say Lord Leigh?"

She paused, hands on her square hips, a grimace on her face.

"You knew?" Leigh asked. "When I applied to be an orderly..."

"'Applied' makes it sound as if we had an advertisement up. You walked in off the street and begged us to let you help." Maggie sniffed. "Which was very odd, in and of itself. Of course, the name rang a bell. Your brother may be the Duke of Dareford, but I was not unfamiliar with the family name."

"Of course," Leigh murmured. "Stupid of me."

"Not so stupid as getting yourself knifed," Maggie remarked. "What was it? A spat over a horse? A lost bet at White's?"

Leigh tried to look repentant and foolish. He hoped he succeeded.

Maggie shook her head. "And you say he is your fiancé, Miss Spencer? I wonder if perhaps you could do better. Find a man who doesn't go about getting himself stabbed on the regular."

"That would be preferable. I shall take what you say under consideration," Marigold agreed with a serious face. Leigh gave her hand a little pinch. "Ouch!"

"Miss Barry, I thank you for the excellent service you have rendered to me this morning. Although my time spent as an orderly in your establishment has been admittedly brief, I have nonetheless seen how your facilities are rather... lacking."

Maggie snorted. "You don't say."

"And while I know my brother has been generously contributing to the dispensary's day-to-day running," Leigh continued. "I cannot help but feel he has still not done enough for this benevolent institution. Particularly when it is one which is so close to my bride-to-be's heart."

"What are you up to, you incorrigible man?" he heard Marigold murmur.

"I would like to move the dispensary to a new location," Leigh went on. "One with windows. Preferably in each room. And at least two floors."

"What's this now?" Maggie said, finally looking interested. "A new location? It would have to be in Seven Dials. This is where our patients live."

"Of course," Leigh agreed. "I am sure something suitable could be found."

He could feel Marigold's eyes on him. "The location will have to be sufficiently large," she said. "For it will need to house two establishments. Both the dispensary and the new institution."

"Yes?"

"Yes, a home for women in desperate straits who find themselves with child. A place where women might come and safely stay." He watched her turn to Maggie, her face rueful. "I admit, I have not thought it all through yet."

"There are many details to be worked out," Maggie acknowledged. She cleared her throat. "But it is a fine idea, Miss Spencer. There is certainly an abundant need for such a place. One in which women do not need to repent of all their supposed sins or work themselves to the bone in order to deserve safe harbor."

She gave them a small smile, then began to turn away. "Well, milord. When you feel well enough to stand, kindly empty the bed. We need it for patients with more serious ailments."

"Of course," Leigh agreed, already trying to sit up.

Marigold pushed him back down. "Rest for a few more minutes, for heaven's sake. I'll go and speak to Lady Fulford's footman. We can't just have you emerge on my arm, shirtless and bandaged." She giggled. "Although it would be a familiar scene, of course."

"So familiar," Leigh agreed, grinning. "I promise, I shan't make a habit of it."

"I fear you already have," she said, lifting her chin and sailing out of the room beside Maggie.

Leigh put his head down on the cot and closed his eyes.

Abruptly, he recalled Bryce's letter. Bloody hell. Had the man been following him? Trying to warn him? Or trying to stop him?

Regardless, Bryce had saved him in the end. If he had not gotten Leigh to the dispensary, he would have remained, bleeding, on the floor of that godforsaken house. Eventually, more of Ascanio's men would have come along and found him.

Or his uncle would have arrived, searching for Leigh, only to find he had come too late.

That goddamned gaming hell owner had redeemed himself slightly, Leigh had to admit.

———————✧———————

Marigold followed Maggie out into the hall.

"We've just had a messenger. Arpan is on his way back," Maggie announced as they reached the waiting room. The two women who had been sitting there were gone. Mrs. Tuck must be seeing to them, Marigold thought. "I suppose you wish to escort your fiancé home?"

"Yes, if you can do without me."

Maggie sniffed. "We'll be fine." She studied Marigold. "Was he serious, do you think? Your young man?"

"He was extremely serious," Marigold assured her. "As was I." She colored a little. "We really are to be married. And as you know, the Duke of Dareford has already wed my elder sister. I shall have wealth of my own. More than I shall know what to do with." Not to mention whatever Leigh had, and she had no doubt it was not an inconsiderable sum. "I can think of nothing better I should like to do with it than build something like we spoke of."

Maggie was silent for a moment. "I met Arpan at Guy's Hospital, you know."

"I believe Dr. Bannerjee mentioned he had studied there," Marigold said with surprise.

"They do not allow women, of course." Maggie grimaced. "Nevertheless, I completed some of the required courses. Most of them, in fact."

"How did you..."

"I know I am not the most beautiful woman in the world, Miss Spencer." Maggie's plain face was determined. "But there are advantages to that. I found a way to pass. To get by unnoticed."

"You dressed as a man!" Marigold stared. "Oh, Maggie. Good for you. How absolutely brilliant."

Maggie seemed pleased. "Yes, well. I received the knowledge, if not the recognition."

"But to come so close," Marigold lamented. "You would make such a fine physician."

"I always thought so. Well, it is all right. I do what I can. More than is properly allowed if truth be told. As you well know." She shot a wry glance at Marigold. "Someday, there will be women at Guy's. And many other places."

"I hope that day comes soon," Marigold said softly. "I should have liked to have the opportunity." Or for her daughters to have it. Or Laurel's or Wren's or Ash's.

"Arpan didn't care that I was a woman. He saw my mind. We formed a friendship. We are partners. In a way, I did not think I would ever be with a man. There was a man once, who I thought I could accept as a husband, but he... Well, enough said about that the better." Maggie shrugged her shoulders. "Now, Miss Spencer, can you find your footman, or should I escort you? How many escorts do you need, Miss Spencer? Off with you now. We need that bed!"

Marigold hid a smile and slipped out from the building.

Chapter Twenty-Seven

Blakeley Manor
A few months later

It was the happiest day of his life, and yet Leigh was feeling something vastly uncomfortable.

Guilt.

"You're so beautiful. I don't deserve you."

Marigold laughed, a lovely tinkling sound. She was radiant in a pale-pink gown of French lace. Her hair was worn loose in flowing curls, with small white rosebuds and pink ribbons mingled amongst the blonde tresses. She looked fresh and sweet, and Leigh could not wait to bury his head in her hair and lay her down... somewhere, anywhere. Perhaps even on the lawn.

He felt the twinge again. Guilt.

"Don't be silly," Marigold said, twirling about in a circle. She had drunk quite a bit of champagne back at the house and had asked Leigh to take her away before anyone noticed her getting silly. Leigh grinned as he watched her. She could be as silly as she liked with him. "It was a perfect day. It was a perfect wedding. You are a perfect husband." She paused. "It will be a perfect night."

Leigh had been looking forward to spending the night with his new wife all day. All through the trip to the church, all through the receiving line with relatives he was quite sure he had never seen before, all through the late lunch, and now all through the evening reception.

"It has been a very, very long day is what it has been," he complained, then felt even more guilty for having done so.

It had been an unusually large wedding. But then, there were extenuating circumstances. Many in the Blakeley family wished to be given an opportunity to finally welcome back the dowager duchess. Those in the Renfrew clan that Briar had married into were eager to visit and make the acquaintance of her siblings—especially the long-lost prodigal son. As a result, it was not the simple affair Leigh had anticipated with a quick service at St. George's and then a small wedding breakfast. This had become a much larger, much louder celebration. Leigh couldn't say it was what he would have chosen, but the happy expressions on the faces of his mother and siblings as they mingled with guests had certainly made the sacrifice of peace and quiet worth it in the end.

Marigold giggled and swatted him. "Just because we have given our dear siblings the wedding some of them didn't get to have..."

"Wren. You mean Wren. Just say Wren."

"And because every Blakeley and Spencer relative, and yes, every Renfrew relative in England, Scotland, Ireland, and Wales has turned out to wish us well," she continued.

"Don't forget the Continent," Leigh grumbled.

"And from the Continent," she amended. "Doesn't mean it hasn't also been a very perfectly perfect day. With a perfectly perfect husband."

Leigh scuffed at the grass. "I am nowhere near perfect. You should not even have married me."

Marigold stopped her twirling, scrunching up her pretty face. "What are you talking about?"

He knew he should stop this self-indulgent moaning. It was pointless. What was he looking for, anyway? Was he really about to spoil his bride's happiness today of all days?

But he couldn't stop. He couldn't help himself.

266

"I don't deserve a perfect day. Or a perfect wedding. Or a perfect wife. I don't deserve to be happy. I don't even know how to be, and I am sure to make you a perfectly terrible husband," he said in a rush. "I'm a rotten man who has done rotten things, and you deserve someone good and kind who will treat you like the queen that you are." He stopped, suddenly struck by an awful thought. "Good Lord, perhaps you should have married Harley."

"He is courting someone else now, I believe," Marigold said, looking thoughtful. "And I don't believe he would have been a perfect husband."

"Well, I certainly won't be," Leigh said, not meeting her eyes. He lowered his voice. "You know what I am. What I've done. The blood won't wash away. What if there is to be a child? What sort of father will I be to them? How could I ever dare to teach a child right from wrong?"

"You would be a perfectly wonderful father," Marigold said, setting her chin stubbornly. "And yes, I shall continue saying 'perfect' and 'perfectly' to my heart's content, and you cannot stop me. Oh, Leigh, where is this coming from? I love you. So desperately. And I know you love me." She searched his face. "Don't you?"

He stepped up to her and cupped her face in his hands. "I love you so much that it terrifies me. I think of what I would do for your sake and that terrifies me as well. My love for you knows no bounds. I would wade through an ocean of blood to ensure your safety. I would brave the depths of hell and sacrifice everything to protect you. I could not bear to lose you. Every moment of every day, the very thought of you in my arms sets my blood aflame. I am utterly unworthy of your love, and yet I believe I should die without it." He stopped, his breathing ragged.

"Well, that is rather dramatic," Marigold said, lifting a hand to smooth his hair. "But also beautiful. Perhaps we should have worked that into our wedding vows. Though I suspect the vicar would not have approved."

Leigh rested his head against hers, burrowing his face in her sweet-smelling hair. "I'm sorry," he said, his voice muffled.

"No, Leigh. No apologies. Is there any woman on earth who could resist being told by the man she loves that he would journey to hell and back for her? If there is, I am certainly not her."

He leaned back to see her face. She was smiling. She had the sweetest dimples, he suddenly realized. Would their children have dimples? He certainly hoped so.

"I hope it shall not be necessary for you to 'wade through an ocean of blood' as you so poetically put it," she said carefully. "But it is indescribably wonderful to think you would not hesitate to do so for my sake."

"Is it?" Leigh stared. "It is?"

"Oh, yes," she assured him. She kissed the top of his nose. "In fact, it fills me with... Well, it makes me feel rather..." She gave a little shiver. Leigh thought that was odd as the night was quite warm. "Oh dear, is that the orangery over there?"

"The orangery?" Leigh looked blankly toward where she was pointing and tried to focus. "Yes, that is it. The white-trimmed glass structure."

"Well, then, come along," she said, taking his hand and dragging him almost impatiently. "I have been longing to see the orangery with you now that we are back."

They strolled hand in hand down the lawn together.

The stars were just beginning to make an appearance. They had walked quite a way from the house, down the front lawn, toward where the formal gardens began.

From behind them came the sound of happy laughter, children shrieking, and a band of musicians playing a lively country dance.

Leigh felt his guilt and fear and panic slowly beginning to give way. He was being a fool. She was here. She was holding his hand. And she would not let go.

It was a beautiful night after all. The stress of the long and busy day was dissipating. The night was what mattered after all. The night was all theirs.

"Did I ever tell you about the dream I once had?" Marigold asked suddenly.

"No," Leigh replied, still feeling rather stupid from his earlier outburst. "Did it involve the orangery?"

He watched his wife smile serenely. "It most certainly did."

Epilogue

A few weeks later...

The baby's name was Alistair.

He was still small for his age, but he was lovely—with Laurel's blue eyes and Dare's dark hair.

Marigold cradled him to her chest, cooing sweet words, as Leigh stood nearby watching.

"You don't wish to hold him?"

Leigh put up his hands and shook his head.

"You have not forgiven him for spitting up all over you yesterday, have you?" Marigold asked, extremely entertained. "He is a baby, Leigh. He could not help it."

Leigh grimaced. "I did not say he had done it on purpose. Though it was certainly not the first occasion."

"He loves you, Alistair," Marigold murmured to the baby. "Don't listen to him. You spit up on your Uncle Leigh as much as you like."

"What are you telling him?" Leigh demanded, stepping toward her.

"Nothing," Marigold said innocently. "He is only a baby."

There came the sounds of animated voices and loud footsteps. Lady Fulford, Dare, and Laurel entered the room.

"Well, what do you think?" Leigh asked, his eyes lighting up. "Will it do?"

"Miss Barry is still conducting her inspection," Dare replied. "I do not believe we can come to any conclusions until she renders her judgment."

"No, that would be sacrilege," Laurel agreed, coming up to Marigold and taking Alistair from her arms carefully. "Miss Barry holds sway."

"She will hold sway on one side of the building at least," Marigold said cheerfully. "But on the other, Lady Fulford will reign supreme." She winked at the older woman who stood regally off to one side, trusty silver-headed cane in hand.

"Yes, well, you have rather roped me in," Lady Fulford said. "I had no idea when I brought you to London for your Season that I would wind up becoming the benefactress to unwed women, babes, orphans, and the like..."

"Don't forget the harlots," Leigh muttered near Marigold's ear. She elbowed him sharply.

"The Lady Fulford Relief Society for Ladies will play an important role here in St. Giles," Marigold reminded Lady Fulford. "Not to mention the rest of London, for we shall turn no one away."

Lady Fulford gave her cane an indecisive little rap. "I am still not certain about the wisdom of referring to all your patrons as 'ladies,' my dear. It suggests a... well, a level of classification that may be misleading."

Leigh coughed. "Would you rather we call it the Female Friendly Society for the Relief of Poor, Infirmed, Aged Widows, and Single Women of Good Character, Who Have Seen Better Days?"

"It is the requirement to have 'good character' which is the issue," Marigold explained patiently. "We know the Female Friendly Society turns away unmarried young women. Thus, someone like Miss Peel would have sadly found no assistance there."

"Yes, that is very true," Lady Fulford admitted.

"Does Maggie know what you are naming the other half of the establishment?" Laurel inquired, bouncing little Alistair in her arms.

"Does Maggie know what?" Miss Barry stepped into the room,

followed by a beaming Dr. Bannerjee. She was frowning slightly, but her pink-tinged cheeks hinted at her excitement. "Well, it will do, I suppose. Shan't fall down in the near future as far as I can tell. Good bones. Strong supports."

"It is a delightful building and a great deal better than where we have been treating our patients," Dr. Bannerjee declared, not bothering to hide his enthusiasm. "So much light! Miss Barry is simply overcome with joy and forgets her immeasurable gratitude."

Maggie scoffed. "Oh, I have, have I?"

"We are so glad you approve, Maggie," Marigold said, a slightly mischievous smile on her lips. "Especially after all you did keeping the St. Giles Dispensary going for so many years. You put so much hard work into it."

Maggie scoffed again, but this time, the redness in her cheeks was even more noticeable. "Yes, well, I didn't do it entirely single-handedly. Arpan helped as well."

"Only part of the year," he reminded her. "But I thank you, nonetheless."

"Because of all your hard work and your care, we wish to honor you, Maggie," Leigh said quietly, stepping up beside his wife. "And that is why when the new dispensary opens, it shall be named the Margaret Barry Hospital for the Residents of St. Giles."

"Oh, you're taking the 'poor' out, are you?" Maggie looked amused. "My name on a building plaque, hmm?" She shook her head but was smiling. "There's no need for any such nonsense."

"The other half is being named in *my* honor, Miss Barry," Lady Fulford informed her stiffly. "Therefore, I do not think it is nonsense."

"No well, you wouldn't, would you Lady High and Mighty?" Leigh heard Maggie mutter.

"Well, now that we have seen the place, why don't we all return to the house for refreshments and discuss what comes next in more detail there?" Laurel said brightly. "Dare, my darling, I believe this little fellow is need of a burping. Will you do the honors?"

"Certainly, my love," the Duke of Dareford said cheerfully from where he stood between his wife and brother.

Alistair gave a faint wail of protest as he was passed over to his father.

"Now you see, Leigh, there is a trick to this," Dare informed him as he began to bounce the baby against his shoulder.

"Is there now?"

"Yes, you must not be too gentle, or the babe shall simply fall asleep with a sore stomach. But neither must you be too vigorous, or the results will be disastrous."

Leigh inspected Baby Alistair, who was currently looking at the wall with a vacant expression and his little mouth open.

"I believe your offspring is leaning toward the slumber end of the spectrum," he informed his brother.

"Oh, is he?" Dare lifted the baby away from his shoulder to check.

"Don't jostle him like that near me," Leigh protested.

The baby turned to look at the source of the noise, just as his father gave him a solid tap on the back.

There was a belching sound followed by a splat.

"Oh dear, Leigh, has it happened again?" Marigold asked with interest. She had a hand to her mouth.

"Indeed it has."

THE END

Thank you for reading *My So-Called Scoundrel?*

This was the last installment in the *Blakeley Manor Series.* Have you read the stories of Leigh's siblings?

Have you read the Christmas novella *The Countess's Christmas Groom*? It's the prequel to this series and it tells the story of Leigh's sister Katherine!

She is his ideal match. The woman he has been waiting for all of his life. The only problem? He's her servant.

This Christmas, two very unlikely individuals are about to realize they are one another's ideal match. And once mutual desire has been sparked, they will never be parted, no matter the price they must face.

Also by Fenna Edgewood

The Gardner Girls Series

Masks of Desire (Prequel Novella)

To All the Earls I've Loved Before

Mistakes Not to Make When Avoiding a Rake

The Seafaring Lady's Guide to Love

Once Upon a Midwinter's Kiss

Must Love Scandal Series

How to Get Away with Marriage

The Duke Report

A Duke for All Seasons

The Bluestocking Beds Her Bride

The Brazen Belles

The Brazen Belles Anthology

About Fenna Edgewood

 *USA Today* bestselling author Fenna Edgewood writes swoon-worthy, humorous stories of love, family, and adventure. In other words, the most important things in life! She is an award-winning retired academic who has studied English literature for most of her life. After a twenty-five-year hiatus from writing romance as a twelve-year-old, she has returned to the genre with a bang. Fenna has lived and traveled across North America, most notably above the Arctic Circle. She now resides back on the Prairies with her husband and two tiny tots (who are adorable but generally terrible research assistants).

Connect with Fenna:

https://fennaedgewood.com

facebook.com/fennaedgewoodbooks

instagram.com/fennaedgewood

bookbub.com/authors/fenna-edgewood

amazon.com/stores/Fenna-Edgewood/author/B0929KJV52

Made in United States
North Haven, CT
15 May 2023

36618168R00171